VOWS OF LOVE

He lifted her chin and said simply, "Serena, I love you."

"Oh, Nicholas, I love you, too," she returned, snuggling against him.

He lifted her chin again and proceeded to kiss her forehead, then her nose, and finally her mouth. This area required a great deal of attention, and they were leaving Green Park before the driver could get an answer from the occupants of his vehicle.

"Where to, guvner?"

Nicholas smiled at Serena and said, "It's only the twenty-fifth of June, my love. Gretna Green isn't that far. You could still win that wager."

With a dreamy smile, Serena pulled his head back down to hers, trying her best to show him her answer.

—from "The Wager" by Donna Bell

* * *

Whether it is Gretna Green, a country chapel, or Westminster Abbey, a wedding is an occasion for celebration. And when the day is sunny and warm, the flowers are bright and gay, and music fills the air, the exchange of vows is a wondrous example of love and joy.

We're pleased to present six delightful Regency authors to lighten our hearts and bring a smile to our lips as they regale us with tales of beautiful brides finding their way through courtship and marriage. So join with Donna Bell, Carola Dunn, Jean Ewing, Marcy Stewart, Phylis Warady, and Winifred Witton as they escort us down the aisle to a Regency-era wedding filled with happiness and joy.

ZEBRA REGENCIES
ARE
THE TALK OF THE TON!

A REFORMED RAKE (4499, $3.99)
by Jeanne Savery

After governess Harriet Cole helped her young charge flee to France—and the designs of a despicable suitor, more trouble soon arrived in the person of a London rake. Sir Frederick Carrington insisted on providing safe escort back to England. Harriet deemed Carrington more dangerous than any band of brigands, but secretly relished matching wits with him. But after being taken in his arms for a tender kiss, she found herself wondering—*could* a lady find love with an irresistible rogue?

A SCANDALOUS PROPOSAL (4504, $4.99)
by Teresa DesJardien

After only two weeks into the London season, Lady Pamela Premington has already received her first offer of marriage. If only it hadn't come from the *ton's* most notorious rake, Lord Marchmont. Pamela had already set her sights on the distinguished Lieutenant Penford, who had the heroism and honor that made him the ideal match. Now she had to keep from falling under the spell of the seductive Lord so she could pursue the man more worthy of her love. Or was he?

A LADY'S CHAMPION (4535, $3.99)
by Janice Bennett

Miss Daphne, art mistress of the Selwood Academy for Young Ladies, greeted the notion of ghosts haunting the academy with skepticism. However, to avoid rumors frightening off students, she found herself turning to Mr. Adrian Carstairs, sent by her uncle to be her "protector" against the "ghosts." Although, Daphne would accept no interference in her life, she *would* accept aid in exposing any spectral spirits. What she never expected was for Adrian to expose the secret wishes of her hidden heart . . .

CHARITY'S GAMBIT (4537, $3.99)
by Marcy Stewart

Charity Abercrombie reluctantly embarks on a London season in hopes of making a suitable match. However she cannot forget the mysterious Dominic Castille—and the kiss they shared—when he fell from a tree as she strolled through the woods. Charity does not know that the dark and dashing captain harbors a dangerous secret that will ensnare them both in its web—leaving Charity to risk certain ruin and losing the man she so passionately loves . . .

FLOWERS FOR THE *BRIDE*

**Donna Bell, Carola Dunn,
Jean R. Ewing, Marcy Stewart,
Phylis Warady, Winifred Witton**

**ZEBRA BOOKS
KENSINGTON PUBLISHING CORP.**

ZEBRA BOOKS are published by

Kensington Publishing Corp.
850 Third Avenue
New York, NY 10022

First Printing: May, 1995

Printed in the United States of America

CONTENTS

THE WAGER   7
  by Donna Bell

A CONFORMABLE WIFE   67
  by Carola Dunn

THE IMPOSSIBLE BRIDEGROOM   115
  by Jean R. Ewing

AN INDEFINITE WEDDING   167
  by Marcy Stewart

DELIGHTFUL DECEIVER   231
  by Phylis Warady

THE VICARIOUS BRIDE   295
  by Winifred Witton

The Wager

by
Donna Bell

The door to the ladies' salon opened quietly, and a small figure stood silently in the doorway.

"Well?" demanded the room's occupant.

"I'm betrothed," answered the petite brunette, crossing the room and stretching out slender fingers to grasp the nearest chair for support.

"Ohhh! You are so-o-o-o lucky, Serena!"

"Am I?" she said softly. Then she squared her narrow shoulders and walked calmly around the chair, sitting down and carefully arranging her skirts. "Lord Redmon is a courteous man, quite presentable, and certainly wealthy. I shall be very happy."

"Yes, happy to have won our wager!" said her friend Angel, plopping into the chair beside Serena's and sitting on one foot, a posture guaranteed to bring censure from her mother. But since her mother was not in the room, Angel didn't give her unladylike pose a single thought.

Serena smiled mischievously and said, "That is certainly one benefit. I shall enjoy that one hundred pounds immensely. Perhaps I'll buy a new horse."

Angel made a moue. "You would spend my money on one of those disagreeable beasts! So, when is the ceremony?"

Serena laughed. "The twenty-eighth day of June—just in time to win the wager. Unless, of course, you've a dark horse and manage to get in under the wire before that!"

Angel shook her head. "I would if I could, but," she paused, placing a hand to her forehead and striking a pose before continuing faintly, "alas, I have not yet encountered my great love."

Serena snorted in a most unladylike manner. "Stuff! If a lady waited for love before marrying, she would find herself with one foot in the grave."

Angel leaned forward, her smooth brow wrinkled with a frown. "Have you no tender feelings for Lord Redmon?"

Just then the door burst open, and the broad shoulders of a tall man wearing the red coat of the Household Cavalry blocked the opening. "I hear there are mice in this house, and they keep Father awake with their childish squealing!"

"Nick! You're home!" cried Angel, leaping up and flinging her tall form on her brother's hard chest.

He bent to kiss her forehead before holding her at arms' length and saying fondly, "You've grown up, Mouse. Outwardly, at least."

Serena, who had stood up at his entrance, waited quietly by her chair. Nicholas Case released his sister and advanced, taking Serena's hand and lifting it to his lips. "Ever the Solemn Serena; it's good to see you."

"And you, Nicholas," she replied, disengaging her hand.

"Don't get all a-tingle," he drawled. He waited for the inevitable blushing protest, and smiled slightly when there was no such reaction. "And grown up on the inside, too," he murmured, before turning back to his sister. "Come into the green salon and meet my friend Alfred Lumsden. I've left him to Mother's tender mercies. He'll want rescuing."

Together, the three of them went down the long corridor and entered a well-appointed drawing room where a short, rotund man was enjoying conversation with Mrs. Case. He stood up at the girls' entrance and bowed low, the top of his head gleaming through the sparse crop of hair. As he straightened, his corsets creaked loudly, and Angel poked Serena in the ribs, quickly unfurling her fan to hide her grin.

"Ladies, this is Alfred Lumsden, a better friend and soldier you'll never find. Alfie, this is m'sister Angel—a misnomer if there ever was one—and her friend, Miss Serena Blessed, my second little sister."

Serena ignored his taunt and curtseyed elegantly.

"Servant, ladies," said the red-faced young man.

"Are you home to stay?" asked Angel, taking a seat beside her brother. Serena seated herself on the edge of the nearest chair and folded her hands primly in her lap. She stole glances at Nicholas, marvelling at the changes six years of rough living had wrought. His hair was the same dark gold she remembered, but his handsome face was a golden bronze with tiny crinkles at the corners of each blue eye—from squinting into the sun, no doubt. His shoulders seemed to have doubled in breadth, and his leg muscles rippled beneath the knitted riding breeches he wore. He had left a boy and returned a man—a man of almost frightening virility.

Serena's gaze left his calves, and she looked back at his eyes—eyes that were dancing with amusement as he watched her perusal. Serena lifted her chin slightly and returned her attention to the conversation.

Nicholas, too, appeared to be paying attention to the mundane discourse, but his thoughts were on Serena. She was not the know-it-all child or the blushing young lady he remembered. She was, he reckoned, twenty years of age—late to be enjoying a first Season, as his mother had written him. But her mother's illness had prevented an earlier introduction to the *ton*. And now, according to his mother, there was no time to be lost. Too bad, he thought cynically, as he took in Serena's fine brown eyes and flawless complexion, that she was so old.

Nicholas grinned at the absurdity of society and fielded his mother's query with, "What do you think, Alfie?"

His friend shot him an annoyed grimace and said, "It's up to you, Nicholas. I don't want to put your family out by appearing unannounced on their doorstep as we have."

Nicholas waited for his sister's and mother's protests to die away before he said, "Very well, very well. We'll stay here until we find bachelor quarters." Serena, he noticed, had not added her voice to theirs. So she had changed in that respect, too; she no longer suffered from her adolescent attraction to him.

So much the better! he told himself. He only wanted fun and foolishness after so many years of war. He didn't want Miss Sobersides following him around!

". . . and they are to be married at the end of the month," finished Mrs. Case, reaching over to pat Serena's hand.

Nicholas frowned and demanded, "To whom?"

Serena's eyebrow rose a fraction, and she said, "Lord Redmon."

"Best wishes and all that," Alfie began, before his friend interrupted.

"Not Gussie Fielding, not that Lord Redmon," said Nicholas.

"Augustus Fielding," said Mrs. Case, waiting for her son's congratulations. After all, Redmon was quite a catch for a girl like Serena who had only a modest dowry.

Serena, however, had heard Nicholas's tone and bristled. "Yes, *that* Lord Redmon," she proclaimed.

"Oh, that one," murmured Alfred Lumsden to himself. All eyes turned his way, and he laughed nervously. "Grown up to be a fine man, I'm sure," he hedged. "We knew him at school, Nick and I . . . But that was years ago! Changed completely, I'd lay a monkey. Oh! Pardon the expression, ladies. Nick, we really need to get settled . . ."

"Well, of course you do!" said Mrs. Case. "Come along. I'll have Burns show you to your rooms."

"I wonder what that was about?" said Angel when she and Serena were alone again.

"Obviously they remember him from school. Boyhood jealousies, that's all," said Serena, standing up.

"Where are you going? Don't you want to go to the dress-maker's and discuss your wedding gown?"

"Not today. It's been a tiring morning, and I'm going for a drive with Lord . . . my fiance this afternoon." How strange that sounded to her ears, she thought. "I'm going to lie down for awhile."

"Oh," said Angel, feeling deflated. "Rest well. We can go tomorrow, I suppose.

Serena entered her bedchamber and sat down on the bed. She removed her shoes and wiggled her toes on the plush carpet, absentmindedly drawing geometric patterns. After a minute, she began to remove her morning dress; it was her best one, a wool crepe in the palest of yellow that set off her dark hair and eyes to advantage.

After donning a lacy wrapper, Serena picked up her diary and re-read the last entry. She closed it with a sigh. Only last night she had expressed a pleasurable anticipation of this morning. She had been nervous, to be sure, as anyone would be at the prospect of a marriage proposal. But she had been sure of her response. Until Nicholas Case returned.

Not, she told herself, that she had any designs in that direction. Nicholas had ever been a capricious young man, not at all the type of man for her. But his presence had dampened her joy. Why, he hadn't even offered his best wishes, she thought indignantly.

Still, what could one expect? He felt no obligation to be courteous to her. She was only his little sister's annoying friend. They had grown up neighbors; being her elder by seven years, he had never treated her with respect. There had been that brief interlude before he left for the Peninsula when she had looked on him with admiration.

She blushed; she certainly hoped he didn't think she'd been dreaming of him for the past six years!

As children, Nicholas had hated his studies, escaping regularly from the rector's lessons and later being sent down from school at least three times for his audacious escapades. She, on the other hand, had begged the rector to teach her Latin and Greek, just like the boys, and had excelled at school.

They were complete opposites. Serena was quiet where Nicholas was garrulous. She was conscientious where he was reckless. She was good where he was . . . not. And he had always teased her unmercifully for it, calling her names and trying to make her cry. She'd never given him that satisfaction—had never shown him his teasing hurt.

Serena pursed her lips. She was being mawkish to allow his lack of manners to affect her mood. With her diary in hand, she padded across to the delicate writing desk and sat down. She dipped the pen in the ink and then nibbled on the end of it thoughtfully.

2e juin, 1816

Cher Journal,
    Aujourd'hui, j'ai eu un rendezvous avec Lord Redmon. J'ai dit "oui."

Serena frowned and put down the pen. She always kept her diary in French since Angel, who was an incurable snoop, had no command of the language. She re-read the French words with a grimace. Even to her sedate nature, the entry sounded dull.

"Met with Lord Redmon. I said yes." She read it aloud in French. Not even the romantic language could erase the blandness of the sentences.

Serena closed the volume and went to the window, staring down at the courtyard. She reminded herself that marriage was not a romance. It was, if anything, a business arrangement based on respect—perhaps followed by friendship. She didn't believe in the love depicted in fairy tales and the romance novels Angel thrived on.

She wasn't completely cold-blooded, she consoled herself. She respected Lord Redmon—Augustus, he had told her to call him. He was courteous and attentive. And he was an excellent steward of his estates.

Since Serena's father's death ten years ago, their lands had gradually fallen into disrepair. When she married, her mother had stressed, her husband needed to be an excellent manager to turn the estate around.

So here she was, in London for the Season, with her mother's words still ringing in her ears. There could be only one Season, because of the expense. This didn't bother Serena; she worried about her mother and didn't want to be gone too long.

An amused smile lighted Serena's face as she recalled discussing all this with Angel before leaving for London. Angel had declared they would make a race of it; the one marrying before the end of June would win one hundred pounds. Their carefree wager had been only half-serious, of course. Neither girl had that kind of money—Serena because of her circumstances, and Angel because she spent her pin money as fast as she received it.

Still, the wager had made for an interesting spring. And an interesting summer, Serena added thoughtfully. She moved to the blue velvet fainting couch and settled herself for a restful nap. It wouldn't do to have tired eyes when Lord Redmon—Augustus, came to fetch her for their drive.

Augustus Fielding was a man of average height and average appearance. He was neither ugly nor handsome, his features regular and undistinguished. His manners were impeccable; when he spoke, his voice was well-modulated and even. When in conversation, he evinced complete interest in the speaker. He was a gentleman.

On this day, he wore a brown coat, buff-colored breeches, and a brown beaver hat on his brown hair. He kissed Serena's hand when he entered the salon and tucked it into his arm possessively as they left the house.

"I have sent a notice to the papers," he said when they were underway.

"Good. I hadn't thought of that," said Serena, the unbidden

thought coming to mind that now it was official. There was no turning back.

"You needn't think about anything, Serena. That's what I'm for . . . now."

The speaking look he gave her was replaced by an uncharacteristic grin as he hailed the occupants of a passing carriage.

He returned his attention to Serena and said, "Where shall we go for our wedding trip? Would you like to see France, Italy? We could spend Christmas in the Greek Isles, if you like."

Serena looked startled and stammered, "Uh, I . . . don't know. I hadn't thought. I assumed we'd just go home."

"Home? To my estate? Not likely. Not with my mother there!"

"Oh! Then perhaps my . . ."

"With your mother looking over our shoulders? I don't fancy that idea either. Besides," he began, pausing and looking down on her with a wolfish expression, "I want you all to myself."

Serena managed a smile to mask her shiver of uneasiness.

Then Augustus laughed and said reasonably, "We'll discuss it later. Perhaps a trip to Brighton would be more pleasant for you."

Then he turned the topic as they continued along Rotten Row, bowing and nodding to acquaintances. "Your guardian tells me there's to be a ball next week and that we can announce our betrothal then, if you like."

"That will be fine. The Cases are very happy for us. I daresay Mrs. Case will spread the news of our betrothal before the papers can. But she may be delayed because of Nicholas's arrival."

"Nicholas Case is at home?"

Serena nodded, and Augustus flicked his whip and sent his leader out of line, executing a turn that sent them away from the crowd.

To her inquiry, he said blandly, "I was impatient with the halting pace. How is Nicholas?"

"Fine, I suppose. He's brought a friend with him, an Alfred Lumsden. He seems to be a very agreeable gentleman."

"Old Alfie, too, eh? You must give them my best."

"That's right. They mentioned they were acquainted with you at school. Perhaps they'll be home when we get back, and you can come in and speak to them."

"I have a very pressing appointment, my dear. You'll have to deliver my message for me."

"Of course," said Serena as the curricle rolled to a stop in front of the Cases' townhouse. Augustus helped her down and bowed formally.

"You can find your way inside, my dear. I really must run. I'll call on you tomorrow. Good bye, Serena."

"Good bye, Augustus."

At dinner that night, conversation was general, and Nicholas and his friend kept the entire family amused with their accounts of life on the continent. Tales of desperation for provisions became amusing anecdotes; freezing cold and heat exhaustion became grand adventures.

Finally Serena asked seriously, "But surely it was not all an adventure. I have read the battle accounts of Cuidad Rodrigo and Vittorio. It must have been ghastly. Especially Waterloo."

Nicholas, seated beside her, looked down at her, his eyes a mask of politeness. "Quite ghastly, as you point out, Serena. But we prefer to forego the grim details at dinner." He bit his words off, spitting them out with dangerous precision. At Serena's sharp intake of breath, Nicholas looked around and smiled. "I beg your pardon, Mother. It's rather difficult to remember how to behave in polite company."

Serena nodded and then bent her head, concentrating on her plate. Her face turned a dull red. How stupid of her! Naturally he would not want to dwell on the gruesome, especially in front of his mother and sister. She knew how they had worried about his well-being. Why had she been so thoughtless as to reawaken their anxious years of waiting when Nicholas had been so carefully easing their minds? Why had she felt the need to force him to think of the horrors of war again?

Thoroughly miserable, Serena stood up with alacrity when Mrs. Case signalled that it was time to leave the gentlemen to their port.

In the salon, Angel played the harp while Serena helped sort the silk threads for the chair cover Mrs. Case was stitching. Separating the greens, Serena came to the conclusion that she owed Nicholas an apology. With this difficult decision behind her, she entered fully into the debate of whether to stitch the flowers in pinks or yellows.

Half an hour later, the door to the salon opened, and Mr. Case entered.

His wife looked beyond him at the empty threshold and asked, "Where are the boys?"

Mr. Case sat near her and picked up his book. "The *men,*" he began, with a broad wink to Serena, "decided they would go out for the evening. I've put Nicholas up for membership at my club. I expect they'll spend the evening with their friends."

"Or at the Opera," said Angel with a knowing nod. "All the young men want to see that new singer—the Italian one. Or is she French?"

"Never you mind, young lady," said her father sternly.

Serena continued to untangle the threads, but she somehow felt cheated. Here she had planned to do the right thing, to apologize, and her audience had deserted her. She hoped he lost at cards!

When Serena entered the breakfast parlor early the next morning, Nicholas was before her, dressed in buckskins and boots.

She wanted to treat him coldly, but he caught her off guard by saying, "Glad to see not everyone sleeps till noon around here. I'm going riding. Would you care to come along?"

She hesitated, looking down at her morning gown. She had promised herself to write letters before her fitting that afternoon. Still, she liked nothing better than an early gallop, and since arriving in London this activity had ceased to exist. The promised treat was impossible to resist.

"I'll have to change," she said.

"I'll wait," he promised with that engaging smile.

Forgetting breakfast, Serena hurried up to her room. When she started back down the stairs, Nicholas was lounging on the buffet in the entrance hall, his long legs dangling casually. He spied her and stood up, his admiring scrutiny bringing color to Serena's cheeks.

"You should wear red all the time," he said softly, taking her hand and tucking it into his arm as they went down the front steps to the waiting horses.

Serena peeked up at him, her face partially hidden by the curling red plume on her hat. "Your mother doesn't think so. I had to fight for this habit. She thinks it improper for a young lady to wear red."

"Why, for goodness sake?"

"It's what society thinks," she said, as if that explained everything.

"Then society hasn't seen you in red yet," he said gallantly as he threw her into the saddle. His hand on her stirrup, he added, "You are breathtaking."

Nicholas released her, and her stallion sidled away, giving Serena a chance to recover her equilibrium.

The streets were difficult to manoeuvre with all the carts and vendors making their way to the market. Servants also bustled to and fro, out to make their morning purchases for the big households. Occasionally Serena spied a man dressed in sadly crumpled evening wear, holding his head or squinting as he wended his way home after a night of revelry.

Up ahead a commotion broke out, and Nicholas drew rein. Serena pulled up also, shaking her head in disapproval as two vendors started screaming while spilled fruits and vegetables continued rolling out of their overturned carts. Street urchins took advantage of the fray to dart into the street and scoop up the bruised produce.

"What a waste," said Serena, frowning.

A crowd began to gather, and several people started pointing to a ragged cripple in front of the wreckage. The two vendors quit trying to shout each other down and advanced on the crippled man, shaking their fists and yelling at the pitiful, tattered creature.

"Wait here," ordered Nicholas.

Serena watched him ride into the mass and urged her stallion forward, keeping its nose on his horse's rump.

"What's all this about?" demanded Nicholas. The crowd quieted at the sound of his commanding voice, and the two vendors tugged at their hats.

One stepped forward and said, "This 'ere man jumped out in front o' me, guvner. Made this 'ere bloke run into me cart."

Nicholas raised a brow, looked toward the crippled man, and drawled, "Jumped?"

"Well, 'e . . ."

"See here, you should think twice before accusing such a man of jumping anywhere. Instead, you should be stopping, tipping your hat, and asking if he would honor you by having a ride across the street."

The vendors started to grumble, but the crowd gathered closer.

"Wot for, guvner?" called one observer.

"What for?" asked Nicholas incredulously. He twisted in his saddle to make certain he had captured everyone's attention. When he saw Serena, he winked at her. "Why, can't you see this man's breeches? Are not those the breeches of a soldier, one of our brave lads who brought to heel that monster Napoleon Bonaparte? One of our lads who protected our shores from French guns, our children from certain slavery, our women from rape and murder! Why, we should all make way for one of our brave soldiers! And gladly, too!"

"Huzzah! Huzzah!" yelled the crowd.

The two vendors sheepishly picked up their wares, offering apples and potatoes to the stunned ex-soldier. The crowd began to disperse, and Nicholas dismounted. He extended his hand to the veteran.

"Thank you, Mr . . . ?"

"Case, Nicholas Case. What regiment?"

"Second Division, Picton's."

"Good outfit. I was with Uxbridge. Have you got a place to stay?" The man shook his head. Nicholas took out his card and wrote something on the back. "Go to this address and show my card to the vicar. They'll give you shelter and food. Then they'll help you find a position."

"Me? I reckon I'm pretty worthless now, guvner."

"I doubt that! Here, take a hackney. It's pretty far." Nicholas handed the man a few coins.

"Thank you, Mr. Case," said the old soldier, tears starting in his eyes.

"It's the least I can do," said Nicholas.

The man straightened and saluted; then he limped away, leaning heavily on his crutch. Serena sat quietly, leaving Nicholas to his own thoughts. He mounted and started toward the park again.

Finally, Serena said, "That was very kind of you, Nicholas."

"It was no more than anyone would do, if they had the chance."

"Where did you send him?"

"It's sort of a home for ex-soldiers. The army has turned them all out without any sort of pension. Some of us got together and set up a sort of refuge for them. Hopefully, they can learn a trade and be sent on their way."

"I didn't know you worked with charities."

Nicholas shook his head. "I didn't think it up; I only help

support it. Lord Wentworth wrote to me about his efforts last fall when I was still abroad. I only contribute financially and help spread the word. It's the least we can do," he repeated fiercely. They had reached the park, and he kicked his mare, calling back at her, "Race you to the other side!"

When they had slowed to a walk again, Serena protested, "You cheated! We would have beaten you by a mile if you had given us a fair start!"

"Why do you think I didn't?" he said, smiling into her glowing face. "Tilly here was bred for endurance, not speed."

"Obviously," said Serena haughtily.

"Remember the races we used to have at home?" he asked suddenly. "I always won!" he boasted.

"Of course you won. You were older and had bigger ponies than we did!"

"If you'd been a better horsewoman—"

"Aha! So now you must cheat to win because I am a better rider than you!" she mocked.

"I didn't say that!"

"You didn't have to; it's the only logical conclusion." With that, Serena waved her riding crop by the stallion's side, and they cantered away.

Nick caught them up immediately and said, "Did you ever consider standing for Parliament?"

Serena only laughed, feeling quite in charity with her companion.

"Let's go over to the pond. There are some benches," said Nicholas.

When they arrived, Nicholas dismounted and turned to help Serena. After securing their horses, he pulled a large white napkin from his pocket and offered her its contents.

"I thought you might like a bite of breakfast since I interrupted it."

"Thank you," said Serena, accepting the piece of toast and rasher of bacon.

Next he produced a silver flask which Serena declined.

Grinning, Nicholas said, "Don't worry, Serena, I'm not trying to weaken your defenses. I put hot tea in it. It's rather tepid now, I'm afraid, but it will wash down the crumbs."

Serena took a sip and then returned it, her hand briefly covered by Nicholas's strong fingers. Her eyes flew up to meet his, but he was obviously not aware of the current of electricity his touch had excited.

She shook off the feeling; it was only a remnant of her old infatuation with Nicholas. He pocketed the flask and leaned against the back of the bench, his long legs stretched out in front of him.

"Nicholas, I wanted to apologize for trying to wring the truth out of you last night at dinner. It was frightfully improper of me."

"Not at all. It's I who should apologize. You were only being curious. I well remember how you strive to learn all the facts about everything. I shouldn't have snapped at you."

"But I shouldn't have—"

"Never mind, Serena. It's forgotten now." He turned the subject and asked, "Are you enjoying your Season?"

"Yes, it's been very nice. But I do miss the country. London is much more confining."

"Then I'm surprised you chose Redmon," drawled Nicholas.

"Why do you say that?" asked Serena, sitting straight and turning to look down her pert little nose at him.

"Everyone knows Redmon lives in town and refuses to so much as visit his estate."

"Nonsense! His estate is very prosperous. Your father looked into it, and—"

"Of course it is!" laughed Nicholas. "His mother runs it. I daresay that's the only reason it is prosperous! She holds the purse strings, you know. You'd best get used to living in London."

Serena raised one brow and said loftily, "How could you possibly know anything about the man? You've been out of the country for six years."

"It's not difficult to find out. It's the talk of the clubs, you know. All your admirers are confounded by your choice," he said with a languid smile.

"So I'm the talk of the clubs?" she asked, her eyes narrowing. "I find it wonderful how the idle have so much time to speculate on the affairs of others. If they would go about their own business . . ."

"Now, Serena, you needn't take that tone with me."

"Why not? Were you not there among the tattlemongers?"

"I wasn't the one—" he began before Serena cut him off.

"Did you at least defend me?" she demanded.

"I said very little, Serena. And considering your choice, had I defended it, they would not have believed me."

"What does that mean?"

"It means my old grudge with Redmon is well known. No one would have taken me seriously had I defended your fiance."

"You knew him as a boy!" she exclaimed, jumping up.

Nicholas grasped her wrist and coaxed her back to the bench, saying, "Let's talk about it, Serena. I didn't mean to make you angry. Surely we have outgrown such childishness."

Serena smiled slightly. "I hope so. But you must understand, Nicholas, that I did not choose lightly. And your father thinks him quite suitable."

"Father is a trusting soul. He knows nothing of Redmon's character," he said, taking her hand and patting it. "It's not too late to reconsider."

Serena extracted her hand, taking a deep breath to calm the butterflies in her stomach which his touch had set loose. "Have you been home yet?" she asked, and Nicholas shook his head. "If you had and had visited Mother, you would have seen why I am marrying. Paradise Point is falling apart. We've lost several of our oldest tenants; the land is in such poor shape. The cottages and the manor house are badly in need of refurbishing."

"Surely my father would help . . ." began Nicholas.

"I couldn't ask him. Besides, everyone knows all it will take is for me to marry the right man."

"And what makes you think Redmon is that man?"

"As my guardian, your father has given his blessing. The matter is closed."

"I could open it again. I think I'll have a word with Redmon."

"Nicholas, stay out of it!"

Serena jumped up, glaring at him. Then she turned on her heel and grabbed the reins. The stallion's head jerked up, and he moved away nervously. Serena tried to lead him to the bench so she could mount, but the horse was too agitated. After a moment, she felt strong hands close around her tiny waist, and she was lifted up to the saddle.

"If you'd ride a horse closer to your own size, you could mount alone," mocked Nicholas.

"Oh, do be quiet!" she snapped and tapped the glossy sides with her crop. The horse reared slightly before taking off down the path. Nicholas climbed on his mare and followed at a more leisurely pace, catching her up at the entrance to the park.

Serena was still visibly angry, and Nicholas refrained from further comment.

Serena spent the next few days pouring over fashion plates, trying to decide on fabrics and styles for her trousseau. Mrs. Case insisted that they concentrate on this important decision alone before allowing anyone to proceed with their lives. Finally, with the wedding gown planned down to the final seed pearl, Mrs. Case announced that they would attend the theater that night.

Dressed in cream from head to toe, Serena added an amber pendant that rested just above the décolletage of her high-waisted gown. She studied her image and nodded, pleased with the effect.

It would be her first evening out as a betrothed lady. They were going to the Haymarket Theater to see Rossini's latest light opera. Augustus was to meet them there.

Lord Redmon greeted everyone with an urbane smile. He took the empty seat beside Serena and leaned over to whisper in her ear, "I've been missing you."

Serena smiled and cut her eyes toward him. How should she respond? she thought. The truth was she'd hardly had a moment to think of him. She felt a twinge of guilt. Between the callers who wanted all the details of the betrothal and the frantic shopping for a wedding costume, she had been too weary to think of anyone.

Except Nicholas, of course. He forced his way into her thoughts constantly.

Since coming to London, the only time Serena ever had to herself was early in the morning. She enjoyed starting her day in quiet solitude. But Nicholas had spoiled all that, bounding into the breakfast room every day without fail. After a hearty "good morning," he always called for black coffee and a full breakfast.

Only the day before, Serena had commented on his energy, trying unsuccessfully to keep the sourness out of her voice.

"What? In a bad mood already? You must learn to enjoy life, Sober Serena," he had said with a laugh.

Serena had looked him up and down and then asked him to pass the toast. Nicholas had spent the remainder of his meal hidden behind the newspaper.

That very morning had been much the same except that he had commented on an article about the corn laws Parliament was considering. Serena had questioned his familiarity with the state of affairs in England, which had led to a heated discussion.

When Nicholas had left the breakfast room, he had touched her shoulder and whispered close to her ear, "We must do this every morning to sharpen my wits." She had managed to ignore the leap her heart made at his touch and had thrown a piece of toast at his impudent head.

"Have you seen *The Barber of Seville* before, Serena?" asked Augustus, recalling her attention.

"What? Oh, yes, that is no. But I have read the work by Beaumarchais. I enjoyed it immensely."

"I think you'll like this better. Reading it is too dry," said Augustus.

Nicholas, who had taken the seat behind them, leaned forward. "Don't tell me you've actually read something, Gussie."

Serena glared at him, and Augustus returned a grimace of a smile and said politely, "It's Lord Redmon, now, Mr. Case." His voice lingered over the "mister," but Nicholas only grinned and sat back in the chair. Serena wished she could box their ears.

The curtains parted, and the performance began. The singing, though not brilliant, was good, and the performances were enthusiastic and contagious. Serena laughed out loud at the antics of Figaro, who thwarted old Bartolo's plots to marry his beautiful young ward, Rosina. The audience cheered as the handsome Count Almaviva and Rosina made good their escape and eloped.

After three curtain calls, Mrs. Case rose and announced it was time to leave. Augustus stood back to allow Serena to pass. Nicholas took her hand and led her out of the box, causing her to throw him a look of surprise and his old rival, one of suspicion. In the crowded corridor, short of shoving and pushing, Augustus was forced to lag behind. He watched in growing anger as Nicholas leaned down, his face just inches above Serena's; she was smiling.

"Lord Redmon, I didn't see you in the audience," said a young man at his elbow. "I wanted to congratulate you on . . ."

Redmon threw the young man a look of such loathing that the youth paused, giving Redmon a chance to forge ahead.

". . . but how silly to elope," Serena was saying.

"I thought all young ladies found it romantic to do so," said Nicholas.

"Only the foolish ones," she replied with a laugh.

"And Serena is anything but foolish," said Redmon over

their shoulders as they stepped into the cool night air. He took Serena's free hand and drew her away from Nicholas.

Nicholas bowed slightly, murmuring, "No, not usually." As he straightened, his gaze was hard, issuing a challenge. Redmon drew Serena closer, his smile self-assured.

When Nicholas came into the breakfast room the next morning, he was dressed for riding again. Serena, too, had chosen riding attire. The morning was bright and clear, and Serena wanted to escape before Mrs. Case remembered some pressing piece of business she needed to perform. The ball the Cases were giving to honor Angel and Serena was the next night, and the house would be at sixes and sevens until it was over.

"Going riding, Serena?" asked Nicholas after pouring coffee.

"I had planned on it," she admitted.

"Do you mind if I accompany you?"

"Not at all," she replied.

"Please tell me if it's not convenient. I'd hate to interrupt a rendezvous with your fiance."

"Nothing of the kind! Are you ready?" she added, standing up and marching to the door. Nicholas took a final swallow and choked on the scalding coffee before following her outside.

They were later than before, and the streets were becoming busy with all manner of people. Nicholas stopped beside a ragged flower girl and bought a bouquet of white rosebuds. Winking, he took out a single rose and returned the rest to the girl. She laughed, thanking him profusely.

Then Nicholas presented the flower to Serena. She lifted it to smell, presenting a charming picture to her swain.

"Here, let me," he said, taking it back and breaking off the stem. Moving his horse closer, he put it through the buttonhole on her lapel.

"Now your ensemble is complete, *mademoiselle,*" he said with a French accent and an elegant sweep of his hand.

Serena, also adopting an accent, replied, "Thank you, my good man."

They continued on their way, entering Green Park and setting their mounts to an easy trot.

"Did that soldier find his way to the home?" Serena asked when she felt the burden of their silence.

"Yes, I checked on him the next day. Seems he was a cook, so I don't think they'll have any trouble placing him."

"And the others? Does your vicar find positions for all of them?"

"So far he has. Oh, a few have gotten discouraged and simply left. But for most of them, it's a chance to start over."

Serena refrained from expressing her admiration for him, knowing it would only embarrass him. He had shown her a side of himself which she would never have guessed existed. The war had changed him; he was not the carefree young man who had left England to fight old Boney six years before. It was not that Nicholas had been unkind to others then, only unaware. He would never have noticed the crippled old man or paid a ragged flower girl an exorbitant price for one flower.

Nicholas slowed his mare as they reached the far end of the park. The herds of cattle with their buxom milkmaids were nearby, and Serena paused to watch them.

Her pastoral reverie was brought to a close when Nicholas asked, "I suppose Redmon will be at Mother's ball tomorrow night."

Serena frowned at the irritation in his voice and said, "I should hope so. Your father plans to toast our betrothal at supper."

"Hmph. I hope you know what you're doing, Serena."

"You needn't worry about me, Nicholas. I've done quite well without your advice for the past six years. I think I can decide what's best for me."

"Considering your choices . . ." began Nicholas. Then he

held up his hands to ward off her angry retort. "Never mind. Let's talk about something else. How's old Sleepy doing? Still boring his young students to death?"

Serena masked her laugh and said severely, "We have a new vicar now; Mr. Pritchett is retired. And he was not boring."

"Not boring! He used to put himself to sleep! And then he would wake up and get angry at us for not paying attention!"

"He never did that during my lessons," she said primly.

"That's because you were always asking questions, weren't you? Why, you even cornered me when I was home from University and asked me about your Latin declensions!"

"Which you couldn't answer!"

"Wouldn't answer; I had better things to do with my time than study Greek and Latin when I was on holiday."

"Holiday? Hah! You had been sent down. What was it? Horse races in the corridors or . . ."

But Nicholas' animated face lost its light, and he said abruptly, "We should be getting back now." With this, he turned his mare toward home.

The next evening, Serena dressed with extra care for the ball. Augustus had been absent from her side since the theater, but again Serena had had little time to think about him. She pushed to the farthest cavern in her mind the niggling doubt that she should have missed him, should have spent a great deal of time thinking about this man she was to wed in less than a fortnight.

Serena doubled the long strings of pearls her mother had lent her and stood back to study the effect. The combs of pearl-encrusted flowers shimmered in her dark hair; a bracelet of pearls graced each wrist. Her gown was ivory with three flounces. It was high-waisted, as was the fashion, and the neckline was cut low, though not immodestly so. She looked pale and opened the rouge pot, adding a touch of pink to her cheeks. Her dark eyes with their long lashes didn't need enhancement.

A quick knock heralded Angel's entrance. Serena glanced up at her friend and grinned.

"Just when I think I look quite elegant, you come in, as long and graceful as a gazelle, your blue eyes shining, your gown a shimmery blue to match. It makes me feel positively dowdy."

Angel laughed and plopped down on the chair, her movements more like a newborn colt than a graceful gazelle.

"I have instructed the musicians to play a waltz at least every third dance."

"A bit daring, don't you think?" said the serious girl.

"Pish, tush. I love to waltz, and it is my ball, too."

"Very well, although your mother may countermand your instructions."

"Not likely. You know she never notices details." Angel chewed on her lip, a sure sign of deep contemplation. Finally, she said, "Serena, what do you think of Alfie?"

"Mr. Lumsden?"

Angel nodded and sat forward eagerly.

"He seems very nice," said Serena noncommittally.

Angel sat back with a pout. "He's quite short, you know."

"Not to me," said Serena.

Angel's shoulders slumped. "He's not quite as tall as I am, even when he's in boots and I'm in slippers. I suppose we shall look quite absurd dancing the waltz together."

Serena suppressed a grin and consoled her friend with, "You know very well the ball will be a sad crush. No one will notice. I think you should do as you please."

Angel stood up, smiling once again. She linked arms with Serena and said, "Come on. Let's go to the musician's gallery and watch the first arrivals!"

Nicholas was lounging against a column near the entry way when a movement from above caught his eye. He turned to get a better view of the staircase as trim ankles were followed by rustling skirts. Then a tiny waist appeared and next, rich, luminous pearls suspended from a delicate neck swaying sensuously over her decolletage and the curve of creamy breasts. But it was Serena's face, the radiance of her dark eyes, that made him come to action, crossing the short foyer to stand before her. He bowed low and offered his arm.

"You look beautiful," he said, his voice as awestricken as a blind poet suddenly granted his sight.

"Thank you, Nicholas," said Serena, her voice suddenly breathless as she noted how splendid he looked.

He held out his arm, and she laid her gloved hand on his sleeve. He bent his head intimately and said, "Will you save me a waltz, Serena?"

"Not sure I want her dancing the waltz with anyone but me, old boy." Redmon stood blocking their path.

Nicholas dragged his eyes from Serena's face and gave a curt nod. "Seems to me that's up to Serena, old boy," he drawled, the anger in his voice barely masked.

Ignoring his words, Redmon took Serena's other hand and pulled her to his side, adding bluntly, "And I don't think I like your using my fiancee's name, either."

Nicholas was tempted to trap Serena's other hand, but he didn't want her to become the rope in a tug of war. He released her.

Serena had turned crimson. What was it, Nicholas wondered. Embarrassment? Anger?

"Now, Augustus, I know you have missed me, but I can't dance every dance with you," she temporized. "And as for my name, you must know Nicholas and I were children together. What should I call him? Mr. Case?"

Redmon bestowed on her a condescending look and guided her toward the ball room where the strains of the first waltz were beginning.

Nicholas watched them go, resisting his initial inclination to escape to the card room. Instead, he backed up against the wall to watch Serena as she waltzed with Redmon, then partnered his father, and finally another young man he'd never met before. He was joined in his scrutiny by his friend Alfie who was equally intent on the dancers, though the object of his attention was tall and blond.

"You know, Nick," the easy-going Alfie said softly, "there are times I wish I still had my sword at my side. A quick thrust—that's all."

Nicholas grinned down at his friend. "Anyone in particular?"

"Right now, I'd say that insolent young pup dancing with your sister. Of course, next dance, it will be someone else."

"Why don't you just step in and dance every dance with Angel? That would stir up the whole of the *ton.*"

Nicholas watched as Alfie digested this bit of advice. Then he shook his head and said, "Guess I should speak to your father first."

"That would be the civilized thing to do," said Nicholas. Shoving off from the pillar he was supporting, his look was anything but civilized. Alfie followed as the music ended, and the dancers began to promenade.

When Serena passed, Nicholas stepped up, keeping pace with her and ignoring the glowering young man on her other side.

"Are you free for the next set?" he asked.

"Yes, but it is to be a waltz. I'm not sure Augustus would—"

"The devil with him. What do you say?" growled Nicholas.

A tiny lifting of the corners of her mouth was the only indication that she was amused by his vehemence. Nicholas took this as his cue and pulled her closer. Serena stopped and turned to her previous partner, giving him an elegant curtsey.

"Thank you, my lord."

"My great pleasure, Miss Blessed."

Nicholas, meantime, signalled to a footman with a tray and took two glasses of champagne. He gave one to Serena.

"Thought you might like something cool. Are you tired? We could go outside."

"Thank you, Nicholas. This will be fine," she said, taking a sip and then turning to fend off two young men with a promise to dance with them later.

As for Nicholas, he watched impatiently, silently wishing, as Alfie had done, that he were wearing his sword. He grinned at his own thoughts. Then the musicians struck up another waltz, and Nicholas thrust his and Serena's glasses at the young men and took her hand.

She felt even more tiny in his arms. He could have lifted her like a flower. Her cheeks were suffused with a delicate pink; her brown eyes were lowered. The other dancers swirling around the room were talking volubly, but Nicholas felt no need to converse. He tightened his hold and twirled Serena around until she was dizzy, clinging to him for support. She threw her head back, looking up at him with those wide, dark eyes, her lips parted slightly, the tip of her tongue just visible. Nicholas pulled her closer, wishing they were alone, wishing they could stop this courting dance and embrace with abandon.

Her rosebud lips were just inches from his. If he bent his head just a fraction, his lips could drink in those sweet . . .

Abruptly, Nicholas curbed his thoughts and set her away from him, holding her at a more-than-proper length. What was he thinking? Just because he was playing knight-errant over her betrothal to Redmon, that was no reason to feel obliged to take her for himself! He wanted to enjoy his freedom; the last thing he wanted was a prudish wife!

But as he looked into Serena's puzzled eyes, he felt like a veritable cur.

"What's wrong, Nicholas?" Serena whispered.

"Nothing, Serena," he lied.

She smiled up at him and teased, "Is Augustus scowling at you? Do you fear his terrible wrath?" she added, smiling audaciously.

Nicholas held her closer and said, "I'm shaking in my dancing shoes. If you weren't holding on to me so tightly, I daresay I would be off cowering in my room."

He began another dizzying turn as Serena said, "I doubt that. You have always plunged headlong into trouble, regardless of the danger."

"Not quite as thoughtless as all that. Otherwise, I would never have come back from the war."

"No, I suppose not. Was it so very awful?"

"I don't care to think about what I saw," he said soberly. "Dreaming about it is harrowing enough!"

Serena's hand that rested on his shoulder moved closer to his neck; she pressed against his black evening coat.

"It has changed you, Nicholas."

He gave his usual irreverent grin and said, "And I was just thinking how much you have changed; I can't really call you Silent Serena anymore."

"Then I suppose I shall be forced to give up 'Nick the Knave'," she said, returning his smile.

"You never called me that."

"Not out loud," she laughed.

The music ended, and Nicholas lifted Serena's hand, kissing it as he bowed. Then he turned to promenade with her, but she was pulled away.

"My dance, my fiancee," gloated Redmon. He started through the dancers to the balcony.

Nicholas watched them go, a muscle twitching in his jaw.

As the evening wore on, Augustus kept Serena by his side, allowing her to dance only with select friends of his. Serena smiled and smiled, her jaws beginning to ache by the time they went in to supper. When Mr. Case stood and announced their betrothal, she and Augustus rose. Serena smiled and nodded to all the company, blushing when Augustus put his arm around her waist and kissed her cheek.

When they were seated once more, Serena whispered angrily, "Augustus, I don't appreciate being made a spectacle."

"A spectacle? I don't know what you mean, my dear. It's

perfectly all right for me to kiss you. And it was only a brotherly peck on the cheek. If I had wanted to make you a spectacle, it would have been very different." He smiled rather oddly down his long nose, and Serena turned away.

She excused herself after supper and retired to her room. She tried to calm herself, but she was still distressed. She excused Augustus, telling herself he was a bit tipsy. But this didn't help; his behavior the entire evening had been overly familiar and possessive. Serena told herself this was simply the way of men in love. Why, then, did she feel distressed, rather than loved?

When she left her chamber, she ran into Nicholas.

"Serena, are you all right?" he said, placing a gentle hand on her shoulder.

Tears started to her eyes, and she shook her head. She blinked and said firmly, "I'm fine, Nicholas. I'm a little tired; that's all." He released her, and she started back toward the ball room. She stopped and turned, saying, "Thank you for asking."

Augustus found Serena as soon as she stepped into the room, and he seemed determined to please. She soon found herself laughing at his stories and at ease with his friends. She began to think it had only been a case of the megrims with her. He really was charming.

It was almost dawn when her world came crashing down again. She had danced with Augustus three times, as was acceptable for a betrothed couple. But Augustus, almost reeling from the champagne he had consumed, took her hand and insisted on another dance. Despite her protests, he dragged her into his arms for a fourth waltz!

Serena quickly reached the decision that complying would be the lesser of the two evils. And hopefully, the company had grown thin enough that no one would remark upon it. But then Augustus pulled her indecently close. Trying to fend him off was impossible; Serena closed her eyes and waited for the music to end.

When it did, Augustus led her onto the balcony and proceeded to kiss her. His hands cupped her bottom, pressing her against him while he forced his wet tongue inside her mouth. She gagged and thrust him away, escaping back to the ball room.

Scrubbing at her lips, Serena realized she was being observed. Several gentlemen grinned knowingly, and ladies talked behind their fans. Then she saw Nicholas, his eyes blazing with anger; Serena fled to her room.

She stripped off the ivory gown and put on a wrapper before sitting down at her dressing table and pulling the pins from her hair. The abigail she shared with Angel picked up the brush.

There was a knock on the door.

Serena ignored it, but the noise became louder, and she nodded to the maid who opened the door.

"Serena, a word with you, if you please," said Nicholas from the doorway.

"Not now, Nicholas."

Nicholas stepped inside and folded his arms, leaning against the wall. Serena dismissed the maid, watching him warily, willing herself to remain composed.

He looked ruggedly handsome in his evening dress, the shadow of whiskers darkening his jaw.

"I sent Redmon home," Nicholas said, rubbing his knuckles.

"Oh, Nicholas," she said, her face flushed with embarrassment that he had been witness to her shame. But pride made her look him in the eye and say, "I'm sure Augustus will apologize when he is more . . . himself."

"More sober," observed Nicholas, dispassionately. "Drunkenness is no excuse for disgracing a lady—especially one's fiancee! You must see, Serena, he's not suitable for—"

"Not another word, Nicholas! You go too far! I know you regard me as your little sister, but I'm not, and I'll not have you dictating my behavior to me!"

Nicholas came closer, his expression tense. Serena wished

she were standing; she felt at a distinct disadvantage sitting in front of the mirror. How could she read him a lecture while dressed in a lacy wrapper and seated, only waist-high to him?

"Serena, you must open your eyes! Redmon's a scoundrel! Always was; always will be!"

Serena stood up, then wished immediately she had not. He still towered over her, his fists clenched, his blue eyes dark with anger.

"I refuse to discuss the matter with you. You're being completely irrational," she said loftily.

Nicholas took her by the shoulders. "I ought to shake some sense into you," he growled.

"And you criticize Augustus' behavior?" she said, raising her chin.

Nicholas dropped his hands and stepped back. He shook his head and said, "You always knew how to take the wind out of my sails, even when we were children." He walked to the door, and Serena sagged against the dressing table for support.

At the door, he said softly, "Serena, if you ever need a friend . . ." Then he was gone.

Serena sank down on the bench and covered her face with her hands. Taking a deep breath, she picked up the brush and ran it through her dark hair before climbing into bed, drawing the covers over her face to shut out the growing sunlight.

Nicholas changed into riding gear and went down to the mews and saddled his mare. When he reached the empty park, he allowed the mare to choose her own path, his thoughts rambling as well.

He could still hear Serena's words. "You regard me as a little sister," she had said. He always had; it was true—a particularly annoying sister. But since he had come home . . . She was hardly the solemn little girl who had had the habit of always being right. She was a very independent thinker, a trait he found peculiarly intriguing.

Nicholas shook his head. Serena intriguing? Or was it simply the old rivalry with Redmon that was egging him on?

Surely he had outgrown such childishness. He grinned and rubbed his hand; it had certainly been satisfying to draw Redmon's cork.

Then he frowned and pulled the mare to a halt. He had wanted to kill the man, a rather extreme desire despite his old hostility with Redmon.

The frown creasing his brow eased and his eyes began to twinkle. By God! he thought. He loved the silly chit! Who could ever have predicted such an eventuality when he had pushed her down in that mud puddle so many years ago.

Nicholas closed his eyes and visualized Serena as she had descended the staircase the night before. She was magnificent! Not at all the quiet church mouse he had taunted and teased. She was full of opinions and wasn't afraid to express them. Most of all, he never found her dull.

He squeezed his knees, and the mare ambled forward. "And now what, Tilly?" he asked his horse. "How can I convince her Redmon's not the man for her? She's every bit as stubborn as she ever was. And as for accepting me, she'll never believe I want to wed her."

Nicholas' fertile imagination envisioned a domestic scene, in front of the fire, Serena with a book in her lap. Or perhaps they would play piquet in the evenings. Then his thoughts wandered from the snug little parlor, up the stairs, to his bedroom.

The mare had stopped again, and Nicholas flicked his riding crop impatiently. Not allowing his thoughts to range any farther, he sent the mare off at a reckless gallop.

Making his way to the city, Nicholas entered a dusty, dank cell of an office inhabited by a young man who could well have passed for a troll.

The man gave a toothy grin and said, "Glad you made it back in one piece, Nicholas."

Nicholas grinned and shook hands, clapping the man on the

shoulder. "Glad you've made it this long without a jealous husband running you through, Jarrod."

"Aye, there have been some close calls."

"I know, I know. What I don't understand is what there is about you that attracts the ladies. Perhaps you remind them of their dolls."

Jarrod drew himself up to his full five foot and five inches and said firmly, "Whatever it is, I'm eternally grateful! Now, Nicholas, what brings you to my office?"

"I need your help. You remember Gussie Fielding from school?"

Jarrod's face lost its smile, and he nodded.

"Good. I need to know why he is marrying and what type of character he has become. Mistresses, other betrothals, family, everything."

"Other betrothals?" asked Jarrod, demonstrating his uncanny ability to cut through to the heart of the matter.

"Yes, he's currently betrothed to a . . . friend of mine. I'm afraid she's in for a shock unless he's changed completely. I'll pay you twice your usual fee."

Jarrod held up stubby fingers and shook his head. "No need. I'll do this just for the pleasure. Besides, I've always wanted to pay you back for rescuing me from that bastard."

Nicholas grinned. "That was my pleasure, if you'll remember. There's one more thing. Time is of the essence. The wedding is less than two weeks away."

"I'll have a report for you in two or three days. Shall I come to you?"

"No, it would be better if I came here. If I can't make it, I'll send Alfie."

Serena kept to her room that day, not descending until time for dinner. They were to attend a musicale that night; she wanted to plead the headache but felt that would be the coward's way out. She needn't have worried. Neither Augustus nor

Nicholas put in an appearance, and Angel was bubbling so, no one noticed Serena's doldrums.

When Mr. Lumsden left them to fetch refreshments, Angel whispered behind her fan, "He is so considerate, Serena. He only danced with me once last night. The other times he sat out with me so I wouldn't get too tired."

"But you love to dance," replied Serena with a wan smile.

"Shh. He doesn't know that," Angel said, turning to greet Mr. Lumsden's return with a brilliant smile.

Nicholas arrived home after everyone else had left for the musicale. He entered the library and poured a large glass of Madeira. Then he settled into the leather sofa, propping one booted foot on the fender of the fireplace. It was a chilly evening, and a small fire burned in the grate. Exhaustion finally overtook him, and he was soon sound asleep.

The clock was striking two in the morning when Serena finally decided to get out of bed and go downstairs to find something to read. They had left the musicale at midnight when Augustus failed to show up.

Mrs. Case had been distressed by his absence, but Serena hadn't been. She had not heard from Augustus all day—no note, no flowers, no apology. And what irritated her even more was that Nicholas had been right about Augustus—at least about his disgusting behavior at the ball.

The memory of that kiss had sickened her at first, but now she was annoyed. Her temper would not allow her to sleep.

Serena crept silently down the stairs and opened the door to the library, closing it behind her. A gentle snore alerted her to Nicholas's presence. She turned to leave, but immediately changed her mind. She would be quiet, she told herself, but she really wanted a book to help take her mind off things.

Holding her candle high, she selected a volume of poems by Byron. Turning, the candlelight fell on Nicholas's face.

Serena's expression softened as she watched the gentle rise and fall of his chest. He was reclining, his head propped up at an uncomfortable angle on the arm of the sofa. Serena took a pillow from the chair and eased it under his neck. Nicholas shifted slightly but didn't wake.

Serena studied him, his appearance in repose so young, so boy-like. She felt the old fascination stirring in her breast. If only . . .

Then, wide-eyed, she backed away, forgetting the book of poetry as she fled to her room.

Why had Nicholas come back home now, filling her mind with schoolgirl fancies of romance? Why had he planted these doubts in her mind about Augustus, she added, conveniently disregarding that Augustus's behavior had not been exemplary.

Most of all, why could she not rid herself of her feelings for him?

The next morning, Serena, wearing a fetching yellow riding habit, entered the breakfast parlor. She poured her tea and seated herself, eating her toast in silence. She had tossed and turned the previous night, unable to put Nicholas from her mind. Since she had not heard a word of apology from Augustus for his behavior, she was not feeling at all charitable toward him. But she had dreamed about Nicholas, a disturbing dream of castles and fairy tales. And she had awakened with a start; as though mesmerized, she had dressed and made her way downstairs. Facing him was the only way to lose her discomfort around him, she reasoned.

But Nicholas seemed determined to ignore her, and Serena set her teacup down noisily. Slowly, the newspaper was lowered, and Nicholas looked over the top, studying her for a moment before speaking.

"Going riding?" he asked casually.

Serena squared her shoulders and nodded. "Would you like to accompany me?" she asked, wondering at her own temerity.

Nicholas didn't seem to mind for he smiled broadly and replied, "All right. But I think we should agree to avoid certain subjects."

"Agreed. Are you ready?"

"And willing."

They rode to Green Park, dismounted, and strolled along with their horses trailing. The pastoral scene made Serena sigh, her thoughts wistful.

"Something wrong?" asked Nicholas.

"No, just thinking about home. The new calves will all be growing up. Mother wrote and told me my old mare just foaled. I love this time of year at Paradise." Serena looked up to find Nicholas grinning. "Why are you smiling?"

"Whenever I hear the name of your estate, it makes me think of your father. He used to laugh himself; he thought Paradise Point such an ingenious name for the estate of a man named Blessed. I always liked your father."

"So did I," she said simply and smiled up at him from beneath the brim of her hat.

Nicholas looked away, frowning. She was such a beauty, so sweet and trusting. He really couldn't stand by and see her marry someone like Redmon. Nicholas closed his eyes, his face reflecting his distaste.

He simply had to find a way to make her reject Redmon. Oh, he wanted to wed her, to be sure, but he had no indication she returned his feelings. Just the opposite; she treated him like an annoying older brother—someone to bicker with.

But even if she wouldn't have him, she couldn't wed Redmon. The very name conjured up an image so appalling he flinched, and school day memories long buried overflowed.

There had been a race. Redmon had spent a fortune on a horse and had challenged Nicholas. He had accepted, riding only a hired horse. Still, Nicholas had won, and a furious young Redmon had started beating his own horse, his riding crop cutting into the horse's flesh. Nicholas closed his eyes; he could still hear the horse's screams. And then he had taken the crop away from Redmon, broken it in half and punched Redmon in the nose. The horse had had to be put down; Nicholas and Alfie had paid for it after Redmon refused to put the crippled animal out of its misery.

"You're very quiet, Nicholas."

He stopped in his tracks and took her hand, lifting it to his lips. Serena's wide brown eyes watched in surprise. He kept her hand captive, and her eyes became dreamy. Time stopped as he gazed down at her.

Then her stallion stamped his foot and snorted, breaking the spell.

"We'd better get back," said Serena, her voice small.

"If you say so," agreed Nicholas without releasing her hand.

"I've a fitting for my wedding gown at eleven o'clock."

"Of course," he said coldly. "Wouldn't want you to be late for that!" So saying, he threw her into the saddle before vaulting into his own and sending his mare off at a brisk trot without a backward glance.

Feeling subdued, Serena followed.

When they arrived home, there was a huge bouquet of pink roses on the buffet in the entrance hall.

"For you, Miss Serena," said Burns loftily. "Shall I have them taken to your room?"

Serena shook her head. "No, they look so pretty here, I think I'll just leave them. Was there a note?"

Burns handed her a stiff envelope, and she moved away from them, a smile touching her lips. The flowers were from Augustus, and he begged her forgiveness for his ardor at the ball. He also reminded her that he was leaving town to bring his mother back for the wedding.

Nicholas turned to the butler and said, "Redmon?"

Burns nodded, dropping his mask of disinterest long enough to reveal his distaste for Serena's suitor.

Nicholas muttered a curse as he watched Serena drift up the stairs.

Several days later, Nicholas left the dingy office of his friend, his visage grim. If he had seen Redmon walking toward him at that moment, he would have throttled the man. That a man like Redmon had entree into society disgusted him. That Serena would be marrying the man in only four days turned his stomach.

Looking for distraction, he went to his club where he found a secluded corner in the library and ordered a drink and a deck of cards. As he played patience, losing badly each hand, he concluded that he would have to lay the facts before Serena, no matter how unpleasant it might prove. Even if she never spoke to him again, she would be safe from Redmon.

"Nicholas, what are you doing? Hiding?"

Nicholas pointed to the chair opposite his and began to deal a hand of piquet. "Sit down, Alfie."

As his friend obeyed and obligingly picked up his cards, he stammered, "Thing is, Nick, wanted to talk to you."

"Hm? What is it?"

Alfie laid his cards down and hunched forward, his corsets creaking. He took a paper from his pocket and pushed it toward Nicholas.

Nicholas picked it up and opened it. "What the devil?"

"Shh! Not so loud. Act casual."

Nicholas lowered his voice and said, "This is a special license to marry! What are you doing with it?"

Alfie smiled for the first time. "I talked to your father, and he gave his blessing, but he said Angel had to be consulted. Thing is, Nick, I'm sure she finds me a dull stick. You know how these young girls are—want a knight in shining armor and all. And look at me!" Nicholas obliged, a twinkle in his eye. "Well?" demanded Alfie. "I daresay they don't even make armor to fit me!"

"But why the special license?"

Alfie nodded and said mysteriously, "Ah, that! It's romantic, don't you see. It will make me seem a man of action!"

Nicholas shook his head. "Alfie, you are a man of action. We were together at Waterloo, remember? You were mentioned in dispatches several times. You don't need this! And I don't want to see m'sister elope! Just come out and ask her!"

"I . . . I guess I could. I'm just afraid . . ."

"You? Afraid? Remember, my good man, 'Faint heart ne'er won fair maiden'!"

Alfie stood up; the cards forgotten. "You're right! I'm going to speak to her right now!"

Nicholas twitched the paper from Alfie's grasp. "Here, let me get rid of that for you. You won't be needing it."

Alone again, Nicholas tapped the paper on the table thoughtfully. "Faint heart . . ."

He smiled, envisioning the blistering lecture Serena would read him if he were to kidnap her to prevent her from marrying Redmon. Shaking his head, he stood up and, placing the paper in his pocket, strode out the door.

Serena settled her newest bonnet on her brown curls and tied the jaunty green bow under her ear. She smiled at her image and hurried downstairs to wait for Augustus.

When she reached the entry hall, the footman opened the front door, and Nicholas stepped inside.

"Serena, I'd like a word with you," he said, striding to the library door and holding it open for her.

"I can't right now, Nicholas. I have plans."

"It will only take a few minutes," said Nicholas, thinking that when he started talking about Redmon, she wouldn't listen to him very long.

"But Nicholas . . ."

The footman opened the door again, and Redmon entered. He swept off his beaver hat and bowed low when he saw Serena.

"Beautiful as ever, my dear," he intoned.

"Thank you, Augustus. Nicholas, perhaps later?"

He gave a curt nod and sneered at Redmon.

Redmon vouchsafed a smug smile. "Good day to you, Case."

"Redmon. Serena, when you come back from your drive . . ."

"I shan't be back for some time. Augustus is going to escort me to the dressmaker after our drive."

"I see. Some other time then."

When they were in the curricle, Augustus said, "If Case is bothering you, I shall speak to him."

"There's no need for that," Serena said quickly. The last thing she wanted was her fiance to exacerbate the situation. With Nicholas's temper . . .

"He's really overstepping the lines of propriety. I've heard about your morning gallops, Serena. That's not at all the thing. I haven't said anything before; after all, we'll be married in a few days, and all that will come to an end."

Serena's grimace was hidden by her poke bonnet. He was so sure of his control over her. But why shouldn't he be? As her husband, he could tell her exactly what to do. And Nicholas? What would happen to their new-found friendship?

"We will be neighbors with the Cases, you know," she said quietly, turning to face him.

Redmon turned his mocking smile on her. "What makes you think we'll be living on your estate, my dear? I absolutely refuse to be a provincial; we'll live in town.

"But I prefer the country."

"You may visit the country, but you'll grow accustomed to town life. It's the only place to live," he concluded firmly.

Serena clamped her jaw closed, refraining from protests. As they reached Rotten Row, she smiled and nodded to acquaintances, but her thoughts were confused. She felt trapped; she had chosen Augustus partly because he seemed a sensible man and would be able to manage her estate. She knew now he had no interest in mundane tasks. Nicholas must have been right; the dowager Lady Redmon ran Augustus's estate.

"You haven't mentioned the flowers I sent before I left town, Serena. Did you like them?"

His voice has so eager, she found herself brightening and said, "They were beautiful! Thank you, Augustus."

"Not as beautiful as you, my dear," he said, fixing his gaze on her. Serena lowered her eyes. "Haven't you forgiven me yet? I'm afraid my ardor frightened you. This month of waiting has been difficult for me. I'm so impatient to make you mine."

Serena smiled as she tried to shrug off the chill his words sent down her spine. It was just nerves; she, too, would feel better after they were wed.

"We'd better get you to your fitting. It's getting late."

Serena dressed with special care for the masqued ball that evening. She wore her costume like armor, the jeweled cowl covering her hair, the green gown with its fitted bodice and gold underskirt hinting of her charms, the wide sleeves banded with gold braids recalling days of knights rescuing damsels in distress.

From the headdress, the abigail pulled a few tendrils of brown curls to dance and tease when she moved. "You make a proper Juliet, miss," she pronounced, stepping back.

"Thank you, Polly," said Serena, smiling at the thought. She, however, had no intention of taking her life; instead she would do her best to accept her husband as he was. She would learn to adjust, and he, too, would make some concessions, she thought confidently. He had to care for her, or he wouldn't have offered for her!

She entered the salon and found Nicholas waiting for her. He wore a scarlet domino; the mask dangled from his fingers.

"Good evening, Serena," Nicholas said, sounding for all the world like a stern schoolmaster.

"Nicholas," she replied, her tone equally serious.

"Is Redmon going as Romeo?" he asked, trying to lighten both their conversation and his mood.

"No, I believe he, too, wears a domino."

Silence reigned until Nicholas broke the silence with, "Serena, I must speak to you alone."

Serena looked around the empty salon, raising her brows in query.

"Not now. There is not time enough. Later, perhaps, at the ball."

"Very well, Nicholas. I don't understand why you're acting so strangely. You can—"

"Serena! How charming! You look just like a lady in a medieval storybook. Why, you might be the daughter of some feudal lord!" Angel exclaimed, hurrying into the room with Alfie trailing at her heels. "Isn't Serena beautiful?" she added, turning to Alfie for confirmation.

But his response made her blush prettily when he said, "Yes, but not as beautiful as you, Angel." Alfie swallowed hard, remembering the other occupants of the room, and he stammered, "That is . . . uh . . . Miss Serena is quite beautiful . . . it's . . . well . . . I'm sorry."

"Never mind," Serena and Nicholas said simultaneously.

The elder Cases joined them, and they headed for the door. The Prentices lived only two blocks down the street, but it would have been sacrilege to walk, so they rode in the huge traveling carriage. It was cozy seating six, but Mrs. Case insisted they all arrive together. When the carriage queued up only three houses down from their own front door, Mrs. Case utilized the time to repeat her homily about the girls' comportment at the masquerade.

"And stay with one of us whenever you are not dancing," she concluded just as the carriage reached the Prentices' door. The house was ablaze with candlelight. There were tall candelabra everywhere, even descending the front steps and into the street.

There was no receiving line, and they stood on the threshold looking down at the ballroom for a few minutes. Peering through the slits of her mask, Serena searched the ballroom for Augustus, but it was impossible to determine which, if any, of the dominos and masks concealed him.

When several friends called them by name, the pair of girls realized quickly that their masks were superfluous. Being petite and brunette, Serena might not have been remarked. But with a tall blond beside her, they were unmistakable.

"We must separate if we're to have any fun," said Angel.

"You heard your mother," cautioned Serena.

"Fiddlesticks! I'll stay with Alfie, and you go with Nicholas."

Nicholas wagged a finger at his sister and said, "How easily you arrange our lives without any concern for our desires."

Serena masked her surprise and turned up her nose, saying haughtily, "There is no need for you to serve as my protector. I have Augustus."

She hurried away. Nicholas turned to Angel and snapped, "Must you always put your foot in it? Take care of her, Alfie. She needs a keeper." He hurried into the crowd which had swallowed Serena.

Serena was carried along by a wave of humanity, her search for Augustus forgotten as she was jostled and squeezed. The voices were louder than at other balls, the behavior of the guests more daring.

The orchestra was playing a waltz, and Serena blushed as she watched several couples pressed against each other. Then her eyes discovered a familiar figure, his brown hair and thin lips unmistakable to her. He was holding his partner as tightly as he could; their thighs moved as one while they swirled and swayed. Serena was not familiar with the woman; she wore a milkmaid's costume, her waist cinched tightly and her bosom overflowing. Through the narrow openings in his mask, Augustus's eyes never left her decolletage, and he kept licking his lips. Then he threw back his head, laughing loudly at something she said.

Serena felt her knees begin to wobble. Her face turned a dull red, and she hurried away. She found the ladies' withdrawing room and accepted the maid's offer of a cool cloth to bathe her face.

Serena wished fervently she had stayed with Mrs. Case, or even with Nicholas, despite his reluctance. Though Mrs. Case had warned them that guests at a masquerade could sometimes forget themselves, Serena was shocked.

The music stopped, and Serena plucked up her courage and left the ladies' room. Outside, voices filled the void left by the music, and she remained by the door.

Then he was there, bowing low before her, the candlelight playing on his dark gold curls, his smile amused below the red half-mask.

"Lady Juliet, might this poor knight beg a dance with you?"

Serena eagerly took his proffered hand, saying, "Oh, Nicholas, I'm so glad to see you. This is not at all what I expected. I was wrong to go off alone like that."

"It was my fault," he said, patting her hand. "I was only teasing Angel, you know. I realized immediately how it sounded, and I followed you. Just stay with me."

"Gladly!" Serena let him guide her onto the dance floor where waltzers were gathering again. He held her firmly but not too intimately. As they danced, Serena began to relax, forgetting about the other dancers and Augustus.

"I think your fiance is here," Nicholas said finally.

"I know. I saw him during the last set."

Her voice was solemn, and Nicholas pulled her closer, whispering, "I wouldn't place too much importance on it, you know. Many people forget themselves at these little affairs."

"I realize that now. Nicholas, it's so confusing; Augustus makes me angry one minute and the next, he is as charming as . . ." She paused, completing her thought silently, "as you are."

Nicholas remained silent, unable to supply the reassuring words she craved. Then he managed a grin and said, "Let's forget about everyone else. We're at a masquerade. Let's be outrageous!"

With this, he began to twirl her faster and faster, spinning as they passed couple after couple, forcing them from the floor. Soon, they had the outer circle of the floor to themselves. In the inner circle, the dancers stopped and watched Serena and Nicholas. He put outlandish lyrics to the familiar music and sang off key in her ear. By the end, she was laughing so hard, she kept upright only by the strength of his arms.

The music faded away; the other dancers began their promenade, moving past Serena and Nicholas. But they remained in each other's arms, the amusement fading from their eyes, leaving a hunger in its wake.

Her hand played with the curls at the nape of his neck. He trapped her other hand against his chest and leaned closer, his lips relentless. Serena held her breath; time and air were suspended. Then he kissed her forehead—a simple, lingering touch full of promise and passion.

"Nicholas," croaked Alfie Lumsden nervously.

Nicholas looked over at his friend and smiled. He led Serena toward his sister and friend.

"Serena, you have torn your hem!" announced Angel loudly for the benefit of all the tittering masqueraders who were staring at her shocking brother and friend. "Come with me to . . ."

"Dearest Serena, how glad I am to have found you in this sad crush."

Everyone turned as one, mouths open at the newcomer's genial tones.

"Good evening, Augustus," said Serena, recovering first.

"You'll grant me the next dance, won't you, my dear?" As he took her hand and led her back to the floor, he whispered tenderly, "Only think, four more days! I'm counting the hours!"

Nicholas started after him, but Alfie's hand held him back firmly.

"Well!" said Angel. "That was certainly good of Lord Redmon to clean up after your frightful behavior, Nicholas! What could you have been thinking!"

Nicholas turned on his sister, his eyes sparkling dangerously. "I was thinking I had finally won Serena." He looked back at the dancers and watched as Serena flashed a dazzling smile up at her fiancee. "Obviously, I was mistaken."

He stalked off toward the card room, leaving his sister and future brother-in-law gaping. To the onlookers, the matter appeared to be closed, and they returned to their own conversations.

Supper was over, and Serena leaned on his arm slightly, content and confident that she had made the right choice all along. Augustus was exactly the type of man she should wed. His manners were impeccable, and he was adept at entertaining not only her but the others seated around them. He had spoken knowledgeably about crops and harvests with Lord Fenwicke. He had traded *on-dits* with old Lady Aimsworth.

And he had been attentive to her every wish. He had even kissed her cheek when they had had the unmasking just before supper was served.

And Nicholas? The last time she had seen him, he had been glaring at Augustus from the doorway of the card room before turning his back on them both. No, he was not at all suitable for an even-tempered, sensible girl such as she. He was as mercurial as ever.

It was quite late when they finally left the ball. Augustus helped Serena enter the carriage and turned to find himself face to face with Nicholas, whose expression was filled with purpose.

"A word with you, Redmon," said Nicholas. "Mother, I'll walk home."

"Very well. Good night, my lord."

"Good night, my dear Mrs. Case. Serena, until tomorrow."

"Good night, Augustus."

The carriage pulled away from the curb, and Nicholas pointed toward home. Redmon fell into step beside him, a smile playing on his thin lips.

"Well, Case, I thought you said you wanted a word with me."

Nicholas stopped and nodded. "Several, as a matter of fact."

"You have my attention," said Redmon.

"I want you to withdraw from this betrothal."

"Withdraw? You must be joking! Why would I do such a thing? Serena will make an excellent, biddable wife. And what's more, I have the added pleasure of knowing I will be making you utterly miserable. I assure you, nothing could make me happier."

"So you're marrying her out of spite for me," said Nicholas, rubbing his fist against his thigh.

"Not at first. But it has made the idea of marriage much more palatable for me."

Nicholas smiled for the first time, disconcerting his opponent. "Oh, that's right. I almost forgot that your mother is forcing you to marry, or she'll withdraw her support, along with her substantial fortune."

"Who told you that?" snarled Redmon.

"The same person who told me about your mistress and how you saw fit to send your two illegitimate sons to some servants' relatives in Ireland. If you had an honorable bone in your body, you would have acknowledged them. I wonder what Serena will say about that?"

Redmon glared at Nicholas, then his expression grew smug again. "Tell her," he said. "After tonight, she won't believe a word you say against me."

"Then you refuse to withdraw?"

"Without question, old boy." With that he turned around

and walked away, calling back with a laugh, "See you at the church!"

Nicholas hurried down the street and caught up with the lumbering carriage as it pulled up at the front steps. He waited while everyone said good night before calling Serena back into the salon.

She covered her yawn with delicate fingers and shrugged, going with him.

"Nicholas, I am extremely tired."

"Serena, I have some things to say to you which you may find distasteful. But they must be said," he added, almost talking to himself.

"Nicholas, I am not in the mood. You have caused me enough . . . uncertainty."

He rang the bell and asked for tea to be served before continuing, trying a different tack.

"It was a wonderful evening, wasn't it? I think the Prentices outdid themselves."

"It was pleasant," returned Serena, her voice losing some of its wariness.

"You know Angel and Alfie are to be married, don't you?"

"Really! How wonderful! I'm afraid Angel and I haven't had much time to talk in the past few weeks. She's always busy with Mr. Lumsden, and I'm always trying something on!" They both laughed, and sat down when the footman entered with the tea tray.

"That will be all for tonight, Cummings," said Nicholas, accepting the cup Serena had poured for him. He helped himself to a biscuit and chewed thoughtfully for a moment.

Then he put down the cup and the biscuit, shaking his head. "It just won't do, Serena. I can't stand by, knowing what I know, and let you marry Redmon. The man's a bounder!"

Serena was on her feet in the instant. "Nicholas, I warned you . . ."

Nicholas stood up also and shouted, "Not this time! This time you're going to hear me out!"

Serena turned on her heel and marched out of the room. Nicholas's nostrils flared in anger; then he was striding after her. He spun her around before she took a step up the stairs and dragged her back into the salon, his frustration spilling over with every step.

With a snap of his wrist, he pulled her against his chest, growling angrily, "This is what I should have done at the ball!" One hand tilted her chin up, and his lips came down on hers. He watched as a single tear escaped down her cheek.

Nicholas closed his eyes and, with amazing restraint, released her. Taking a deep breath, he said softly, "I'm sorry, Serena. I was angry. I apologize for . . . my behavior—both now and at the ball."

As Serena's heartbeat slowly returned to normal, her anger grew. First he wanted to kiss her; then he apologized for it. He didn't want her for himself, but he didn't want Augustus to have her either. She had had enough!

"I hope we can still be friends," Nicholas continued.

"No, Nicholas, I don't think so! You accuse Augustus of all sorts of unnamed horrors, and then you turn around and treat me in the most appalling manner! No, I don't think we could ever be friends!"

She turned and walked to the door. She paused, waiting for him to follow her. When he didn't, she continued up to her room where she threw herself on the bed and cried.

Nicholas made his way to the library and proceeded to get very drunk.

Serena was still abed when she received a note from Augustus. It confirmed her opinion that her choice was both romantic and sensible. He would pick her up at two o'clock, it stated, and take her to meet his mother. He begged her not to worry, saying he was certain his mother would love her as much as he did.

A single red rose accompanied the missive, and Serena

picked it up to sniff the sweet fragrance. "Ow!" she said, looking at the dot of blood oozing from her pricked finger. She put the flower back on the table and nursed the hurt.

Serena climbed out of bed and padded to the window. Rain! How she hated rainy days. And foggy; she could barely see the street in front of the house. She returned to the warm bed and drank the hot chocolate the abigail had brought.

There were more wedding presents to be unwrapped, Polly told her. Serena nodded but she made no move to get up.

"Shall I lay out the lavender gown, miss?"

"Lavender?" said Serena, making a moue. She didn't know why she had allowed Angel to talk her into that gown. It didn't suit her coloring, and the style was all wrong. Still, she hadn't worn it yet, and she didn't want it to go to waste. "Yes, make it the lavender. I might as well finish ruining this dreadful day. What does Griggs's bad knee say? Will it rain all day?"

"No, Miss," said the maid seriously. "He thinks as how it should be better by evening."

"I hope he's right; I do hate dreary days like this."

"Mr. Griggs is never wrong, Miss," adjured the abigail, helping Serena out of her nightrail.

True to his word, Augustus called for her at precisely two o'clock. He helped her on with her coat and then tugged his beaver hat down around his ears against the rain. He took her arm and whisked her down the front steps and into the waiting carriage.

Shaking the raindrops from her hair, Serena looked around in surprise. It was a traveling carriage, spacious and well-appointed, but dark with the curtains drawn at all the windows.

Augustus said solicitously, "Let me light the lamps, my dear. It will help dispel the gloom."

"Is this yours, Augustus?"

"Yes—that is, it is my mother's. She rode in it to London. I don't have another enclosed carriage, and I didn't want you exposed to the elements—not when our wedding is only three days away!"

"Oh, of course. How considerate of you," said Serena.

"Serena, did Nicholas talk to you last night?"

"No. That is, not exactly."

"He's blackmailing me, you know."

"No, Augustus! He would not!"

"Well, I suspect he would like to have you for himself," said Augustus, putting his hand on her shoulder and playing with a loose curl of dark brown.

"I don't think so," said Serena, turning to face him. His hand rested heavily on her shoulder, and she shivered.

"Cold, my dear? I should have had warm bricks at your feet. But then, we won't be in here too much longer."

"Augustus, why would you say Nicholas wants me for himself? I assure you he has never indicated to me . . ."

"And that spectacle you made of yourselves last night wasn't an indication? Oh, come now, my dear, everyone could tell he wanted to take you then and there. I wonder, would you have resisted?"

"Augustus!" she exclaimed angrily. Then his fingers gripped her shoulder, and she cried out. "Let me go!" When he had complied, she said severely, "I think you had better take me home, Augustus!"

"Home? To your Nicholas?" He moved the curtain to one side, and Serena peeked out.

"Where are we? Surely this isn't Grillon's Hotel."

A rumble of laughter filled the carriage as it rolled to a stop. "No, my dear bride. It isn't. This is a Miss Hampton's house."

He opened the door and jumped down. Then he reached inside and took her hand, dragging her out roughly. Before she could protest, he had rushed her up the short flight of steps and into the house.

A beauty, somewhat faded, was standing in the doorway to a neat salon, her eyes fearful.

"Augustus," she began, but stopped when he cursed her.

"Augustus! Take me home at once!" exclaimed Serena, but he only laughed and pushed her into the salon.

As he passed the woman, presumably Miss Hampton, he pulled her close, kissing her as he fondled one breast. He laughed again at Serena's gasp, and entered the room, still clasping Miss Hampton's hand. He took a chair beside Serena's and pulled the other woman into his lap.

"No, Serena, I don't want to take you home. Perhaps tomorrow, but not now."

Her thoughts tripping over each other, Serena perceived only that her fear was feeding his insanity—and insane he had to be to have conceived such a bizarre plot.

Keeping her voice pleasant and even, she said, "Augustus, I wish you would call your mother down so that I may meet her."

"Mother? By God, woman, you must be mad. Why on earth would my mother be at my mistress's house?"

Serena's feigned composure slipped, and she whispered weakly, "Mistress?"

"Oh, pardon my lack of manners, ladies," he said with a laugh. "Serena, this is my mistress, Miss Hampton. Eugenia, this is my fiancee, Miss Blessed. Now, say how d'you do." They did as they were bid, though Serena felt a hysterical laugh welling up inside her. "Eugenia, get me a drink. Have something yourself. Serena?" She shook her head.

When he had drained his glass, Serena said, "I should really be getting back. The modiste is supposed to deliver my wedding gown."

She watched while Miss Hampton fetched another glass, and Augustus poured it down his throat as well. With a violent snarl, he flung the glass against the stone hearth where it shattered and fell to the floor.

"You would have me believe you still intend to wed me? I won't be gulled, you stupid chit. I saw how you looked at Case; even if you're too blind to admit it to yourself."

"You're wrong, Augu—"

He leaped from his chair, dumping his mistress on the carpet. He grasped Serena by the nape of her neck and pulled her close to his face. Serena struggled, and he wrenched her head, forcing her to look at him.

"You'll find, over the years, that I am never wrong. Won't she, Eugenia?" he asked without looking away. The mistress whimpered her agreement. "But I will wed you, and you will be begging me to do so after you spend the night here in my company."

"What are you going to do?" Serena whispered fearfully.

He released her suddenly, laughing loudly when she fell backward. He pointed toward the table of decanters, and Eugenia scurried to pour him another drink.

Serena took the opportunity to cast about the room for some weapon. Her eyes came to rest on the poker that leaned against the stone fireplace.

Nicholas groaned as he opened his eyes. He shut them again and turned over. Touching leather, he opened his eyes once more and thought back to the previous night. Oh yes, he remembered, you're in the library. Too drunk to make it to your room.

He sat up gingerly, resting his elbows on his knees and holding his head in his hands.

The door opened and Angel exclaimed, "Oh, it's you, Nicholas. Have you seen Serena this afternoon?"

"No," he croaked, his mouth dry and his voice practically non-existent.

"Mrs. Pruitt is here for her final fitting, and she's nowhere to be found."

Nicholas sat up straight and paused for the pain to subside. "What time is it?"

"Almost five o'clock. I've been looking all over for her."

Frowning, Nicholas pushed himself up slowly.

"Ooh, you look awful," observed his sister. "I thought you two had a fight last night. Why do you do that, Nicholas? What do you have against Augustus? He's always courteous. When he picked her up for their drive, he helped her on with—"

Nicholas squeezed her shoulder and said sharply, "What time?"

"What? Oh, at two, I believe."

"And she's not back yet?"

"I don't suppose so. I've turned the house upside down searching for her."

"That bastard. If he—"

"Nicholas! You're beginning to frighten me. What's wrong with Serena going for a drive with her fiance?"

"Not now," he said, pushing past her. He ignored the pounding in his temples and rushed upstairs, his sister's long legs carrying her along at his heels, her mouth ever questioning.

She stopped when they had entered his room, watching as he threw water on his face and took a second to stare at his rough appearance.

He pushed past her again, returning to the library where Angel's queries became more frantic as she watched him prime and load two dueling pistols.

When he would have passed her again, she threw herself in front of the door and demanded, "Where are you going and what are you going to do?"

Nicholas noticed her for the first time. "I'm going to find Serena and kill Redmon. Someone has to, and I was ever the lucky one."

"Nicholas! Why?" she shrieked as he set her aside and hurried to the front doors.

"Ask Alfie. I told him all about Redmon."

Nicholas's mare was saddled and waiting for him. He knew of only two places to look. One was Redmon's rooms; the other his mistress's house beyond Curzon Street. As fast as the rain would allow, he rode to St. James' Street. He pounded on the door for several minutes before it opened.

"Lord Redmon?"

"Not here," said a slovenly servant who then tried to close the door.

Nicholas shoved past him. The servant shouted an obscenity and then stood back as Nicholas snarled at him savagely.

"Redmon! Redmon!" roared Nicholas. He dared not call Serena's name. Her reputation would be shattered.

Back at the front door, he grabbed the servant by the collar and shook him.

"Where's your master?"

"I don't know! He doesn't tell me anything!"

The genuine fear in the man's eyes made Nicholas believe him. Nicholas dropped him and strode outside, bending the brim of his hat against the steady drizzle.

Curzon Street it was! He sent the mare along at a canter, not slowing even as he dodged the occasional traffic. He passed the neat houses and rode into the next street, trying to recall the number Jarrod had revealed to him.

Serena watched as her fiance drank steadily, his interest focused mainly on his glass and not on her or his mistress. He walked to the window occasionally and peered outside, grunting with satisfaction.

It was growing dark, and she knew she had to make her move soon. As it was, however, he stayed between her and the front door. She had to stir things up a little.

"Why are you doing this, Augustus? I am a woman of my word."

"Hmph!" he grunted.

"I am. I always do what I start out to do. Didn't I come to London to find a husband? And I have found one! Now, why don't you take me home so I can get some rest. You don't want your wife all tired, do you?"

"You'll be tired enough when I get through with you," he laughed.

"Augustus, please," whispered the mistress.

"Shuddap!"

"But she says she'll still marry you!"

"She's lying. She thinks I'm too drunk to know that, but I'm not completely legless. Yes, sir, we'll stay right here until she's got no one but me who will even have her. Not even her precious Nicholas Case!"

His wicked laugh made Serena shudder. "Do you intend to . . . molest me?" she asked coldly.

"Molest you? Oh, I like looking at it that way." He turned to watch her. But he was neither as mad nor as drunk as he appeared. He shook his head. "I might let you watch, but I'll wait until we are wed before I bed you. My mother might get wind . . . No, I'll wait. But perhaps you can learn a little about how to please me from Eugenia. What do you say, Eugenia? Come here and give me a kiss."

The mousy mistress walked to him, wringing her hands. But as his kiss endured, Miss Hampton put her arms around his neck and pressed her body against him.

Serena lifted her skirts, cleared the low table in front of the sofa and dived for the iron poker. Before she could get to her feet, she heard the front door crash open! Then she screamed as Redmon's heavy form landed on top of her, knocking the breath out of her!

"Serena! Are you all right?" Nick shouted, shoving Redmon to one side and leaning down to pull Serena into his arms.

Gasping for air, she couldn't speak. "Serena! Blast it all! Say something!"

"Some . . . thing," she just managed to impart, a weak smile on her face.

"Some . . . Serena, I could . . ." He leaned down and kissed her lips.

Serena gasped for another breath of air and tried to rise. "Let's get . . . out . . . of here."

"Not until I . . ."

Serena and Nicholas looked down at the inert figure sprawled on the floor. Miss Hampton glanced up at them anxiously, but she continued to pat Redmon's limp hand.

"What are you going to do?" said Serena, her voice brimming with laughter, whether true amusement or hysteria, she couldn't have said. "Kill an unconscious man?"

Nicholas's gaze lingered on his old enemy. "I would have," he said coldly.

Just then, Redmon opened his eyes and groaned. He wriggled away when he saw Nicholas. "Case!"

"Yes, Gussie, it is I," said Nicholas.

"I didn't touch her!"

Nicholas turned to Serena, and she shook her head. "Good for you, Gussie. At least you've learned something. Now, I don't want to see you, hear about you, or even smell you. Ever again. Understood?"

His eyes on the dueling pistols tucked into Nicholas's breeches, Redmon nodded eagerly.

"Good. We understand one another. You don't mind if I borrow your carriage, do you, old boy? You!" he said to Miss Hampton, causing her to jump. "Send to the stables."

She did as she was bid, and Nicholas leaned down beside the cringing lord. "Just so we don't misunderstand one another. I expect you to leave the country as soon as possible. In the meantime, if anyone should ask why Serena rejected you, your story had best be very flattering—to her."

"And I suppose you'll be taking my place in her bed," sneered Redmon.

Nicholas stood and placed one boot on the man's neck. "That didn't sound flattering, Gussie."

Redmon gasped, "All right, all right. I'll keep quiet."

"See that you do," said Nicholas, removing his boot from Redmon's throat and his hand from his pistol's grip. "Let's go home, Serena," he said gently.

When they reached the street, the rain had stopped. Nicholas helped Serena inside and told the driver to take a turn through Green Park. Serena began to shiver, and Nicholas pulled the rug around her shoulders. Trying to control the chattering of her teeth, Serena found it impossible to speak.

And what could she say, she asked herself. Nicholas had been right about Augustus all along. Knowing Nicholas, he was probably gloating over his own cunning. Why couldn't she have escaped sooner? Why had he had to find her in such mortifying circumstances? Nicholas, of all people!

"Serena, you're safe now. He can't hurt you again. I'll see to that!"

"You!"

Nicholas sat back frowning. "What do you mean—me? I saved you, didn't I?" When she didn't reply, he demanded again, "Didn't I?"

"I was taking care of myself!" she shouted.

"You were on the floor!" he cried.

"Nevertheless," she said, her nose in the air.

Nicholas fumed in silence. Then he said, "Aha! I know what you're mad about! You're angry because you lost that infantile wager!"

Serena, who had long since stopped shaking, moved to the opposite seat.

"If that's all it is, I'll pay you back!" Nicholas blustered on.

Serena pursed her lips and glared at him.

"Well?"

"You, Nicholas Case, are without a doubt the most thick-headed, dull-witted, self-indulgent dolt in the whole of England! No! In all the British Isles! In all . . ." Serena began to cry, her body convulsed with great, wracking sobs.

Nicholas sputtered and spewed, his jaw slack, an astounded expression on his handsome face. Then he opened his arms, and Serena fell into them, pressing her face against his chest, completely ruining his coat. And Nicholas smiled.

When her sobs had faded to occasional sniffles, and he had settled her more comfortably on his lap, he lifted her chin and said simply, "Serena, I love you."

"Oh, Nicholas, I love you, too," she returned, snuggling against him.

He lifted her chin again and proceeded to kiss her forehead, then her nose, and finally her mouth. This area required a great deal of attention, and they were leaving Green Park before the driver could get an answer from the occupants of his vehicle.

"Where to, guvner?"

Nicholas smiled at Serena and said, "It's only the twenty-fifth of June, my love. Gretna Green isn't that far. You could still win that wager."

With a dreamy smile, Serena pulled his head back down to hers, trying her best to show him her answer.

A Conformable Wife

by
Carola Dunn

"Benedict! My dear, how delightful to see you." Juliet Faulk beamed up at her tall brother from the chaise longue in her pink and white boudoir. She held out her hand and he bowed over it correctly, then unbent sufficiently to lean forward and kiss her cheek. "Pull up a chair and sit down."

He obeyed. "You look very well, Ju."

"Why should I not? Pregnancy is not a disease. Oh, don't poker up, Ben! You cannot consider it improper to speak of my condition to my own brother."

Benedict gave her a rueful smile which transformed his austere face. "No, of course not."

"Especially after you helped me through the last months with Timmy when Faulk had to go to Vienna."

"How is Timmy?"

"Flourishing. Learning his ABCs already. You will go up to the nursery, will you not? He'd be sadly let down if he knew you had called without visiting him. His favourite uncle!"

"The effect of bribery. As a matter of fact, I've brought him a cuckoo whistle," he added gruffly. "I hope he'll not drive his nurse mad with blowing on it."

Juliet laughed. "Probably. But what brings you to Town, Ben? No, don't tell me: either business or a debate in the House." What a pity he did not live farther from London, she thought, not for the first time.

Without any desire to cut a figure in politics, Benedict, Viscount Clifford, took his parliamentary duties seriously. If it weren't so easy to come up for a day or two, he'd be forced to spend the Season in Town and he might even come to enjoy the amusements of the Polite World.

As it was, simply because attendance was expected of him as a member of that world, he endured the occasional ball, rout, card party, or ride in Hyde Park at the fashionable hour. Only concerts and the theatre aroused any enthusiasm, though he did take pleasure in evenings at his club with political cronies.

"There's to be another debate on climbing boys," he told her.

"Faulk says it's prodigious eccentric of you to go into battle for chimney sweeps' brats," she said incautiously.

His expression became stony. "Not at all. Many members of both Lords and Commons feel as I do about the appalling suffering. We just haven't quite been able to muster a majority yet."

"But you will," she hastened to assure him, filled with remorse. How could she have come to tease him on that subject of all others?

To be eccentric was the worst sin in Benedict's book. Their parents had exhausted several generations' allowance of eccentricity. The late Lord and Lady Clifford, perennial butt of the gossips, laughingstock of the *Ton,* had abandoned home and family to explore the world. After surviving Africa, China, Indonesia, the Americas, they met their deaths in a flash flood in the Great Australian Desert, their ignominious end immortalized in caricature by Gillray.

Juliet had compensated for their desertion by seeking security in an early marriage to an older man, of whom she had fortunately grown excessively fond. Benedict had responded to their notoriety with a rigid adherence to convention. His aim in life was to be respectable, staid, *ordinary.*

His manners were formal; his dress impeccable without the least hint of dandyism; his thick brown hair cut in a severe Brutus crop—no casual Windswept for him. His friends he chose from among the highest sticklers, those who eschewed any form of unconformity. He had concentrated his considerable energies on his long-neglected estate. The introduction of carefully chosen modern agricultural methods resulted in his rents increasing annually without the least hardship for his tenants.

He was altogether admirable, but he never relaxed except with his little nephew. Even by Benedict's stern standards, nothing a small child did could be considered eccentric.

In a roundabout way, Juliet realized, his love for Timmy explained his concern for sweeps' boys. Still, she wished he'd take life just a little less seriously.

"Heaven forbid you should have come to Town in search of pleasure," she said with a sigh.

"Well . . ." He hesitated, self-conscious, smoothing the sleeve of his perfectly smooth blue morning coat.

"What is it, Ben? You *are* going to stay a while? My dear, that's splendid! Now let me see, I can procure invitations . . ."

He held up his hand. "No, no, wait. The fact of the matter is, I've decided it's time I became a Benedick."

"But you already are— Don't laugh at me like that, you horrid wretch. I'm not a complete featherhead. You're talking about *Much Ado about Nothing*? Oh, Ben, you are going to be married? Who is it?"

"That's what I've come to consult you about. There is no one eligible at home, and I've never met a female in London I could wish to wed. I don't want a frivolous miss fresh from the schoolroom, nor a worldly widow. I'd like you to introduce me to someone suitable so that I can go straight to her guardian for permission to address her without all the Marriage Mart fuss and bother first."

Juliet was dismayed. To be sure, he needed an heir, and nothing could be more conventional than a marriage of convenience. Yet she had always nursed a secret hope that one day he'd meet a woman who'd take him out of himself. Besides, it was a huge responsibility to heap upon her.

"You'd trust my judgement to that extent? But I have not the least notion what sort of wife you *do* want."

" 'Rich she shall be, that's certain; wise, or I'll none; virtuous, or I'll never cheapen her; fair, or I'll never look on her; mild, or come not near me; noble, or not I for an angel; of good discourse, an excellent musician, and her hair shall be of what colour it please God.' But above all, Ju, what I'm looking for is simply a conformable wife."

A conformable wife! What he thought he wanted was someone as ruled by propriety and convention as himself, but there were chinks in his armour. How many gentlemen, asked what they wanted in a bride, would or could spout Shakespeare? He'd be bored to tears by a conformable wife!

Rich, wise, virtuous, fair, mild, of good discourse, an excellent musician—forget the conformable part. "Ben, I do believe I have already hit upon the very person: Lady Eleanor Lacey."

"Lacey? Who is she?"

"Lord Derrington's sister. She was my dearest friend at school, and we've always kept up a correspondence."

"She's your age? Why have I never met her? Why isn't she married? Though I don't insist upon beauty, I don't care to face an antidote across the breakfast table every morning."

"Nell made her come-out when I did, then her mother died and she took over running the household for her father. She comes up to Town for brief visits but she never had a second Season. I must say she has always seemed perfectly contented. She prefers the country."

"That is something in her favour. Derrington? Ah, yes, the Lacey Stables. The old earl died some eighteen months ago, did he not?"

"Yes, so she kept house for her brother instead, until he married a few months since."

Ben gave her a shrewd look. "And now Lady Eleanor's nose is out of joint because she has to give precedence to her sister-in-law."

"Nell would never be so petty! Though I do think it must

be difficult when she has been mistress of the household for seven or eight years. Heavens, how old that makes me feel!"

"At any rate," he said impatiently, "you believe she is no longer so contented with her lot that she is unwilling to marry. She sounds suitable. I shall have to meet her before I make an offer, of course."

Again Juliet was dismayed by his cold-blooded approach. "You may go down to Brantwood with the excuse of meeting a few carriage horses before you make an offer on *them*," she snapped.

"An excellent notion. In any case, I daresay I shall have to purchase a barouche or landau and pair for my coachman to drive Lady Eleanor about in—if she proves acceptable. I'll write to Derrington today. And now, my dear, I'll pay my duty visit to the nursery. Thank you for your help."

Juliet glared at his oblivious back as he strolled from her boudoir. Her only consolation was that Nell was free to refuse him.

Nell struggled to keep her face blank as Phyllis's peevish voice besieged her. That's what it was, not an attack to be repulsed, but a siege to be endured. How *could* Bertie have married the woman?

". . . And his letter says most particularly that he looks forward to meeting his sister's dearest friend, so it's perfectly obvious he has more on his mind than carriage horses." Phyllis laughed with a ghastly roguishness. "He is just of an age to wish to be setting up his nursery."

Where Phyllis was concerned, Lord Clifford's supposed desire to find a bride was pure wishful thinking, fuelled by her own desire to rid herself of her sister-in-law. Unfortunately, Nell knew she was right. Juliet's letter had disclosed her brother's intentions, as well as promising to take no offense should Nell refuse him.

Juliet might forgive a refusal, but Phyllis never would, nor would she ever let Nell forget it. Unless she positively disliked the man, she'd accept his offer. At six-and-twenty she was far too old to dream of love, and Brantwood was no longer a haven.

She glanced sadly around the pretty, comfortable morning room, its flowered chintzes bright in the April sunshine. The new Lady Derrington's plans for it included sphinxes, black lacquer, palm trees, and faux bamboo.

"There is nothing to be done about your height," Phyllis said discontentedly. "It will never do to hunch your shoulders. You must endeavour to remain seated as much as possible when in his company. As for your hair, that may be hidden under a cap. How fortunate you are more than old enough to be putting on caps."

"Why on earth should I hide my hair?" Nell demanded, shaken out of her apathy by the attack on her only vanity.

"Gentlemen abominate red hair." She tossed her own golden curls. As a bride of a few months, she had not yet taken to caps herself. "We shall have a cap or two specially made for you to hide every wisp. Of course, while he is here you will read only the most respectable novels and light verse—no Byron and no philosophy! Gentlemen abominate a bluestocking. And none of your political talk. It is quite shocking the way you will be always trying to persuade Bertie with your radical fancies."

"Hardly radical, merely reformist."

"I am sure no *lady* knows the difference. You must play for Lord Clifford, that goes without saying. Your performance upon the pianoforte is really quite adequate, my dear Eleanor. But pray avoid that horrid, noisy, new German composer whose music you recently received."

"Avoid Beethoven?" she asked, surprised.

"Far too *passionate*," said Phyllis delicately. "Not at all ladylike. Haydn is much more decorous. Which reminds me, on no account must you drive your dog-cart about the countryside. A gig with a single placid horse is acceptable, provided you stay within the park. A dog-cart is a gentleman's vehicle, and to take a lively pair on the public roads is not at all proper, as I have previously had reason to advise you."

"I don't own a gig," Nell pointed out, "nor is there a single nag in Bertie's stables I should describe as placid."

"There will be no need for you to drive anywhere while Lord Clifford is here. If you require exercise, a stroll in the shrubbery will suffice—none of your cross-country rambles! Of course you will leave the parish visiting to the vicar's wife. One must be charitable, but it is quite beneath the dignity of the sister of an earl actually to call upon labourers and people of that sort."

"If someone has need of me, I shall go. Besides, a stroll in the shrubbery may conceivably suffice me for a few days, but it will not do for Maera." She reached down to fondle the ears of the shaggy beast stretched in watchful repose beside her chair.

"One of the stable-boys may exercise that horrid great mongrel of yours. It will have to be confined to the stables in any case. The only unexceptionable dog for a lady is a pug."

Nell knew the only reason Maera was still allowed indoors was that Phyllis had not yet managed to break Bertie of bringing in whatever spaniel or pointer happened to be at his heels. Sooner or later she would succeed in banning dogs from the house.

She must have been storing up a list of her sister-in-law's faults. It was not as if Nell ever did anything outrageous. Papa had not minded how she spent her time as long as she made him comfortable and did not scare the horses, so she quietly went her own way. She had been her own mistress for years.

In fact, Bertie had taught her to drive a pair and Papa had given her both the dog-cart and Vesta and Vulcan, her spirited, perfectly matched chestnuts. To match her fiery head, he'd said. Papa hadn't abominated red hair.

Tears rose to her eyes. She fiercely blinked them away.

"I shall lend you some of my French perfume," said Phyllis graciously.

That was the last straw. She had to draw the line somewhere. "If Lord Clifford doesn't care for lavender water," she snapped, "he may go to the de . . . depths of the ocean!"

"Well, really!" Phyllis was thoroughly offended. "I'm only trying to help. At your age you must seize your chance."

With difficulty Nell mastered her temper, as Miss Lindisfarne had taught her years ago. "But, Phyllis," she said in desperation, "if I behave as you suggest, Lord Clifford will not know what I am really like."

Phyllis stared, astonished. "Good gracious, Eleanor, once he has come up to scratch and you are safely married, what has that to say to anything?"

So that was why poor Bertie had married her. He had mistaken a carefully constructed facade for reality, and discovered the reality too late.

Was Nell prepared to play the same trick on the unknown Lord Clifford? It was not as if she had any desire to make him live beneath the cat's paw. She would make him comfortable, as she had Papa, and perhaps he'd allow her a little freedom in exchange. He would want children, at least an heir. No more dying of envy whenever she saw a woman with a babe in her arms. No more wondering whether she should marry a man she did not care for, solely for the sake of children.

As Phyllis nagged on, anything seemed preferable to staying at Brantwood.

"I believe Lady Eleanor is in the music room, my lord."

Benedict thanked the butler with a nod and made his way towards the music room. In five days at Brantwood he had yet to speak to Lady Eleanor alone. The Derringtons were all that was hospitable. There were other guests, many of them interested in purchasing the young earl's fine carriage horses. Days were filled with shooting parties, outings on horseback with the ladies in carriages, a hunt with the South Berkshire. Every evening there were more guests to dinner, followed by music and cards and billiards.

He would have thought no one guessed his real purpose were it not for Lady Derrington's constant hints and determined chaperonage of her sister-in-law.

He was well satisfied with what he had seen of Lady Eleanor. She seemed at ease among her brother's guests and, he gathered, had played hostess to admiration in her equally hospitable father's time. Her dress was neat and proper, neither dowdy nor excessively fashionable. Her face was pleasant, distinguished by neither daunting beauty nor plainness. She was neither fat nor thin, and she moved with grace. When she played Haydn or Scarlatti upon the spinet in the drawing room after dinner, her touch was light and sure. Benedict looked forward to musical evenings in his own home.

If Lady Eleanor had a fault, it was that she was rather too quiet. On the other hand, Lady Derrington talked enough for two, enough to convince him the last thing he wanted was a garrulous wife. He had decided to propose.

His interview with Lord Derrington proved most satisfactory. Lady Eleanor possessed a considerable fortune in her own right—naturally he'd settle it upon her and her children. He had no need of her money but at least it proved she wouldn't be marrying him for his wealth.

He was not ill-looking. He had every intention of being a considerate husband, and he'd provide her with a family and an establishment of her own. What more could any woman desire?

The music-room door was closed. As Benedict opened it, a flood of sound engulfed him, urgent, demanding, troubled. Startled, he stepped forward. The music came to a sudden halt.

Lady Eleanor sat at the pianoforte, her hands still on the keys. She stared at him as if turned to stone by his sudden appearance.

"What were you playing?" he asked to put her at her ease, advancing towards the instrument.

She jumped up, closing the music. "A new piece, Lord Clifford. I fear I have by no means yet mastered it. Were you . . . were you looking for me?"

"Yes. I have something particular to say to you, Lady Eleanor. Will you not be seated?"

"No, thank you," she said with an odd hint of defiance. Tall and elegant in leaf-green sarsenet trimmed with white Valenciennes, she moved to the window where she gazed out at a glinting April shower.

For the first time, Benedict felt a hint of awkwardness. After all, he had never before proposed marriage. But gentlemen did it every day. It was nothing out of the ordinary. There was even a prescribed form of sorts—stuff about hands and hearts. However, he was not going to lower himself to offer Spanish coin. Hearts had nothing to do with the matter.

"I have spoken to your brother," he said. "He has given me permission to address you and reason to hope that you will not look unkindly upon my suit. Lady Eleanor, you will do me the greatest honour if you will grant me your hand in marriage."

She turned. With the bright rectangle of the window behind her, he was unable to read her face, but he thought her regard was searching. Surely she wasn't trying to find a courteous way to tell him his hopes were unfounded!

After a moment, she said with quiet dignity, "Thank you, sir, I am happy to accept your flattering offer, and I shall do my best to be a good wife to you."

And now, Benedict found, came the truly awkward part. He could not take this cool, self-possessed woman in his arms and kiss her as instinct bade him. He would not lie and tell her she had made him the happiest of men. In any normal social situation, precisely the correct words were always on the tip of his tongue, but now he found himself at a loss.

"You are very kind," he said. "I shall do my best to be a

good husband. You do not care for a long engagement, I trust? I believe a June wedding is traditional if you can be ready in time."

"June will do very well."

She held out her hand to him and he bowed over it, venturing to touch his lips to her knuckles. There didn't seem to be anything else to say, so he left her.

She had accepted him. Why, then, this chilly, hollow feeling of disappointment?

As he politely closed the music room door behind him, he realized he didn't know the colour of her hair or eyes.

"I can't do it, Agnes, indeed I cannot!" Staring into the looking-glass, Nell saw the panic in her voice reflected in her grey-green eyes. Her face was pale above the white nightgown.

Her misgivings had grown during the four weeks since Lord Clifford's proposal, and had come to a head during evensong that very evening. She hadn't seen her prospective husband since the day after his offer, when he had bowed to her wish for a quiet wedding in the village church. Sitting in the church today, she had tried to imagine herself standing with him before the altar, promising to love, honour and obey a stranger. Impossible!

Her abigail paused with the hairbrush in one plump hand poised above the flowing copper tresses. "Then you shan't, my lady," she said soothingly. "Though when all's said and done, he's a handsome, well-set-up gentleman, with a good handle to his name and no need of your fortune, from what I hear."

"Handsome? He might be handsome if there were only a little animation in his face. His features are well enough, but so impassive I never saw him smile, or even frown. When we discussed the arrangements for our wedding—even when he proposed to me—we could have been planning the dullest of dinner parties."

"There's some men don't care to show their deepest feelings, dearie."

"Even to the women they're going to marry? I don't believe he has any feelings. How can I spend the rest of my life with a block of wood? A block of ice!"

"His valet said he's a good master, a good landlord, and a good brother."

"But I should not be his servant, his tenant, nor his sister."

"Ah well, 'tis not the end of the world," said Agnes philosophically, resuming the brushing of Nell's hair with long, rhythmic strokes. "You've turned down others afore."

"But never after first accepting them. And then I had a happy, peaceful home . . . Oh, Agnes, I miss Papa so! If he were still alive, I'd not have considered accepting Lord Clifford."

Their eyes met in the mirror. Nell never directly criticized her sister-in-law to any servant, but her abigail knew well enough what was driving her from Brantwood.

When Bertie married, Nell had welcomed the new Lady Derrington and willingly turned over the reins of the household. That was not enough for Phyllis, whose chief joy in life was the exercise of authority. First, Miss Lindisfarne must go.

Lindy, Nell's governess before she went away to school, had returned as her companion when her mother died. But Nell needed no companion, Phyllis said, now that her brother's wife was living at Brantwood. Nell would have fought, but Miss Lindisfarne, foreseeing endless battle, chose a graceful retirement.

At once Nell made plans for them to set up house together. Her personal income was adequate for a perfectly comfortable existence with as many of the elegancies of life as interested either. Phyllis was horrified. Everyone would say she had driven her husband's sister from her home.

For Bertie's sake, Nell stayed. Envying Lindy her escape, she frequently visited her friend at her cottage near Hungerford some five-and-twenty miles distant. Phyllis promptly made it plain that she didn't actually *want* her sister in Brantwood. It was Nell's duty to find a husband and remove herself in an unexceptionable way for which no one could hold Phyllis to blame.

So Nell had accepted Lord Clifford.

"I cannot live with a man who never laughs," she said firmly as Agnes loosely plaited her hair for the night. "We shall go and live with Miss Lindisfarne."

"Just give me the word, my lady, and I'll pack."

"Bless you, Agnes. What should I ever do without you?"

Nell felt much better for having come to a decision. She fell asleep quicker than she had in weeks, but when she woke in the small hours of the morning all the difficulties seemed overwhelming.

The moment she revealed that she meant to cry off, the nagging would start. Phyllis was quite capable of following her to Lindy's and making both their lives a misery. In the end, if only for the sake of peace, she'd give up and return to Brantwood. She'd find herself tied for life to a man she didn't know.

Throwing a wrap around her shoulders, she went to sit on the windowseat. Maera scrabbled out from under the bed and came to lay a heavy, loving head in her lap. Outside, beneath a full moon, white candles bloomed on the chestnut trees in the park and the fragrance of lilac wafted in through the open window. Under the calming influence of the May night, the answer came to her.

If she disappeared the day before the wedding, it would be too late for anyone to fetch her back.

To desert him at the last minute was not very fair to Lord Clifford, she acknowledged, but it was not as if they were to be married at St. George's, Hanover Square, before half the peerage. Besides, it allowed him three more weeks to reveal to her what sort of man he was. If he showed himself to be a real person with feelings to be hurt, she would reconsider.

If he remained distant, impassive, uninterested in discovering what sort of person *she* really was, let him look elsewhere for a bride.

She went back to bed and slept soundly.

In the three weeks to follow, Nell received two letters from her betrothed. One informed her that he was at his country house, refurbishing and redecorating the apartments which would be hers. Apparently it did not dawn on him to consult her taste in colours and furnishings. The second letter informed her that he'd be unable to arrive at Brantwood until the eve of the wedding as he had business in London the previous day. He failed to explain his business and expressed only the most polite, proper, perfunctory regret.

Both missives addressed Nell as "Madam" and were signed with equal formality, "Your most obedient, humble servant, Clifford." She didn't expect professions of undying love, but still . . .

Nell told Agnes to pack.

"I wish you could come with me," she said, "but Miss Lindisfarne's cottage is far too small. You shall join me as soon as I have found a suitable house to rent. In the meantime, I wish you would take a holiday and visit that brother of yours who is forever inviting you. Of course I shall pay the coach fare and your salary and a living allowance."

"And you'll look for a house right away, my lady?" the abigail asked anxiously.

"Oh, yes, at once. Maera will scarcely fit in the cottage and I don't like to entrust Vulcan and Vesta to outside stables. Now, how are we to smuggle my bags down to the dog-cart?"

"Any of the footmen'll do it, my lady, and gladly, and won't none of them nor the grooms give you away to . . . anyone."

That was part of Phyllis's trouble, Nell realized. Brantwood's staff were still loyal to her, not to their new mistress. Well, she'd be taking advantage of their devotion for the last time.

She smiled at Agnes. "I shall leave it to you, then. Don't pack more than is absolutely necessary for a few weeks. I shan't take any jewelry. I'll leave immediately after luncheon, claiming I need an airing to calm my nerves. With luck I shall not be missed until dinner."

By three o'clock on that fine June afternoon, Nell was well on her way. Beside her on the seat of the dog-cart Maera perched, her black nose in a constant state of twitching ecstasy. Vulcan and Vesta, chestnut coats gleaming in the sun, trotted westward through the maze of lanes between hedges twined with wild roses and the white trumpets of bindweed.

In the exuberance of her new freedom, Nell took off her blue-ribboned Leghorn bonnet and set it under the seat. "A few freckles are a small price to pay for the warmth of the sun on my face," she told Maera. "No one is about to see except the haymakers in the fields, and little they care if Lady Eleanor Lacey is so lost to propriety as to go hatless."

In the hamlets she drove through, an occasional villager stared as she passed. She waved blithely and Maera barked a greeting.

Maera began to pant, her tongue lolling from the corner of her mouth. Vesta and Vulcan were sweating. Next time they came to a patch of woodland, Nell drew rein in the shade of a huge old oak to rest the horses and let them cool off.

Maera leapt down from the carriage. First she went to touch noses with her equine friends, then she loped off beneath the trees on the scent of a rabbit or a squirrel. Nell knew she would not wander far.

Though dressed in thin blue muslin rather than a shaggy brown fur coat, Nell herself was hot and glad of the shade. The flask of lemonade she had brought with her was very welcome. Her neck was sticky where her hair had started to come down, and her face in particular felt hot and rather tight. Guiltily she pushed in a few loose hairpins and put on her bonnet.

Corking the lemonade, she called for Maera.

Nearby bushes rustled and shook. From them emerged not a large, happy dog but a large, masked man with a pair of pistols in his hands.

And both pistols were aimed unwaveringly at Nell.

"Stand and deliver!"

She held herself rigid. "I cannot stand any stiller," she pointed out, hoping she sounded more reasonable than terrified, "and I have no valuables with me."

"As to vallybles, we'll see about that, missy, but it's them prads as interests me."

"Prads?" she asked uncertainly.

"Hosses." He moved forward, larger and more threatening with every step. "That's a fine pair o' prancers you has there."

"Wh-what does a footpad want with a pair of horses?"

"Footpad! Here, you watch who you're calling names, missy! I'm a bridle-cull, a gentleman o' the road, I am." He wore riding breeches and boots, she saw, shabby but clean, as were his green coat, shirt, and the yellow Belcher handkerchief at his neck. The mask hiding the upper part of his face was incongruous black satin, fit for a masquerade ball. "My Rumbo were shot out from under me," he continued, "and it's another nag I . . . hey, you keep away!"

Maera had appeared from nowhere. Stiff-legged, teeth bared, she stalked towards the man, a low rumble issuing from her throat. The thick hair on her neck bristled in a ruff, making her appear even larger than usual.

The highwayman turned his pistols on her.

"Don't shoot!" Nell cried. "Maera, down! Stay!"

The dog glanced at her in disgust but obeyed. Every muscle tensed, she hunched down, lips still drawn back in a snarl, the ominous growl still rumbling, baleful stare fixed on the stranger.

"That brute's yourn?" he asked incredulously. "You do what I says, missy, or it's dead. Drop that whip, geddown, and hurry up about it."

Nell's knees wobbled as she scrambled down. She didn't dare reach for her own pistol, under the seat. She might take him unawares but the thought of Maera bleeding, dying . . .

"Open up the boot."

As she trudged around to the back of the carriage, he moved to where he could both watch her and keep an eye and a pistol aimed at the dog.

He made her take all her bags and boxes out of the boot. When they were piled in the dusty road, he said, "Right, now get the dog in there."

"But she's never shut in there! She's far too well-behaved to need to be—"

"In!" He waved a gun.

"Maera, come." Her voice was sharp with fear. Maera slunk to her feet. "Good girl. Up."

With a look of bitter reproach, the big dog sprang up and lay down in the confining space.

"Latch it."

Her heart in her half-boots, Nell obeyed. Despite the louvred ends, on such a hot afternoon poor Maera was going to stifle.

"That's better," grunted the highwayman, approaching. The pistols were trained on her now. "Let's have them bags open, and be quick about it."

Luckily she had hidden her roll of banknotes in a concealed compartment under the seat cushions. Hurrying to undo buckles, straps, and catches, she ventured to protest again, "Truly, I've brought nothing of value with me."

"Well, missy, if you values your life, go and stand under that tree there and don't move a muscle."

She watched as he set down one pistol and rifled through her possessions, flinging out gowns and chemises, slippers and shawls, sheets of music and her favourite books. His gaze and the second pistol never wavered from her except when he cast a quick glance in each container to make sure it was empty.

"Bloody hell!" he snorted in disgust. "Got your gelt in your pocket, eh?" He eyed her as if considering the best way to approach and search her without risk of her snabbling his pistols.

"Just a few shillings," she said hastily and tossed her small, netted purse to him.

It jingled as it landed at his feet. He swiftly bent to retrieve it, but gave another disgusted snort as he weighed it in his hand. "No more'n a guinea or two. What's a gentry mort like you doing wi'out a good supply o' the ready rhino?"

"I don't need money when I'm going to visit friends. They are expecting me and will come looking for me if I am much longer delayed."

"Ho, they will, will they? Then Nimble Jack'd best be on his way." He stowed the purse in a pocket and pulled out a knife.

"W-what are you going to do?" Nell stammered.

Tramping across heaps of clothes on his way to the front of the dog-cart, Nimble Jack looked surprised. "Why, cut the harness, missy. I ha'n't got time to fiddle wi' buckles."

"But you can't take Vulcan and Vesta!" she cried. "They're not even saddle horses."

"Then I'll have to ride bareback, won't I? You keep back now, and don't let that dog out till I'm out o' sight."

A moment later he vaulted onto a startled Vulcan's back and, leading Vesta, galloped off down the lane.

Nell stared after him in despair. An encounter with a highwayman was a just punishment for treating Lord Clifford rather shabbily, she acknowledged, but to lose her beloved horses was too much! She hurried to release Maera, hugging the big dog, who licked her face before jumping down and padding off to investigate the situation.

A sudden gust of wind fluttered the papers scattered in the lane. Stooping to collect them, Nell tried to think what to do next. She hadn't passed a house for two or three miles. Surely, here in heavily populated Berkshire, there must be some kind of habitation not too far ahead.

A stronger gust caught at her skirts as she stuffed the sheet music into a box and hoisted it into the boot. Silks and muslins stirred. An invisible hand turned the pages of a book lying open on its back. She started to pick up the precious volumes.

Maera returned to whine at her. Trotting off a few paces, she looked back and whined again.

"What is it, girl? Yes, I know they're gone, but the villain can't keep a pair of matched blood-horses hidden for long. We have to find a constable or a magistrate and they'll soon find Vulcan and Vesta."

Maera yelped. As Nell moved towards her to retrieve the last book, she started off again. Nose to the ground, she passed the dog-cart and continued down the lane.

Obviously Maera knew exactly where she was going and had no doubt as to the right thing to do. She was no blood-hound, but she could hardly mistake her stable-mates' trail. Nell didn't dare risk letting that trail fade. Dumping the books in the boot, she slammed it shut and abandoned her wardrobe without a backward glance.

Maera waited for her, white-tipped tail waving impatiently. Pausing just long enough to possess herself of her pistol and her money, she joined the dog and together they tramped onward.

Riding ahead of his crested travelling carriage, Benedict reached Brantwood shortly after four o'clock on the eve of his wedding day. His temper was decidedly ruffled, though he knew from long practice that nothing of his resentment showed on his face. On the way, he had encountered not only his sister and her husband, as expected, but several aristocratic friends and acquaintances bound on the same errand.

Lady Eleanor had herself requested a quiet village wedding, which suited his taste exactly. She might at least have consulted him if she had capriciously changed her mind!

His annoyance was not in the least lessened by a vaguely guilty feeling that he had rather neglected his bride to be. After all, spring was the busiest season both on his estate and in Parliament. Somehow he had managed to find time to set his affairs in order in view of his changing circumstances, and even to have her rooms redecorated. It wasn't as if it was a love match, he thought, a trifle wistfully. He and Lady Eleanor had the rest of their lives before them to get to know each other.

Nonetheless, guilt as well as etiquette had a hand in the choice of the bride-gift reposing in his breast pocket. He had noticed she favoured green gowns, so he had purchased emeralds and diamonds, a magnificent necklace in the form of a garland of leaves sprinkled with dewdrops. If she was miffed at his lack of attention, that would quickly restore him to favour.

Setting aside his annoyance over the wedding plans as unworthy of him, he was eager to witness her pleasure at his munificence. As soon as Lady Derrington's effusive welcome showed signs of ending, he asked Lady Eleanor's whereabouts.

"I am not certain where she is," said the sharp-faced countess guardedly. "She went out for a drive earlier, just to take the air, you know. I shall send to see if she is returned."

Benedict waited impatiently in the hall. He frowned as the footman sent to fetch his bride returned and whispered urgently with his hostess. Both hurried away.

Pacing back and forth, he wondered whether Lady Eleanor could possibly be refusing to come down to punish him for his lack of attention. Juliet had claimed she was not petty, but how well did Juliet know her? Had he committed himself to a capricious female who indulged in the sulks whenever she imagined herself crossed?

Too late for misgivings: no gentleman could cry off and continue to consider himself a gentleman.

Derrington approached, looking distinctly sheepish. A large young man, more horse-breeder than aristocrat, he handed Benedict a sheet of paper, folded and sealed, and a tiny package wrapped in tissue paper. "Phyllis told me to give you these," he said gruffly. "She got them from Nell's abigail."

Benedict had no need to open either to guess the contents. "She's calling it off?" he asked, his voice ringing harsh in his ears. "I must talk to her."

"She's gone," her brother confessed.

For a moment Benedict poised between relief and wrath.

Then wounded pride came to the fore. After inviting half the *Ton,* she was jilting him, making him a laughingstock. It was not to be endured.

"I'm going after her." He stuffed the unopened note and ring in his pocket with the necklace. "Tell me how to find her."

"Phyllis says she has gone to her old governess, in Hungerford."

"Along the Bath road, then."

"No, she avoids driving on the post-road. I can direct . . ."

"She drives herself?" Benedict asked, incredulous, recalling the quiet, demure female to whom he had offered his hand. "Well, at least it means I shall catch up with her the sooner."

"Don't count on it. Her pair are no slugs and the dog-cart is—"

"A dog-cart and pair? Good gad!" He had a bewildered notion they were speaking of two different people.

"I'll lend you my speediest nag," said Derrington, eager to make amends for his sister's disgraceful behaviour, "and explain exactly the way she always takes."

"Then I'll be off," Benedict said, adding grimly, "and make no mistake, come hell or high water I shall get her to the church on time."

As he cantered down the drive on a splendid bay gelding, he met the Faulks' carriage just arriving. Juliet's astonished face at the window brought his feeling of ill-usage to the boiling point. Saluting her curtly, he rode on.

A gusty wind arose and the sunny June day swiftly clouded over. When rain began to fall, at first Benedict welcomed the laying of road dust and the relief from the humid heat. Soon, under a steady drizzle, the dust turned to mud, the relief to damp discomfort. It did cross his mind to wonder whether Lady Eleanor was worth the trouble, but anger and his dread of ridicule drove him on.

Entering a wood, he saw a vehicle ahead, abandoned at the side of the lane. As he approached, he recognized it as a dog-cart and drew rein. The ground behind it was strewn with sodden clothing, gowns, bonnets, pelisses, gloves, handkerchiefs, chemises, nightdresses, tossed about in wild abandon. The carriage appeared undamaged, but the traces were cut. No sign of the team or their driver. What the devil had happened?

It must be Lady Eleanor's equipage. Had she run mad?

The uneasy sensation in the pit of his stomach flared into alarm. If she were fit for Bedlam, naturally he couldn't marry her, but at present he had to consider himself responsible for her safety. The only proper course was to follow the route her brother had described and to hope he came upon her quickly.

At the first crossroads he came to, his instructions were to turn left. However, his eye was caught by a strip of white fabric tied to a twig in the hedge on his right. He dismounted to examine it.

It was a piece of lace, torn and dripping wet but clean, not at all yellowed by exposure to the elements. A sign? Even if Lady Eleanor did not expect to be followed, she might leave a trail for herself in this labyrinth of identical byways. If so, was it the cunning of madness or intelligent forethought?

Benedict was horribly afraid she was in trouble—trouble not of her own causing. He turned the bay down the right-hand lane.

Another piece of white lace where the road forked, and then a third. Watching for a fourth, he almost missed the next marker, a blue satin ribbon. Thank heaven she was wearing blue. He'd never have found green among the leaves.

He cantered around a bend and there ahead of him a hunched, bedraggled figure in blue plodded along, topped with a soggy, drooping straw bonnet. Thank heaven!

Hearing the jingle of a harness, Nell swung round and found herself practically nose to nose with Bertie's favourite hack.

"Hallo, Grenadier," she said, too weary—and too glad—to be surprised her brother had found her. She raised her eyes. "Hallo . . . Lord Clifford! What are you doing here?"

He glared down at her, his brow like thunder. "It may have

escaped your memory," he said bitingly, "that we are to be wed tomorrow. I've come to take you back."

How could she have thought him impassive, indifferent, insipid? He was a brute!

"I'm not going back," she said, bristling. "You cannot dictate to me. We are not married yet and never shall be. I'm going to Miss Lindisfarne's—as soon as I have rescued Vesta and Vulcan." Angrily she brushed away the silly, involuntary tears.

"Your cattle?" he asked in a much more moderate tone of voice. He swung down from Grenadier's back. "Come, let us not brangle. Tell me what happened."

She thought of Nimble Jack and shivered. Now that Lord Clifford was on a level with her and not scowling, his resolute, respectable presence was a decided comfort. "All right, but we must go on before the trail grows too faint." As she spoke, she turned and trudged on.

Leading the bay, he walked beside her. "Too faint? I see no . . . What the deuce?"

Maera bounded into sight, her ragged tail held high. Admittedly she was not a prepossessing vision, her shaggy coat matted with mud, but her teeth were bared in a friendly grin. There was no need for Lord Clifford to shout and wave his whip as if she were a man-eating tiger. Nell grabbed his arm.

"It's Maera. She has come back to show me the way."

"That creature is yours? Good gad!"

"I don't care for pugs," she snapped. "No pug would have tried to defend me against the highwayman, nor followed Vulcan and Vesta all this way in the rain."

"Highwayman!" Astonishingly, he grinned at her. "No, I can't imagine a pug outfacing a highwayman. I don't care for them either."

"Pugs or highwaymen?"

"Neither." Maera came up to sniff at him and he fondled her floppy ears. His boots and riding breeches must bear the familiar odour of Grenadier, for she accepted him without hesitation. "You mean to tell me you were held up by a highwayman?"

"At first I thought him a footpad." As they followed Maera, Nell told him the story, omitting to mention the little ivory-handled pistol Papa had had Manton make for her. On the whole Lord Clifford was bearing up admirably under all the shocks the day had dealt him. Perhaps a confession of feminine frailty might further soothe him and encourage him to lend his aid. "I was quite frightened," she admitted.

"You deserved to be," he said censoriously. "I was under the impression that you were an unexceptionable, gently bred, well-behaved female. Had I guessed that you drive—unescorted—a dog-cart and pair about the countryside and that you keep a monstrous mongrel as a pet, I'd have thought twice before proposing marriage."

"I wish you had! It would have saved both of us a great deal of trouble. I might add that I prefer Beethoven to Haydn, I enjoy long walks better than short strolls, I read the Classics and Byron and Hume and Voltaire, I hold definite political opinions, I visit the poor in person—"

"You do?" He stopped to stare at her.

". . . and my hair is red," she concluded, pulling off her ruined bonnet, no difficult matter as its ribbon had been sacrificed to mark the way. She dropped it in a puddle.

"I have no objection to red hair," he said stiffly.

"How kind of you!"

"It's coming down."

Nell ran her hand through her hair. The last few hairpins fell out and dripping locks descended about her shoulders. "What does it matter, considering the state I'm in?" Defiance fading, dispirited, she looked down at her damply clinging, mud-bespattered gown. The hem was miry brown to above her ankles.

Lord Clifford had followed her gaze. He flushed and quickly looked up. "You must be excessively uncomfortable. It's—"

"Don't you dare tell me it's my own fault!"

"I was going to say, it's a pity this lane seems unlikely to lead us to a respectable inn where we might hire a vehicle."

Instantly her momentary flash of guilt at her ungraciousness vanished. "So you can take me home in disgrace and drag me to the altar."

"There is no question of dragging you anywhere," he said, stiffer than ever. "If you wish, I shall escort you to your friend's residence in Hungerford, though I admit my first thought when I set out in pursuit was to avoid the ignominy of being jilted at the altar."

But now, of course, after viewing her bedragglement and learning of her peculiarities, he was congratulating himself on a lucky escape. It was just what Nell wanted, yet her spirits sank lower than ever.

At least the rain was lightening, the clouds thinning.

"I cannot go anywhere until I have found Vulcan and Vesta," she said. "Pray do not feel bound to accompany me. Maera and I will do very well."

"Don't be idiotish. I cannot in honour abandon you now." His asperity unexpectedly changed to compassion. "You must be very tired, and this lane is becoming no more than a cart-track. Will you not take my arm? If only I had thought to bring a sidesaddle you might ride Grenadier."

"I daresay I could manage him without." At his shocked glance, she added hastily, "But perhaps not. I have not ridden bareback or astride these ten years and more." To make amends, she took his arm, finding it a strong support, well-muscled beneath the damp brown cloth. "You must be tired, too, after journeying from Town."

"I hope I am not such a poor—look, here comes your dog again. Maera, is she? And Vesta and Vulcan—I'd have guessed you to be familiar with classical literature even had you not told me."

Nell sighed. "Phyllis calls me a bluestocking, an honour to which I have never aspired. Well, Maera, where to next? The cart-track is turning into a bridle path, I vow."

"You're sure she knows where she . . . ah, never doubt a dog!"

They stopped. Ahead, the hedge on their left gave way to a whitewashed, windowless wall topped with a thatch roof. At its far end, a five-barred gate led into a muddy yard behind a small, square building, also whitewashed and thatched. Two stories high, this sported two rows of small, square windows and fronted upon a lane not much wider than the bridle path. Smoke rose from one of the chimneys, suggesting a kitchen fire. Nell realized she was hungry.

Maera sat at their feet panting, her happy grin wider than ever. "We've arrived," she seemed to say.

"Vesta and Vulcan must be here," Nell cried. "Come on."

Lord Clifford held her back. "Wait. We cannot just march into a strange farm and accuse the residents of highway robbery."

"Oh, stop fretting over propriety!"

"It's not a matter of propriety," he said, offended, "it's a matter of safety. I am not armed. Good Lord!" He stared at her as the clouds parted and the evening sun shone on them. "You are alarmingly flushed. My dear Lady Eleanor, have you a fever? I fear you are unwell."

"I'm not delirious, if that's what you wish to imply. My face does feel hot," she conceded, "but I took off my bonnet for a while and I believe I am a little sunburned." Incautiously she raised her hand to her cheek. "Ouch!"

He didn't read her a lecture on the fruits of failure to observe due decorum. Instead he said practically, though with an odious laugh in his voice, "A compress of cold tea is the best remedy I know for sunburn. Come, let us seek aid. In case they should prove innocent, we shall claim to have had a carriage accident. While the lady of the house is ministering to your face, I shall investigate the stables."

"If we had a carriage accident, why are you leading a riding horse?"

"A good point. I'll hide the saddle and reins under the hedge, and leave just a strap to lead him by."

With swift efficiency he stripped Grenadier of his accoutrements and, stepping over a bank of nettles, thrust them deep into the base of the hawthorns. His hat fell off and a thorn left a bloody track down his cheek, but he stepped back to the path looking pleased with himself. Maera watched with interest.

"There, I don't think anyone will find them."

"Nor shall we, without a marker. I shall sacrifice the last scrap of lace on my petticoat, which is already quite ruined. Pray turn your back, sir."

He obeyed, but as she raised the filthy hem of her skirt he said in a stifled tone, "I fear your garment may not be the only thing ruined. It is too late to reach your home or your friend at a respectable hour."

"If you mean that I shall have to marry you after all, you are out in your reckoning." Not that she was any longer totally averse to the prospect. However, since he had changed his mind about her suitability for the exalted position of his wife, she refused to be married solely for the sake of her reputation. "For my sake Miss Lindisfarne will be willing to swear I reached Hungerford hours ago, and no one in this god-forsaken spot can possibly recognize either of us."

The sound of stitches ripping and birds twittering in the bushes filled the weighty pause before Lord Clifford responded. "Nonetheless, I shall tell the people here we are man and wife." The back of his neck was dull red. "I have your . . . the betrothal ring in my pocket. You can wear it backwards to hide the stone."

"If you wish," she said, subdued. "Here is the marker. Will you tie it in the hedge?"

He turned and in exchange for the scrap of lace he handed her the small package she had left for him. Unopened, she saw. For the first time she imagined his feelings on arriving at Brantwood and finding himself cast off without warning.

"I'm sorry," she said remorsefully as he stepped back across the nettles to the hedge. "It was an utterly horrid thing to do."

"It came as a bit of a shock." He tied the lace to a twig with unnecessary care. "I was unaware of having offended you."

"You didn't offend me, not precisely. That is, it was not anything you did, it was what you didn't do. Oh, I am making a mull of this! I simply realized that I didn't know whether there was a person inside the perfect gentleman."

"I have always striven to be a gentleman, though I'd scarcely claim perfection." The dry statement failed to hide his hurt. He avoided her eye as he returned to the path. "Shall we go?"

"Yes." The ring was back on her finger, reversed and hidden beneath her glove. "Maera, heel."

"She won't rush off to hunt for your horses and give the game away? You may be recognized, but the longer they remain in ignorance of our surmise the better."

"Not if I tell her to stay. I'd best describe Vulcan and Vesta so you will recognize them."

"I'm scarcely likely to find a profusion of blood cattle in this 'godforsaken spot.' Still, tell me."

The brief recitation of facts restored her equanimity. Turning the front corner of the house, they saw an inn sign over the front door: a lighted candle in a candlestick. The place was too small to be considered more than a hedge-tavern, though it appeared remarkably clean and prosperous for a hostelry on such a narrow, ill-travelled lane.

"It doesn't look like a haunt of highwaymen," Nell said dubiously, observing window-boxes overflowing with scarlet geraniums.

Lord Clifford read the crooked lettering on the door lintel and his lips quirked. "You really must learn to trust your dog. What did you say the highwayman's name was?"

"He called himself Nimble Jack."

"And here we have The Candlestick, proprietor Wm. Quick. Straight from Mother Goose, don't you think?"

" 'Jack be nimble, Jack be quick, Jack jump over the candlestick.' I'd not have expected you to recall a nursery rhyme."

He coloured. "I sometimes read to my nephew," he excused himself, as if it were something to be ashamed of. Hurriedly he continued, "No doubt Jack's depredations account for the general air of affluence. Now, don't give the least sign that we are suspicious, and with luck they will do their utmost to avoid arousing our suspicions. Are you ready?"

Silenced by sudden qualms, Nell nodded. He tied Grenadier's bridle to a post and ushered her through the open door, directly into a low-ceilinged taproom, uninhabited.

"House, ho!" cried Lord Clifford, knocking with his whip on a table.

A short, stout woman in a spotless pink gingham apron came through a door behind the bar counter. The sight of the newcomers flustered her and she stammered, "Begging your pardon, sir, but the Candlestick don't cater to the quality." Then she glanced at Nell and added, "Nor draggle-tails, neither. And, heavens above, here's a nasty, dirty creature come in after you. Out, you monster, out I say!" She seized a broom and waved it at Maera.

"That is my Greek harpy-hound," said the viscount frostily, "an extremely valuable animal. And this is my wife."

"Oh lor, sir, madam, I didn't mean no harm, I'm sure," babbled the woman, dropping the broom and curtsying as Nell suppressed a slightly hysterical fit of the giggles. "But 'tis the truth, I've got nothing fit for gentry-folk, nor dinner nor lodging."

"Whatever you have must suffice. We have suffered an accident to our carriage and my wife can go no farther this day."

The landlady at once became motherly. "Tut, the poor dear. Of course you shan't stir another inch, madam. Just sit here and rest your bones, dearie, for there won't be a soul in afore dark, tossing the hay after the rain as they be, 'gainst the mildew. The girl only comes in days, but I'll make up the bed in the back room myself, comfy as you please, and there's a nice, toothsome rabbit pie browning in the oven this minute. And you'll be wishing for a dish of tea, I don't doubt. The kettle's always on the hob."

"Thank you—Mrs. Quick, is it?" said Nell faintly, dropping into the chair Lord Clifford held for her. "A cup of tea would be heaven."

"And don't forget a compress of cold tea for your face, my dear. If it will not be too much trouble, Mrs. Quick? To compound my wife's misfortunes, she has unwisely exposed her face to the sun."

"My bonnet came to grief in the accident," Nell hastened to explain, "and the sun was horridly hot. Cold tea is the best remedy for sunburn, I have it on the best medical authority."

"You were also soaked by the rain, Eleanor," said Lord Clifford solicitously, not blinking at being referred to as a medical authority. "Do you wish for a fire?"

"No, I am quite warm. I believe I shall soon dry without."

"Then cosset yourself while I go and stable the horse."

The landlady blenched. "Oh, no, sir, I'm sure it's not fitting for you to be seeing to such things. Quick'll take care of your horse in a winking. William!" She hurried to the door by which she had entered, and Nell and her spurious husband exchanged significant glances. "William? Drat, where is the man!"

"That's quite all right, Mrs. Quick. I've no objection to looking after Grenadier myself." The viscount turned towards the front door.

"William!" bawled Mrs. Quick.

A short, wiry man in a leather apron and jerkin appeared in an open doorway on the far side of the taproom. "I were down the cellar, Madge," he said mildly. "Don't take on so. What . . ." He saw the strangers and stopped with his mouth open.

"It's the gentleman's horse, William. Take it round the stable and mind you take good care of it. Quick knows horses, sir," she anxiously assured the viscount as the landlord scuttled out. "A jockey he were once on a time, and won enough purses to set up in business. He'll do all that's needful. Why don't you sit you down with your lady wife and take a glass of wine?"

"Thank you, I'll try your homebrewed." Resigned, Lord Clifford sat down opposite Nell. She shot him a fulminating look. Was he so easily persuaded to abandon poor Vulcan and Vesta? "If I go now," he whispered under cover of the drawing of ale, "I'll be met with a pistol. I'm afraid we'll have to stay at least part of the night and I'll search when all's quiet."

She nodded, mollified. It was really excessively gallant of him to come to her aid, especially after the shocking way she had treated him. He wasn't at all the insensible block, the shell of cold perfection, she had supposed. In fact, she rather suspected he might even possess a sense of humour.

Taking off her driving gloves, she contemplated the lying band of gold on her finger with a certain degree of wistfulness. She should have known the brother Juliet adored couldn't be entirely lacking in human qualities.

As the landlady set a brimful tankard before him and bustled off to make tea, Ben was also thinking of Juliet. She'd be astonished to see him now, but not half so astonished as he was at his own behaviour.

He was suffering from a fit of madness from which he would presently recover. Since Derrington handed him Lady Eleanor's letter and the ring, the world had a nightmarish cast—no, that wasn't quite right—a dreamlike intangibility which freed him from the demands of convention. Sternly suppressed emotions were bubbling to the surface. In a peculiar and alarming way, he felt more alive than he remembered feeling since childhood.

Was this what life with Lady Eleanor would be like? He regarded her as she sat opposite him, sea-green eyes lowered—not, he was sure, in modesty. Her hair, beginning to dry, spread in a tangled, coppery cloak about her shoulders. Would she let him brush it for her? The thought sent a wave of warmth through him.

But they hadn't a hairbrush between them. They shouldn't be here at all, planning to at least begin the night in the same chamber. It was all her fault. She was impossible!

And anyway, she didn't want him.

He had let himself become embroiled in this ridiculous quest for her precious horses. They should have gone straight to the nearest magistrate. Certainly he should not have let her join him in an escapade dangerous both to her reputation and possibly to their lives. At the time, there had seemed to be no alternative, or rather, it had seemed quite natural.

It was *her* escapade, he reminded himself. Moreover, he doubted he could have stopped her, short of resorting to physical violence. She was impossible. He ought to thank heaven he had found out before tying himself to her for life.

In the meantime, the best he could do was to accept whatever this dream had to offer and take what enjoyment from it he might. The demands of reality would return all too soon.

Maera's heavy head appeared on his knee and she gazed up at him with an appeal in her brown eyes.

"Water for my . . ." What had he called her? ". . . for my harpy hound," he requested as Mrs. Quick brought the tea. Lady Eleanor's little snort was undoubtedly a suppressed giggle. Her eyes met his, bright with amusement. "And a bowl of scraps," he added firmly.

Promising to see what she could find, the landlady departed.

"How fortunate that your harpy hound does not require a special diet," said Lady Eleanor, pouring her tea.

"If she were too well fed," he responded, "she'd lose interest in hunting harpies."

"I daresay she would. Are they not reputed to be as foul-smelling as they are sharp-clawed? Poor Maera!"

"I felt she'd prefer a new profession to the ignominy of being chased out with a broom."

"Certainly, although she'd not have stirred without my word. However, I did not appreciate your defending your dog before your wife! What precisely is a draggle-tail?"

"It is not a word a lady need know," Ben said severely.

"I can guess, then." Her delightful smile faded. "Lord Clifford, we must—"

"You must remember to address me as Benedict." He hesitated. Only his sister used his nickname. Why did he feel impelled to offer it to this irrepressible woman who had rejected him? "Ben, if you prefer."

"Ben will do nicely. Benedict is a splendid name to be saved for special occasions. My friends call me Nell."

She accepted him as a friend? Inexplicably his heart lightened. "We cannot discuss our plans here, Nell," he said quickly as the landlady returned with two dishes for the dog. "Later."

In any other female, he'd have assumed her acquiescence to be the result of feminine submissiveness. In Lady Eleanor—Nell—it could only mean that she understood and agreed. Fortunate indeed that her understanding was quick; otherwise, no less resolute than stubborn, she would argue until convinced.

He would always know her opinion—except that there was to be no always. The most he had to hope for was occasional meetings as friends.

"I'll have the bed done in a jiffy, madam," said Mrs. Quick, "and then you can lie down till dinner's ready, with a compress for your poor face. More ale, sir?"

"Thank you, no, but it's excellent."

"The men walks over from miles around for a sup of our ale," she said, beaming, and once again bustled away.

"She *cannot* be in league with that dreadful man," Nell exclaimed. "All right, not another word on that subject. Juliet says you often go up to Town to speak in Parliament. My father and Bertie never bothered. Tell me about it."

By the time Mrs. Quick came to fetch her, he had discovered that at least on the subject of chimney-sweeps and the Corn Laws her political opinions coincided exactly with his.

"Maera needs to go out," she said, rising. "Would you mind . . . that is, perhaps you could take her into the yard, Ben."

"Oh, madam, that would never do," Mrs. Quick protested at once. "There's the chickens back there."

"Mae . . ." Nell began indignantly.

"Maera is far too well trained to chase chickens," Ben broke in, "but I can take her into the lane if you prefer."

"If you please, sir. She's a big creetur, and chase or no, I'd be afeard they'd be scared out of laying. This way, if you please, madam."

As the women departed through the far door, Maera watched, ears pricked, puzzled. Since Ben had claimed the dog as his, Nell had been able to say neither "come" nor "stay." A proper clunch he'd look now if his valuable, perfectly trained harpy hound refused to go out with him.

"Well," he said to her, "are you going to make a fool of me?"

She gazed up at him hopefully. The white tip of her tail quivered.

"Come." He started towards the door. Maera hesitated, glanced sadly back at the door where her mistress had disappeared, and followed.

Her relief when they returned to the Candlestick was not flattering. She was overjoyed when Nell came down for dinner, her hair combed, her face less painful if no less red.

They ate in the corner of a room now filling with weary, thirsty farmhands, most of whom scarce spared a glance for the strangers. After dinner, Ben was in a quandary. Even in the present outrageous circumstances, he couldn't bring himself to suggest that they retire to their shared bedchamber.

Lingering over a gooseberry tart, Nell seemed equally reluctant to make so indelicate a proposal, but at last she sighed and said, "We must make plans. I'll go up. Do you mind taking Maera out again?"

Perhaps they could claim Maera as a chaperon, Ben thought wildly ten minutes later as he climbed the narrow stair, the big dog padding at his heels. Whatever Nell said, her reputation was liable to end up—like her petticoat—in shreds. Honour would force him to marry her.

Somehow the prospect no longer appalled him.

She was sitting on the bed, her knees clasped in her arms. Her face brightened as he entered—but not in welcome for him. "Oh, I was afraid you'd leave her downstairs. Thank you."

Though she sat on top of the patchwork coverlet, Nell was swathed in a voluminous white cambric nightgown. It was not an enticing garment, but Ben couldn't help staring. Was her lack of propriety more profound than he had supposed? Was she not merely unconventional but unchaste? Despite his shocked dismay, his loins stirred. Was she inviting him . . . ?

A blush intensified the scarlet of her sunburn. "Mrs. Quick insisted on lending me a nightrail. I put it on over my clothes lest she should come back to see if I needed anything more. She won't come now. I'll take it off."

Fully dressed beneath she might be, but he studied the low, sloped ceiling as she knelt up on the bed to disrobe. In the tiny chamber, bed, clothes press, and washstand took up all but a small strip of floor, most of which Maera occupied.

"Mrs. Quick did not query our lack of baggage?" he asked in a strangled voice.

"No. I believe she is too flustered by our presence and dare not ask questions for fear of arousing our curiosity. She or her husband must have spoken to Nimble Jack by now. There, that's better." With the removal of the suggestive attire, she appeared to have regained her *sang-froid*. "There is no chair. You will have to sit on the bed while we make our plans."

Ben perched perforce at the foot of the bed, leaning back against one of the posts. They agreed to sneak down to the stables as soon as all was quiet, lead out the horses—by now they were both convinced the chestnuts were there—and make off at once. Retribution for Nimble Jack could wait.

That decision led to talk of the Law, thence to the plight of the poor, to Parliament, to London's music and theatre, to literature and philosophy. More often than not their opinions coincided, but even when they argued Ben was constantly conscious of the candlelight on her hair, the alluring swell of her breasts, the glimpse of a neat ankle when she shifted.

If this were madness, who would choose sanity?

The sound of voices below gradually died. Footsteps sounded on the stairs; a latch clicked. The old timbers of the house creaked and groaned, settling for the night. Maera slept the sleep of the just, raising her head once to stare at the door, then drifting back to foot-twitching dreams of rabbits—or perhaps of harpies. The passionate song of a nightingale drifted through the narrow casement, open to the warm night.

"Was it Beethoven you were playing that day?" Ben said abruptly.

She did not need to ask which day. "Yes. The *Appassionata* sonata."

"You had not played any of his works in the evenings."

"Phyllis said you would . . . prefer more decorous music." She studied her hands as if she had never seen them before. "I let her persuade me to deceive you shamelessly, to make you believe I am the soul of demure conformity."

"But why? Why did you accept my offer?"

"To escape from her. I have had other offers, you know, quite a few over the years, but never a suitor worth leaving my father for. Then he died and Bertie married Phyllis. You must not suppose she is a bad person, or intentionally cruel, yet *anything* seemed preferable to staying at Brantwood!"

"Anything!" The word burst out from the pain within. His parents had not cared for him enough to stay at home. Lady Eleanor Lacey, a spinster at her last prayers, desperate to escape, did not want him. He had striven to make himself utterly unexceptionable and thought he had succeeded. He had deluded himself. What was wrong with him?

That question he could not ask. Nell was looking at him with concern, about to speak. "You should have told me you wanted a fashionable wedding," he said harshly. "I'd not have refused."

"But I didn't! Phyllis insisted on inviting all the nobility she could think of with the slightest connection to either family. As many as will fit into St. Mary's, at least. I assumed she had consulted you."

"No. I begin to see why you are eager to leave."

"I should not have involved you in my difficulties. I didn't really mind hurting your pride, and I didn't believe you had feelings to be hurt."

"A gentleman does not display his feelings."

"A perfect gentleman," she said thoughtfully. Recalling Juliet's tales of her parents' notorious peculiarities, she fell silent. The silence of their surroundings closed in around them. Nell bit her lip. "A perfect gentleman—nonetheless, you must not feel obliged to help me rescue Vesta and Vulcan."

"Having come thus far, I'd not miss the adventure for the world." Ben reached out to take her hand and she gripped hard, the stone of the ring digging into his palm. "Nervous?"

"A little. Shall we go now?"

"I'll just take my boots off. They'd make a noise on the stair. I had best carry them down."

Struggling to remove Hoby's once-glossy creations without the aid of his valet, he watched with a tender smile as she tidied her hair in the tiny mirror on the washstand. Unconventional, eccentric even, but no less feminine for that! She picked up her gloves, he took his and his hat and, squeezing past the now-alert dog, he reached for the door-latch.

"Locked!"

"It can't be! Your hands are full, let me try." She tugged in vain. "We'll have to go through the window. There's an outbuilding roof just below. I saw it earlier. I was trying to see the yard and the stables but it cuts off the view." They turned as one to contemplate the tiny window. Nell groaned. "You cannot possibly fit through that. Your shoulders are far too broad. I'll have to get the horses and go for help."

"Not alone!" he protested, but she slipped past him, slithered out, and dropped from sight. Maera, surprised but game, bounded after her.

He stuck his head out. By hazy moonlight he saw both of them slide down a thatch slope and disappear again. A soft call reached his ears: "We're down."

The rash, intrepid little widgeon! He had to go after her, had to squeeze through that window if it killed him. He stripped off his coat, stuffing her necklace into the pocket of his riding breeches.

He made it. He tore both shirt and waistcoat, and wrenched his left shoulder, but he made it. A moment later he strode in his stockings across the muddy yard after the dark figures of woman and dog.

Maera headed straight for the far end of the long, low stable building. Nell followed. She didn't dare look back, for if she did she might turn and run, might try to regain the cosy nest and the reassurance of Ben's masculine strength.

With a low whine, Maera scratched at the next to last door. Instantly it swung open. A man stood silhouetted against lamplight, a burly man, with an object in his hand which glinted evilly.

"Ah, 'tis the gentry mort come a-visiting, eh?" said Nimble Jack. "I seen you from the hayloft. Tell that bloody brute to stay, and come in, missy, come in." He reached out and grabbed her wrist.

"Stay, Maera!" Nell said sharply to the snarling dog.

The highwayman pulled her towards him, into an empty loosebox. In the stalls on either side were two black horses. One put his head over the partition and whickered a soft greeting. The other pricked her ears forward.

"Vulcan? Vesta? You have *dyed* them!" cried Nell.

"Aye, and they won't be the only ones what's died, missy," he said regretfully. "I can't let you go. I c'd run for it, but you'd turn Madge in. She's me sister. She been good to me and never asked no questions, and . . ."

A flash of white shirtsleeves passed Nell. Ben's fist caught

Nimble Jack on the chin. The highwayman staggered backwards, dropping his pistol, but Ben clutched his shoulder with a moan. His left arm hung limp.

Jack recovered his balance and rushed in. Ben blocked a hefty fist with his right arm, then Jack's second punch met his eye and it was his turn to stagger back, through the doorway. Tripping over Maera, he landed flat on his back in the mud.

With a cry of triumph, the highwayman stooped to retrieve his pistol. But before he could do so, Nell shot him.

Bellowing in surprise, pain, and fury, Jack in his turn clutched his shoulder, but he managed to grasp the gun. Maera, her snarl rising to a bloodcurdling growl from deep within her chest, leapt forward. Her jaws closed on his wrist.

Jack dropped the pistol. "Call it off!" he pleaded.

"Not bloody likely," said Nell, taking profound pleasure in the vulgarity. She seized the gun. "Good girl, Maera. On guard."

"I'll bleed to death!"

"Good." She was already out in the yard, where Ben struggled to sit up.

"I strained my shoulder climbing through the window," he explained in a shaky voice, "and now I think I've sprained my ankle. I'm sorry, I'm not much use as a rescuer."

"You were simply splendid," she said warmly. Kneeling at his side, she put Jack's pistol in his good hand and pocketed her own. "I'd be dead by now but for you, and you were positively heroic, rushing in with an injured arm. You need a sling first, I think. Your neckcloth will be perfect." She untied the neat, unobtrusive knot, unwound the rectangle of muslin, and quickly fashioned a sling. "That's better. Can you rise?"

"If you will give me . . . a hand."

Not *your* hand, with its echo of his proposal, she noted sadly, helping him to stand. To cap her many ineligible habits, she had used shocking language and she had shot a man.

"Heavens, I must try to stop Jack bleeding to death. I confess I was aiming for his heart, but all the same, I should not like to have his death on my conscience."

She supported Ben into the stable. When he was seated on the manger, the pistol trained on Jack, she called off Maera and started to bandage the highwayman's shoulder and wrist with strips of her desecrated petticoat.

"Don't know why you bother, miss," he said gloomily. "I'd as soon bleed to death as end up on the nubbing cheat."

"The nub . . . the gallows? Oh, I hope it won't come to that. Purely for your sister's sake," Nell added severely. "She was kind to me. I shall discover who is the local magistrate—I daresay I am already acquainted with him—and ask him to inform me if any more highway robberies take place in this district. If they do, I shall tell him where to find you. If you reform, he shall learn nothing from me."

"What about the gentry cove?"

She followed his gaze to Ben, who appeared stunned by her forbearance.

"After all," she defended herself, "Maera and I have done Jack far more damage than he ever did us. But, oh dear," she added guiltily, "I believe *you* are going to have a perfectly dreadful black eye!"

Benedict, Viscount Clifford, stiffest and starchiest member of the *Ton,* burst into helpless laughter and laughed till he cried.

Ben did not dare let Nell return to the house for his boots. There was no knowing what the Quicks might do. In any case, his ankle was swelling and he'd be no better off with one boot than none. As for his hat, if she had no bonnet, why on earth should he feel the need of a hat?

She found an oaken staff to support him. She had to lead all three horses, but they followed her willingly. They left by the side gate and Maera took them straight to Grenadier's saddle.

"I need not have sacrificed my lace," said Nell with forced lightness, "though after bandaging Jack's shoulder not much is left of my petticoat anyway."

Her frank mention of the intimate garment no longer had the power to shock him. "I wager Maera will lead us back to the dog-cart, too," he responded in the same tone.

"Oh, Ben, I'd forgotten, Nimble Jack cut the harness. I'll have to cobble together a makeshift rig."

"I'm sure I'll be able to give you a hand with that, but I fear you will have to drive." To her friend's house, he thought dismally. "I'm more of a hindrance than a help to you."

"Not at all. I need you right now, to hold the horses while I retrieve the gear."

Nell muttered unladylike curses as she ploughed through the stinging nettles and reached into the thorny hedge. Nor was saddling her brother's restive fifteen-hand hack an easy task. Not until it was done did Ben realize the real problem.

"I think I can mount, but I doubt I can control Grenadier with one arm and one leg. You will have to leave me after all and go for help.

"Fustian! I shall ride in the saddle, and you shall sit behind and use your one arm to hold onto me."

"It's not a side-saddle," he reminded her.

"Riding astride is much easier."

"Astride!"

"No one will see, it's dark," she said stubbornly, then wailed, "Ben, I don't *want* to go on alone in the dark!"

He infused his voice with all the cheerful encouragement he could muster. "Then somehow we shall manage it," he vowed.

Somehow they managed it. His ankle throbbed; his shoulder throbbed; his eye throbbed; but he was far more conscious of his arm about her supple waist, her back pressed to his chest, her silky hair tickling his chin, the lavender scent of her. As

Maera led the way, the white tip of her tail bobbing ahead, Ben was happy.

Though reality had shaken him when Nimble Jack's fist sent him flying, Nell's bandaging of the highwayman had assured him that he was still dreaming. Anything could happen in dreams, couldn't it?

"Nell, will you marry me?"

She stiffened. An endless pause before she replied, her tone strained, "I do not consider myself compromised, I promise you. My reputation—except as a jilt—is quite safe."

"To the devil with your reputation!" He buried his face in her hair and groaned, "Oh, Nell, Nell, see what you have brought me to: swearing before a lady, dismissing her reputation as irrelevant. If you won't have me, I shall spend the rest of my life only half alive."

"But I'm not at all the sort of female you thought you were offering for, the sort of wife you want."

"The sort of wife I *thought* I wanted. Why should only women be privileged to change their minds?"

Still Nell hesitated. He was kind, gallant, brave, sensitive, forgiving, and only a man with a lively sense of humour could have laughed as he had in the stable. And yet . . .

"If I say yes, you will not mind having Maera in your house?"

"Our house. Certainly not. I have met many a dowager with less acceptable manners."

"You won't stop me driving myself?"

"As long as you take a groom along—or me—to guard against highwaymen."

"You will let me play Beethoven?"

"I'll buy you all he ever wrote for the pianoforte, and take you to hear his symphonies and concertos in London."

"You will not insist upon directing my reading?"

"I venture to say you will find my library a considerable improvement over Brantwood's."

"Neither Papa nor Bertie was ever fond of books," Nell admitted. "You will not try to change my opinions?"

"Oh yes I shall, but I shall respect them, and you for holding them."

"And I may visit the poor?"

"Unless there is danger of contagion." His voice thickened. "If I should be so lucky as to win you, you cannot expect me to risk losing you."

"Oh." She wished she could see his face.

"Have you any other shocking habits I should be warned of?" he teased.

She guessed at a valiant effort to subdue his emotions, to put her at ease, but his query had the opposite effect. "I have never done anything really shocking before," she said penitently, "nothing scandalous . . . except running away from you."

"I don't want you to marry me for fear of scandal!" He straightened, drawing away from her. "All my life I have sought to avoid being a subject for tattlemongers' tongues, but I had rather suffer ridicule for being left in the lurch than have you wed me to save me from that fate. Which leaves you with no possible reason to want me. I'm quite useless to you."

"Oh Ben, I don't want a man who won't let me do things for myself, who won't let me help him. You *are* a perfect gentleman. If I agreed to marry you it would be because . . ." She hesitated.

"Because?"

After all her other questions it was going to sound petty, but she had to know whether she had misinterpreted the warm light in his eyes up there in their shared bedchamber. "Benedict, you truly don't object to red hair?"

"Object! My dear, my dearest Eleanor, if you had not kept it hidden from me, I'd have fallen in love with you weeks ago instead of proceeding in my dispassionate way. I doubt I am so perfect a gentleman I'd not have shown you . . . my passion."

His arm tightened about her waist as once again he buried his face in her hair. His lips found the nape of her neck and his kisses sent a glowing tremor through her entire being. She forgot the night, the dog in the vanguard, the patient, plodding horses, the predicament awaiting with the dawn.

"Because?" he whispered in her ear.

"Because I love you."

Maera led Grenadier to the dog-cart. Nell and Ben emerged from their dream to repair the harness with knotted strips of Nell's abandoned, ruined clothes, and they set out again. Vesta and Vulcan, now patchily black, pulled them at a steady trot eastward into a sparkling sunrise perfumed with honeysuckle. And as she drove, Nell's apprehensions returned.

Ben's acceptance of her quirks was all very well in the middle of nowhere with none but a highwayman and his accomplices for witnesses. How would he feel when the moment came to appear before the *Ton?*

As the bridegroom's closest relative, Juliet Lady Faulk sat in the front pew in the little church, next to the empty place where her brother ought to be. Only the calm, reassuring presence of her husband at her side stopped her pulling off her glove to bite her nails, or running out into the churchyard to question Lord Derrington.

Her doubts of Lady Derrington's increasingly anxious excuses had become certainty. Ben and Nell were missing. Which had cried off, which had jilted the other, she could not pretend to guess. Perhaps it was mutual. In any case, it was a major disaster and it was all her fault.

She held Faulk's hand tight as the whispers behind her

turned into scandalized remarks audible above the organ's persistent drone.

Heads turned as the sound of hooves and wheels was followed by a ragged "Huzzah!" from the village urchins waiting outside. Cheering? Jeering? A curious mixture of the two. Juliet craned her neck. Had the bride arrived at last only to be humiliated by the groom's absence?

If so, she'd *kill* Ben.

Bertie Derrington appeared, looking stunned, and raced down the nave to speak to the vicar. Behind him, two figures stood silhouetted in the arched doorway.

The organist embarked uncertainly upon Handel's *Arrival of the Queen of Sheba.*

The bride wore a magnificent necklace of emeralds and diamonds. Her head was wreathed with honeysuckle, from which her unbound hair fell in a fiery veil about her shoulders. Her simple gown of blue muslin was sprigged with . . . mud? Mud! . . . to match the ankle-high strip of dried mud around the hem. She walked slowly between the rows of gaping guests, very slowly, for she was supporting . . .

Juliet closed her eyes, unbelieving, and reopened them to the same sight.

Ben had one arm across Nell's shoulders. His other arm was in a sling and he limped heavily as she helped him towards the altar, *in his shirtsleeves and stocking-feet!*

Torn shirt, without neckcloth, and filthy stockings, Juliet noted, beyond incredulity. And one eye was red and puffy, swollen almost shut.

"Someone has darkened his daylight for him," murmured Faulk, grinning.

Yet Ben did not look angry. He was not embarrassed, nor even self-conscious. In fact, as he bent his head to whisper in Nell's ear, he was positively radiant. So was she.

So was the huge, filthy dog of uncertain parentage who pranced after them exuding triumph.

They stopped before the flower-laden altar. Ben's back was

caked with mud from the crown of his head all the way down to his heels. Nell's face, now turned up to him, was a curious, uniform scarlet quite unlike a maidenly blush.

The organ music ceased. Before the flustered vicar could pronounce his "Dearly beloved," Ben once again bent his head. To the aghast amazement of the noble congregation, his lips met Nell's in a long, loving kiss.

The Impossible Bridegroom

by
Jean R. Ewing

For my sister, Mary,
who speaks Welsh.

"Beth! There's a carriage stopped at the door! Papa says to come at once, because he's most dreadfully afraid it's our cousins Honeywell!"

Elizabeth Lindsay looked up from the linen she had been sorting for mending and grinned at her little brother. "His very words, no doubt! I suppose I had better take off my apron. And you, young man, will go and wash your hands and face immediately. Is Mrs. Honeywell very grand?"

"Grand enough to sour milk," replied Joseph, looking seriously at his grubby fingers. "And that's what Papa said too."

Beth choked back her amusement and a few minutes later ushered a slightly damp Joseph into the parlor. As for herself, she had removed her apron and smoothed down her honey-colored hair, but she still wore the sensible plain blue dress which served her perfectly well for everyday chores. Since her mother had died, ten years before, Beth had acted as sole housekeeper for her father and little brother, and she did much of the work herself. Mr. Lindsay didn't make enough in his legal practice in Much Haven to hire many servants; he took on far too many charity cases and cheerfully went without any luxuries for himself. Beth took whatever burdens she could from his thread-bare shoulders and bypassed finery without a backward glance. The same could hardly be said for the Honeywells.

Fanning herself furiously, Beth's Aunt Honeywell was already ensconced in Mr. Lindsay's favorite armchair. Her bounteous bosom supported several frills of scarlet silk, which rose and fell with her rapid breathing and contrasted most unfortunately with her hot round cheeks. Harriet Honeywell sat opposite her on the sofa, pretty as a china figurine in a fetching blue and cream muslin, liberally sprinkled with silk bows. Trapped between them at the hearth, Mr. Lindsay looked distinctly miserable. Beth noticed with a small pang of dismay that he had a new hole in his sleeve.

"Ah, Elizabeth," he said with open relief as she entered. "Here are Mrs. Honeywell and Miss Honeywell stopped by to pay their respects on their way to London. Miss Honeywell is to be married in June—at St. George's in Hanover Square, no less."

He winked quickly at Beth, as she held out her hand to her aunt and cousin. The freshly scrubbed Joseph was allowed to escape to the window, where he could occupy himself admiring the Honeywell carriage, but Beth must take a seat next to her exquisite cousin and ring for tea. It would have to be the best China tea, of course, and there wasn't much of it left.

"How very splendid!" she said, smiling.

"Wait till you hear the name of the bridegroom, Beth! It is such a crown to our consequence!" The import of this prospect entirely robbed Mrs. Honeywell of breath. She began to pant a little and was forced to fan with even more vigor. "Tell your cousin who has promised to wed you, Harriet."

"Henry Fitzroy, Lord Ravenstoke!" announced Harriet. "What do you think of that, Beth?"

"Lord Ravenstoke?" Beth looked at her cousin in open astonishment. She had never heard of the man, but how extraordinary that the daughter of a dealer in best China tea should land a lord! Perhaps the fellow was out-at-pocket and in need of Harriet's dowry? Or maybe he was a toothless old rake, content enough to marry youth and beauty where he found it. "What's he like?" she asked with real interest.

"He's a viscount!"

"Yes, but I mean—what kind of a man is he? What are his interests?"

"Oh, I've no idea," said Harriet with a toss of the head.

"But he's fabulously handsome, you know. All the girls are green with envy."

"He has at least twenty thousand a year, Beth dear," said Mrs. Honeywell, going straight to the heart of the matter. "Think of that! And he's a renowned Corinthian, cuts a dash among the *ton*—or so we're led to believe. Many a peer's daughter has cast her cap in his direction without success. Quite a triumph for our Harriet!"

So the fellow was certainly not in need of Harriet's portion and it didn't sound as if he were otherwise ineligible. Which made it all the more odd. Of course Harriet was very pretty, perhaps this Lord Ravenstoke had fallen in love? Though the aristocracy were supposed to be above such vulgar emotions and certainly not marry for them.

"And does he have a large family?" asked Beth's father, whose quick thoughts were very closely following those of his only daughter.

Mrs. Honeywell shifted her bulk in the armchair and smiled complacently at Mr. Lindsay. "Not at all. He is sole heir to his father's fortune and titles, and from what we hear, the old earl can't be long for this world. The family seat is reputed very grand and in the meantime, there's a neat little property of his own—Ravenstoke Hall."

"Have you ever been there?" asked Beth.

"My dear, the place is in Wales! I declare I could wish that Harriet were to settle somewhat closer to London, but there it is, one can't have everything."

The maid had come in with the tea tray, allowing Harriet to catch sight of herself in the hall mirror. She had been adjusting her glossy ringlets and smiling at her own reflection, but at this she turned back to the company. "Oh, I shall make him take a lease on another house closer to town, something modern. You won't catch me going to horrid old Wales. Ravenstoke Hall is some kind of dreadful ancient manor that's been in the family since the Middle Ages. I changed the subject very smartly, I can tell you, when he began to tell me about it."

"Perhaps he has no care for it," Beth said sympathetically. For no good reason she began to feel for the viscount.

"Oh, no, it's his passion, of course. He's touchingly devoted to his tenants—all that kind of stuff. You know how men are! But his agent can take care of the place and it will provide a very pretty income, I'm sure. He's to be married now and a gentleman's first concern should be to please his wife. Now, Mama, mayn't I have the lime-green bonnet with the white daisies that we saw in Much Haven? Ravenstoke said once he hated fake flowers, but it'll make the other gentlemen's eyes turn, I shouldn't wonder."

Beth caught her father's eye and had to look down to avoid disgracing herself. Mr. Lindsay almost choked in his tea and disguised his laugh with a small cough. "I'm surprised you would find anything in our little main street grand enough to tempt you, Miss Honeywell," he said as soon as he recovered.

Harriet dimpled prettily at him. "Well, normally you can't get a thing down in the country, of course, and if I'm to be Lady Ravenstoke, I must be in the first stare. Mama and I are to do no end of shopping in London, aren't we, Mama? Yet when I see a thing I like, I must have it, you know."

"Then you shall, my dear," said Mrs. Honeywell. "For I declare I don't know how I shall drag myself around the shops when we get to town. This must be the hottest May in years! To think of all the things we shall need, I am exhausted at the very idea. You will have to go out with your maid, Harriet. You know how very delicate my health is in hot weather."

"Nobody of consequence goes shopping with just a maid, Mama!" said Harriet, pouting. "And for my trousseau! I want a lady to accompany me."

"You have no care for my nerves, Harriet," complained Mrs. Honeywell. The scarlet frills began to flutter as mother and daughter looked stubbornly at each other. "You know I have a very dainty constitution. You shan't bully me when I'm not well!"

"No doubt the London shops will be so exciting you won't notice the company, Miss Honeywell," said Mr. Lindsay in his best professional manner.

Harriet ignored him and turning to Beth gave her a sudden brilliant smile. "Beth shall come to London with us!"

Mrs. Honeywell sat up. Beth was caught with the teapot in one hand and a cup in the other as the attention of the whole room centered on her. "Why, I declare, it's the very thing! Now don't say no, Elizabeth. It would be the perfect answer. And don't worry about the blunt. Mr. Honeywell will settle everything, of course. I don't imagine you eat more than a bird and the clothes you have will do very well. An amiable spinster like yourself will make Harriet a very respectable companion, indeed. As Harriet's cousin, who could be more suitable?"

Beth swallowed her indignation at being called a respectable spinster, though of course at six-and-twenty she was thoroughly on the shelf. "Aunt Honeywell, you are more than kind, but I can't possibly accept."

"But it would only be a month—just until the wedding!" said Harriet. "Do come, Beth. We'll have no end of larks!"

"But Papa needs me here, Harriet. You do see that it's impossible, surely, that I leave home so suddenly."

But Mr. Lindsay was looking very hard at his daughter and a frown line had appeared between his brows. His darling Elizabeth had turned into a spinster, had she? Her youth was passing her by, while she was wearing her fingers to the bone on his and Joe's behalf without a word of complaint. And he hadn't noticed! "No, Elizabeth," he said suddenly. "I think you should go with your cousin. You deserve a holiday."

"Papa, who would take care of you and Joe?"

"We'll manage very well, my dear. Joseph's thirteen now, he doesn't need his sister to mother him any more. We'll shift for ourselves for a bit and come to no harm. You shall go with your Aunt Honeywell and I'll hear no more about it."

"Then that's settled," said Mrs. Honeywell, struggling out of the chair. "Pack a few things, Elizabeth. Harriet and I will go after that bonnet and then we'll come back for you. We can make room in the carriage, I'm sure."

Beth watched them go out in dismay. "Father, how could you? I am perfectly content here with you and Joe. You know you cannot endure the company of Aunt Honeywell yourself for more than two minutes, yet you condemn me to live with her for a month in London. How shall I stand it?"

"Now that is nonsense, my dear girl. Mrs. Honeywell will barely stir from the house and Harriet's harmless enough. Her companionship will make it possible for you to see the sights. You will love it and I could never otherwise afford to send you. There'll be walks in the Park and parties and dances enough, no doubt. You're to thoroughly enjoy yourself and come back to your Papa with roses in your cheeks."

"But supposing you should need me?"

"You'll not be more than an hour and a half away, my dear." His eyes twinkled. "Besides, you'll meet the redoubtable viscount. Think of that."

"I am thinking of that," said Beth with a sudden giggle. "And I'm not sure that I'm looking forward to the experience."

Mr. Lindsay laughed aloud. "Indeed you may be right, my dear, for if he's fallen for Harriet, he must be either a nincompoop or a popinjay."

Henry Fitzroy, Lord Ravenstoke, was thinking much the same thing as he tooled his curricle up the Oxford Road into London the following week. How on earth could he have allowed himself to become entrapped by Harriet Honeywell? It had seemed harmless enough to stop in the shires for the last of the hunting and accompany his friends to the local balls. Miss Honeywell had caught his eye for a moment, but as soon as she opened her mouth he had discovered that there wasn't much inside that pretty head. He had thus paid her no more than casual attention and at each event, correctly danced once with each girl in the room. The night before he was due to leave, he had thankfully escaped outside for a breath of fresh air. The next thing he knew, Harriet was in his arms and kissing him passionately on the mouth. He could not deny that he had returned it, at least for a moment. She was very pretty and her kiss seemed experienced enough. Only afterwards did he think that it might have been planned that her father discover them there together. Harriet had started to cry.

"I'm so sorry, Papa. Don't be angry! Lord Ravenstoke meant no harm by it, I'm sure. I had no idea that a London gentleman would . . ."

"Be quiet, Harriet! Damn your eyes, sir! This is a respectable town and we're a respectable family. What are your intentions by my daughter? For if they're not honorable, I'll meet you, sir, damn me if I won't!"

". . . and since we had reached an understanding." Harriet was blubbing.

A little group of interested spectators had begun to gather. "Sir, I beg of you," Ravenstoke had said quietly. "If you have a care for your daughter's reputation, pray do not escalate this scene."

But Mr. Honeywell was spluttering and red in the face. "She's an innocent, sir! It may be the way of you town gentlemen to flirt with a child, then entice her into the garden to steal her virtue and ruin her reputation without a backward thought, but not down here, sir! I say again, what are your intentions?"

Harriet had clung to his arm and looked up at the viscount with tear-drenched eyes. "It doesn't matter, Papa. For a gentleman like Lord Ravenstoke to pay me the honor of his regard . . ."

"Then your intentions are honest, my lord? I am very glad

to hear it and welcome you into our family. We may be in trade, but I'll do what's right by my daughter."

Henry Fitzroy knew then that the jaws of the trap had sprung shut. "Of course, sir," he had said stiffly. "I have the honor of asking your daughter to be my wife."

Afterwards he thought of a thousand other ways he could have handled it, but that wouldn't help now. He was committed, and in less than a month, Harriet Honeywell would become Lady Ravenstoke unless his plan worked to prevent it. What an absurd situation for Viscount Ravenstoke, the man who had been avoiding the matrimonial traps of the *ton* for ten years, to be captured against his will by the empty-headed daughter of a cit! And now, as if to add to his bedevilment, it was building up to a thunderstorm.

Beth looked around in exasperation. It had started to rain, the sky was turning pitch black, and Harriet had disappeared. Mr. Lindsay had been entirely wrong. She was not having a good time. Firstly, she hadn't visited any sights: Harriet was interested only in shopping. Beth had been enthralled for a while by the riches displayed in the London shops and spent the little bit that her father had given her on a few ribbons and some trimming, but regretfully, she wasn't passionately interested in Harriet's trousseau. Secondly, she was of course thrust into Aunt Honeywell's company every day. Thirdly, the bridegroom seemed to be out of town, so she hadn't had the opportunity to discover if Lord Ravenstoke was either a nincompoop or a popinjay, and thus assuage her natural curiosity. Harriet wasn't in the least concerned about the whereabouts of the groom. He had gone to Wales, she thought, to wish good-bye to Ravenstoke Hall and did Beth think the gentlemen would like her better in the pink sarsenet or the primrose? Beth had pushed aside her irritation and tried to give her honest opinion, but when she looked up from the bolts of fabric in Green's Emporium, Harriet was gone.

Beth ducked under the cover of her umbrella and hurried up the street to where she thought they had left the carriage. It wasn't there. Instead a big-boned chestnut with one white leg was tied to a post at the curb. She seemed to have been completely abandoned. Perhaps Coachman hadn't liked to keep the team standing longer. Or had she mistaken the direction? These London streets all looked much the same. As she hesitated, there was a distinct growl of thunder and the heavens opened. Under the onslaught of water, the crowds rapidly melted away. Perhaps if she tried the other way?

"Can I 'elp you, miss? You look lost."

It was a crossing-sweeper, a boy no older than Joe, who was peering hopefully at her from beneath a fringe of water-logged locks.

"Thank you. Can you direct me to a cab?" Beth reached into her reticule and pulled out a penny. "I must get home to Russell Square by myself, it seems."

"And another penny when we get there?" The boy eyed her cheekily as Beth nodded. "Just follow me, then!"

The boy grabbed the coin and scurried away with Beth at his heels. The rain had become blinding and her umbrella obscured the houses and shop-fronts. She paid no attention to where they were going until the stones beneath her feet gave way to rough cobbles. She looked up. Ahead lay rows of small tenements and another few blocks would take her into what looked like a positive warren. With a sinking heart, Beth stopped in her tracks.

"This can't be the way to a respectable cab!" she said indignantly.

"I was promised another penny," said the boy stubbornly, holding out his hand.

The rattle of carriages and the wet splash of water from the pavement behind her must surely indicate a main thoroughfare? She may be fresh from the country, but Elizabeth Lindsay wasn't entirely a pea-goose. If she stayed safely within reach of the traffic, no doubt she could find a cab by herself, but to venture any further in the company of this urchin might land her thoroughly in the mire. Beth reached into her purse for another penny.

"Thank you for your help," she said kindly—and the urchin tore her entire reticule from her hand.

In the next instant, he was racing away with every penny she possessed into that tangle of tenement houses. Beth shouted and then was deafened by the sound of a shot. The boy stumbled and the reticule fell from his hand. A bullet had just whizzed over her head and cut the purse strings. Fortunately—or unfortunately, perhaps—the boy didn't seem to be hurt, for he picked up the fallen bag and turned and danced a little jig, all the while defiantly waving his prize towards her and his assailant. Then he turned and whooped and was soon swallowed up in the gloom.

"I hope I didn't startle you, ma'am," said a most attractive voice behind her. "I thought to act the knight-errant, but failed most dismally in retrieving your purse from that vagabond. And then the dance was so entertaining, I hadn't the heart to fire again."

Beth swung around to meet the gaze of a gentleman at the reins of a very dashing curricle. He was just putting up his pistol, but that wasn't what caught her attention and robbed her of breath. Perhaps it was the way his brown hair curled at his temples or the laughter lurking in the warm brown eyes. Her would-be rescuer was an extremely good-looking young man—though not, she thought with a relief that was patently absurd, all that young. She judged him to be twenty-eight or nine, at least.

"Are you lost?" said the gentleman. He looked Beth over thoughtfully. Her frank blue eyes were fixed on his face and she had the most lovely soft gold hair which was curling enticingly in the damp air. But her clothes were plain and positively countrified, and she must be five-and-twenty at least. Perhaps she was a governess?

"If you could direct me to a cab, sir, I would be most grateful. I have no idea where I am and I must get back to Russell Square."

"You are now on the Oxford Road and your goal is close to two miles off. Without a purse, though, you'd be hard pressed to find a cabby who'll take you there." He smiled. There was something in his expression that made Beth's heart beat a little faster. "But I'm sure you are a lady of infinite resources. After all, you didn't even flinch when I fired past your head."

"Didn't flinch? I nearly jumped out of my skin! But you have a rotten aim, sir, and it cost me my money."

The dark eyebrows shot up and the brown eyes went instantly from warm courtesy to open laughter. "Do you think I should have killed the scoundrel? How very bloodthirsty of you. Next time, perhaps?"

"Well, not killed him, certainly." Beth wrinkled her forehead. She was delighted that he had known instantly that she wasn't serious. "Or even wounded him. But you did take that risk when you fired so carelessly, didn't you?"

"Do you dare to question my aim, ma'am? I thought I brought off an impossible shot with the greatest display of derring-do. It is only with hindsight that it appears a foolish target, since it left the prize in the hands of the ruffian. And then a moment's weakness prevented me from instantly dispatching him, which any no-nonsense knight-errant would have done without compunction. But pray, don't impugn my aim. I hit exactly what I intended, I assure you."

"Stuff," said Beth wickedly. "It can only have been a lucky shot!"

"Do you wish to stand here in the rain and debate the issue? I could give you a demonstration of my prowess, perhaps? That's a remarkably ugly statue." He indicated an equestrian monument at the end of the street. "I could make it more so, I suppose, by taking off its nose." He raised his pistol as if to aim at the offending sculpture.

"I pray you will do no such thing, sir!"

"Then I shan't, of course. Besides, uncertainty is so much more exciting than proof, don't you think? In the meantime, I am getting very wet, and I think that having failed so dismally to rescue your purse, I am now in honor bound to take you to your destination."

Beth hesitated for a moment, but there was another growl of thunder and who knew how long it would take her to get back to Russell Square by herself? The brown-eyed gentleman had already handed the ribbons to his tiger and leapt down from the curricle. Without more ado, she allowed him to hand her up into his carriage.

"How do you know that I'm not also a scoundrel, ma'am?" said the gentleman as he took up the reins and the horses sprang forward. "Now I have you in my carriage, you are completely in my power. What a horrid predicament for a lady fresh from the country. You are fresh from the country, aren't you? Don't try to deny it, I recognize the lack of town bronze at a glance. Perhaps you have leapt from the crossing-boy's frying pan into my fire? I might have all kinds of dastardly and nefarious purposes in mind in rescuing you."

Beth glanced at him. His profile was cut like a statue, but he was smiling. It carved deep creases down the side of his cheek. She had already noticed that he had perfect white teeth. "I'll admit that our urchin mistook me for a sausage, but your fire can hardly burn very hot in this downpour," she said firmly. "What could a villain hope to gain by abducting me? I have no money left to steal and although my person is worthless, I should defend it to the last gasp with my umbrella."

The brown eyes met hers in delight. "You think I'm not serious?"

She smiled back. "I trust to your honor, sir!"

"Perhaps I don't have any."

"Which I don't believe at all. I will even confess that I suspect you're truly a very good shot and I'm glad you didn't hurt that boy, in spite of my purse."

"You're a lady of great generosity, I see. But I assure you

it's only the presence of that fearsome umbrella that assures your safe return to Russell Square, rather than a horrid abduction to the Castle of Otranto."

Beth laughed. "And there you entirely misread me, sir. Right now, a gothic castle might well be more welcome than my uncle's house."

"Ah, an uncle. And in Russell Square—the preferred abode of all prosperous burghers. Perhaps I can hold you to ransom?"

"He wouldn't pay."

"Then there's no hope for my career as a villain and I suppose we must introduce ourselves." He gave her a courteous salute with his whip. "Henry Fitzroy, Viscount Ravenstoke, at your service, ma'am."

Beth almost dropped her fearsome umbrella. "Oh no!" she said.

"Good heavens! Does my name offer even more offense than my shooting? That's particularly damnable, isn't it?—because I'm stuck with it. And at the very moment when I had decided to reform and follow the path of virtue, after all. Or have you heard of my fearsome reputation for carrying off fair maidens?"

Beth shook her head. She felt the most unaccountable despair. "Oh, dear! Lord Ravenstoke, you don't understand. We are on our way to Mr. Honeywell's house. I'm Elizabeth Lindsay and Harriet Honeywell is my cousin."

There was silence for a moment, then Ravenstoke began to laugh.

"All my children's names begin with an 'H'," said Mrs. Honeywell triumphantly. "Harriet, Henrietta and Hannibal Honeywell. A very pretty conceit, wouldn't you say, my lord?"

Ravenstoke nodded politely. He had returned Beth safely to Russell Square, where Harriet had upbraided her for being so silly as to get lost. "I was only in the muslin room," she said with a charming little giggle. "They have the most divine muslins in that shop, Ravenstoke. I bought no end of stuff. I intend to impress you when you see my trousseau."

The viscount had bowed and said nothing. Beth had already told him how she had hunted for Harriet throughout the shop before venturing onto the street to look for the carriage and he thought Miss Lindsay's account far more likely to be true than his fiancée's. A thought which brought him no comfort at all. But it was also unlikely that Harriet had anything other than muslins on her mind, so perhaps Beth was mistaken after all? Yet how easy would it be to disappear in the fabric bazaar? Never having been there, he had no idea. He shook his head.

"My lord?" said Mrs. Honeywell. "A very pretty notion, don't you think?"

He looked up and smiled at his future mother-in-law. "Indeed, madam. Should Harriet and I continue the tradition, do you suppose? We could have any number of small Horaces and Hortensias running about at Ravenstoke. Then we should have a house full of 'H's."

"And you are a Henry yourself! I declare it's too delightful. But your surname is Fitzroy," objected Mrs. Honeywell.

"Why, so it is! I shan't be able to be part of the household unless I change my name to Fitzherbert."

"But that doesn't start with . . . oh, you're teasing me, my lord. So very droll!"

"I don't see where it's in the least funny," said Harriet with a pout.

"Neither do I," said Henry Fitzroy, Viscount Ravenstoke, but under his breath. And then he inadvertently caught Beth's eye and they both had to suppress their inevitable reaction. For Beth it was a comfort to find relief in the absurdity of the conversation, for otherwise she might have to ask herself why the notion of Harriet Honeywell bearing Lord Ravenstoke's children was causing her such distress.

* * *

Ravenstoke had already learned that Beth Lindsay longed to see something more of London than the fashionable shops on Bond Street. He also knew that nothing else held interest for Harriet Honeywell. It was thus obvious to suggest that they visit the Tower the next day and when Harriet began to demur, to insist on it. He arrived late, however, and the ladies had been left waiting in Russell Square for the best part of the morning.

"I declare, it's too bad of you, Ravenstoke," pouted Harriet, when he finally arrived. "I could have been to the Emporium and back by now. Oh, good gracious! What on earth are you wearing?"

The viscount glanced down at the shabby shooting jacket he had selected with such care that morning. "My favorite coat, of course," he said. "Don't you like it?"

"Really, my lord. We aren't going out for a brace of partridges!"

"Now, Harriet," interrupted Mrs. Honeywell, whose active mouth had actually fallen agape for a moment when he had first arrived. "I'm sure his lordship may wear as he pleases." She pulled Harriet to her and said in a loud whisper: "The aristocracy may do as they like, my dear. A charming eccentricity, I'm sure. No one will notice."

But Harriet continued to pout. "I'll be the laughingstock, Mama! His stockings don't even match! And his cravat looks as if it's been slept in!"

But she turned to Ravenstoke and held out her hand with a pretty smile. Half an hour later, they had passed in front of the white pillared face of St. Clement Danes and were bowling up Ludgate Hill and past St. Paul's. Beth was enchanted. This was the most ancient part of the City of London, where all those romantic historic events had taken place about which she had read throughout her childhood. Nothing should spoil her mood. She felt she was at the center of the universe in all the bustle of these busy streets. Ravenstoke's odd attire did indeed attract some stares, but Beth was oblivious to them.

She also refused to be fazed by his rather erratic driving style, though it did seem strange that he could hardly manage his team after driving the same horses with such aplomb the previous day. And then he began to sing.

"Oranges and lemons, say the bells of St. Clement's. / I owe you five farthings, say the bells of St. Martin's . . ."

He didn't have the best of voices. Harriet looked at him aghast. Beth suddenly felt overwhelmed with delight. She didn't sing that well herself, but what could be more appropriate than the old nursery song? These were the very streets and churches whose names had become immortal. What possessed her to do so, she would never know, but instead of supporting Harriet's censorious looks, she joined in with gusto.

"When will you pay me? say the bells of Old Bailey. / When I grow rich, say the bells of Shoreditch. / When will that be? say the bells of Stepney. / I'm sure I don't know, says the great bell of Bow."

The crowds on the streets began to turn their heads. But these were magical places: the Strand, the Temple, Fleet, St. Paul's, Cannon and Eastcheap. Beth had so forgotten herself as to clap her hands in time to their music. Even the tiger standing up behind had so forgotten himself as to join in. His rough voice made up in enthusiasm what it also lacked in harmony. The result was close to Bedlam. They reached the glorious finale in a fine discord of voices. "Oranges and lemons, say the bells of St. Clement's. / Here comes a candle to light you to bed and here comes a chopper to chop off your head! / Chop, chop! The last man is dead!"

Harriet had so forgotten herself as to look openly furious.

"The Tower of London, ladies," said Ravenstoke, springing the horses into a sudden canter. "Started by the Romans, built by the Conqueror, improved by the Henrys, detested by Elizabeth, neglected by the Georges, and admired by us."

Beth was clutching at her bonnet and laughing. Harriet, in a sulk, was pulling her skirts aside from the dirt that was splashing up from the street.

"Once we're married, my lord," she said acidly. "I promise you I'll not ask to go driving with you again."

The horses jerked to a walk and Beth was thrown against the squabs. "Once we're married, Miss Honeywell, I trust you will do as you are told."

Harriet almost began to look rebellious, but then her attention seemed to be caught by something behind them and she turned back to Ravenstoke with a sunny smile. "Of course, Ravenstoke. I know how you like to tease! I'll be the perfect bride, you'll see!"

And you're going to be an impossible bridegroom, aren't you, thought Beth, looking at the handsome face that was grinning back at Harriet. Then she made herself look away, because it was somehow very unsettling to allow her attention to dwell on him too long. At that moment she noticed a big-boned chestnut horse with a white leg just turning away into a side street. The rider wore a dashing red coat. Some officer, no doubt. London was full of them.

Now that the bridegroom had returned to town, Harriet declared to Beth's relief that they needn't do any more shopping right away. Instead they should take a stroll in the Park with the viscount. "You will wear something more suitable, won't you, my lord?" Harriet had asked when they returned from the outrageous jaunt to see the Tower. "I have a new outfit in lime green with the most dashing little hat."

"I'll endeavor to look my best for you, my dear," said Ravenstoke gravely. "I'll have my tailor run up something that's the latest stare."

Beth heard the shriek as she came down the stairs. Ravenstoke stood in the hall, bowing to Mrs. Honeywell. He was blinding in brilliant yellow pantaloons and burnt-orange jacket. It was Harriet who had shrieked. Her fetching lime-green walking dress and the bonnet with the fake daisies clashed biliously with Ravenstoke's attire.

"How could you? Oh, you want to do nothing but vex me!"

"My dear Miss Honeywell," said the viscount, raising his eyebrows. "Whatever do you mean?"

"That jacket! And the yellow!"

Ravenstoke looked innocently at his legs. "All the latest crack or so I'm led to believe. You didn't care for my shooting jacket, so—"

"Now don't refine so, Harriet," said Mrs. Honeywell. "I'm sure his lordship looks very well."

"I shall have to go and change!" announced Harriet and followed by her remonstrating Mama, she pushed past Beth and ran up the stairs.

Beth stepped into the hall to find the viscount leaning against the bottom balustrade almost helpless with laughter.

"Good Lord! Oranges and lemons, indeed," she said, as the full glory of his dress hit her like a blast from a furnace. "Definitely a popinjay!" And then she blushed scarlet.

"No, no," said Ravenstoke, recovering his breath. "I do agree, Miss Lindsay. Yet you say that as if it were an estimate of my character you'd heard before?"

"It was my father," Beth confessed. "When he heard you were to marry Harriet he said you must be either a popinjay or a nincompoop, but he hadn't met you, of course."

"Then he is more than astute, for I believe I must be both. Do you think my yellow limbs will be sufficient to carry me to the altar?"

"I'm sure they can carry you wherever you like. Though whether the bride will be there to admire the effect, I can't say. Didn't Harriet mention that she had a new lime-green bonnet? Do you deliberately provoke her?"

"Now why should you think that? I believe, Miss Lindsay, that you don't agree that I look bang-up-to-the-nines. I went to a great deal of trouble and it seems that no one appreciates it."

Beth bit her lip and looked at him. Even the garish clothes couldn't hide the grace and strength of the form they concealed. "Something is missing," she said, as seriously as she was able. "Let me see. I think you need a buttonhole."

She ran over to a bowl of full-blown roses that sat sweetly on the hall table and picked out one in a strong deep pink. Against the orange jacket the effect was sure to be hideous. She turned, rose in hand, to find Ravenstoke at her elbow. Without hesitation, she reached up to put the rose into his lapel.

"How very perfect," he said, looking down at her.

But Beth was frozen where she stood. Something was happening to her arms and legs. They seemed slow and heavy, and she could feel her hands tremble as a wave of warmth spread throughout her body. The touch of his jacket felt delightful under her fingers, his clean scent enveloped her. It was as if everything else in her mind was gone except the pleasure of his presence. She wanted to lean into his chest and put her arms around his neck. In confusion, she dropped her head and stepped back. Ravenstoke took the rose from her numb fingers and pinned it onto his jacket. Then he plucked a white bud from the bowl and as Beth stood helpless, he fixed it to her plain straw bonnet.

"There," he said gently. "We are almost matched in sartorial perfection, Miss Lindsay."

When Harriet rejoined them, dressed now in white muslin, her cousin and her fiancé were chatting casually about the weather, as if nothing at all had happened.

Harriet stayed in a sulk for the entire ride to the Park and refused to take Ravenstoke's arm when it was offered. They were thus strolling in silence beside the Serpentine when a young man hailed them.

"Good God! Ravenstoke? What the devil is this? You're normally the soberest of fellows! Follower of the Beau and all that. Don't say you've taken a wager to blind the entire *ton?*

If so, you've won it! Good morning, ladies. James Gregory at your service."

He gave them each a deep bow.

"I declare you've hit upon it, sir!" Harriet smiled gratefully at the newcomer and turned to the viscount. "How can you tease me so, Lord Ravenstoke? You intend to win money from your cronies by your wicked apparel, don't you? Well, I shan't be a party to it, my lord! I shall walk with Mr. Gregory and leave you to Beth. She doesn't care what she looks like!"

"As you wish, my dear," said the viscount with a wink at Beth, whose simple dark frock set off his own brilliance. "Mr. Gregory's black coat is a perfect complement for your charming white dress. Let Miss Lindsay accompany the daffodil and spare you any more blushes."

So Beth must put her hand on his arm and walk ahead with him beside the water. There was the faintest of summer breezes moving the leaves on the trees and sending little ripples across the lake, fashionable ladies and gentlemen strolled about on the grass, frustrated children tugged at the hands of their nursemaids, but Beth didn't notice. She had lost herself in his company. She couldn't remember when she had last been so enthralled and so entertained. She lost all thought of what jacket he might be wearing or whether her pink rose wasn't the most hideously successful clash of colors ever invented. Instead she noticed that there were little flecks of black in his brown eyes and a small mole high on his right cheekbone, and that she must challenge her wits to match his. She had lost all track of time when Ravenstoke turned to look over his shoulder.

"Now where on earth is my betrothed?"

Beth looked back. Mr. Gregory was standing staring about himself in a daze, with a bunch of limp flowers clutched in his hand. Harriet was nowhere to be seen.

"I say, Ravenstoke, I've lost her! She asked me to go and fetch this little nosegay from the flower girl and when I got back, she'd disappeared!"

"Don't be so silly," said Harriet, hurrying up to them from behind a small stand of trees. Her face was flushed with color, her eyes sparkling like wine. "You disappeared, sir! I just had to stop and adjust my boot."

"Whatever you say, of course," said Mr. Gregory with a small bow.

"Well, no gentleman's company means a thing to me except my fiancé's," said Harriet, taking Ravenstoke possessively by the arm. If she had been put out by his sunny outfit earlier, it seemed to mean nothing to her now. Harriet was beaming.

Ravenstoke looked curiously at her as she rattled on. "When we're married though, my lord, promise me you won't take any more wagers!" Harriet gave the viscount a dazzling smile. "Now I wish to go home. I'm fatigued. All this walking about in parks is so silly, don't you think? And I declare, Beth looks ready to drop." She reached out a little hand and patted Beth on the arm. "You look as if you have the headache."

Since Beth had never felt better in her life, she could only assume that Harriet meant she looked plain. Which since it was the way she expected to appear, didn't bother her in the least. Unless, she thought wistfully—no, perish that thought immediately.

Harriet proposed a trip to Vauxhall Gardens the following night. She had heard so much about the fabulous pleasure grounds on the other side of the Thames! All her friends were going there to drink sherbet, dance, and walk the verdant pathways before admiring the most splendid display of fireworks imaginable.

"You will take us, won't you, my lord?" Harriet gave him a pretty smile. "Beth is my chaperone, so it'll be quite proper. And wear what you like; I'm sure I don't let it worry me."

Vauxhall had a slightly dubious reputation; in the suspicious minds of most Mamas the dark leafy alleyways were only too likely to invite indecorous behavior. Of course, innocent Beth,

fresh from the country, couldn't be expected to know that and
Miss Honeywell didn't care as long as Mama thought it suitable, which she did.

"I can think of nothing more to my purpose," replied Ravenstoke, with a charming grin.

Which Beth thought was a very odd reply, for Beth could
think of nothing but Henry Fitzroy. As soon as he had come
to call again, she had known with certainty. She had tried to
suppress it, but she could not forget the way he had first smiled
down at her from the curricle, or the mercy he had shown to
the young thief. The curl of his lip at the corner of his mouth,
the shadow of his cheekbone, his outrageous sense of humor
and obvious intelligence, the sense of controlled strength she
noticed in his movements, everything about him haunted her.
Not even the yellow pantaloons had hidden his attractiveness.
The result was the worst thing that could possibly happen to
her. Out of the blue, at six-and-twenty, she had at last met the
man she could love and he was engaged to her cousin Harriet.
How on earth could it have happened? And now to have to
chaperone the happy couple about London! She must root out
this insistent attraction and crush it, which would be the hard-
est thing she had ever done. So though she knew nothing of
its reputation, she still was very much afraid that Vauxhall
would be a disaster.

Yet, as they arrived at Vauxhall Gardens, Beth was instantly
entranced. Thousands of tiny lanterns lit the paths and pavil-
ions, which thronged not only with fashionable members of
the *beau monde,* but also with the more prosperous citizens
of London with their wives and daughters. The night air was
filled with the music of a band playing the latest dances and
there was a merry undercurrent of talk and laughter.

Harriet was hanging onto Ravenstoke's arm. She looked be-
witching in silver muslin sown with tiny spangles. Beth, in
contrast, wore the same plain blue frock in which she had been
sorting linen. She had dressed it up a little with some navy
piping around the hem and square neckline, but for the first

time in her life the knowledge that she must look positively dowdy caused her real pain. The wicked fact that she wanted Ravenstoke to approve of her appearance added to her consternation. The viscount seemed to have abandoned his attempts to shock with his attire, for he was quietly and respectably wearing black. In spite of her resolutions, Beth's heart had turned over when she saw him.

"Oh, look!" squealed Harriet as they came out into the central square near the bandstand. "There's Sally Rutledge! Coo-ee!" She let go of the viscount's sleeve and waved wildly. "Sally! Over here!"

A plump redhead in ice-green and ivory turned and grinned widely, then picked up her skirts, ran over to them, and threw her arms around Harriet.

"Harriet! It's been this age! You darling thing, how have you been since Bath?"

This simple greeting seemed enough to throw both girls into giggles. Harriet recovered first and tossed her head. "Oh well enough, I'm sure. This is Lord Ravenstoke, of course—oh, and my cousin, Beth Lindsay." Hands were shaken all around. "Now let's take a turn together about the pathways, Sally dear, and you can tell me all the latest news. You don't mind, do you, Beth? Ravenstoke will keep you company."

She gave her fiancé an arch smile as he bowed his assent. Then she slipped her arm around Miss Rutledge's thick waist and the girls strolled off together.

"Well," said the viscount. "You are once again left with only my sorry company, Miss Lindsay. May I bring you some lemonade?" He cocked a brow and then laughed. "No, nothing so staid, I think. Let's dance."

"My lord, surely it's not suitable . . ."

"Nonsense! Come, when have you ever had the opportunity to dance outside under the stars before? I insist."

There was nothing Beth could imagine in the world she would rather do than dance with him. It was undoubtedly foolish, given the unsteady state of her heart, but she might never come to London again, never be asked to dance to the giddy music of a bandstand again, never meet someone so very entrancing again.

"I'd love to," she said, and let him take her fingers and lead her onto the small stone-flagged area set aside for dancing.

It was merely a country dance, which involved several complicated figures where the dancers wove patterns around each other. There was nothing more intimate than the occasional touching of fingers with one's partner and the meeting of eyes when they bowed and curtsied. Yet Beth noticed every touch of Ravenstoke's hand. I have fallen from the frying pan into the fire, she thought frantically; I've fallen in love with my cousin's bridegroom and I'll never be content with my lot as a spinster again. I hardly think this is what Papa had in mind when he sent me to London. They whirled and stepped, passed up and down, and then it was over and she was curtsying once again to his bow.

"Now, the lemonade, Miss Lindsay."

He found her a seat at a table and fetched her an iced drink.

"Are you really from Wales?" she asked a little desperately. "Mrs. Honeywell said you had a place there."

He gave her a smile. "I'm from the Marches," he said. "Which is close enough. My ancestors fought Prince Llewelyn and his descendants for centuries and won nothing for all concerned but misery, of course. Ravenstoke Hall is solidly on the English side of the border, but some of the tenants are Welsh-speaking. They're a proud people with an ancient tongue. It's a privilege to know them."

"My father had a Welshman come to him once with a case about a horse," said Beth. "We had to get Dai Davies, our local tailor, to translate. It's a beautiful language, isn't it? You're lucky." She looked up and caught a fleeting expression on his face which she couldn't interpret. It was as if he were seeing something for which he longed, yet couldn't have.

"Let's walk," he said, suddenly jumping up. "You've seen nothing yet of the gardens."

He offered his arm and Beth slipped her gloved hand into the crook of his elbow. He felt very warm and enticingly solid next to her as they strolled down a network of pathways between the flower beds and greenery, and he entertained her with stories about Welsh history. Beth longed to sparkle and be witty in return, but she felt her tongue grow clumsy in her mouth. How dare she want to attract him when any such feeling between them was forbidden by every rule of decency? And yet . . . the thought of the quiet life with her beloved father which before had always filled her with contentment, suddenly seemed to stretch away into barrenness. Dear Papa, she thought, forgive me if I come back to you positively peaky and without a single rose in my cheek.

"Ah," said Ravenstoke at last. "There are my betrothed, Miss Honeywell, and her interesting friend, Miss Rutledge. Thank you for the dance, Miss Lindsay, and for your entrancing company."

Beth expected him to give her a polite bow as she released his arm. Instead, he suddenly caught her by the shoulders and pulled her into his arms.

"I'm damned if I planned exactly this!" he said, as he bent his head and began to kiss her.

It was both agonizing and delightful, and Beth knew she ought to be forever disgraced for allowing him to do it. Yet when you've fallen so very desperately in love with a gentleman and he kisses you, surely it's beyond human strength to pull away, even if the man's fiancée is watching you both?

"Oh, la!" said Harriet's voice. "How can you be so very naughty, Ravenstoke?"

He released Beth, who was staring at him with eyes like saucers, and gave Harriet a bow.

"I think you're about to marry a dreadful flirt, Harriet," said Miss Rutledge archly—as if to find your friend's bridegroom kissing a respectable spinster were an everyday occurrence. "Have you been imbibing too deep, Lord Ravenstoke?"

"Oh, he's just trying to vex me for leaving him alone for

so long, aren't you, my lord?" Harriet tapped him on the sleeve with her fan. "Well, you shan't faze me. And I know Beth wouldn't stoop to offer you any encouragement for your rakish behavior, so you shan't make me jealous!"

As Ravenstoke stood looking at his bride in dismay, Harriet possessively slipped her arm into his and leaned up on tiptoe to kiss him on the cheek before waving good-bye to Sally Rutledge. The viscount hardly noticed the retreating skirts of the redhead or the affectionate gestures of his betrothed, he was damning himself for so using Beth. How could he? For he had not only used, but hurt her, as her stricken expression when he released her had made only too plain. And the ruse hadn't even worked. If a careless kiss had been enough to trap him into this engagement, it appeared obvious it wasn't going to release him from it. Harriet wasn't going to cry off from jealousy, and to exploit Beth was the most unforgivable thing he had ever done.

Beth spent the rest of the evening in a numb daze. Even the fireworks left her cold. What had he meant by kissing her? Ravenstoke didn't speak another word to her except essential platitudes and barely acknowledged her when they said good-bye in Russell Square. She had been kissed before, of course. But it had never had such an impact on her senses. You're being silly, she told herself, to refine so much on something so casual. Whatever it might cost her, when she next saw Ravenstoke, she was determined to greet him with at least a surface equanimity.

The dance at Lady Berry's was quite a small affair. Harriet dressed for it with her usual flamboyance and Beth brought out the one fairly fashionable dress she had. It was an old-gold silk with ivory trimmings which warmed her pale skin and set off her blue eyes. She had no fancy jewelry, except for a gold chain which had been her mother's. She put that around her neck with no regrets or embarrassment at all. Ravenstoke was there, of course. Her eyes met his as soon as she entered the room and he winked like a conspirator at her. Out of deference perhaps to Lady Berry, he was not wearing an old shooting jacket nor the yellow pantaloons. Instead, he looked impeccable in navy and cream as he came over to greet them. He did not, however, ask Beth to dance. While Mrs. Honeywell looked on with an indulgent smirk, Harriet gave him an arch smile and demanded the first waltz.

He bowed over her hand. "My dear, how very unfortunate," he said with exaggerated regret. "I have already promised it to Miss Somerset and you know I can't disappoint her. We're so close; did you know? We practically grew up in each other's arms."

"Oh pooh! You're to be married soon, my lord. Dance with the other ladies all you like while you can, I say."

And Harriet turned away and allowed several other swains to fill her dance card. Beth didn't expect to dance. At six-and-twenty, she wasn't exactly a prize on the marriage mart, after all. In fact, she supposed she should have worn a lace cap.

"Come, Beth," said Mrs. Honeywell, as if to confirm her thoughts. "Let's go and get a seat or the dowagers will have all the chairs and I declare my constitution is too dainty to allow me to stand all night."

So Beth spent the evening watching the dancing and watching Viscount Ravenstoke as he moved gracefully around the room with a succession of partners. In particular, a very lovely blonde in blue net seemed to be constantly at his side.

"Lord Ravenstoke is very marked in his attentions to Miss Somerset, Mrs. Honeywell," said one of the dowagers, plumping herself down next to Beth. "I thought he was to wed your girl the first weekend of June?"

"Yes, indeed, Lady Pin. But Harriet attracts the gentlemen like bees to a honeypot. Her admirers won't allow her fiancé too much of her time, I'm very sure, even if he is a viscount."

The dowager looked archly at Mrs. Honeywell and lurched to her feet. "Well, Ravenstoke has known the Somerset girl all his life. They're so fond of one another. Felicity Somerset is very lovely, is she not? I'm surprised she's not wed. We all thought to see her settled by now."

She gave Mrs. Honeywell a tight smile, before sailing off down the room.

"There!" said Aunt Honeywell. "I shouldn't wonder if Ravenstoke planned on offering for Miss Somerset, until he met Harriet, of course. What a triumph! I can't get over it! That my girl should beat out the Somersets and become Lady Ravenstoke. It's quite a feather in my cap, I can tell you, and Mr. Honeywell hasn't been behindhand in his satisfaction, either."

So that must be why the viscount so obviously wanted to be free from his engagement. He was already in love with someone he'd known for years. It made Beth's feelings all the more ridiculous, didn't it? When they finally went home from the dance, she was determined to destroy everything she had allowed herself to feel for him. She was a respectable spinster, wasn't she? Good heavens, she might as well be a green girl to have her head turned by a handsome face and a passionate kiss.

For several days she saw nothing of him, except to exchange a glance in the hall or a few words over tea. Beth was proud of her poise and Ravenstoke seemed as full of good humor as ever. He took Harriet for carriage drives in the Park where no chaperone was necessary, or he met his fiancée with her parents at evening dances or the theater, which Beth made excuses not to attend. It was impossible to tell how he might dress next, yet Harriet seemed oblivious to his sartorial efforts.

Even though Ravenstoke was behaving outrageously, as she told Beth, Harriet was in alt. The viscount had shocked everyone by racing his curricle around the Serpentine with the result that Miss Honeywell's bonnet had gone flying into the water. He had brought a female with him to the theater who could not be quite respectable—in fact one Mrs. Honeywell suspected might be a member of the *demi-monde*—and brazenly introduced her. And he continued to fawn over that Felicity

Somerset. But of course, that was just how one expected the aristocracy to behave, wasn't it? If Harriet had been put out by his behavior on the day they went to the Tower, it seemed that it no longer bothered her what he might do.

"And actually, Beth dear, once I'm Lady Ravenstoke, who cares how he conducts himself? I'm sure I shan't be the kind of wife who expects her husband to hang about her petticoats. And now I'm going walking with Sally Rutledge. You'll be all right here with nothing but that book?"

Beth nodded, but she was not really all right. Lord Ravenstoke's features kept intruding on the page and making her lose interest in the otherwise charming Mr. Darcy, hero of her novel. She sighed and set the book aside. Was it really better to have loved and lost than never to have loved at all? She had been perfectly happy in Much Haven before she'd ever met the fascinating viscount. Now how would she cope with the rest of her life? The door opened and the face which had been haunting her dreams was smiling down at her.

"Miss Lindsay? I'm glad to catch you alone for a moment. May I sit?"

Beth knew that color had flooded her cheeks. She leapt to her feet to offer him a chair and then collapsed back onto the chaise longue as she caught her foot in the hem of her skirt. "Of course," she said.

"I was supposed to take Harriet out for a drive this morning, but I'm led to believe she has gone out with Miss Rutledge?"

"They're very close friends, my lord."

He laughed. "Indeed. Harriet seems to do nothing but disappear these days in the company of her bosom companion. I can never keep track of her—and only a week until our wedding. You'd think she would want to spend every moment with the groom, wouldn't you?" He watched as Beth relaxed a little and smiled at him.

"Mrs. Honeywell is getting most distressed about the arrangements," said Beth, who had been the one to take the brunt of her aunt's hysterical frenzy of preparation. She would prove to herself that she could calmly discuss it, even with him. "She is determined that your wedding will outshine the Duke of Harrow's."

"Yes, I know. She wanted the Prince Regent for a guest; thankfully he is otherwise engaged. But I didn't come here to talk about that." Then Ravenstoke leaned forward and his voice became quite serious. "Miss Lindsay, I owe you an abject apology which there has never been the opportunity for me to make. Yet you continue to smile on me with equanimity and grace, and put up with every absurdity. I hope you will accept this small token of my very real feelings—of humility in your wise presence and mortification if I have damaged you in any way, at least."

He reached inside his coat and brought out something wrapped lightly in paper. Beth stared at him with her heart in her mouth, but she took the present and unwrapped it. It was a small wooden carving in the shape of a spoon, but the handle was made of an intricate set of little hearts, shields and flowers, all topped by a wooden key on a wooden chain.

"It's beautiful," she said. "But I couldn't . . ."

"Nonsense, of course you can. It's what the Welsh call a *'llwy-serch'*. It's just a spoon, after all. And if you will accept it, it will help me face the rest of my life."

"Whatever are you talking about, Lord Ravenstoke?"

"Will you forgive me for kissing you at Vauxhall? You see, I wanted—want—Harriet to cry off. I thought if I behaved badly enough, perhaps she would. But I had no justification for using you for my nefarious purposes, none at all. If it's any consolation, I didn't plan it."

What he didn't say was that it was also Beth's wide blue eyes and her honey-colored hair that had made him want to kiss her then and still made him want to kiss her now. Instead he stood up and began to pace the room.

"Then you're not in love with my cousin?" asked Beth as soon as she could speak.

He spun on his heel. "You ask in jest, I assume?"

"Can't you withdraw from the engagement?"

"Never. Unless Harriet releases me, I am in honor bound to wed her. I asked her to marry me in front of several witnesses. And the wedding is imminent—the church booked, the parson on hand. I can't jilt her, Beth. So I hoped she would jilt me—vainly as it turned out. But I didn't want to hurt or involve you. Now say you forgive me for my recklessness."

Beth looked down at the lovely little carving in her lap. He had kissed her, as she had guessed, because of his own problems, not because he returned her feelings. In the circumstances, that must be a consolation. It was one thing to go through life suffering from unrequited love while single. But what a hell for him if he felt as she did when married to someone else. Unless he was in love with Miss Somerset, but she couldn't help that, could she? Either way, if she loved him, she mustn't let him see how much she was hurting. She put all the warmth of humor that she could find into her voice. "You did warn me when we first met that you might have dangerous ulterior motives. Of course, I don't hold it against you that you kissed me. It meant nothing at all and we shall be cousins soon. Let's put it behind us and be friends."

Proud of her own bravery, Beth couldn't understand why he should look so very devastated as he bowed and left the room.

To drive to Much Haven was Harriet's idea. Beth should see her family for the day. It would be a delightful outing away from the dust of London. All the wedding preparations were becoming just too exciting, even for Harriet. "And I want to show Miss Rutledge that cunning little milliner's in the main street. You wouldn't think to find such charming bonnets in such a nowhere place, but it's a positive find! Ravenstoke can take us all in the barouche."

Which he did. Harriet sat beside her betrothed on the driver's seat and squealed and giggled as the viscount tooled his team along the country lanes. It was a glorious summer day, such as Beth fervently believed could be found nowhere in the world beside England. The sky blazed blue above their heads as they passed green hedgerows and a panoply of fully leafed trees. Fields of hay were already getting ripe for the scythe and the grass was embroidered with ox-eye daisies. High in the clear air, skylarks spiraled and sang. In any other circumstances, Beth would have felt thrilled to be out on such a day. But there were Harriet and Ravenstoke on the box, and Miss Rutledge sat beside Beth in the barouche, her red head shaded by a silk parasol.

"Why, that fellow has been following us for an age," she said archly, looking past the two footmen who sat stiffly at the back of the open carriage. "Do you see that, Harriet? There's a fellow on horseback on the highway behind us."

Harriet spun around on the seat above Sally and Beth, and looked back down the road. "Oh, it's only some silly officer," she said, and giggled. "Why must you refine upon every handsome gentleman that comes along, Miss Rutledge?" She turned back and smiled at Ravenstoke, then said lightly over her shoulder: "Did Mama give you some tea, Beth, to bring to your papa?"

Beth had been looking back at the red-coated rider with an odd misgiving. Although he was some way behind them, she was almost sure she had seen the horse before. Just such a big-boned chestnut with one unusually long white stocking had been tied outside the muslin shop where she had first lost Harriet. Then she had thought she saw it again on the trip to the Tower and that rider had been an officer too. Oh well, no doubt there was more than one such horse and they were on the main turnpike. The horseman would hardly still be behind them when they took the side road to Much Haven.

She turned back to Harriet. "Why, yes, thank you," she said, and then had to grin when Ravenstoke looked over his shoulder and gave her a wink. He had been there when Mrs. Honeywell had made her generous overture.

"You must take some of our China tea down to your family,

Beth dear," her aunt had said. "Let me ask Mr. Honeywell if we have an ounce or two that is damaged in some way, then I'm sure we can let you have it wholesale."

The viscount had been forced to pretend to cough into his handkerchief to cover his reaction to this extraordinary suggestion. As soon as he recovered, he offered to purchase a pound of the finest grade for Beth to take. "I am a connoisseur of China tea, you know, Mrs. Honeywell. No doubt Mr. Honeywell has some that would meet even my standards. And I insist on paying full retail price," he had said.

"Oh, no, my lord, you are too kind. I'm sure we have some that's good enough for Beth in our warehouses. I shall have Mr. Honeywell see to it."

Nevertheless, it was several pounds of the very best tea that China and the Honeywell warehouses had to offer which Beth was carrying home to Much Haven. As the carriage pulled into the familiar main street, she felt a flurry of emotions. At least Papa and Joe needed her and would welcome her back after Harriet had married the viscount, and for Papa's sake, until then she would pretend she had been having a wonderful time in London.

"Here's the shop, Sally," cried Harriet, as they came up to the milliner's. "Let us off here, Ravenstoke. Then take Beth to her papa and pick us up later. You're not interested in ladies' fashions and I'm sure Beth never wore a decent bonnet in her life."

"Very probably not, my dear," said Ravenstoke gravely. But he pulled up the horses and helped Sally and Harriet step down from the barouche. Moments later, Beth was running into the open arms of Mr. Lindsay, with Joe proudly carrying the present of tea. The viscount waited for a moment, then allowed Beth to introduce him to her father. As they went into the house, the men fell into natural conversation. Joe hung back, then blushed furiously when Ravenstoke turned to him and smiled.

"And you are Master Joseph, no doubt," he said simply. "I am pleased to meet you, sir."

Joe pumped the viscount's proffered hand, then blurted out, "I say, my lord. Are you really from Wales? It's a wild country, isn't it? Harriet said she'd never go there!"

Ravenstoke laughed. "Oh, wild enough," he said. "I'm a descendant of the Marcher barons, you know. But Miss Honeywell will have to go there if she's to marry me, won't she?"

"And do you speak Welsh? There's a fellow in the village from Monmouthshire. He speaks it, I've heard him. Can you say something in Welsh for us?"

Ravenstoke turned to Beth and asked very seriously, " *'Wi'n dy garu di. 'Wnei di 'mhriodi i?'* "

"What does that mean?" asked Joe.

"I asked Beth if she admired my horses," said the viscount without missing a beat.

"Did you?" said Beth, surprised. She had no idea what he'd said, but that didn't seem quite right. "I thought the word for horses was *'ceffylau'*? I remember thinking it was such a pretty word when Dai Davies had to translate in that case for us."

"No doubt Lord Ravenstoke knows what he's talking about," said Mr. Lindsay, who knew no Welsh at all. "Now, my lord, may I offer you some refreshment?"

"You are very kind, sir. Perhaps later? I think it's your son who would like to admire my horses and you should be allowed some time alone with your daughter." He bowed to Joe and indicated the waiting carriage. "Would you like a turn at the ribbons, young man?"

Since nothing could be closer to heaven in Joe's estimation than to be allowed to be close to horseflesh, he could only blush scarlet and nod his head. A few minutes later, he was sitting next to the viscount on the high box of the barouche and tooling away down the lane. Mr. Lindsay turned to Beth.

"Well, dear child," he said with a grin. "I was wrong."

Beth raised a questioning eyebrow.

"Neither a popinjay nor a nincompoop, I think. I'm horribly afraid I rather like Harriet's bridegroom."

"Now, Papa. Why 'horribly afraid' when you like someone?"

"Because the fellow deserves better than Harriet Honeywell, of course. I wonder how such an impossible engagement came about?"

Which was a question Beth had asked herself a million times. But she was determined not to talk to her papa about the viscount. No one was more likely to discover her shameful secret than her father, so instead she turned the subject to learn how the house had been running without her. She wasn't sure whether to be glad or upset to find that Mrs. Scone, the neighboring widow of a retired colonel, had been taking excellent care of everything in her absence, even to the playing of cards in the evenings with her papa.

"So you see, we do very well here, my dear. I wish I could think that London agreed better with you?"

So he had noticed that something was wrong, however much Beth nobly tried to hide it. She was saved from a reply by the return of the carriage and the thud of her brother's feet as he ran into the hall, then burst bright-eyed into the drawing room.

"I say, Beth! Lord Ravenstoke has the most bang-up team of cattle you can imagine! And he let me spring 'em! It was top notch!"

"And where did you learn such cant?" said Mr. Lindsay gravely.

"I'm afraid I taught him, sir," confessed Ravenstoke with a bow. "Your son drives like a professional; he has the making of a fine horseman, you know."

If only we could afford horses, thought Beth. What future was there for Joe when they were so poor? Then she looked down at her hands. Don't say the stay in London was spoiling her acceptance of her poverty as well?

"And we saw a splendid beast in the village, didn't we, my lord?"

"Indeed we did."

"There was a big chestnut, Beth, with a white stocking quite over the knee, tied up to the hedgerow in the oddest place. And Lord Ravenstoke said he could tell it was an officer's horse, because of the saddle. You'd think a traveler would stop at the inn, but this was almost beyond the houses."

"That is odd," agreed Beth. She felt a little shiver go down her spine. Could it be the same animal who had followed them from London? This was becoming more than coincidence. Did the viscount have enemies?

"And there was no sign of Harriet or her friend. We stopped at the milliner's to see if we could give them a lift back, but they'd never been there. What do you think of that?"

"I think," said Mr. Lindsay, "that your cousin's whereabouts are none of your business, young man. No doubt the young ladies stopped at the inn for tea or saw another shop that took their fancy. Now, my lord, . . ."

Conversation became general. They took a turn in the gardens, where Ravenstoke admired the strawberry frames and the pleached alley. Tea was taken under a bower of roses that Beth had spent so many years in training and that Mrs. Scone had lovingly kept trimmed in her absence. Beth said hardly a word as her father and the viscount roamed over every topic. Dutifully, she joined in the laughter and even managed to make one joke of her own. Harriet and Sally eventually appeared, a little breathless and windblown, and it was time to return to town. No more mention was made of the chestnut with the white stocking and as they trotted through the village, the horse was nowhere to be seen.

Dai Davies arrived the very next morning with strawberries. After promising her father to bring some back for Mrs. Honeywell, Beth had forgotten. It seemed that her mind was turning to mush, she thought ruefully. *The sooner Harriet marries him and they go off together, the better. I shall return to Much*

Haven and be happy. And then she had sat down and cried. By the time the Welshman turned up at the door with a basket, however, Beth was her usual composed self.

"I was coming anyway," said Mr. Davies. "And your dad said you'd be grateful for these." He held out the basket.

Beth insisted the diffident tailor come in and take some tea. All the Honeywells were out and she had the house to herself. It didn't take much to get Dai to wax poetic about his homeland, although Beth realized it was a kind of self-torture to encourage him.

"I have something from Wales," she said, after a bit. "I'll show you, Mr. Davies. Perhaps it may remind you of home."

It only took her a few moments to fetch Ravenstoke's present from beneath her pillow. She arrived back in the drawing room a little breathless, and then when she put the spoon into the tailor's hands, she knew she was going to find out more than she had bargained for.

"Well, a *llwy-serch* to be sure," said the tailor. "There's a lovely thing."

"Does it have any special meaning?"

"I should think you would know that, Miss Lindsay," said Dai Davies with a kindly smile. "If a young gentlemen was to be giving this to you, now." He turned the little spoon over in his hands and ran his stubby fingers over each of the carvings. "The key offers his home, the shield his protection, the flowers are for gentleness, and the heart is for love. Why, it's a token between sweethearts and we Welshmen have given them to our lady-loves since time immemorial."

Beth swallowed hard. Why had Ravenstoke given her such a thing? Whatever had he meant by it? He was to marry Harriet in two days, for heaven's sake.

Then Dai Davies went on. "Well, if you've won some gentleman's heart, I'm not surprised. And Mrs. Scone has taken ahold of your Papa's, you see, so it's a fine ending for everyone."

"Mrs. Scone?" asked Beth after a moment.

"There'll be a wedding there right enough, upon my word."

And Beth's despair was complete. She had hung onto the thought of how badly her father and Joe needed her to give her the courage to face Ravenstoke's wedding to Harriet, and now it appeared that her family didn't need her any more after all. Mrs. Scone would make her Papa a lovely wife. Beth was fond of the widow herself. But it was her own absence that had allowed her father's romance to grow. Would her return rob her father of happiness? And Joe would soon be a young man. Beth had raised him after her mother had died and their relationship was very special, but Joe didn't need any more mothering now than Mrs. Scone would be perfectly competent to give. Dai Davies put the spoon back into her hands.

"How would you ask in Welsh if you admired someone's horses?" asked Beth suddenly.

"On'd ydyn nhw'n geffylau ffein?"

Which was not what Ravenstoke had said to her at Much Haven at all. Then the Welshman was bobbing at the door and taking his leave. Beth saw him out and retired to her room to nurse the most frightful headache of her life.

She hadn't come down to supper, but retired early. So perhaps it wasn't strange that she should wake suddenly and find it still night. Beth sat up in her bed and pushed the hair from her face, then stopped with her hand still at her forehead. Someone was in the room.

"Don't be afraid, Beth dear," said warm tones. "It's only me. I have the wrong room, it seems."

Beth reached for the tinder box beside the bed and lit a candle. Viscount Ravenstoke was sitting on the windowsill, watching her. Instead of appearing like a scarecrow or a fop as she had seen him so often recently, he was dressed in neat evening clothes. His cravat still looked as crisp and perfect as it must have done when he first tied it several hours before. If he had climbed up the drainpipes, it didn't show in his clothes. Yet how else could he have arrived? She took a deep breath and tried to steady her pulse.

"What are you doing here, my lord? How long have you been on the windowsill?"

"One question at a time, I think. I have been here for an hour or more." He tipped his head and smiled at her. The moonlight lit the planes of his face and glanced off the sheen of his hair.

"Why? It can't be very comfortable."

Ravenstoke stood and stretched. Because I couldn't tear myself away, he thought painfully. Because I wanted to drink in the beauty of your honeyed hair on the pillow, my dear, and your long lashes on your soft cheeks. Because the sound of your breathing is more precious to me than a symphony. Because I'm condemned to wake up and see a different face for the rest of my life unless I do something dramatic and at once.

"I thought to wake Harriet," he said instead. "I should have known that an open window would lead to your room."

Beth's heart thudded in her chest. Were he and Harriet already lovers? She felt sick. "What time is it?" she asked.

"Very nearly dawn, I should think." And then as he went on, she began to breath again. "I thought I might get thoroughly foxed and creep unbidden into the hallway. It's time, don't you think, for a little pandemonium?"

So at least Harriet was not expecting him to visit her in her bed. Which was small comfort considering that they would be man and wife in two days. What on earth was he planning by getting drunk and climbing into the Honeywell house at night?

"And are you?" she said.

"Foxed? A little."

"What kind of pandemonium?"

He grinned. "Well, I admit I did think of an attempted ravishment. There would be tremendous screamings and wailings, I believe. But then, what if there weren't and Harriet held out her arms to my reluctant embrace? That would be a great irony, wouldn't it? No, I think I had better be sadly three-sheets-to-the-wind and throwing myself on her not-so-tender mercies to admit my utter ruin. Ravenstoke Hall is lost; the creditors are coming for the curricle, horses, guns, clothes, even the yellow pantaloons. What would she think of dramatic despair over my gambling away my entire fortune, do you think?"

"Did you?"

"No, not yet. But if she doesn't cry off, perhaps I will. Poverty is a great deal more appealing than servitude. I could always make another fortune, but once the parson's mousetrap snaps its jaws, I can't take another wife. Do you think Miss Honeywell is so devoted to my person that she would be content to live with me in a cottage and keep pigs?"

Beth tried hard to concentrate on the problem at hand and not allow her see-sawing emotions to get in the way. "Suppose it doesn't work? My aunt and uncle love money, of course. Yet Mr. Honeywell is fixed on the idea of a title for his oldest daughter and you'd still inherit from your father eventually, wouldn't you? So there'd be riches in the offing, as it were. Perhaps Harriet would hesitate, but then her father might offer to set you up in comfort until you inherited and to be Lady Ravenstoke is something, isn't it? More than Harriet might be willing to let go. You might give up Ravenstoke Hall and everything you love, then still be obliged to walk the aisle with my cousin."

"I thought of that," said Ravenstoke quietly. "But what else is left? I have embarrassed her, scared her, neglected her, paraded a supposed mistress before her." Even kissed you in front of her, my dear, he thought. And my other hope is running out of time. "She is only the more determined. It doesn't matter to Harriet whether I like her or not, nor whether we should be happy together. Perhaps the lack of the blunt will be enough?"

"And if it's not?" Beth swung her legs over the side of the bed and caught up her dressing gown. "Should you be found in her room, they will make you marry her regardless."

"Ah, you are right, as always, Miss Lindsay. As a matter of

fact, I thought more of a splendid scene in the hallway. Mr. and Mrs. Honeywell in nightcaps and wrappers, maid-servants screaming, the butler valiantly taking up the poker to defend the household, Harriet fainting away in horror at the thought of there being no curricle and having to send out for a job-horse. Surely there would be enough witnesses to protect her virtue and reputation? It seems worth the risk. I have nothing left to lose, Beth."

"You are foxed, aren't you? But I have a better plan," said Beth impulsively. And she felt her heart begin to shake in her chest. "What if you're found in here?"

"Beth! Dear child!" He walked over to her and touched her cheek. "Do you think to be the sacrificial lamb, *'nghariad?'*"

Beth held her ground though she could feel her legs sway under her at the force of his presence. "Stay here for the rest of the night. Let the maid find you with me come morning—as if we were lovers. Not even Harriet could overlook that! She must cry off then, surely?"

He was gazing down at her with the light of something she had never seen before in his eyes. Yet his voice was still light and teasing. "Sweet Elizabeth Lindsay. It couldn't be a pretense."

Beth knew she was blushing furiously. She could smell his scent and the faint odor of brandy on his tongue. All her blood yearned for him: for his fine hands to touch her body, for his firm lips to close once again over hers. Any thought of the consequences fled away like dead leaves in the face of a gale. "I don't care," she said.

He took her face in both hands and bent and gently kissed her on the forehead. There was a tension running through him that she could feel. "But I do," he said quietly.

Beth stepped back and sat suddenly on the edge of the bed. She had misread everything. He didn't love her or want her. He wanted to be free for Miss Somerset. The spoon had been nothing but a token of apology, after all. "I'm sorry," she said stiffly. "I can't think what made me say something so outrageous."

It seemed that it took him a moment to regain control. "The moonlight?" She couldn't see his face for he had turned away and was gazing out of the window. " 'It is the error of the moon; She comes more nearer earth than she is wont / And makes men mad.' " Then he turned towards her and his face was entirely in shadow for a moment. "Brave Beth! Suppose I stay with you, as you suggest. What if Harriet insisted on the wedding regardless? Nothing else has turned her from it. You pointed out yourself that even my penury would probably not be enough and she cares nothing for you or your reputation. It's not a risk I'm prepared to take, even if you are. Besides, you don't know what it is you're asking and what it would mean, *'nghariad*. And I do."

" *'nghariad?* "

"It means farewell, I think. Or it will be too late. Forgive me, Beth."

And with that he suddenly stepped to the window and swung himself over the sill. Beth watched him leave, then crawled back between the sheets. She was five years on the shelf, an amiable spinster. She would likely never know anything of passion. Did he think that she had blindly reached for the chance, since another might never come her way? Or that she in her turn was trying to trap him into marriage? For if Harriet had cried off because he was found in her bed, he would have felt obliged to offer for her in turn, wouldn't he? Did he think that was her motive? The humiliation sank into her soul like a stone. She had no idea that she would ever be able to fall asleep again, but she must have done so, for it seemed barely a minute had passed before the sun was streaming in at the window and there was indeed pandemonium in the hall.

Beth snatched up her wrapper and flung open her door. Mrs. Honeywell, in her dressing gown and with her hair tied up in rags above her puce cheeks, stood screaming and weeping at the open door to Harriet's bedchamber. "My poor heart! Oh, I declare I've never been so put out! I shall have palpitations! My salts! A burnt feather!"

Beth ran to her aunt. "Pray, calm yourself, Aunt Honeywell! What has happened? What has Lord Ravenstoke done?"

Mrs. Honeywell turned to her with a look of genuine astonishment. "What? Why should the viscount have done anything? It's Harriet! Harriet who has disgraced us!"

At that moment Mr. Honeywell came out of Harriet's room, followed by a weeping maid. "She has left us a note, ma'am," he said to his wife.

"And where is she gone?" wailed Mrs. Honeywell.

"Harriet has gone?" asked Beth in total confusion.

The weeping maid nodded her head. "Oh, miss, her bed's gone unslept in and all! She's taken her best dresses and her jewelry. I discovered it myself this morning when I went to pull back her curtains. Miss Honeywell's flitted and nobody knows where."

Beth stood silent for a moment, as Mr. Honeywell unfolded the note and began to read it. What had Ravenstoke done? Had he been so desperate? She had the most dreadful vision for a moment of him dragging Harriet from the house by her hair and doing away with her in some horrid fashion. Then she shook her head and pulled herself together. Whatever else he might be prepared to do, the viscount would never harm a living soul, not even Harriet.

"What does she say?" wailed Mrs. Honeywell.

"Read for yourself, madam," said Mr. Honeywell in tones like thunder, thrusting the note into her hands.

"I declare, I cannot read a thing. Oh, my poor heart! Read me the note, Beth."

Beth took the missive and began to read aloud. Harriet had obviously written it in a great hurry. "Good Lord!" she said when she had finished it. "What do you intend to do, sir?"

"Send for Ravenstoke and that Miss Sally Rutledge, of course. Harriet must be stopped; she shall be stopped. Barnes!

Fetch a footman! I want to send a message! For God's sake, Mrs. Honeywell, shut your mouth. It was your scheme, madam, and look what has become of it!"

They were all dressed and sitting downstairs when Lord Ravenstoke arrived and joined the family in the drawing room. Mrs. Honeywell had prostrated herself on the chaise longue and was wrapped in several shawls. Some foul-smelling tincture sat beside her on a small table. As Ravenstoke entered the room, she sat up and held out a wobbly hand.

"My lord! You find us overcome! We are mortified! You will go after her, of course, and bring her back to the bosom of her family? And the wedding—not two days off!"

"My dear Mrs. Honeywell, I am sorry to find you so afflicted. May I ask what has happened?"

But Mrs. Honeywell could do no more than raise her handkerchief to her eyes and wail.

"My daughter has shown herself to be an ungrateful and wayward chit!" exclaimed Mr. Honeywell. "I trust to you, my lord, to put all to rights!"

Ravenstoke bowed stiffly, but there seemed to be the slightest glint of laughter in his eyes. "I would be more ready to offer my assistance, sir, if you would be kind enough to inform me of the circumstances."

Neither of the Honeywells, however, seemed to be able to put anything further into words. Would it fall to Beth to give him the news? She was afraid she would betray herself if she did so.

"Why," said the voice of Miss Rutledge from the doorway. "I can tell you. Harriet has eloped, my lord. What do you think of that?"

Ravenstoke seemed overcome for a moment. "Eloped?" he said after a moment. Then he sat down on a spindly chair and threw back his head and began to laugh.

"My salts, Beth!" cried Mrs. Honeywell. "The viscount is

distraught! And no wonder! To think that a daughter of mine should be so disobliging! After all we've done!"

"You will go after them, my lord," stated Mr. Honeywell, as if he were speaking to one of his underlings at the tea warehouse. "Bring her back and I'll get her to the altar with you, never fear. She'll not turn down a title and a fortune for some penniless, runt-faced, spindly-legged, jumped-up fellow in a scarlet coat—not over my dead body, she won't."

"Why don't you go yourself?" asked Sally cheekily, seating herself next to Beth on the sofa. "She's your daughter."

"Miss Rutledge! I'll have you know I have business in the City that can't wait. Nor do I have a fast carriage like the viscount's curricle. He's her betrothed, for God's sake. If the man has any pride, he'll fetch her back forthwith and see the redcoat hanged."

"May I ask," said Ravenstoke, as he recovered himself, "with whom she has eloped? Do you tell me that I have a rival for her affections?"

"My brother, of course," said Sally smugly. "Captain John Rutledge of the Blankshire's. They met in Bath. It was only Mr. Honeywell that didn't think John good enough for her, and Mrs. Honeywell who so longed for a lord for a son-in-law. But Harriet's been seeing him in London all along. I helped them."

"What, miss? Under our very noses? I forbade her to accept him! I thought your brother was with his regiment in the shires or I'd never have allowed you to visit Harriet!"

"I never heard of such a thing for a pair of sly minxes," wept Mrs. Honeywell. "My daughter to follow the drum? When she could have been a lady! It's too much, I declare!"

Miss Sally Rutledge wasn't in the least overawed. "It's been the greatest lark imaginable! I saw Harriet at the muslin counter at Green's Emporium and John was outside. He'd just ridden into town on leave. She sneaked off right away and met him. I arranged everything and very smartly too, though I say it myself. They left to take a turn together in your carriage, Mr. Honeywell."

"Leaving me to find my own way home?" asked Beth dryly.

"And he was in the Park and at Vauxhall, of course. And came down to Much Haven behind us. She's met him ever so many times. The betrothal with Lord Ravenstoke was the most perfect cover! No one suspected a thing! I declare it's been more fun than a merry-go-round at the fair."

"And Captain Rutledge has a chestnut horse?" asked Beth.

"With an unusual white stocking," added Ravenstoke.

Sally nodded smugly. "So you did notice! Harriet was afraid you might. She gave me the most frightful roasting for pointing him out on the road to Much Haven, I can tell you. But it didn't matter, did it? They'll be well on the way to Gretna Green by now."

Mrs. Honeywell began to moan. "Captain Rutledge! He has ginger hair and eyebrows and a frightful set of mustaches! And nothing but his pay! What consequence, what position can I hope for as Captain Rutledge's mother-in-law, I'd like to know? Oh, my poor heart!"

"Pray discipline your heart, madam. You will catch them before noon, my lord," insisted Mr. Honeywell.

Ravenstoke leaned back in the chair and smiled. "My dear sir," he said quietly. "I really don't think that I shall."

"Nonsense," said Mrs. Honeywell. "Your curricle would outrun them. She said in the letter they had gone in a post-chaise, didn't she, Beth?"

"I believe so, Aunt."

"There, you see?"

"But I shall not be in pursuit, Mrs. Honeywell," said Ravenstoke gravely. "I apologize for adding to your distress, dear lady, but I think we are better to let them escape together, don't you? Far be it from me to stand in the path of true love. I think I must take my defeat like a gentleman."

The following severe palpitations necessitated a prolonged session with burnt feathers, which was almost enough to drive them all from the room. Beth ran to the French windows into the garden and opened them.

"But the wedding!" exclaimed the invalid. "All the arrangements! The flowers, the music, the guests! St. George's in Hanover Square is booked!"

"I see no reason why I can't still use them," said Ravenstoke calmly. "I shall reimburse all your expenses, of course."

"Still use them?" stuttered Mrs. Honeywell. "Then you have a plan to recover our wayward Harriet? Oh, Lord Ravenstoke! How very thrilling!"

"You entirely misunderstand me, madam. It might entail slightly different guests, of course, but I think I shall use the flowers, the music and St. George's to marry someone else."

At which Beth's heart stood still and died within her. And for the first time in her life, she fainted dead away.

She awoke to the sound of bird-song and the sweet smell of roses. She was lying on a garden bench with her head cradled against a blue superfine coat and strong fingers gently stroking the hair from her forehead. Ravenstoke was smiling down at her.

"Feeling better?" he said with a grin.

Beth sat up, but he didn't take his arm from her shoulders.

"Good heavens," she said. "Don't say I actually fainted like the goose-girl who saw the fox in the basket."

"No, more like someone overwhelmed with happiness, I hope," he said.

Beth struggled not to allow herself to weakly lean a little closer into the strength of his embrace. "Overwhelmed with happiness? Why ever should that be so?"

"Because I shan't marry Harriet, of course."

"And I should be happy for you? I am."

"I rather hoped you'd be happy for yourself too."

Beth sat up straight and looked deep into the brown eyes. "Now why should I be that?"

He slipped his arm from her and instead took her fingers in his. " *'Wi'n dy garu di. 'Wnei di 'mhriodi i?"*

"That's what you said at Much Haven, isn't it?"

"Why, I believe it is," he said with a wicked grin.

"Do I admire your horses?"

"That's not what it means—as you guessed."

"Then you might have the grace to look at least a little sheepish for so misleading me. What does it mean?"

" *'Wi'n dy garu di*: I love you. *'Wnei di 'mhriodi i?*: Will you marry me?"

"Please, don't tease, my lord. What about Miss Somerset?"

He looked blank for a moment. "Felicity? Good heavens, I've known her all my life. We're like brother and sister. Anyway, she's going to marry James Gregory. Did you think there was ever anyone but you, *'nghariad?"*

"You've barely known me a month. How could I have told?"

"Because I asked you to marry me and gave you the lovespoon, of course."

"Yes, in Welsh, which I couldn't understand—and you told me the spoon had no meaning. Now I learn you had the nerve to ask me to marry you when you were still engaged to Harriet."

"I never could have married her. I was an impossible bridegroom."

"So you were. Thank goodness she was in love with her captain all along, or you would have broken her heart."

Ravenstoke laughed. "She didn't give much thought to mine, did she? Perhaps it is just as fortunate that I was in love with you, *'nghariad."*

" *'nghariad?"*

"Sweetheart. Now please answer, Beth, before it's my turn to go into a decline. Will you marry me?"

"You said yourself you're an impossible bridegroom."

He took her hand and carried it to his lips. "But I'll be a much better husband, I promise. It's June, Beth. The birds are singing; the roses are blooming; St. George's is booked. And I'm going to kiss you again."

His lips touched hers and she surrendered willingly into his embrace. There was that mysterious undercurrent of energy that she had felt in him the previous night in her room, but this time nothing was held in check. As he allowed his passion full rein and his kiss became deeper, she understood and welcomed it. At last he released her and smiled into her eyes. They were wet with unshed tears.

"I love you, *fy nghariad,* my sweet; *fy nghalon,* my heart; *'mlodyn,* my flower. You're supposed to smile about it, not weep. Now say you love me."

"I do," said Beth. "And if you want to live in a cottage with me and keep pigs, that's all right, but I would like to see Ravenstoke Hall. Did you go out and gamble it away?"

"Not yet, thank God. I had a far more dishonorable plan to escape Harriet—it was just that I wasn't sure it was going to work."

"Which was?"

"I'll never tell you. But Captain John Rutledge is a richer man today than he ever expected to be. Quite a stroke of luck that he had such an unusual mount: it was so easy to trace. Will you let me get a horse for Joe?"

"How can I stop you?"

"And buy you a new dress and a bonnet for the wedding?"

"As long as they're not orange or lemon."

"That suit has been burned and you'll never see me in anything so vile again—as long as you will marry me in St. George's in Hanover Square?"

"If we can get my father and Joe and Mrs. Scone here in time."

"Of course we can. Now, will you marry me? Say yes."

"Yes," said Beth.

An Indefinite Wedding

by
Marcy Stewart

Standing before the long mirror in the Duke of Weston's finest guest chamber, Lady Sarah Millbright viewed her bridal dress and blinked back tears.

Her companions were too absorbed in the fitting to notice her distress.

"Your daughter is beautiful, my lady," said Madame Tellesand around a mouthful of pins, her fingers measuring a length of lace against the bodice of the most modest wedding gown she'd ever been required to make. "But it is a pity you do not allow a décollètage instead of the high collar."

Lady Millbright, who half-reclined on a nearby divan, raised her chin and said reprovingly, "Sarah is the daughter of an earl and must not flaunt herself as a courtesan would."

Madame Tellesand glanced down at her own revealing neckline and, after a few words in French, was heard to mutter about dictatorial mothers who refused to consult their daughters about their own wishes.

The countess was unwilling to let this pass. "Sarah is an obedient child, Madame Tellesand," she chided. "My husband and I raised her with wisdom and kindness; therefore, it is ever her desire to please us. Is that not so, Sarah?"

"Yes, Mother," the young lady said dutifully, and Madame Tellesand sighed and shook her head at the wistfulness of the words.

Sarah stared dismally at her reflection. She was not disturbed by her wedding dress; in spite of Madame Tellesand's objections, she thought it quite romantic, very like something a tragic heroine in a novel might wear. The gown was of white satin with an overlay of Irish shamrock lace sprinkled with seed pearls; and though the skirt was cut fuller and the fitted waistline lower than fashion decreed, the gathers emphasized the existence of a small waist, and the long, pointed sleeves made her hands appear delicate.

She presented an elegant figure in the mirror and knew it, without false modesty or pride. Some might think her too tall, her form too mature for eighteen years of life; but none could find fault with her flawless skin, shining eyes, a straight, fragile-looking nose, and deeply etched lips. Sarah often felt the lack of a distinctive color of hair, the golden locks of childhood having recently faded to a nondescript shade; and she might wish her eyes to be a more startling blue than their indeterminate hazel; but nothing could be done to change that. She was pleasing enough; she had had sufficient compliments and warm, gentlemanly glances to know it was so.

Thus it was not her appearance that caused her low spirits, nor was it the fact that her mother hadn't consulted her on the pattern of her gown. Rather, it was the note lying on her dressing table, and the deeper meaning behind it. Unwillingly, her gaze wandered toward the letter once more.

"Please to be still, Lady Fidget," complained Madame Tellesand, whose reputation as a French modiste *non pareil* allowed a certain familiarity with her customers.

"Yes, what is wrong with you today, my dear?" asked the countess. "Oh!" she exclaimed, suddenly remembering. "You're not still distraught over Elizabeth's refusal, are you?"

Sarah's eyes brimmed anew. "How can I fail to be when my dearest friend declines to serve as maid of honor?"

"And why has she refused?" demanded the countess. When Sarah remained silent, she exclaimed, "Oh, how vexatious! You cannot mean she still believes you and her brother should wed?"

Sarah's face flushed. "Gerry and I—we . . ."

"Do not speak of childish promises," Lady Millbright interjected. "I well know the three of you have been inseparable from the cradle, but a squire's son cannot wed an earl's daughter." She scanned Sarah's face and added more kindly, "It you wish to replace Elizabeth, we can dispatch messages to your friends at Miss Packerdy's. Or the duke will know of someone."

"The duke?" Sarah cried, a note of hysteria creeping in. "That will be very nice, and most appropriate! Yes, let us ask him, for why should I not have strangers to attend me at the wedding, when the bridegroom himself is unknown to me!"

"That is not precisely true," the countess said, and looked pointedly at the seamstress, whose averted eyes shouted her interest. "Your father knows him, and knew his father; what better recommendation can there be? Moreover, the duke was considerate enough to invite us here to High Ridgely for the final month before the wedding in order for your acquaintanceship to grow. Besides, there will be a lifetime in which to know him better."

"And yet in the fortnight we've been here, I've learnt nothing about him," Sarah declared. "He seems a cold man, and uncaring. I don't know why he wishes to marry me."

"How could anyone not wish to marry you?" proclaimed her mother loyally.

"I cannot understand it," Sarah continued heedlessly. "You and Father have always been so protective of me. How you could betroth me to this—this *rake* is beyond everything!"

"Sarah! Mind your tongue." Lady Millbright pressed her handkerchief to her lips. "Weston has reformed; he has even taken to attending chapel, and though it is Church of England and not Methodist, one can make allowances. Many young men are undisciplined in their extreme youth."

"Mother, he is nearly thirty!"

"I had forgotten how ancient that must sound to you. But consider, my dear, that the match is financially and socially advantageous to both lines. Think, Sarah; you will be a *duchess!*"

"I care not about titles."

"That's because you have never known the lack of one," the countess said dryly. Madame Tallesand could not resist grunting her assent at this remark, and the two older ladies knew a moment's agreement.

Sarah longed to tear the wedding dress off her body; she wished to throw herself upon the bed and howl. Instead, she stood stalwartly while Madame Tellesand finished her alterations.

As her mother had said, she was an obedient child.

But her heart was not so easily calmed. *Gerry, Gerry,* it cried, while her mind tormented her with memories of a pair of soulful brown eyes.

At that moment in the small library of High Ridgely, Artemis Shallot, the Duke of Weston, placed his empty tea cup on the tray and settled comfortably in his favorite armchair. The look he gave his two companions, however, was less comfortable than wary. Lady Druscilla Duncan, the pretty young woman sitting across from him on the settle, thought his eyes the most frigid blue she had ever seen.

"I assure your grace that my wife is capable of the utmost discretion," said the lady's companion, a tall, auburn-haired gentleman dressed impeccably in shades of brown. "You may trust her as you would myself; and, given the limitations of time, I believe her assistance will prove invaluable."

While Lady Dru prayed her lips would not smile at this high-blown praise—only she could know what it had cost her husband to speak so—the duke leveled an appraising stare at them both. As the pause became prolonged, Dru sensed her spouse's gathering ire; and while Duncan was not a high-tempered man despite being half Scot, she knew he was capable of abandoning the assignment just as quickly as he had accepted it. He had become a private inquiry agent to relieve the boredom of the indolent life of a wealthy baron, and he could choose and discard his causes as he pleased. Knowing this, Dru held her breath and hoped he would not take offense at the duke's doubts, for Duncan could not, *must not,* become angry and leave, *not on her very first investigation!*

Fortunately, the duke seemed to come to a decision, for he inhaled sharply and said, "I'll trust your judgment, Lord Duncan. As I wrote to you, our mutual friend, Sebastian Montgomery, highly recommends your work. He told me that his wife and Lady Duncan are sisters, and that you rescued his lady from a kidnapping attempt."

"Yes, he did," Dru said quickly, before Duncan could disclaim modestly as he was wont to do. "Duncan posed as a footman at the Hall, using the disguise both to gather information and to protect us. We became acquainted during the weeks of his investigation."

"And so the footman married an earl's daughter," the duke said, his expression thawing at her speech. "Lord Duncan, you must tell me sometime how you managed to accomplish that."

The newlyweds exchanged small smiles. They very nearly hadn't bridged that social gulf, false though it had been.

Weston crossed one well-shaped leg over the other and straightened an infinitesimal wrinkle at the knee of his unmentionables. "I suppose we'd better speak of my . . . dilemma now, though it pains me to reveal my folly before such a charming lady." He cast an appreciative glance in Dru's direction, and she felt herself reacting to the power in his extraordinary eyes even as she felt her beloved's breath on her cheek.

Weston did not appear to be aware of his magnetism and was the more dangerous for it, Dru judged. She shifted slightly closer to Duncan.

"I wish we had more time to accomplish the task I've set before you," the duke was saying. "However, the Weston gems have been stolen and *must* be recovered before my marriage. Unfortunately for your investigation, no one can know of the theft. Otherwise, the wedding will very likely be cancelled.

And that must not be allowed to happen, because my marriage is a financial necessity."

His mouth tightened bitterly. "It's a problem for which I've only myself to blame. The embarrassing truth is that certain pieces of the gems are now forfeit to a friend of mine, John Lyons, due to a lost wager. John is an honourable man and can be trusted not to speak of the debt, but I cannot deceive myself that he will remain quiet do I fail to meet my obligations. And if Lord Millbright discovers I've made another wager, he will forbid the marriage, for such was one of the conditions of the agreement between us. The Millbrights, you see, are staunch Wesleyans and take a dim view of gambling. That's why I must ask you to pose as wedding guests. No one can know of the theft or your investigation."

The duke walked to the window. "There is more," he said, and turned his face to observe the downpour outside. "I don't suppose you've gone about in Society without hearing something of my reputation."

Dru's eyebrows lifted. Few indeed were those who hadn't heard of the profligate duke.

Weston turned and leaned into the wide windowsill. He combed his fingers through his dark hair, mussing slightly the attractive edge of silver at his temples. "Not all the stories are deserved," he said. "I hope I've been discreet in those areas of my life which might sully Lady Druscilla's ears. But I've not been wise in my love of wagers, though never have I endangered the estate before. However, my last few gambling debts have depleted my resources and have, shall we say, reformed me more surely than Lord Millbright could."

"Meaning the estate might now be forfeit?" asked Duncan, his voice carefully neutral.

"Not directly, but such could prove the final outcome."

"And marriage to Lord Millbright's daughter will restore your fortune . . . ?"

The amassing of wealth through marriage was not uncommon, and Weston took no offense at Duncan's query. "It's not quite so simple as that, though her portion is considerable," he replied.

The duke's thoughts seemed to turn inward, his eyes growing cool. "You must understand that for the whole of my life I've been promised a considerable inheritance from my maternal grandmother. And while I make no excuses for my behavior, I confess I've depended upon her eventual bequest to resolve financial embarrassments. When she died last September, imagine my surprise when I discovered she'd added a codicil to her will."

He chuckled with little mirth. "She'd been at me to wed since my parents died. She often reminded me I had a responsibility to the title, being the only child; said I needed the steadying influence of a good wife. But I ignored her. In the end she had her way. The codicil requires that I marry a lady of untarnished reputation within a year of grandmother's demise. If I do not, my cousin Charles will inherit all. If that happens, I'll be forced to sell off portions of the estate to meet my debts. That's why nothing must interfere with my wedding."

The duke's expression darkened, and despite the fact his problems were of his own making, Dru's heart skipped a beat in sympathy.

"After the will was read, I began looking for a suitable lady," Weston continued. "Since my reputation preceded me, this was more difficult than I supposed; many fathers viewed my attentions with suspicion. I was also hampered by my own distaste for the vapid airs the young ladies adopted. Until I met Lady Sarah."

"And you loved her immediately," said Dru, who was still very much a newlywed, and ever a romantic.

Weston coughed. "Well, if not that precisely, let us say that I didn't take her in dislike. Sarah is beautiful, intelligent and well-mannered. And though she's as shy as one would expect from not having the advantage of even one Season, I feel satisfied she will soon grow more polished."

"Oh," Dru said numbly.

"Don't think me hard-hearted," the duke said. "I was charmed enough to promise her parents to reform myself. I did very well, too; even took myself from London to refrain from the clubs. Then John wagered his bay could beat my black in a race from Bath to Bristol. I was sure I'd win, but Pacer took a stone in his hoof."

"And this is when you wagered the gems?" asked Duncan.

"Yes, a diamond and sapphire set against John's jewelled sword hilt, which is said to have belonged to the Bonnie Prince. I've long admired it."

"When did you discover the jewels were missing?"

"They disappeared this Tuesday last. Tobias—he's my butler, you met him when you arrived—was cleaning the settings that morning in preparation to my giving them to John. All was well when Toby replaced them in the safe, but that evening they were gone."

Weston left the window, returned to the chair, and leaned forward earnestly. "I put John off with a story that the necklace needed a clasp replaced. He *must not* know the gems are missing. John knows the Millbrights' views and has pledged to keep the wager secret. But if I default, he cannot be expected to remain silent."

Dru, torn between exasperation and amusement, knew the situation to be potentially tragic were the duke not so otherwise a masterful and compelling figure, though not as wonderful as her own dear spouse, of course. But Weston was hopeless!

When she was certain her voice would remain steady, she asked, "Is there anyone you suspect of the thievery?"

Weston sighed. "I've thought long about it, and I can only hope it was one of the servants. But don't think for a moment it was Tobias, because he has been with the family for twenty-five years. I wouldn't be surprised if John himself took them for a prank, merely to put me in this spot."

"Quite a risky venture for a jest," Duncan said. "What about your cousin? Does he know of the earl's requirements for a

GET 4 REGENCY ROMANCE NOVELS FREE

A $16.47
value.
FREE!
No obligation
to buy
anything, ever.

bridegroom? He would benefit greatly were you unable to marry during the time limit."

"The marquess has greater need for the funds than I, and he *does* know the earl is a religious man; but I don't like to think it could be my cousin. Besides, Charles had no knowledge of the wager."

"We mustn't fail to consider the gems could have been stolen for their own value," Duncan commented.

"I suppose that is true," Weston said reluctantly.

"Did both of these gentlemen have access to the safe on the Tuesday in question?"

"Yes, both are here for the wedding. Well, now that you've heard all, what think you of my prospects for success?"

"I never make promises," Duncan said. "But we'll do our best, Druscilla and I, to ferret out answers without disclosing your secret. And now if you'll give us an itemized list of the missing gems . . ."

Returning to their bedchamber some moments later, the Duncans found Pizzy still unpacking their valises. The little maid was summarily excused.

As soon as the door closed, Dru flung her arms around Duncan's shoulders and molded her body to his. Her embrace was returned with equal enthusiasm; but when she began loosening his cravat, Duncan laughed softly and stilled her hands. "Ach noo, lass," he whispered. "We're nowt at home noo."

Dru's eyes stared dreamily into his. "Use that accent at your own peril, then," she said, and began unfastening the buttons at her throat. "I've not had your arms around me for hours, and I grow lonely."

"Druscilla, we must be about our investigation," he said sternly, but his eyes fell to the soft flesh emerging from her dress. Swallowing hard, he continued, "Don't forget that I'm allowing you to help at your insistence, and only because I don't believe there's an element of danger in this particular case. However, you must *help,* and not *distract,* do you wish to assist me again."

"Very well, but I must change," Dru said. With an air of indifference, she stepped from her gown and loosened the fastenings of her chemise. "How shall we begin, dearest?"

Turning to face the door, Duncan said resolutely, "We must interview the guests and servants, of course, and find their whereabouts on Tuesday afternoon. That will give us a start."

"I find the duke a fascinating man," she said abruptly.

Duncan immediately turned back. "Oh, do you?"

Smiling, Dru said, "He is austere, yet charming. But if I were a child of Lady Sarah's age, I would think him frightening."

"Child?" he snorted. "She cannot be more than two years younger than yourself." A moment later he added, "Austere and frightening . . . these are the qualities which you find attractive?"

"Every lady has a tender spot for a rake," Dru said, the chemise falling to a silken puddle at her feet. "The naughty boy whom only she can reform."

Flames burned within Duncan's eyes as he walked toward his wife. "And do you account yourself such a reformer?"

"Oh, not entirely," Dru said, and laughed victoriously when she was deposited upon the bed. "You, for example, I would not reform at all."

When Lady Millbright finally took her leave of her daughter to dress for dinner, the young lady's abigail rushed to Sarah's side, held out a battered envelope, and whispered, "Begging your pardon, my lady, but I've been dying to give this to you. A messenger delivered it on the sly this afternoon."

Paling, Sarah accepted the note and said, "Er—thank you, Myrtice, I—I should like to be alone for a moment."

"O'course you would," the maid said, her brown eyes knowing in a pert little face. "I'll be in the dressing room do you need me."

Sarah watched her departure with wild eyes, then tore open the letter. As she suspected, the message was from Gerry, who asked to meet her at the duke's maze after the household went to bed.

So he was here! He'd come all the way from Sussex to be with her. She couldn't refuse to meet him, not after he'd traveled so far. But what if they were caught? With her heart beating as frantically as the rain pounding the windows, she refolded the note and, after considering several hiding places, thrust it between the mattresses.

During the next few moments, she was scarcely aware of Myrtice's last-minute adjustments to her hair and dress. Nevertheless, she was ready when her parents knocked.

"You look a treasure," said Lord Millbright from the corridor, his eyes beaming beneath bushy white eyebrows. "That green gown becomes you exceedingly, and I like your hair all done up in curls. The duke will find you most fetching this evening."

"Enough, Reggie," warned Lady Millbright. "You'll make her self-conscious, if not proud."

"Not our Sarah. She's an excellent girl."

Sarah looked into her well-loved sire's face and knew guilt; but instead of confessing, *There is a note from my sweetheart beneath my mattress* as she was tempted to do, she smiled wanly and accepted his free arm.

The three of them descended to the first-floor drawing room where all the duke's guests appeared to be present; they chattered like magpies, Sarah thought. She noted an unfamiliar couple, very attractive, and wondered why her own hair could not have remained as golden as the lady's. Weston stood near the fireplace talking to them, his tall figure defined to perfection in black evening clothes. Sarah's heart lurched painfully as it always did when she saw him, particularly when his icy blue eyes met hers as now. Dry-mouthed, she watched him nod briefly to his companions and walk toward her.

The Millbrights were brought forward to meet the new couple, a Lord and Lady Duncan. Before she realized how it was accomplished, Sarah's hand had been enfolded within Weston's arm while her parents, after a few words of greeting, wandered off to speak with other guests. Feeling abandoned, she found solace in the warm eyes of Lady Duncan.

"I understand you're from Sussex, Lady Sarah," the baron's wife said kindly. "Do you live near the sea?"

"Yes, my father's favorite residence is outside Worthing," Sarah answered, adding pensively, "It is very beautiful along the coast."

"And steadily becoming overgrown with an influx of travellers," Weston commented. "A sad result of the betterment of roads and the growing wealth of the merchant class. Town dwellers are converting their establishments into boarding houses, and new buildings are being raised to accommodate even more people. The merchants hope to emulate Brighton, but don't realize they exchange the advantages of village living for avarice."

Sarah's cheeks reddened. In a strained voice she said, "There is a wonderful bath at Wickes's, and we now have Spooner's and Stafford's, two excellent libraries."

"I can understand how a young lady would find the libraries interesting," Weston said tolerantly. "But nothing compares with our mountains and those of Derbyshire. Here nature runs riot as it should, unrestrained by man. You'll soon understand the difference."

There was no mistaking the spark in Sarah's eye, but any answer she might have made was swallowed by a roar of thunder. Several ladies uttered little squeals of terror; when Lady Duncan jumped, her husband placed his arm around her waist.

The duke laughed. "Nature at work at its most elemental. Another instance of our magnificent northern climate."

"And your betrothed didn't so much as flinch," said a darkly handsome gentleman approaching their group. Though his evening attire was not of the latest fashion, it in no wise diminished the charm of his demeanor. "She's brave as well as beautiful, as is this other lady."

"Charles," said the duke, "may I present the Right Honourable Lord and Lady Duncan. My cousin, the Most Honourable Marquess of Beasley."

"I am delighted," said the marquess, his eyes intent upon the baron's wife. "Artemis, you've managed to do the impossible—you've assembled a houseful of guests wherein every lady is devastating."

Sarah was pleased to see how smoothly Lady Duncan brushed aside his flattery. The marquess had often made flirtatious remarks to Sarah, but she'd only responded with speechless embarrassment. It would not be amiss to observe this lady's polished manner, for such might prove useful after the wedding should the duke's other contemporaries become over-familiar.

Thinking of the wedding, Sarah's face flooded with color; then, remembering her assignation with Gerry was only hours away, she grew pale again. The duke, unmindful of her inner turmoil, chose that moment to pull Sarah away to mingle, and all thoughts of learning from Lady Duncan were forgotten.

Had Dru known her behaviour was admired by Lady Sarah, she would have been chagrined; for only moments after the younger lady departed, Dru watched her husband with all the gentility of a hellcat. Duncan now stood several paces away, his attention having been caught by a vaguely familiar female who appeared entranced by his every word. The woman wore an orange dress that was cut dangerously low and left nothing to the imagination. With a sense of outrage, Dru observed her husband responding to her coquettish mannerisms.

Dru was left alone with the marquess, who observed her with amusement. "Are you acquainted with the lady who

speaks with your husband?" he asked. "She is Olivia Wingate."

"Oh, yes, I recall her now. She's cousin to my brother-in-law
Sebastian and attended their wedding."

None of which excused the woman's familiarity with Duncan, especially since he hadn't been present to meet her then.

"Quite a taking little thing, isn't she?" the marquess said
slyly, drawing closer. "So demure, so subtle . . ."

Startled, Dru looked at him, then laughed. "You are teasing
me, my lord."

"I only hope to draw a measure of the green fire within
your eyes for myself. The baron is a fortunate man."

Dru was too much in love with her husband to answer the
marquess's flirtatious gambits, and she looked away. Unfortunately her eyes again fell upon Duncan and Olivia. *How can
he attend her so?* she thought. *He treats her no differently
than he does me!*

Her heart fell. It was obvious Duncan did not burn for herself as she did for him. If he loved her as completely as she
adored him, if his every waking thought was dominated by
thoughts and memories of their times alone together, he could
not laugh and banter so urbanely with scandalous flirts like
Olivia Wingate.

She tried to justify his behaviour. Perhaps he only attempted
to learn Olivia's whereabouts on the afternoon of the robbery.
But he needn't go about it with so much enjoyment, surely?

When Tobias entered the drawing room to announce dinner,
she wasn't surprised that Olivia begged Duncan's escort to the
dining room, nor was she surprised when he capitulated so
easily. It was fortunate for her the marquess offered his arm;
otherwise she would have had to be content with the shrug
and wink her husband so generously offered as he passed by.

Sarah suffered through the four removes of dinner with a
steadily growing silence. The duke seemed to regard her every

attempt at conversation as the blatherings of a schoolgirl; therefore her responses became monosyllabic and curt. Weston appeared to find nothing unusual in this and made no attempt to draw her out.

Something very like rage began to fill the young lady's heart. It was an unfamiliar and unpleasant emotion, but it overwhelmed the muddle of other feelings whirling in her brain during the past hours. Guilt, excitement, and fear over the upcoming meeting with Gerry could not prevail against her anger with the duke. Even worse was her increasingly distraught feelings toward her parents.

Being an only child, Sarah had always enjoyed the exclusive attention and protection of her mother and father. They had been unusually close; had travelled and played together as few families did. But now, simply because Artemis Shallot had the distinction of a dukedom and had manifested a change in his morals (a change she doubted), she was to be sacrificed on the altar of marriage. Never mind that she preferred the comfortable childhood relationship with Gerry to the incomprehensible aloofness of the duke; her opinions were not to be considered, not in the most important decision of her life!

It was unfair.

Over the next few hours, Sarah moved normally through the forms of convention; she spoke sweetly if not frequently to the guests when they reconvened in the drawing room; she resumed work on her bead-and-shell sewing box project while others gathered at the card tables. But inwardly, a change was taking place.

The gentle, meek-hearted girl was disappearing.

In her place a rebellious spirit was being born.

Instead of fearing to meet Gerry in the maze, she looked forward to it.

The hours clicked by slowly. When her parents retired, she followed and submitted to Myrtice's assistance in preparing her for bed. After the maid left, however, Sarah exchanged her bedclothes for a simple plaid morning gown and lay on the bed to wait.

Perhaps the rain caused the other guests to grow as sleepy as she did, for shortly past midnight she heard the last of them ascend the stairs. When the house grew silent, Sarah put on a hooded cloak, seized her umbrella, and turned the doorknob. Not daring to use a candle, she crept down the stairs and out the kitchen door, then ran toward the maze.

The weather was truly nasty, she saw, as mud splashed onto her skirt and shoes. Poor Gerry must be soaked through by now.

Sarah made several turnings among the high hedges and hoped Gerry hadn't gone to the very center, for what if they became lost during this downpour? But around the fourth bend she saw his familiar, sturdy form hunched forward on a wooden bench, the umbrella he carried tipped carelessly over his head.

He stood when he saw her, and Sarah ran gladly into his embrace.

"I've missed you and Elizabeth so much!" she exclaimed, then laughed as their umbrellas became entangled and had to be sorted out. "I hope you don't catch cold from waiting in this awful rain."

"It's too late for that now," Gerry said, and swept a sodden handkerchief across his face. "Thought you'd never come, Sarah!"

Slightly miffed at this unloverlike complaint, she said mildly, "I came as soon as I could. It wouldn't do for anyone to see us together." Then, observing his dejected, boyish face with its sprinkling of freckles, the stubby nose and wide brown eyes, her irritation faded. "I am sorry you had to wait."

"No, you're right, old girl. Can't take the chance of Weston seeing us." He chuckled uncomfortably and ran a hand through his wiry red curls. "No telling what he'd do."

"That's true enough, since he seems to regard me as property," she said bitterly. "I've heard he's accounted a fine shot."

Gerry's face whitened the darkness. "I don't want to hear about the duke," he said determinedly. "I came to see *you*. Are you happy, princess? With him, I mean?"

Fighting tears, she said, "You know I am not. We spoke of it before I left Worthing."

"I recall it; I only want to make certain nothing has changed."

"Nothing has," the newly rebellious Sarah declared. Her ears echoed with the sound of Weston's haughty voice even now. "I cannot *bear* the thought of wedding him."

"Then come away with me," Gerry said urgently, and clasped her hand within his own. "We'll go to the Border and be married."

Sarah's heart seemed to stop. "I—I don't know what to say, Gerry! What—I mean, when—"

"There's no better time than now! I have a carriage waiting down the lane. By the time they discover you're missing, we'll be halfway to Scotland!"

Sarah's fingers loosened, and she stepped back a pace. "Gerry, I—I cannot just disappear. My parents would be frantic." Not that she cared, of course . . .

"We'll send them word as soon as we wed. They'll endure no more than two days of anxiety. Don't be overly mindful of them, Sarah, not in this! After all, have they not sentenced you to a lifetime with someone you cannot love?"

Sarah's thoughts churned frantically. The old Sarah would never have considered Gerry's audacious proposal. The new one did consider it with a growing taste for revenge. Would such an action not be a fitting retribution for her parents? And more importantly, the proud duke would be brought low by a runaway bride. Still . . .

"Why do you hesitate?" Gerry demanded. "Can it be you've grown fond of Weston?"

"Don't be absurd!" she cried, her lips curling at the thought. "But you must give me time to think, Gerry. I cannot run away on a moment's notice."

Frustration lit his face. "We haven't long to wait, Sarah. Remember how quickly your wedding approaches. Send me a message at the Silver Trumpet when you've made up your mind; I've taken a room there." And so saying, he tossed aside his umbrella, wrapped his arms around her, and kissed her furiously.

Sarah pulled back, her hand flying to her mouth. It was their first kiss, something she had often dreamed about. But never had she imagined it like this, a desperate stolen thing dampened by rain and tears. With a soft cry, she turned and ran.

When Sarah disappeared around the hedge, Gerry bent to retrieve his umbrella, then hurled it angrily toward the center of the maze.

"You're worse than a wild boar," said a feminine voice behind him. Gerry turned and saw a woman emerge from one of the interior hedges; her thin, worn cloak was as saturated with rain as his own clothes.

"Be quiet, Myrtice," he snapped. "She might hear you."

"In all this rain? And what if she does? If you can't do no better than that with her, what use is keeping our love a secret?"

Gerry's mouth twisted. *"Our love?* You give the relationship more importance than it deserves."

"You mayn't think it's important now," the maid said, her eyes narrowing. "But if you don't provide for your unborn child like you should, your papa's going to think it's *very* important. Especially after his hoity-toity friends find out his first grandchild's a bastard. And what'll Lady Proper think about you then, do tell?"

"You grow tiresome in your threats, Myrtice. You forget that you're the one who will be more censured than I."

"That may be true of other young gentlemen sowing their wild oats, but Lady Sarah still says her prayers every night. You want her good opinion, you'll get me a little place where I can raise our child comfortable. I only want food and clothes, a roof overhead, and a visit from Daddy now and then. It's not so much to ask, is it? It's not like I expect you to marry *me.*"

Gerry closed his eyes. "What if I deny being the father?" he asked softly. "What then, Myrtice?"

She was quiet for a long while, and he opened his eyes and looked at her. The rain had flattened her hair into dripping ribbons. Her face was pale, and the little curved mouth he'd once found so enchanting was grave. Even as he wondered what could have made him fall so haplessly into her web, he felt a stirring of the old feelings. Myrtice saw it as she seemed to see everything, and her eyes softened.

"You couldn't lie to yourself, though, could you, Master Gerry?" she whispered. "And I've marked this child. As I live and breathe, the babe will have your red hair and brown eyes. There'll be no denying it then."

"My father will cut me off."

Her arms slipped around his waist, and she looked up entreatingly. "That's why you've got to marry Lady Sarah. It'll be a rough patch for a while, but *her* sire will forgive her anything. Never would he cut *her* off. And then you can have the best of both worlds, Master Gerry. Lady Sarah for your fancy ways; me for when you want comfort of another kind. Get her to marry you if you have to steal her to do it. And that might be the only way; you know she's afraid to go against her folks. It'll be a happier end for everybody."

Myrtice leaned her head against Gerry's coat and pulled him near. Reluctantly, as though the action were beyond his will, his arms crept around her shoulders, and he rested his cheek upon her hair. But his eyes were restless and troubled in the dark.

Dru awoke to the sound of rain. Her head throbbed in a similar rhythm, and before she could wonder why it did so—she seldom suffered headaches—she rolled over, saw her husband, and remembered.

Duncan grinned at her squinty-eyed look and slid his hands around her waist, pulling her toward him. Every nerve ending in her body immediately responded, and Dru cursed herself for a fool for wearing a silken gown to bed instead of some old thing of thick cotton. But she didn't possess an old thing of thick cotton, and his roaming hands were making her wild. Nevertheless, the virtue of anger won over the weakness of the flesh, and she stiffened.

The baron's grin faltered, and his hands stilled. "What's wrong, lass? Don't you feel well?"

"I am fine," she said in clipped tones. She wriggled from his arms, tugged her gown into place, and rolled onto her back.

Duncan pulled himself to a sitting position and propped a pillow behind him. "You were fine last night when I tried to speak with you, but too sleepy to talk. This morning you're fine again, but are what—too awake to talk?"

Averting her eyes from his bare chest, Dru said, "I should think you'd extinguished a month's supply of speech last evening with your fawning companion."

"Oho! So that's the way of it, you little green-eyed cat!"

"You may laugh, sir, but you made a perfect fool of yourself. And If I am a cat, you were like a dog at a bone!"

"I don't suppose you thought I might be trying to gather Olivia's trust in order to solve our mystery."

"I am certain you gathered more than her trust," Dru said, her chin rising.

"Then you're in error, Lady Thunder. I learned a very important detail that eliminates many suspects. It seems most of the duke's guests attended a picnic given by Weston's neighbor last Tuesday."

"Including the helpful Olivia, no doubt," she sneered.

"Yes, she did attend, but the ones who didn't are more to the point. The servants remained here, of course, as did the marquess and Lyons; Lady Sarah pled a headache, and the duke had estate business."

When she said nothing, he gave her a mild look. "Druscilla,

it's occasionally necessary to play roles during an inquiry. If you wish to be my partner in business as well as life, you cannot react jealously when I interview females. You'll notice I didn't mind when you entertained the marquess's attentions."

"I? I could hardly be said to have entertained his attentions; a more apt description is that I was abandoned to his chivalry in the absence of my husband." When he made a sound of disgust, she added quickly, "But I learned about the picnic too, and that the marquess was sleeping in his room all Tuesday afternoon."

Duncan looked surprised. "He said that? How did you discover such personal information?"

"Why do you ask?" she responded heatedly. "Do you think I told him I am helping my husband investigate a robbery and that he's a suspect? Have you so little regard for my intelligence?"

"Druscilla . . ." Duncan said warningly.

"Oh, very well, but you're treating me like a simpleton. I merely asked him what activities one might expect at High Ridgely for entertainment. He told me that outings frequently take place in the afternoons and cited the picnic as an example. Charles remained in his room because he detests picnics."

"So he says, but it's easily confirmed by talking with the servants, which is what I intend doing today. I also hope to speak with Lyons; the duke said he should return this afternoon from his excursion to the Peak. You'd do well to spend a little more time with the marquess; he might incriminate himself in an unguarded moment. And do try to speak with Lady Sarah; she seemed to respond well to you last evening."

"Why Lady Sarah? Surely you don't suspect *her?*"

"Druscilla, in an investigation *everyone* is suspect. There are a multitude of reasons for people's actions; it's our work to find them."

He rolled from the bed and began to dress. With her head still turned toward the ceiling, Dru watched him from the corner of her eye. "I think you're trying to distract me with the least likely candidates."

"On the contrary. The marquess is very high on my list."

"Oh, pooh. I cannot believe it is he. Charles is a gentleman and utterly harmless, if I am any judge of character."

"You must keep your mind open. It's not our place to form opinions; otherwise, we can unintentionally reject evidence that contradicts our thoughts."

"Good advice," she said. "Do remember it when the exceedingly buxom Miss Wingate next claims your attention."

He made no answer to this. After he finished dressing, Dru dragged herself from the bed and rang for Pizzy. She reflected sourly that Duncan hadn't even noticed her use of the marquess's given name. So much for making him jealous in retribution. Apparently her husband had total confidence in her affection, and for good reason; she could never disguise her feelings for him. She had better become accustomed to the fact that her love for Duncan ran deeper than his for her.

Perhaps he was incapable of feeling intensely. Perhaps she was not worthy of such devotion.

Dru was still downcast an hour later when she left their chamber. Duncan had long since departed without mending their rift. It was not an accustomed or welcome feeling to be estranged from him; thus, when she heard soft sobs emanating from the curtained window seat near the library, she thought at first the sounds were of her own making. But when her steps paused, the cries stopped as suddenly, and she knew another poor soul was in pain.

Dru slowly parted the drapes and saw a huddled figure regarding her with startled, puffy eyes. "Lady Sarah!" Dru exclaimed. "What's wrong, dear? May I help you?"

"No one can help me," said the younger lady, but she withdrew her knees from the seat to make room for Dru. "Please— please close the draperies again."

Dru did as she was bid, though she knew their hiding place would deceive no one with their slippers and knees protruding like lumps from the cloth; hopefully no one would pass by until the young lady composed herself. Dru squeezed Sarah's hand sympathetically and asked, "Should I call your mother or your maid?"

"No!" Sarah cried. "And please don't tell them you saw me like this."

"Of course not, if you don't wish it," said Dru. She waited a moment while Sarah struggled for control, then added gently, "If you tell me of your problem, perhaps I *can* help."

Sarah glanced at her, then returned her gaze to her hands. She felt an instinctive liking for Lady Duncan and was inclined to trust her, but they were little more than strangers. Nevertheless, Sarah's heart was so close to breaking that she hardly cared if the baron's wife told the duke himself. There came a time when unburdening oneself was more important than caution.

"I—I don't believe there's anything you can do, Lady Duncan," Sarah said finally. "It is only that I am most unhappy." As if to confirm her statement, fresh tears began to flow.

Dru put a comforting hand on the girl's shoulder. "But this won't do, you know. Your wedding day is drawing near, and you should be happier now than at any other time."

"That—that's why I am so unhappy," Sarah sobbed. "I am afraid of the duke, and he doesn't like me, and—and Gerry wants me to run away with him!"

"Gerry?" Dru asked, dumbfounded. "Who is he?"

"Gerry is my best friend," Sarah said, her chin wobbling. "We've planned to marry since we were children. But Mother and Father betrothed me to the duke without asking *me!* Weston is an unfeeling, monstrous . . . *old man* who is probably only marrying me for my fortune. He certainly doesn't love me, and I'll be unhappy forever if I wed him!"

Dru's mind reeled. She longed to comfort the young lady, but she was unfortunate enough to know that much of what Lady Sarah suspected was true. "Sometimes . . ." Dru said slowly, "sometimes love comes after marriage. And I am certain the duke is fond of you—"

"He doesn't show fondness for me in any fashion," Sarah disputed. "He won't grant me even normal civility; I cannot make the simplest comment without his contradicting it. Weren't you present when he cast aspersions upon my home last evening? Accusing our townspeople of avarice, indeed! I vow he's more guilty of that sin than they!"

You're probably correct, thought Dru, but Sarah needed encouragement, not confirmation. The duke *was* thoughtless in many ways, but Dru still found him a charismatic, exciting man. Surely Sarah felt *some* attraction for him; could part of her distress be caused by his apparent neglect? Dru hoped so, for if not, this marriage *would* be a sad one.

Perhaps she and Duncan were trying to save a wedding that shouldn't be taking place at all. She would do her best to find out. Lady Sarah's happiness was more important than the duke's financial welfare.

"This . . . Gerry," Dru said tentatively. "Do you love *him,* Lady Sarah?"

"Yes," Sarah said, sniffing. "I do love Gerry. I have told you, he's my best friend."

"Friendship alone is not the best reason for marriage. There should be something more . . ." Duncan appeared unbidden in her mind's eye, and Dru breathed deeply and continued, "Something more vital; an element of mystery, a compulsion to be in the other's presence. Do you experience this sort of excitement when you're with Gerry?"

"I am always happy to see him," Sarah answered after a moment.

Dru recognized an evasive answer when she heard one. With a little smile she asked softly, "How do you feel when you're with the duke?"

"My heart beats like a drum, but that's because I fear him."

At least she doesn't dislike him, Dru reflected. Perhaps what the girl interpreted as fear was the beginning of a sweeter and more powerful emotion. Dru recalled that, before learning the truth about her feelings for Duncan, there had been a time when she thought she feared him. "Promise you won't run away with Gerry; at least not until you tell me," Dru said decisively. "I want to help you, but you must be patient."

Sarah wiped her eyes with her handkerchief. "You won't tell anyone of our conversation, will you?"

"Not if you promise to wait. Have I your word?"

Without daring to hope, Sarah stared at Dru and wondered what that lady could be planning. At the very least, her agreement would delay having to make a decision. "I won't do anything until I speak with you," Sarah pledged.

While Dru was congratulating herself on a well-conducted interview, the duke sat motionless in the library next door. An article on the science of breeding superior racehorses lay open and unheeded on his lap. His face was expressionless, but a tumult of emotions boiled within his breast.

Call him *old,* did she? He was a *monstrous old man?* Did not regard her opinions? Was *uncivil?* Angrily he thought of a long list of ladies who had been proud to be courted by himself. They hadn't found him so terrible.

Who was Sarah Millbright to disparage *him?*

And who was this ruffian who thought to make away with his bride? If he lost Sarah, he would be ruined. He should find the devil and call him out. But a duel would cause scandal, and the Millbrights would frown upon that.

Feeling hamstrung, he raged silently for a moment; then his temper began to recede. He thought of his betrothed's pronouncements and snorted. Perhaps he *had* taken her too much for granted. As a duke, he was accustomed to others toadying to *him;* it was one of the more boring aspects of his life, but he had learned to expect it. Sarah had misinterpreted, thought him *unfeeling,* if it could be believed. Poor chit; maybe it was time to exert the charm for which he was known. It would be more sporting than fighting a lad, and far more respectable.

A glimmer appeared in his eye. Actually, the notion had the

feeling of a game. It was a wager he could make with himself: *I shall make her love me,* he decided.

By luncheon, Duncan had interviewed the household servants. In the role of restless guest, he wandered from room to room and isolated maids and footmen, the butler and the cook as they worked. Fortunately many of them unknowingly vouchsafed for one another's whereabouts on the day of the robbery. Lady Sarah's maid nervously assured him that she had watched her lady sleep the afternoon through—her mistress's headache was *that* bad—so Lady Sarah appeared out of the running as a suspect. The same could not be said for the marquess, however; a footman recalled seeing him walking upon the grounds; evidently it was a thing Lord Beasley did every afternoon.

Why had the marquess lied about sleeping in his room? In spite of Druscilla's protestations, Duncan had a bad feeling about the man.

But perhaps that was because Lord Beasley's ingratiating manners with ladies disgusted him, especially when those attentions were centered on his wife. Duncan remembered telling Druscilla to remain objective; should he not do the same? The task was not an easy one, especially when the marquess flirted outrageously with her as he did at luncheon. At one point Beasley boldly whispered something in her ear, and Duncan was surprised to see her nod solemnly in agreement. There was no opportunity afterward to ask what it was about, since Druscilla slipped away while his head was turned to attend Olivia's conversation.

He was beginning to regret his instructions to Druscilla about spending time with the marquess. She was following his directions a little too well for comfort.

After luncheon, while most of the others went upstairs to rest, Duncan took an umbrella from the stand in the hall and wandered outside. If the rains did not soon stop, they would all go mad.

It was a different world in the stables. He breathed in the earthy scents of horseflesh, straw, leather and wood and felt peaceful for the first time that day. The duke kept a fine stable; Druscilla's bay, Cinnamon, and his own grey, Kibo, were in good company among these proud steeds. He visited both horses, offered them lumps of sugar, and began questioning the grooms and stableboys.

Within moments he learned that four of the grooms had attended the picnic to mind the horses; the ones who remained had polished leather harnesses and saddles and cleaned the stables as they always did.

After watching them work a while longer, Duncan decided to return to the house. Druscilla might be in their chamber, and mayhap they could repair their disagreement. If only he could avoid Olivia . . .

Before re-entering the rain, he spotted a horse and rider approaching on the duke's long drive. A moment later the man rode swiftly into the stable, his saturated mount scattering clumps of earth in all directions. To avoid a mudbath, Duncan stepped backward from the doorway.

When the stranger saw the damage he caused, he said in a hearty voice, "So sorry!" He dismounted, flung his reins at the grooms, instructed them to give his beast an especially fine rubdown for carrying him in such weather, and walked toward Duncan with his hand outstretched. "I'm John Lyons," he said. "Didn't mean to splash you. This deuced downpour makes a man forget his manners."

Duncan shook his hand and introduced himself. Lyons was a giant of a man, standing taller than the baron himself, and had the look of a blond bear. Duncan knew the massive hand shaking his could easily have crushed his bones, but Lyons's grip was gentle.

After exchanging a few civilities, Duncan said, "I understand you've been exploring the Peak."

"Yes, had to get away. After a day or two in the drawing room, I start feeling like a zoo animal."

Duncan had often felt the same. "Do you ride every day?"

"Ride or shoot or climb or . . ." His face flaming a brilliant red, Lyons's attention shifted to something outside the stable.

To Duncan's consternation, Olivia entered. "John!" she cried, then tossed back her hood and shook raindrops from her umbrella. "I watched your arrival from my window. I wondered when you'd re—" Suddenly noticing Duncan, she flushed. "Oh! Lord Duncan!" For several instants she struggled for words, then dimpled prettily and laughed. "How fortunate to find both of you here. I declare I've never attended a house party with so many delightful guests!"

"And I wish you well of them," Lyons growled, and stalked out of the stable into the rain.

A look of genuine distress appeared on Olivia's face. She murmured a distracted excuse in Duncan's direction and ran after Lyons crying, "John! Wait!"

The baron, hearing the sound of laughter behind him, turned curiously.

Roger Trowell, the head groom, threw a brush at the offending stableboy. "Shut yer mouth," he said.

"Can't help it," the boy wheezed. "After treating him how she did, it's wot she deserves, ain't it?"

Roger glanced at the baron. "Not our place to say, Dipper."

More than interested, Duncan asked, "Has she wronged the gentleman?"

Sensing sympathy rather than censure at their speaking of a member of the Quality, Roger said warmly, "More'n a bit, my lord. Quite the flirt is she. Had Mr. Lyons wrapped around her finger, 'till she spoilt it with the marquess."

"Lord Beasley, do you mean?"

The groom nodded. "Promised to meet Mr. Lyons for a ride, she did. Came back early from the outing and everything, but went off with the marquess instead. Traded a real man for a dandy and thought she could get away with it. But Mr. Lyons, he saw 'em together in the summerhouse."

Duncan's pulse began to beat rapidly. "When did this happen?"

Roger squinted thoughtfully. "Last week, I think it was. Day of the picnic."

While the baron questioned the grooms further, Dru approached the duke's suite with some trepidation. It was not proper to enter a gentleman's chamber, but the opportunity for a private interview would probably not present itself otherwise—not with a houseful of guests. When the footman informed her that his grace was resting, she decided to risk it. However, she could not help feeling daunted by the look of disapproval in the servant's eye when, after receiving his grace's permission, he admitted her to the sitting room.

This intimate chamber contained several satinwood Adams chairs, a chaise longue, and a thick, plum-colored carpet. A small fire in the hearth dispelled the damp. The door to Weston's bedroom was closed. Dru took a chair beside the fire and prepared to wait.

She was dismayed when the duke appeared a moment later in an embroidered blue silk dressing gown, his hair in wild disarray. "Please forgive me for disturbing you," she said, embarrassed. "I didn't mean to awaken you."

Weston's eyes were not as chilly as she feared they would be, and she was heartened to see his lips quirk upward. "I awoke the instant before you came," he said gallantly. "May I offer you tea?"

"No, thank you, I shall stay only a moment. I have a personal matter to discuss concerning Lady Sarah."

"Lady Sarah," he said thoughtfully. "And here I had guessed you brought news of your investigation."

"Investigation?" she asked stupidly, her concentration drawn away by the puzzling look in his eyes. Why did he look so amused? Coming to herself, she said, "Oh! Of course, the investigation! Yes, it is proceeding well, I hope. But it is an unrelated matter which brings me here."

"You have come to speak of Lady Sarah," the duke prompted.

"Yes." She gave him a fleeting, worried glance, then began to fidget with the material of her skirt. "I hope you won't think I am meddling; I mean only to help." Not an auspicious beginning; why hadn't she given more thought to what she was going to say? And how could she offer advice to a duke without offending him? Clearing her throat, she said, "A wedding is—a very important day in a woman's life. Perhaps the most important."

The duke raised his eyebrows. "It's important to the man as well."

"Naturally that is so. But for a woman, the wedding day is something she anticipates all her life." Remembering her own ceremony, Dru's recent disagreement with Duncan receded, and her expression grew misty. "She knows her life is changing forever. No more will she be a daughter in her father's house; henceforth she will run her own household, perhaps become a mother. These things are wonderful but frightening. Yet the fears are easily overcome if the bride feels her husband loves and cherishes her."

"I believe you speak from experience," the duke said. "You make me envy Lord Duncan when I perceive your regard for him."

"It can be the same for you and Lady Sarah," she said earnestly. "It *should* be the same."

"I judge you feel Sarah and I don't possess a similar closeness," he said, his eyes twinkling. "Has my betrothed spoken with you about our relationship?"

"It is a thing I've observed," she said carefully.

Weston nodded. "Thank you, Lady Duncan, for your observations. You've helped me realize I must be more considerate of my bride's feelings if I wish her to think as highly of me as you do of your husband."

Elated, Dru rose from the chair. The interview had gone so much more easily than she'd anticipated. The duke was a gracious man in spite of his aloofness, and she hoped her efforts would make Lady Sarah happy.

Thinking he'd not had so much fun in an age, the duke escorted Lady Duncan to the door. How much better to let her believe she'd influenced him than to confess he'd eavesdropped in his own library instead of leaving the room as a better man would have done. And after observing that lady's loyalty to her spouse, he grew more eager to win Lady Sarah's affection. If he must wed, the experience might as well be as pleasant as possible.

At the corridor door, the duke bent to kiss Dru's hand, and she blushed and curtseyed. As she walked away, Weston turned to his footman and pressed a finger to his lips in an unmistakable gesture of silence demanded. The footman nodded and resumed his post.

None of the three saw the baron, who had for some minutes been wandering the house looking for his wife. He had just ascended the stairs when he caught sight of the affecting scene at the end of the corridor. Immediately he stepped around the corner and out of sight, his face white with shock.

Dru hurried to her chamber, straightened a few strands of hair that had escaped from Pizzy's bonds, and patted a small amount of rice powder on her cheeks. Her eyes were still shining from the satisfying talk with the duke.

Judging herself adequate for her next appointment, she rushed from the room and down the stairs to the conservatory. At luncheon the marquess had asked her to meet him there at three o'clock, and it was already a quarter past.

She hadn't entered the conservatory before, and at its threshold she stopped in amazement. The large, three-story structure was composed entirely of glass and supporting metal; plants were gathered into artistically arranged squares like a garden; wrought-iron benches were scattered here and there upon the white tiled floor.

The marquess left his examination of a miniature fountain and hurried toward her. "Isn't it wonderful?" he asked, seizing her hands. "The conservatory is a popular place on rainy days, and we're fortunate to have it to ourselves. I had hoped the others would be resting during the afternoon, and it appears they are."

Dru slowly withdrew her hands and began to walk. "The duke possesses many fine things," she said. "This room is astonishing."

Keeping pace with her, Beasley replied, "No more astonishing than you are. There's not a lady in residence who can surpass your beauty."

"You flatter me, sir," she said, barely keeping the annoyance from her voice. The marquess was likable in spite of his flirtatious nature, but he grew wearisome. Were it not for Duncan's command that she question him, she would rather be napping. "Isn't the duke's home extraordinary?" she went on. "Sometimes it seems unfair that one person should have so much. Do you not find it so?"

"I don't know; I'm quite fond of my cousin, and at least he enjoys his inheritance. That's what I'd do, if I had one worth speaking of!"

Beasley took her arm and urged her to sit. She did so reluctantly, and was further piqued to find how snugly he sat beside her. To compound matters, a large fern frond behind them poked her head every time she moved.

"Then you don't resent the fact that he possesses such a fortune?" she persisted, slapping the fern away.

"When I have so little, you mean?" he chuckled. "No, why should I? As long as I enjoy good friends, what need have I of material wealth?"

That's because those friends provide your living, Dru thought. To hide her disappointment, she shifted once again to contemplate the inconsiderate growth pattern of the fern.

Beasley gently turned her toward him. Before she could protest, he kissed her. Repulsed, Dru pushed him away and jumped to her feet.

"How could you?" she demanded indignantly.

He looked surprised. "This is not what you expected when I asked you here? I thought—well, since your husband appeared taken with Olivia—forgive me," he finished lamely.

He appeared so woebegone that Dru almost absolved him. "I am sorry if I misled you," she said with dignity.

"What goes on here?" came a voice from the doorway. To Dru's dismay, Olivia Wingate entered the room.

The marquess stood and stepped a few paces away from Dru. "Nothing goes on, Olivia; Lady Duncan and I have been admiring my cousin's indoor garden."

Olivia eyed him ironically. "Wouldn't have you, would she? Look to her husband and discover the reason."

"How very unkind," said the marquess. Somewhat snidely, he added, "Have you been *drinking,* Olivia?"

"If I have, what concern is it of yours?" she asked peevishly, approaching them with unsteady steps.

Beasley put a supporting hand on her arm. "Poor Olivia," he said. "Would John not forgive you?"

"No, he would not," she whimpered, and pressed her cheek to his lapel. In response, the marquess gave her a sympathetic embrace.

Happy to be forgotten, Dru murmured an excuse and slipped away.

"Ow!" cried Sarah as Myrtice jerked the brush through her hair.

"I'm sorry, my lady," said the maid. "I'm so nervous I don't know what I'm doing. His grace's invitation has got me feeling rushed, that's all. Why does he want to meet you alone for dinner, anyway?"

A half-hour earlier, a footman had delivered a message requesting Lady Sarah's exclusive company at dinner. She and the duke were to dine in the library.

"I am sure I don't know," Sarah replied. "I'll be too nervous to think of anything to say to him." But it was not an entirely unpleasant nervousness, and at least she would be able to cease thinking of Gerry for a little while.

Lord and Lady Millbright stopped by on their way to the dining room to exclaim over the unusual invitation. "He wants to know you better," declared the earl. "With all these people around, how else can you become acquainted if you don't isolate yourselves?"

A footman arrived to escort Sarah down at half-past six. She wore a yellow gown with a tight-fitting bodice topped by a fichu of billowing chantilly lace; matching lace extended from the long sleeves, and horizontal strips bordered the hem. It was a demure dress, but the colours complemented her complexion and hair. In spite of Myrtice's frowns, she felt confident of her appearance.

Entering the library, she saw a small round table had been placed near the fireplace. The table was covered in white linen and set with the duke's finest silver, crystal and china. A small vase of white roses served as the centerpiece.

The duke rose from the settee to greet her. He was dressed formally in a black jacket, blue waistcoat, and grey pantaloons. She thought he looked very fine, though intimidating in spite of the kind expression in his eyes. Sarah could not recall him looking kindly at her before, and she wondered if he was ill.

After seating Sarah at the table, Weston took the opposite chair and nodded to the footman, who immediately placed bowls of chilled chicken consommé before them. During the several removes which followed, the duke spoke politely of his properties in London and Bath and his goals for the High Ridgely farms; he paused often to ask Sarah's opinions on such matters as tenant housing and the need for refurbishment of the downstairs rooms. Sarah felt inadequate to venture answers, but when her first attempts were encouraged rather than spurned, she found that she did indeed have opinions and offered them with increasing confidence.

"When my father rebuilt our worker's cottages, the farmers' production increased," she said at one point. "There seems to be less sickness among the families, too. Father says that a happy worker is more loyal."

"I agree that such action is humane, and I've often heard of similar good results," he said. "At the time of my father's death, I had intended to update the cottages. Somehow I never got around to it."

Without thinking, Sarah said, "I imagine it is difficult to remember such things while enjoying London."

Weston's face immediately became unreadable, and Sarah's eyes widened in dismay. She'd probably made him angry. And why should she feel so crushed if she had? Assuring herself it was merely against her nature to give offense, she whispered, "Forgive me, your grace. I didn't mean anything."

Sarah was relieved to see the duke's expression soften. "I think perhaps you did," he said. "And you're correct; I *have* neglected my duties for love of the cards. I've no excuse to offer, other than the fact that I continue a family trait. The Weston line has ever enjoyed the pleasures of gaming, though perhaps not to the extent my father and I have. Had you heard of my sire, Lady Sarah?"

"I know only that my father respected him for his generosity to the Retired Minister's Fund," she answered.

Weston blinked in surprise. "Er—yes. He was an excellent man. He had a manner about him which drew people, as did my mother. Together, they were . . . magical. The two of them spent much of their time with the London set." Weston's eyes lost focus. "I think I was something of an unexpected intrusion in their lives."

Visualizing a sad little boy left alone, Sarah said, "No, that cannot be. They must have loved you deeply."

"Oh, certainly they did," he said, returning to the present. "I don't mean to indicate otherwise. But my father and I didn't begin to enjoy a true relationship until I was grown. And we were never more companionable than in the midst of a wager of some sort."

The footman placed a dish of stuffed trout in front of Sarah. She picked up her fork and said, "Then it was your father who began your love of gambling?"

"Oh, no, don't think so for one moment. I was gaming by my Eton days. It's in our blood." His gaze dropped to his fish, and he began to slice it with surprising vehemence. "In point of fact, it was a wager that killed my father. One of his friends challenged him to race to the summit of Dove's Rest; you can see it from the window there. Father had climbed it many times, but on this occasion he slipped." Weston took a sip of wine; he seemed to have trouble swallowing. "My mother didn't live long afterward; she never recovered from the loss."

Sarah slowly replaced the fork on her plate. "That is the saddest story I've ever heard," she said. Tears began to spill down her cheeks.

Somehow the tears flowed not only for the heartbroken, doomed Lady Weston, but for herself. She thought of Gerry; she thought of the duke; she wished for a love so strong she could not survive without it. In a moment she was sobbing uncontrollably.

Aghast, the duke rushed to her side and led her to the settle. The footman looked to be as distraught as Sarah herself and paced uncertainly between the table and serving cart while wiping his eyes and nose on his sleeve. Weston irritably waved him from the room.

"There, there, Lady Sarah," said the duke, and hesitantly placed an arm across her shoulders. "I didn't mean to upset you so. All of this happened a long time ago; please don't cry."

Why the devil had he even mentioned his parents, he thought miserably. He'd meant to charm Lady Sarah, not destroy her. He'd planned to draw her out, make her feel valued for her thoughts; it was an approach that always won feminine hearts. Instead, led astray by a pair of wide, innocent eyes, he'd rambled off course into personal matters. And to what results? Disaster!

When he saw Sarah's handkerchief had become soaked through, he offered his own. "I—I am sorry," she said, taking it and wiping her eyes. "It is not your fault. I seem to cry at every opportunity of late." She attempted to laugh. "It is a shame to waste so much water. Next time I shall try to weep over a vase, or a flowerpot."

There should not be a next time, Weston reflected, and felt an unfamiliar constriction in his chest. Tenderly he placed a finger beneath Sarah's chin and nudged her face upward. Even a torrent of weeping hadn't destroyed her beauty, he noted. Her skin hadn't gone all splotchy and red, and her lips were fascinating. Why had he never before noticed how expressive her mouth was, and how eminently kissable?

What would the strictly-raised Lady Sarah do, he wondered, should he kiss her?

Before caution could restrain him, he leaned forward and pressed his lips to hers. He was conscious of a sweet, yielding softness that made him long to possess the girl completely. He wished to show her, gently and with an aching slowness, the pleasures of a man and woman together. At the same time he knew an overwhelming desire to protect her happiness.

Astonished at these unfamiliar feelings, he pulled back and stared into her eyes.

Sarah returned his gaze with equal wonder. When she saw he meant to kiss her, her first impulse had been to run from the room. She was glad she hadn't, for the experience had been quite agreeable. But now her emotions were in a greater muddle than ever, and she dropped her eyes in confusion.

Misreading her expression, Weston said slowly, "If it's our approaching marriage which brings you so often to tears, Lady Sarah, then I'll release you. I cannot make you so unhappy."

The duke straightened. Had he really said those words? Was

he run mad? Looking intently at Sarah, he thought perhaps he was.

Sarah felt her stomach tighten. Here was an easy escape. She would be free to marry Gerry without hindrance, for her parents could not force her to wed the duke if he didn't want to marry her. Perhaps the kiss had made him realize how little he cared. It was rather a pity, however, now that his former, forbidding manner had seemed to disappear. He had been so interesting at dinner and had made her feel very adult, especially when seeking her opinions on running his estate. Gerry never asked her anything. And Gerry had never kissed her like that.

Sarah's eyes began to sting. "I've always believed that love should be the basis for marriage," she said.

"Perhaps you've formed an attachment for someone else," said the duke, gritting his teeth.

"What? Oh . . . no," said Sarah, startled to hear herself. Gerry's familiar face seemed to float before her eyes. She did love him; she would always love him. But in the past hour with the duke, she had felt a great stirring in her heart, as though she were about to embark on an exciting, unknown journey.

Could her parents have been right after all? How painful to think so, especially after she had decided to rebel.

"There's no one else," she said finally.

The duke watched her hopefully. "If you are looking for love," he said, "I believe you will find it here." And if it was too soon to lay claim to that worthy emotion, Weston reflected, he soon would. He knew it as surely as he felt doom, entrapment, foreboding, and dawning exultation claim his feelings, one after the other.

Sarah's face began to glow. Unwilling to raise unrealistic dreams, the duke said, "I warn you, I am not good as you are. Others have called me proud, uncaring, wicked, and a wastrel." Gloomily he added, "I am trying to be better."

"I cannot believe you deserve such unkind epithets," said Sarah, forgetting she had called him a rake.

Enjoying her defense of him, he said humbly, "At the very least, I must be named improvident, rash, or—or inconstant."

"It is the future that matters, not the past," she asserted.

Trembling, Sarah placed her hand in his.

Dru made her excuses to the others and retired to her room by nine-thirty, but it was nearing eleven before she ceased looking out the window and went to bed. She hadn't seen Duncan since luncheon and was frightened and angry. They often had disagreements—she was volatile, she had to admit, and perhaps not easy to live with—but never had he gone off for hours without telling her where he was.

At dinner she'd been forced to fabricate a story about him visiting an old friend in a nearby village. The marquess and Olivia had exchanged glances and given her falsely commiserative looks the entire evening through.

Before going upstairs, Dru had checked the stables and found Kibu was missing. Now she imagined all sorts of things. Perhaps Duncan had fallen and was lying in a ditch. Maybe he'd discovered the identity of the robber and had been shot.

But her thoughts kept returning to their argument. Duncan had been disappointed in her. He was probably so tired of her jealousy that he wished to be rid of her. She would *have* to curb her feelings, rein them in like a runaway horse.

Yet as the hours ticked by, she grew angrier. Nothing except an accident could excuse him now. By midnight she was distraught enough to rise from bed and light a candle in order to dress. She decided to saddle Cinnamon and search for Duncan. It would be better than lying awake all night.

And then she heard the sound of Duncan's step outside the door, and she sat abruptly on the bed, relief making her knees weak. When he entered the room, she sprang to her feet again.

"Where have you been? You're soaked through and covered with mud!" she exclaimed.

"So it would appear," he said, and began removing his outer clothing. "Is there water here? It's too late to disturb the servants."

"There's a full pitcher behind that screen, but it is cold," she said impatiently. "What has happened, Duncan? I've been so worried!"

"Have you?" he asked tonelessly. He went into the dressing room and returned with his robe, then retreated behind the screen. Muddy clothing soon appeared on the edge of the divider, and little splashing sounds could be heard.

Dru walked around the screen. At the sight of his tall, lean, muscular body, she felt her indignation melt away.

Duncan looked up from the basin. Wordlessly, he wrapped a towel around his waist and returned her to the other side.

"Well, I beg pardon!" she huffed. "You didn't used to be so nice, sir!" She crossed her arms and plopped onto the bench at the dressing table. It was all she intended to say until he spoke; *she* could play the silence game as well as he.

A short while later he emerged, tightening the sash of his robe. His eyes flashed in her direction. "I wouldn't cast aspersions if I were you. At least *I* can be trusted to honor my vows."

Dru's heart turned to stone. "Whatever can you mean by that remark?"

"Did you think I wouldn't know? I saw him kiss you."

"You *did?*" Dru visualized the open expanses of the conservatory. Had Duncan hidden among the ferns? "How did you manage that?"

"How? She's concerned with *how!*" he said dramatically, addressing the gilted mirror over the mantel as he would an audience. "Notice she doesn't offer explanations! Druscilla forgets that detecting is my vocation, but even so, anyone could have spied her leaving his bedroom as brazenly as brass!"

"His *bedroom!*" Dru cried. "Oh! Of which kiss are you speaking?"

An ominous silence fell. "Of which kiss are *you* speaking?" Duncan asked grimly.

Enraged, they glared at one another for a long length of time. And then the silliness of the misunderstanding struck Dru, and she began to giggle helplessly. Naturally her laughter only increased his wrath, and seeing it, she became quite overcome.

When her amusement showed no signs of abating, he said, "Enjoy yourself, madam. I shall sleep in the dressing room."

"Oh, no, you will not," Dru gasped, dashing tears from her eyes. She then proceeded to recount her afternoon's activities, though she was discreet about her time with the duke, telling Duncan only that a private matter concerning Lady Sarah had caused the interview. She had, after all, promised to keep the girl's secret.

He was not entirely appeased. "You should never go into a gentleman's bedroom, no matter how refined or safe you think he is. And certainly not into the room of someone of Weston's reputation and, er—person."

"We were in his sitting room only, and his manners were impeccable," she said, adding meekly, "But I shan't ever do that again, Duncan."

"See that you don't," he said gravely. "And as to this Beasley business . . . I'm beginning to think the method of inquiry endangers you. You're too young and beautiful to speak privately with gentlemen without their misconstruing the situation."

"You are jealous," Dru accused, and caught her lips between her teeth to prevent further expressions of delight.

"I suppose I am," he admitted. "And I thank you for not reminding me that I recently scolded you for behaving similarly."

Dru *had* been about to remind him, but instead she said airily, "Oh, you mean the awful Olivia. After this afternoon's experience in the conservatory, I can only pity her relentless pursuit of men. But I must admit it was *your* attention to *her* which disturbed me."

In a sudden movement that was almost frightening, he gripped her arms firmly, pulled her from the chair, and walked her steadily backward until her spine was against the wall. "You're the only woman I shall ever love," he said, his face a heartbeat from hers. "Therefore, I am reclaiming these lips."

His kiss left her breathless. "Duncan . . ." she whispered. "Do not . . . I must tell you . . ."

He braced his hands on the wall on either side of her head and murmured impatiently, "Tell me what?"

"I think there was a connection between John Lyons and Olivia, and another attachment between her and the marquess. I don't know if it means anything."

"This deuced case," he sighed. "There's no getting your mind off it. I know about the liaisons, and that Olivia and the marquess were together during part of the afternoon of the robbery. Before Olivia arrived from the picnic, the marquess's whereabouts are unknown. He had ample time to rob his cousin."

"So he lied about being in his room," she mused. "But that was probably to protect Olivia. I simply cannot believe he did it." She looked up defensively. "I don't think he has the will necessary to carry out any sort of plan, Duncan, even a robbery. He seems content to drift along."

"That may be what he wishes us to think," Duncan said, tracing his finger up and down her cheek. "We're at an impasse, Druscilla; tomorrow I'll ask the duke to get everyone away from the house so that we can search the rooms. But the rain could delay us a few days."

"Speaking of the rain . . ." She paused to kiss his finger. "Where were you this evening?"

"After I saw you with the duke, I went for a long ride while I contemplated the ethics of calling out my employer."

"Please say you never considered such a thing!"

"I did. However, my murderous thoughts were lost when I came upon a coach stuck in the mud. The west road has flooded just before it meets the bridge; the driver turned off at the last moment to avoid the waters. We struggled a long while to free the wheels, but had to abandon it when one of them broke. I helped shuttle the passengers to a posting house." He pulled a face. "The Golden Duck, it is called, and specializes in lamb stew you could float a rock in. The grateful passengers insisted I remain for supper and an evening of dart-throwing. It was just what I needed to return me to sanity."

Dru attempted to turn her laugh into a less offensive sound. "My—my poor dear," she hummed, and touched his hair with shaking fingers.

A very wicked glint came into his eyes. "Laugh at me, will you? You would do better to say your prayers, young lady."

Some time later, her eyes closed in ecstasy, Dru did precisely that.

The slowing of the rain became the main topic of interest on the following day. For whole long minutes the rain would cease entirely, only to begin again. As the day progressed, the spells of dry patches lengthened until Tobias was moved to wander into the various receiving rooms and utter, "Luncheon is now ready in the small dining parlour; chipped beef in wine sauce is the especial feature of the day, along with apricot pudding and fruit compote; all will be served without rain."

The Duke of Weston, whose attention was halfway engaged by his reluctant but virtuous study of the steward's yearly report, was less astonished than he would normally have been at his butler's attempt at humor. The duke set aside the report in relief, walked to the library windows, and said, "You're right, Toby." His gaze shifted in John's direction; his friend shuffled and re-shuffled a deck of cards with stony concentration. "It's a pity the ground is too wet for outdoor activities though. We all grow restless."

Sarah looked up from her embroidery, glanced from the handsome duke to her parents, who were reading quietly to one another at a table in the corner, and thought, *I am too happy to be restless.*

After luncheon, Sarah sought out Dru and begged her company for a few moments. Dru, who didn't know whether to be alarmed or encouraged by the girl's excited manner, followed her upstairs to Sarah's bedchamber and was urged to sit in one of several Queen Anne chairs surrounding the fireplace.

Sarah sat in the chair closest to her and smiled shyly. "I wish to thank you for your patience with me yesterday when I was so upset," she said. "I am sorry for being such a bother. And thank you especially for offering to help me resolve the difficulties which troubled me."

"It was no bother," said Dru, easily dismissing the argument with Duncan which had resulted from her little *tête-à-tête* with the duke. Had not the reconciliation been worth it? "I am happy to assist in any way I can."

"Well, that's why I wished to see you immediately, before you *did* go to any bother," Sarah said, and lowered her head, not entirely disguising the faraway look in her eyes. "It is no longer necessary, you see. I tried to speak with you last evening, but you'd gone to bed by the time Artemis and I finished with dinner."

Dru, who had begun to fear the girl had decided to run away with her childhood friend after all, found her flagging spirits suddenly caught by this name. *"Artemis?"* she asked meaningfully.

"He asked me to call him that," said Sarah, blushing like a rose. "We had such a nice time over dinner, Lady Duncan; for the first time I learned a little about him. He was so— so—"

"Attentive?" supplied Dru teasingly. "Fascinating?"

"Yes, those too," Sarah giggled. "But more importantly, forthcoming. I now understand he wears his cold manner like a mask. Behind the facade is a very fine man. I've decided to marry him after all."

"Sarah!" Dru exclaimed. "I am most happy for you." And could not help feeling a heady sense of power. *I must have made a greater impression on the duke than I thought!* But a wave of concern for the girl prompted her to say, "This is a large transformation in a short time. Your background and the duke's are so different. Did Weston promise to alter his behavior?" Meaning, *Did he lie to you?*

"I cannot pretend to believe life with Artemis will be as soft as I've dreamed," Sarah confessed. "He has a few shortcomings in his character, and I don't believe these will change overnight. Perhaps they never will. I am not even sure I love him yet. But he—he *intrigues* me so. He stirs me in ways I never dreamed. And I'll admit to you, Lady Duncan, that my interest was caught long before last evening. It is only his reciprocation that has released my own feelings."

"And you don't have the same feelings for your friend?"

She shook her head sadly. "Gerry seems like a child to me now. And I am too comfortable with Gerry." Her eyes became startled. "Is that what love is? A lack of comfort? A feeling of unbalance?"

"There can even be pain," said Dru, offering the vast experience of several months of marriage. "But I believe comfort comes later; a different sort of comfort, though; the kind which results only after weathering the storms of youthful love."

"I rather like those storms," Sarah said wistfully. "I hope they never fade."

Dru admitted she felt the same and, looking at her pocket watch, recalled she was to meet her husband shortly.

"Well, I thank you again, Lady Duncan," Sarah said, and accompanied Dru to the door. "I appreciate your willingness to help, even though you didn't have to do anything after all."

"Think nothing of it," Dru beamed. "And for pity's sake, please call me by my given name. You make me feel so old."

After she closed the door, Sarah walked to the window, hug-

ging herself and sighing deeply. Though the sun had appeared
briefly at luncheon, churning, boiling clouds now darkened the
sky. A great wind had risen and blew knots of straw, gorse,
heather, and barley across the green. Young trees and the sodden flowers in the garden knelt toward the ground; hefty gusts
shook at the shutters and tore at the eaves. Something rattled
across the gutters and fell; she hoped it was not a small animal
or bird. Shuddering slightly, she pulled the draperies closed.

Deciding not to call Myrtice, she walked toward the dressing
room to exchange her morning dress for a nightgown. Sarah
had been too excited to sleep much last night—had even kept
Myrtice awake with her newfound hopes—and now she needed
a nap.

Several paces short of the closet door, she stopped Perhaps
it was the sound of the lonely wind calling outside, or perhaps
her weary ears deceived her, but she thought she heard noises
within the closet—noises like voices, whispering angrily.

Was High Ridgely not only besieged by forbidding weather,
but haunted as well? She would ask Artemis. Immediately.
Turning cautiously, Sarah began to retreat.

When she felt a rush of air behind her, like that of a door
opening and closing, Sarah broke into a run. She heard no
sound of someone or something chasing her, however, and
couldn't resist looking back when she reached the safety of
the door.

"Gerry!" she squeaked.

"Yes, it is only Gerry," said her visitor dismally. "Comfortable, childish, unexciting Gerry."

"Oh, my dear," Sarah said, her heart aching at his expression. "You heard everything." She went to him and touched
his sleeve. "Come, sit down and tell me why you're here."

"It's obvious, isn't it? You didn't send a message, so I came
to you. Thought you'd be ready to fly away with me. Thought
you'd be sick to death of Lord Lofty-Head." He leaned his
elbows on his thighs and looked at the floor. "Shows how
wrong a fellow can be."

"Oh, Gerry, I am so very sorry. More than anything, I regret your learning about my decision in this way. But how did you come to be in my closet?"

The young man thought rapidly. He could hardly say he'd spent the night in the maid's room and waited until luncheon to creep downstairs and hide.

"I hid in the cellar last evening," he said, not meeting her eyes. "Then I found my way to your dressing room while everyone was at luncheon."

"How did you know which room was mine?"

Gerry reddened, then said defensively, "Why so many questions? Oh, I suppose you're worried the duke might hear there's been a man in your bedroom. His manner would become less pleasing then, I daresay. Wonder if it would be worth my spreading the rumor?"

"Gerry!"

His gaze dropped to his boots. "All right," he said miserably. "I won't say anything. I trust I know when to cry quits."

Sarah blinked rapidly. "I hope you will always remain my dear friend, Gerry."

He gave her a deep look. "We cannot have everything, old girl." When this comment was met with a heavy silence, he said, "Oh, don't cry, princess. Maybe one day when I have my pride back . . . for now, I must go. Why don't you look to make certain nobody's in the hallway? Can't ruin the duchess's reputation."

Sarah nodded and walked to the door. Finding the corridor empty, she closed the door again and gave him a tearful embrace. Before releasing him, she said, "Gerry, just before you left the dressing room, I thought I heard voices."

"Oh that," he said, and edged away, waving his hand dismissively. "You're aware the closet door opens into the corridor. After your visitor left, I was so hurt I almost decided to leave without talking with you. Just as I opened the door, two servants walked by disagreeing about—about who had duty at dinner, I believe. It must've been them you heard."

It wasn't a bad lie, he felt, and was much better than confessing he and Myrtice were arguing about how to make Sarah run away with him, and that Myrtice had left in a huff.

"But that door is always locked, and my abigail has the key," Sarah said, frowning.

"Well, this time she didn't," he said irritably. "The key was in the lock." When Sarah continued to stare at him, he cried, "What do you want me to say, Sarah? That I was talking to myself?"

She patted his arm. "Now *that* I *can* believe. Goodby, dear friend. I *do* love you."

"Yes," he said sadly. "Like you would a dog."

A brief knock sounded at the bedroom door, and before either of them could react, Myrtice entered carrying a tea tray. With her eyes downcast, the maid said, "Begging your pardon, Lady Sarah, but someone in the kitchen told me Lady Duncan was visiting, and I thought you might like a cup of tea."

Myrtice looked up then and saw Gerry without surprise. For one long moment, the three of them stood as still as actors in a tableau. Sarah became pale; Gerry's face flushed in splotches; Myrtice returned her gaze to the tray.

"Excuse me, my lady," said the maid.

"Myrtice, it is not what you think," Sarah said wretchedly.

"Why are you here?" Gerry demanded.

"I know you wouldn't do nothing wrong, neither of you," Myrtice said quietly. "Don't you worry about me telling anyone, Lady Sarah. Looks to me like you two was saying goodbye. Why don't you have a cup of tea before you part, since I've already brought it?"

Gerry gave the maid a hard, searching look. She felt it and glanced up defiantly. An instant later, she looked away.

"Very well," Sarah said faintly, and gestured toward the wing chairs by the fireplace. "Have a cup of tea, Gerry, before you leave."

The young man didn't move, but when Sarah sat down and looked at him curiously, he slowly followed.

Myrtice pulled a small walnut table directly between the two chairs and set down the tray. Bending over it, she poured steaming liquid into a porcelain cup painted with blue roses.

Gerry watched her every movement. He was conscious of the sweet smell of freshly-washed hair.

"Here you are, my lady," Myrtice said, breaking the strange silence which had fallen over them. "Two lumps of sugar and a double measure of cream; just as you like it." She set the cup on the tray before Sarah, who nodded at Myrtice to continue pouring.

"Your tea, sir," the maid said a moment later. "I remembered you like one lump and a twist of lemon." She placed the cup in Gerry's hands, her eyes drilling his.

He looked at his cup, then Sarah's, which still rested on the table. Reluctantly he returned his gaze to Myrtice. Handing his cup back, he said, "I would like cream also."

"But you don't take cream," Myrtice protested.

His mouth tightened. "My taste for tea has changed," he said. "Cream, if you please, Myrtice."

The maid took his cup, replaced it on the tray and lifted the cream pitcher over it, her hands shaking. The pitcher suddenly slipped from her fingers to the floor and shattered.

"Myrtice, what is wrong with you?" Sarah cried.

"I'm sorry, my lady," Myrtice said, wiping at the stained carpet with a cloth. "I'll have to go to the kitchen for more. Please forgive me." She rushed toward the door and cast a pleading look in their direction as she left.

"I cannot understand it," Sarah said, reaching for her cup. "She's acting so oddly."

"Don't drink that," Gerry said.

"Pardon?" asked Sarah, an uncertain smile tugging at her lips. "Did you say something?"

Moisture dotted Gerry's forehead. He couldn't explain what he thought Myrtice had in mind. Though he was certain the maid didn't plan murder, he had to prevent Sarah from drinking. Would another broken dish arouse her suspicions?

"Trade with me," he said suddenly.

Sarah laughed. "Trade?"

"Yes. My cup for yours."

"But I despise lemon."

"Wait for a new cup then. I'm very thirsty."

Sarah looked at him strangely. After a moment she said, "Oh, very well. Here."

Sighing deeply, Gerry accepted her cup and placed his on the tray. "Thank you," he said, and stared at the tan-coloured liquid as though it were poison.

"Well?" Sarah's eyebrows lifted. "Aren't you going to drink it?"

"I beg pardon?"

"You said you were thirsty. You have confiscated my tea, and now you won't drink it."

"Oh." A tiny muscle in his eyelid began to quiver. Sweat dripped down the sides of his face. He gave a garish imitation of a smile, lifted the cup to his lips and swallowed twice.

"Better?" she queried.

He replaced the cup on the table as carefully as he would handle a loaded pistol. "Much better, I thank you."

A sudden, loud knocking was heard at the door. "Message for Lady Sarah from his grace," announced a nasal voice.

Sarah and Gerry stared at one another in terror for an instant, then both dashed to their feet. "Go into the dressing room, Gerry," she hissed, then rushed toward the door and called, "Wait one moment!" turned, saw the tea paraphernalia, and returned to Gerry's side, all before he had moved more than a pace toward the closet. She whispered furiously, "Drink your tea and and take the cup with you!"

"God knows I cannot," he said desperately.

"Then give it to me and I'll drink it; we cannot have another spill, and the footman mustn't see two cups!"

"No, I'll take it. I won't . . . spill it." Gerry began walking toward the dressing room. A wave of dizziness stilled him momentarily, then passed. He looked at the cup, then at Sarah, who watched him with frantic urgency. *Don't dare to spill it,* she seemed to say.

At that moment the closet door opened, and Myrtice stood on the threshold carrying a pitcher of milk on a golden salver. Gerry supposed she must have seen the footman and entered through the dressing room. He glanced back at Sarah to see if she understood the implications, but the young lady only widened her eyes with impatience.

A pleasant weakness washed over him then, and tea sloshed onto the saucer. He *was* going to spill it after all. Sarah needn't worry, though; the footman probably wouldn't notice. Why would the servant care if there was a stain? No more than he himself would care if he drank the tea and fell into a thousand-year slumber. And if he did? No one would miss him. Well, perhaps his mother and Elizabeth would, and Myrtice, for he was her ticket; but certainly not Sarah, who had been destined to be his from the beginning of time, if only she knew it.

He looked at Myrtice, his eyes shining defiantly. With great deliberation he drained the cup, walked into the dressing room, and pulled the door shut behind them. "I've just finished Sarah's tea," he whispered, and laughed carelessly.

"You never! Oh, God, say it's not so!"

A gentle fog was beginning to descend, but he was alert enough to feel a distant alarm at her distress. Perhaps he had been wrong. "Was it . . . poison?" he asked, his voice cracking a little.

"No, you fool, but the milk had enough laudanum to make her sleep for a day at least!"

The closet was small and growing smaller; moreover, it had an annoying tendency to spin. To steady the room, Gerry propped one hand against a shelf. "Why, Myrtice?"

"I figured if I got her to sleep, you would be willing to take her away tonight. We could've made it to the border before she woke up. By then the duke wouldn't want her no more.

Everything would've been perfect if you'd let me do things my way!"

Gerry rubbed his eyes. "I could never have taken her unwillingly. You . . . should know that much . . . about me."

"Then you're a bigger idiot than I thought. And now look at you, tottering on your feet! What's to do when someone finds a man sleeping in the closet?"

Gerry eased himself to his knees. "You must . . . help me, Myrtice. Help me get away. Cannot . . . ruin Sarah."

"Well, I can't, Master Gerry. You've forced my hand and I've got myself to look after. Once Lady Sarah finds out I tried to dram her I'll be in too much trouble to stay here."

He groaned. "I never thought . . . forgive me. What will you do?"

"I've planned for trouble, never fear. A wise girl has to, if she's got nobody to do it for her."

The carpet was calling to him, and he sank toward it. The hems of dresses and pelisses caressed his face like tender leaves. Everything smelled of Sarah. He peered upward, tried to find Myrtice's face. "The baby . . ."

"Don't trouble your head about it," she said pityingly, throwing things into a portmanteau. "There's no baby, though there would've been one soon, if you'd got me that cottage. I had to lie to make you fight for Lady Sarah. We'd of had a nice future, had it worked."

"No . . . baby," he said wonderingly, and closed his eyes.

"I was really very fond of you, Master Gerry," Myrtice said, and knelt to kiss him on the lips, then hurried away.

Not long after, Sarah finished writing her answer to the duke's note and gave it to the footman. Would she join him for dinner again that evening? Artemis had written. And, What is your favourite colour? She was urged to wear something in that hue, for he meant the table linens and flowers to match. Further, *he* would choose a cravat or shirt in the same colour, provided her chosen shade was not *pink*. Sarah chuckled and thought it all very romantic, but would have enjoyed it more had she not known Gerry waited in the closet.

She gave the footman ample time to be away before entering the dressing room. She smiled at the sight of Gerry sleeping; obviously his spirit was not too wounded. But when he did not answer her soft entreaties to awaken, she bent and shook him. His head lolled back, exposing a white face; his body remained limp; she was not sure he even breathed.

Stifling a scream, she thought, *Where is Myrtice?* The abigail had been in the dressing room only moments ago. Never had anyone been so needed.

In spite of her panic, a certain incongruity struck Sarah forcibly. How had Myrtice come to enter the dressing room? If the key had been inside the closet as Gerry said, how had the maid known the corridor door was open? When Myrtice realized her key was missing, wouldn't she have used the bedroom entrance? But if she knew the closet door was open, she had to know Gerry was inside . . .

Sarah saw the empty cup and saucer lying askew on the floor beside Gerry. She was reminded of the broken pitcher, and Gerry's insistence on drinking her tea. Her eyes darkened with speculation.

Sarah slowly stood to her feet, horror sweeping through her soul like a keening wind.

The baron and his wife were preparing for an afternoon of socializing and inquiry when they heard a furious knocking at their door. Dru opened it and discovered a very distraught Sarah.

"Please, Lady Dunc—Druscilla," Sarah chattered. "You must come with me." Spying Duncan in the background, she added, "Alone, I beg you."

Dru could not refuse, and within moments she was kneeling beside Gerry while Sarah explained, her words flowing as disjointedly as her thoughts.

"And I cannot tell Artemis, not when we are becoming so close, and my parents would slay me, do you think Gerry will live, he's so still, so pale, Myrtice must be mad, trying to poison me, and I've never been in so much trouble in my life!" concluded Sarah.

"I think Gerry will be all right," Dru said, pulling herself to her feet. "Surely if he'd taken poison, he would be violently ill, perhaps dead. I believe he's had a dose of sleeping powders. My sister used to suffer headaches and occasionally used them; her sleep would be unnaturally deep like this."

"Thank God," Sarah said. "But—but what shall I do with him until he wakes up? My parents often visit me during the day; they are bound to discover him."

Dru thought for a moment, then said, "I believe we'd better take Duncan into our confidence." When Sarah protested, Dru continued, "No, he'll be discreet when he understands the matter. There's naught else to do unless you wish to leave Gerry here; I am not strong enough to carry him, are you?"

"Oh, I suppose you're right," Sarah groaned. "But promise you won't tell your husband I considered running away with Gerry. Please?"

"I'll say only that he's an old friend who came to bid you goodby," Dru said.

But Duncan wasn't so easily fooled. "Are you certain there's been no impropriety between these two?" he asked Dru when she returned to their room. "You're asking me to walk in a grey area, Druscilla. I've been employed by the duke to solve a mystery which will ensure his wedding. If Lady Sarah is no longer pure, shouldn't I warn him?"

"How prudish you sound!" she snapped. "Weston is my employer also, and at no time have I heard him ask us to guard his bride's virtue. But as to that, I am certain she still possesses her *purity,* as you call it. Just as I am positive I do not."

"You are become very wicked, my sweet," he said.

"And who is responsible for that, I wonder?"

"Very well," he said, feigning defeat. "I shall do as you ask."

Sarah was too embarrassed to look at the baron when he entered her chamber. After she led him to Gerry, Duncan agreed with Dru's diagnosis, though he thought it wise to find the maid. "Have you searched for her?" he asked Sarah. "Since we cannot rouse him at all, there's a small chance he's been given an overdose. He's hardly more than a lad and weighs little."

"She's gone," Sarah answered worriedly. "My largest portmanteau is missing, along with several articles of clothing."

"I'll look for her as soon as we move your friend to our dressing room. No one will find him there if we give Druscilla's maid a holiday."

Instructing them to guard the two turnings of the hallway between their respective chambers, Duncan hoisted Gerry onto his shoulder and carried him easily to their bedroom. The two ladies quickly made a pallet on the floor and covered Gerry with blankets.

"Keep trying to awaken him," Duncan said, then headed for the stables. Firing questions, he learned none of the horses were missing; but the muck-boy admitted seeing a woman hurrying along the west road. Duncan saddled Kibu and rode off in pursuit.

Fortunately it hadn't rained again, but the windy conditions caused Kibu to snort and balk nervously. Duncan was forced to go slower than he liked; even so, it was not long before he spotted the maid walking briskly toward the bridge.

The winds had dried much of the water off the road since yesterday, but no one had rescued the abandoned carriage yet. He saw Myrtice look into its interior as she passed; finding nothing of interest, she hurried on her way.

Evidently she didn't expect to be followed, for she never looked back. Duncan's approach was further disguised by the noise of the wind. When he hailed her, she nearly dropped the portmanteau in surprise.

"Don't walk upon that bridge!" Duncan called. "The rains may have weakened it!"

She looked at him with a desperate expression, hugged the bag closer to her body and rushed on. Duncan tapped his heels into Kibu's sides, and the horse lunged forward.

When he reached the wooden bridge, Duncan dismounted, threw Kibu's reins around one of the landed posts, and started across. Myrtice was nearing the other side; she glanced over her shoulder and gave a little scream when she saw him. "It's no use running!" he cried. "We know what you've done! The question is, *why?*"

"Why?" she shouted over the roar of the river. "Can't you figure it out?"

"You were jealous of your lady, is that what you mean?" he asked, continuing to walk toward her.

"Me? Jealous of Lady Proper? Not a bit!" She edged backward, her eyes fixed on him. But 'twas my turn to have something! Why can't I never have anything but work?"

Her answers were incomprehensible. Duncan's steps faltered. And then, without warning, one of the center pilings cracked and fell inward, pulling the middle span toward the river. Duncan fell with it, clinging desperately to his end of the bridge as he submerged. He fought and kicked his way upward, managed to keep his grip on the wood though the current tore at him. He shook the water from his eyes and saw Myrtice clinging to the other side, but the struggle to hold onto the portmanteau was too much for her strength. Screaming in rage, she finally released it and pulled herself to safety on the opposite bank.

"I couldn't help it!" she cried to him, then crouched and reached her hands beseechingly toward the bag, which had wedged itself between two boards of the bridge. "They was so beautiful and there for the asking!"

Realizing at last that she could not retrieve the portmanteau, she rose and wiped her eyes, looked at him a final time, and ran.

Elation replaced bewilderment. But all was not well yet. Duncan looked across the water at the portmanteau; the river would soon tease it loose as it now carried off other remnants of the bridge. He turned his head to view the span behind him; the remaining planks were anchored to land for the time being, and he should climb to safety as Myrtice had, though he had farther to go. His head swiveled forward again. Water splashed into his face; the roar of the wind and river was deafening. He was beginning to shiver. The portmanteau rocked between the boards like a babe caught in a cradle.

Duncan tightened his lips, took a deep breath, and plunged into the river.

On the morning of the wedding, an anemic sun hid behind sweeping veils of clouds. Bets were laid among many of the duke's guests as to the probability of rain during the ceremony. Weston himself refused to participate in the wager, though it was evident it pained him to decline.

Once again the Duncans sat in the duke's library; on this occasion Weston was more relaxed in his manner. More content, Dru thought. He looked dashing in his formal black coat and white pantaloons, and his shirt of unadorned white linen seemed the more costly for its simplicity. On his lapel he wore a red rosebud. Sarah's favorite colour, he had explained.

Weston blotted his signature, walked around the desk and handed a bank draft to Duncan. "Most generous, your grace," Duncan said.

"Not generous enough," the duke said. "Had it not been for you—both of you—I wouldn't be awaiting the sound of chapel bells. Though I still cannot like your risking your skin as you did to retrieve my gems, Lord Duncan."

Dru hadn't liked it either, and told Duncan so with her eyes. The baron laughed and said, "Just be certain Tobias doesn't leave the room the next time he cleans your collection. Not with the combination lying in plain sight on the desk."

Weston shook his head. "He's too trusting. I suppose there were many opportunities for Sarah's maid to open the safe after he was done. But where could she have hidden the gems? If they were stored in the house as you seem to think, how did she know I wouldn't search every nook and cranny?"

"Sometimes I believe servants know more than anyone," Duncan answered. "She may have learned of the wager and your need for secrecy. I suppose we'll never know unless she's caught."

"The important thing is that I have the gems back and was able to give John the sapphires. Not to mention the fact that my wedding will take place because the Millbrights never learned I made that final wager." A little crease appeared on Weston's forehead. "I must admit I feel badly about not telling Sarah."

"Sometimes secrets are necessary if no good can come from their disclosure," Duncan said. Immediately he felt Dru's gaze upon him, sharp as knives. He shifted uncomfortably. "I mean, not in the ordinary course of events would one *hide* anything from one's spouse, but if the information could only *hurt* them, one might not . . . Actually," he said in louder tones, "I believe you *had* better tell Sarah. Honesty is always best, or so I've found."

"Er—yes," the duke said, his lips twitching. "I'll tell her . . . someday."

The clock on the mantel chimed the hour, and they all exclaimed at the time. The duke walked them to the door and said, "I find it interesting, Lord Duncan, that your original suspicions concerning my guests didn't prove true."

"That often happens in an inquiry," Duncan said. "Everyone is suspect, and sometimes the least likely person is the guilty party. Occasionally the answer is found by chance. Had it not been for my wife's connection with Lady Sarah, we wouldn't have known of the maid's departure in time to recover the gems. Druscilla is actually more responsible for solving the mystery than I."

"You both take my breath away," the duke said. "This mystery solving sounds rather like a game. Perhaps I should try it sometime."

Duncan agreed that he should, then bowed and walked toward the stairs.

Dru lagged behind, saying quietly to the duke, "I haven't had the opportunity to tell you how much your conversations have meant to Sarah, your grace. She has become radiant during the past week."

A mischievous gleam appeared in Weston's eyes. Pressing her hand, he said, "The credit belongs to you, dear lady."

"Nonsense," Dru said, her heart singing. She curtseyed and rushed to join Duncan, who had watched them curiously. Paying no heed, she began her ascent saying pertly, "I remember when you thought the marquess was guilty, but I knew he was not."

"That's because he kissed you," Duncan said, taking her arm. "One successful inquiry, and you're in danger of becoming proud."

"That may be true, but I hope I've proved you need my observations," she retorted. "And at least *I* don't keep secrets from my husband," she added for good measure, standing aside while several guests in their wedding finery passed them on the stairs. "Not important ones, anyway. And if you have any, as your speech to the duke would indicate, you had better tell them to me."

He started to reply, but Sarah's new maid appeared at the head of the stairs and summoned Dru. With Duncan's admonitions to hurry ringing in her ears, Dru followed the maid to Sarah's room. The maid closed the door, leaving the two ladies alone.

Sarah stood before the window watching the guests leave for the wedding. She turned and smiled at Dru's entrance. The young bride was resplendent in her wedding white, and the muted sunlight seemed to cast a glow around her. She hadn't pulled the veil across her face yet, but a wreath of red roses and baby's breath could be seen through the netting.

Dru sighed. "You are simply magnificent," she said.

"Do you really think so?" Sarah asked, her eyes sparkling like sunlight on water. "Thank you! I am so happy I could burst!"

"Well, please don't. The duke wouldn't take kindly to his bride exploding."

Sarah giggled. "He won't take kindly to my being late at the altar, either, and I know we must hurry; but there's something I must ask you." Her face sobered.

"Perhaps you had rather ask your mother?" Dru inquired hopefully.

"My mother?" Sarah repeated, confused. "Oh! It is not about *that,* Dru. Rather, it is Gerry who concerns me. No, no, I am not regretting my decision; what I mean is . . should I tell Artemis about how closely I came to running away? That Gerry spent two days recovering secretly in your room, and that he confessed of his liaison with my maid, and her planned treachery against me? Or would it be better to hide these things because they might make Artemis angry, or perhaps even jealous?" She stared at Dru anxiously. "It is only that I don't wish to keep anything from him."

Reflecting that this certainly seemed a day for discussing secrets, Dru said, "You shouldn't tell him now. This day, and many, many days afterward, should remain yours alone; there must be time to strengthen the bond between you. However," she said thoughtfully, as though discovering the truth of her words even as she spoke them, "one day far from now, when he has become accustomed to you—perhaps even takes your affection for granted—you might want to mention Gerry. Casually, and without obvious intent, of course."

Sarah's doubtful look slowly faded. For a moment, both young ladies smiled at one another in perfect understanding.

Later, while seated in the chapel, Duncan leaned toward Dru and whispered, "You look very pleased."

"I am," Dru said, and gazed around the stone-walled sanctuary with great interest. Olivia and the marquess were sitting together, she noted. The duke had hired a small orchestra for the occasion. The strains of a Vivaldi concerto now faded away, and a cheerful Purcell wedding tune began. The vicar entered, followed by the bridegroom and his best man, John Lyons; John shifted his weight from one foot to the other and looked ready to bolt. Dru was pleased to see Sarah's friend, Elizabeth, proceed down the aisle; Gerry had convinced his sister to serve as maid of honor after all, even though he had not the heart to attend himself. Elizabeth was a darkly pretty girl and looked fetching in a pink satin gown.

Weston was an imposing, commanding figure as he awaited his bride. All eyes were drawn to him, and he in turn scanned the room. After a moment his gaze found Dru, and his face brightened. He smiled and bowed slightly in her direction. Then Lady Sarah entered on the arm of a beaming Lord Millbright, and Weston's eyes were hers alone.

The shuffling sound of many people rising to their feet ensued, and almost everyone looked at the bride. There were a few sighs for her beauty, and some tears.

Duncan was not looking at Sarah, but at his wife. Nodding his head in the duke's direction, he whispered suspiciously, "What was *that* all about?"

Dru's mouth curved upward in a smile—a small, secret smile.

"I cannot say," she answered.

Delightful Deceiver

by
Phylis Warady

PRELUDE . . .

Nineteen-year-old Hester Astell tapped her foot in time with the music. Perched on the edge of a shield-back side chair, her stormy gaze was fixed on her twin sister dancing the quadrille with Charles Stuart. It hardly seemed fair that, simply because Hannah was a mere seven minutes older than she, Charles felt obliged to approach the elder twin before requesting a place on Hester's dance card. She let out a great sigh. She'd once had a schoolgirl crush on the bespectacled Charles. And while she'd long since outgrown such romantic notions, just once she longed to be first on his agenda.

"Dearest, your spine is as rigid as a broomstick. Do relax," advised Lady Pardo gently.

Hester shifted her gaze to her mother, the former Margaret Astell who had been wed for the past six years to the Earl of Pardo. "I'm too up in the boughs not to be tense, Mama. I'm tempted to wring Ned's neck for forcing me to play wallflower at my own come-out ball."

Her gaze sympathetic, Margaret patted her daughter's gloved hand. "Pray do not make a Cheltenham tragedy out of one missed dance. Obviously, he's been detained. Now, do leave off tapping your foot and pin a smile upon your face."

"Smile? I've nothing to smile about and I'm dying to sport a toe."

"Sport a toe, indeed! Hester, I beg you to cease using cant terms unbecoming to the gentler sex."

"Yes, Mama."

Hester snapped her fan shut. Mama was right, she grudgingly conceded. Ned was the best of brothers. Never would he deliberately stand her up. Still, what could be keeping him from doing the pretty as promised?

The elegantly appointed ducal coach, with family crest emblazoned on both carriage doors, slowed to a crawl. Peregrine Simpson, Fifth Duke of Alden, vented his displeasure with a wide yawn. Nothing quite equaled the tedium of being caught in a crush of carriages inching forward at a worm's pace, he reflected. Never mind that the evening looming before him promised to be a dead bore. Waiting meekly in line like an emasculated sheep until his coach finally drew up to the entrance of the Earl of Pardo's town house was simply too much to stomach for a man of action.

Perry tapped smartly on the carriage roof with his hickory cane and, once he gained his driver's attention, ordered him to halt. John Coachman, well aware that his grace did not suffer fools gladly, obeyed with alacrity. Like clockwork, the carriage door was flung open by a liveried footman. Unfolding his brawny frame, Perry moved down hastily lowered carriage steps with surprisingly nimble grace for such a solidly built man.

Lengthening his stride, he forged ahead, his zest for the evening revived now that he was no longer trapped in a hopeless quagmire of carriages. Only when he reached the torch-lit portals did fresh qualms give him pause. Come-out balls were not his cup of tea. Yet his honor demanded that he endure the tiresome ritual, all because of a deathbed promise his father had wrung out of him.

Perry's lips twisted in cynical amusement. After fifteen years of putting his straitlaced sire to the blush, he'd caved in at the last minute. He'd vowed to mend his rakeshell ways in order that his father could die happy—which explained his decision to attend the come-out ball the Earl of Pardo was hosting to introduce his twin stepdaughters into society. Rumors were rift at the gentlemen's clubs that the Astell twins were slated to be the belles of the London Season.

Besides, Perry mused, as he waited for the gimlet-eyed butler to announce him, aside from the obvious advantage of there being two to choose from, it stood to reason if he could fix his interest early in the season, he need not attend any more of these farcical affairs that set his teeth on edge.

At the starched-up butler's nod, the duke squared his broad shoulders and entered the ballroom. There was no receiving line, which meant the ball had already begun. His shrewd gray eyes skimmed the crowd, seeking a familiar face.

Not recognizing anyone, he decided to look into the card room, reasoning if any of his cronies were here, they'd rather play cards than dance. Intent on his mission, he didn't see Viscount Stuart emerge from the refreshment alcove until too late to prevent a collision that made his head reel and his ears ring.

Miles Stuart opened his mouth with the intention of delivering a scathing setdown. Instead, his jaw dropped. "Good God, Perry. Whatever are you doing here?"

"Would you believe looking for the card room?"

Miles snorted. "Cut line, Alden. You abominate chicken stakes. White's or Watier's is more your style. What the deuce are you up to?"

A lock of reddish-brown hair had fallen onto Perry's forehead. He swept it back into line, his expression defiant. He'd be damned if he'd tip his hand before he chose to.

"I fancy a gamble," he said blandly.

Perry salved an uneasy conscience by telling himself, in a larger sense, he spoke the truth. After all what could be more of a gamble than plunging pell mell into matrimony? Still, he couldn't keep dodging pointed questions indefinitely. A change of subject was called for.

"Humor me, Miles. What's in the basket?"

"Henrietta's indisposed. Barred from attending her sisters'

ball, the minx bade me not to return home without garnering treats from the refreshment table."

"Under the cat's paw, are you?"

Miles's eyes grew chilly. "If I were you, I'd refrain from jumping to conclusions."

"I beg your pardon. Your marriage is your own affair, of course."

Perry started to turn away, but Miles's restraining hand on his sleeve caused him to freeze in his tracks. He peered at the viscount quizzically.

"I had no call to rip up at you," Miles admitted. "Sorry."

"Not at all. Forget it."

"You see, Henrietta expects our third child shortly. And given her condition, it pleases me to indulge her."

"Perfectly understandable." There was slight pause before Perry thought to add, "Permit me to congratulate you on your growing family."

"Thank you." Miles beamed a rueful smile. "Forgive my odious curiosity, but I'd still like to know why you came."

The duke gave a deep sigh. Obviously Stuart would hound him until he was satisfied. Nothing for it but to come clean.

"Keep this under your hat. I'm in the market for a wife."

"Are you serious?"

"Would I joke about getting leg-shackled?"

"You astonish me. You've always taken pains to avoid the parson's mousetrap."

"So I did. But with thirty-five years in my dish, it's high time I married and set up my nursery."

"So you've come to look the Astell twins over?"

"Yes. Can I rely on you for an introduction?"

"I must fly else Henrietta will wonder what's become of me. But don't fret. I'll get Ned to do the honors."

"Ned?"

Miles nodded. "The twins' older brother. Also my brother's closest friend since Harrow."

"Excellent choice. But before you go, tell me—how does one tell one twin from the other?"

"Good question. They've been known to fool their own mother. However, tonight—at her insistence—they carry different fans. I believe Hannah's has a mother-of-pearl sticks and guards, whereas Hester's are blond tortoiseshell."

"Thanks for the tip. Lucky for me that I ran into you first."

"Lucky? That remains to be seen. Wait here whilst I fetch Ned."

Margaret cast Hester an anxious glance. She had not meant to thoroughly squelch her. Yet it was necessary to put her foot down now and again—lest her daughter's vivacity land her in the suds.

By rights, her twin daughters should have made their bow to society last spring, she mused. But while her second marriage was a happy one, no relationship is without its share of sorrows. A shadow darkened Margaret's brown eyes at the recollection of the miscarriage she'd suffered the previous spring. Never mind that she'd already born the earl a son and heir. Though five-year-old Marcus was a joy, the loss of the precious babe had left her blue-deviled.

At that point, Lucian had insisted his stepdaughter's come-out be postponed a year and then whisked his family off to the seashore. There, Margaret had gradually recovered both her health and sunny disposition.

Returning her thoughts to the present, Margaret glanced about the ballroom. In honor of the occasion, the ivory walls were draped in rose satin and, while April was a bit early for most blooms, baskets of delicately-scented white lilies appeared at regular intervals about the room's perimeter. Furthermore, each cut glass teardrop suspended from the crystal chandeliers created refracted candlelight that cast a romantic aura over the entire scene.

As for her twin daughters, Hannah and Hester looked coolly

elegant in matching ice blue satin slips overlaid with net frocking, trimmed with a deep flounce of blond lace. Now if only society would clasp both girls to its bosom, Margaret needn't worry about launching any more daughters onto the marriage mart, being as her eldest, Henrietta, was already married to Viscount Stuart.

Catching Hannah's eye as she glided past on her partner's arm, Margaret smiled warmly. Hannah was such a comfort. Quiet, unassuming and biddable—whereas Hester was more of a handful, much like Henrietta in temperament. Glancing askance, the rebellious spark she detected in Hester's cornflower blue eyes made Margaret's heart sink. She was getting too old to cope with this mischievous imp, and she prayed fervently that Hester would find her soul mate during the course of the London Season. After all, her eldest had settled down once she'd become a wife and mother. Doubtless so would Hester—provided her natural vivacity could be sufficiently dampened until some eligible suitor made her an offer. A circumstance that Margaret feverently prayed would happen sooner rather than later.

Sensing himself the cynosure of all eyes, Perry stifled a groan as he bent over Margaret's hand. He might have known his presence at a come-out ball would stir up a breeze.

Straightening, curiosity overcame good manners and he regarded her intently. He was amazed by her youthful appearance, having learned from Ned that the mature beauty was the mother of six offspring, ranging from Henrietta, twenty-four, to Marcus, five. Yet, the only sign of aging were a few silver strands highlighting her chestnut tresses.

"A pleasure to meet you, my lady."

Seemingly from nowhere the Earl of Pardo materialized. Taking root behind his wife, he clasped her bare shoulder and glared at the duke.

Sensing that Margaret's well-set up husband was itching for

an excuse to tap his claret, Perry prudently transferred his attention to Hester, whom Ned was in the process of introducing to him.

His breath caught. His heartbeat accelerated. It was instant enthrallment. Never mind that she had neither her mother's coloring nor her serene beauty. No question, Heather Astell was a very pretty girl with flaxen curls, blue eyes faintly tinged with purple and a pert up-tilted nose that made him smile.

"Charmed," he murmured as he made her an elegant leg.

"Your grace," she acknowledged.

Taken aback by her coolness, he asked, "Have I somehow offended you, Miss Astell?"

"Not at all," Hester assured him. She eyed her brother darkly. " 'Tis Ned I'd like to see keel-hauled."

"Dash it!" Ned Astell exclaimed. "You've no call to tear a stripe off me. I tried to get here in time to lead you out, but Miles collared me and dragged me off in the opposite direction."

"Humph! A likely story."

"That will do, Hester," the earl said firmly.

"Oh, but Papa, Ned deserves a scold."

"Hold your tongue, miss!" cried Margaret.

Mortified, Hester retreated into a sulky silence.

Perry stirred uneasily. He fully expected hostilities to resume any second. Wondering how best to divorce himself from the domestic squabble he'd unwittingly wandered into, his gray eyes met the earl's dark gaze. Noting ironic amusement flickering therein, it dawned on the duke that Pardo, curse him, had read his mind and was amused by his predicament.

Thinking he'd like nothing better than to draw the arrogant earl's cork, he fought to keep a lid on his own temper. For it would never to do to alienate his future father-in-law, now would it?

The worst of the unbearable tension eased when the earl drawled, "Ned, would you be so kind to fetch the ladies a lemonade?"

"A capital idea, sir!"

Some people have all the luck, Alden thought glumly as he witnessed Ned's escape. Too much of a cynic to think his host was about to let him off the hook as well—not with twin step-daughters to fire off—he scoured his brainbox in search of an acceptable excuse to withdraw, but his mind was a blank.

He was still trying to think of a graceful way to extricate himself from this awkward situation when he caught the earl eying him speculatively. Time to fish or cut bait, Perry decided.

A gambler at heart, he cast Hester a mesmerizing smile. "Care to dance, Miss Astell?"

Hester perked up immediately. This was the first chance she'd had to take a good look at him without seeming forward, and she eagerly took advantage of it. He was a large man with an engaging smile that softened his rugged features. But, al-though she was eager to know how it felt to be held in his arms, there were proprieties to consider.

"You should ask Hannah first."

"Since she's engaged elsewhere, I doubt it will set tongues wagging if we reverse the order. Especially if I have your par-ents' permission."

The duke's gaze shifted to Papa. Hester smiled. She liked his grace's style. And she was highly flattered that he wanted to dance with *her*—not Hannah. It made her feel . . . special and somehow unique.

"Do I have your permission, my lord?" Alden asked the earl.

The earl grudging gave his consent, and Perry decided to try his luck once again with the intriguing Miss Astell, whose seeming reluctance to dance with him was belied by her dainty foot keeping time with the music.

"My fate rests in your hands, Miss Astell. Pray don't dis-appoint me," Perry pleaded.

Hester peered at him so long he wondered if she were trying to stare him out of countenance. Yet when her eyes drifted to something beyond his right shoulder, Perry felt utterly abandoned. An instant later, she awarded him a dazzling smile that bowled him over.

"Indeed, your grace, I should love to dance."

Perry helped Hester to her feet. Her fingertips resting lightly on his coat sleeve filled him with a sense of pride as he led her onto the dance floor. Quite suddenly she clutched his sleeve. He shot a wary glance barely in time to see vexation swiftly veiled in her blue eyes. Seeking the cause of her disquiet, he found nothing amiss, but noted in passing that their path was about to converge with that of Hester's twin sister, Hannah. That was fine with him. He welcomed a chance to make comparisons.

However, to his consternation, when both couples drew parallel, Hester stuck her retrousse nose in the air and sailed past. An astonished Perry stumbled along in her wake.

Waiting on the dance floor for the orchestra to strike the first note, Hester sent a silent prayer heavenward. If Mama ever found out she'd cut Hannah, there'd be the devil of a dustup.

Just the same, she wasn't sorry. Whoever said "Revenge is sweet" was right. For once in her life, stealing the march on her older sister felt wonderful. And knowing she—not Hannah—would dance with the Duke of Alden first felt marvelous. So did delivering the setdown Charles Stuart richly deserved for hurting her feelings. Now, if she could just muzzle her guilty conscience, she'd be set.

"Tell me, Miss Astell, do you make a practice of snubbing your twin in public?"

Hester crimsoned. God help her if he guessed her snub was motivated by jealous spite. It'd be sure to give him a disgust of her.

"I didn't cut her—not exactly. I merely felt a nod would suffice."

"You aren't close, then?"

"We like each other well enough."

He gazed down at her, clearly baffled. "Do you know, I

have a hard time believing you are as cold-hearted as you sound."

His condescending manner riled her so much she was tempted to walk off the dance floor, leaving him stranded. But snubbing her sister was one thing; snubbing the duke quite another. Mama would be in a rare taking if she dared to insult any eligible suitor, much less a peer of the realm.

Personally, Hester cared nothing for titles. What lay within a man's heart was what mattered. Still, why alienate her mother? She was in enough trouble already. She'd best behave herself. Better yet, she'd best mend her fences.

"Your grace?" she queried softly.

Wary gray eyes peered down at her.

"I owe you an apology for embroiling you in a sisterly tiff. Do forgive me."

Hester hoped her softly spoken plea would suffice. Instead, his gaze narrowed suspiciously.

"I'm not the one you owe an apology. You owe that to Hannah."

His setdown inflamed her. Though exactly why the remark of a virtual stranger should affect her so strongly puzzled her. But stranger or no, no man had ever aroused her emotions to fever pitch before. The fact that Alden had that power frightened her so badly she was tempted to flee. But only cowards retreated. She would stand her ground.

Deciding subterfuge was her best bet, she said sweetly, "If I promise to make amends for treating her so shabbily, can we cry pax?"

"Meekness is scarcely your metier, Miss Astell," Perry observed dryly. "The musician's have struck the first note. Let's dance, shall we?"

With that, he drew her into his arms, and although he hadn't said he forgave her, Hester didn't quite dare press the point. Anyway, actions spoke louder than words, did they not? And Alden was holding her as if she were a precious jewel. Once again, he made her feel special.

After a turn or two, she realized that despite his husky build, he was amazingly light on his feet. But it was his hands, not his feet, that she fell head over heels in love with. For as they whirled about the dance floor, the hand residing at the small of her back, evoked deliciously wicked sensations that robbed her of breath.

Glancing up at his rugged features, she longed to trace his determined jawline with her fingertips. His fine-textured hair had the endearing tendency to hang in his eyes. But by far his most remarkable feature were pewter gray eyes that mirrored his moods whether stormy or calm.

He was a very large man, well over six feet, and Hester soon discovered that to peer up at him for any length of time was to invite a crick in her neck. Yet, she kept stealing peeks.

"Like what you see?" he asked gruffly.

"That, your grace, is a very impertinent question."

"Granted. What's your answer?"

"I haven't made up my mind yet."

After a lengthy pause, the duke said dryly, "When you do, be sure to let me know what you decide."

ADAGIO . . .

Her cheeks aglow from her morning gallop, Hester pulled to a halt in the stable yard. No slug-abed, she'd risen at dawn to don her smart new habit and tuck her flaxen curls beneath a black felt hat.

Never mind that she'd had less than three hours sleep. The young managed nicely on less than their elders. Which was fortunate, since she'd been too keyed up to sleep after her come-out ball. Her mind had kept churning up bits of trivia regarding the Duke of Alden, whose unexpected appearance at the Astell twins' ball had threatened to turn their debut into a three-ringed circus.

Not that she was in any position to cast stones, Hester conceded. Despite Margaret's stern warning that the debonair duke was a notorious rakeshell capable of ruining young innocents without a flicker of remorse, Hester had chosen to ignore her mother's advice to avoid him. A rebel at heart, she'd thumbed her nose at society by dancing with Alden three times in the same evening.

Foolhardy? Yes, indeed. Especially when she knew propriety dictated that, unless betrothed, two dances were the limit. But dash it, he'd egged her on. For certain, without Hannah's quick thinking, her reputation would now be in shreds.

Hester's brow furrowed. She didn't pretend to understand what had prompted her to defy society, but she had a sneaky suspicion it had something to do with the challenge in his grace's pewter gaze. Bluntly put, the rogue intrigued her. Not that she had any intention of throwing in her lot with a rake. She had better sense than that. Yet, there was no denying she was inexplicably drawn to him. Just as there was no denying that the wealth of emotions he could stir up within her whenever he chose frightened her. Nor did the current rumors being bandied about help ameliorate her fears.

She'd heard he had been a rake for most of his adult life; she heard he was such a superb lover former mistresses looked wistful whenever his name cropped up. She heard he'd ordered his town house in Park Lane refurbished. She heard he was hanging out for a wife.

The grooves in her forehead etched even deeper. If she meant to discourage the notion that she was willing to countenance a marriage of convenience, she'd better think about sending out different signals because he seemed on the verge of fixing his interest on her. Choking back a surge of panic, she'd tried to think of a viable alternative to what at best promised to be a loveless marriage. And, wonder of wonders, she'd come up with a brilliant idea. Consequently she'd drifted off to sleep with a smug smile on her lips.

However, when she awoke she'd realized her plan needed judicious tinkering. Knowing she did some of her best thinking on horseback, she'd stolen down the servants' stairs and slipped out the back door without a soul in the slumbering household the wiser.

Hester unhooked her right leg and slid from her side saddle to the ground. She landed hard enough to raise a dust cloud. "Fudge!" she muttered.

As she handed over the reins to the stableboy, Morning Star's soft whinny called to her. Shifting her gaze, she winced at the rivulets of sweat streaming down the mare's chestnut coat. She hung her head, thoroughly ashamed of herself for pushing the thoroughbred beyond her limits.

Not that she'd meant to mistreat her mount, of course. She was very attached to Morning Star, who'd come to her as a young filly. But her thoughts were in a muddle and, in hopes of clearing out the cobwebs, she'd gone for a brisk gallop long before the *ton* finished sipping its morning chocolate.

Another whinny called to her. She stroked the thoroughbred's forehead, all the time murmuring words of praise for her stamina and her adventurous spirit.

"We're two of a kind, m'dear," she whispered in the mare's ear. "Both of us hate being fenced in. Whenever we manage to break free, we tend to overdo things."

Gratified by signs that Morning Star was regaining her wind, Hester fixed her gaze upon the stableboy. "Walk her until she cools down. Mind that you give her a good rubdown before you return her to her stall."

"Aye, miss."

"Give her an extra ration of oats at feeding time. She's earned it."

"That I will. Niver fear."

Minutes later, Hester tiptoed across the kitchen floor. It was still early, barely ten o'clock, and given that the ball hadn't ended until the wee hours, she thought she had a good chance of reaching her bedchamber without incident. But as she'd tried to sneak up the backstairs, she ran smack into the housekeeper.

"What can you be thinking of Miss Hester? Use the front stairs, as befits your station."

Hester had barely reached the foot of the curved staircase that graced the entrance hall when her stepfather overtook her and marched her straight into the library. Since the book room was where the earl chose to discipline mischief makers, Hester sensed she was in for a scold.

"Sit down, Hester."

Having ridden for over two hours, she preferred to stand. Nevertheless, she sat. Because while, in general, her stepfather was kind and considerate, when riled, his temper could be formidable.

Lucian paced up and down. Little had he realized when he'd married Margaret that he was also taking on the responsibility of raising four stepchildren. Happily for him, Henrietta was already wed to his cousin, Miles Stuart, else by now he'd doubtless be a raving lunatic.

Now, six years later, it was his duty to deal with Hester, who was very much like Henrietta in temperament. Both were inclined to be impulsive; both were capable of outrageous acts guaranteed to turn gray hair white overnight.

If only, he lamented, Hester could be made to behave more like her sister, Hannah, who was a perfect lamb. But since it was well nigh impossible to change human nature, the challenge before him was to find a way to modify Hester's behavior without breaking her spirit.

"Your mother and I want you and Hannah to enjoy your come-out. However, it won't do to flaunt society's rules. And well you know it!"

"But Papa, some of them are so silly. And there are far too many."

"I don't dispute that. Still, I expect you to obey them—for your own sake as well as Hannah's. Do I make myself clear?"

Lucian thought he saw a flash of defiance in Hester's cornflower blue eyes, but she lowered them so quickly he couldn't be certain. This young lady was difficult to reach. Yet she had many admirable qualities and would make a fine wife and mother, if only she didn't ruin herself first.

His dark eyes pensive, he decided candor might work.

"I love your mother and consider her recovery nothing short of miraculous. Yet there's no denying her health's more fragile than before her illness. I must ask you not to provoke her by indulging in any more childish pranks."

"I'm sorry if I cut up her peace, sir. I assure you I wouldn't have actually danced with the duke a third time—had not Hannah and I switched fans first."

"To be sure it was very good of your sister to dash to your rescue. But allow me to point out that should you sink beyond the pale, not only will your own reputation be ruined. Your sister's season will be in shambles. And will break your mother's heart."

The interview had ended on that gloomy note. But, being a born optimistic, Hester had bounced out of the doldrums by the time she found the abigail she shared with Hannah awaiting her pleasure inside her bedchamber.

"Iris, I'm famished. Ring for a tray."

"It'll get here faster if I fetch it."

"Then do so."

Iris was almost out the door before Hester thought to add, "While you're about it, tell cook I fancy a bath and ask her to put water on to boil. I've an important engagement this afternoon and wish to look my best."

"Oh, but miss, by then you'll be deluged with admirers come to pay a courtesy call after last night's ball. Your mother will expect you to be on hand to receive them."

"Oh botheration! I'll consider rescheduling it while you fetch my tray."

While Iris was off on her errand, Hannah paid her a visit.

Peace between the twins had been restored due to Hester's handsome apology after the ball.

"Sleepy head!" Hester teased.

Hannah blushed. "Was not last night's ball a splendid affair?"

"Indisputably," Hester agreed.

Later still, Hannah looked on while Iris helped her twin don a gray kerseymere pelisse trimmed with ruby-colored velvet round the hemline and up from the floor to the base of her throat.

Hester tied on a bonnet composed of ruby velvet intermixed with levantine and catching her sister's eye, asked, "Will I do?"

"Admirably. You look positively regal."

Hester beamed her a fond smile as she drew on her gloves. "Thank you for the vote of confidence. And thank you for covering for me this afternoon."

"Pray don't dwell on it, Hester, though I shouldn't be helping you to pull the wool over dearest Mama's eyes. How is it, I wonder, that you always manage to twist me round your finger?"

"For the last time, I swear it! And only because my errand is of vital importance."

Hannah eyed her ruefully. "So important you refuse to reveal where you're going and what you intend to discuss with whom?"

Hester responded with a tinkling laugh capable of charming birds from their perches. "Very provoking, to be sure. But I promise you, both our futures depend upon me keeping this engagement."

The long-case clock in his private sitting room pealed four times. His expression morose, the Duke of Alden deserted his favorite armchair and strode over to a set of french doors that opened onto a walled-in garden. Peering out, he admitted he'd toyed with the idea of taking part in the daily promenade in Hyde Park in hopes of running into the captivating Miss Hester Astell. However, an hour ago a thick fog had rolled in, making such an excursion impractical.

He should pay a courtesy call at St. James's Square, but competing with a pack of fuzzy-cheeked suitors for a scrap of attention from his chosen bride was not his style at all. Far better to wait a day or two before he began serious pursuit, Perry reasoned.

That way, should he change his mind in the interim, he wouldn't be guilty of raising false hopes. Because, while last night he'd found Hester an utter delight, and while he admired her rebellious spirit, he couldn't quite quell a niggling suspicion that turning the amusing little renegade into a reasonably compliant wife might take more energy than he cared to expend.

"Your grace?"

Discerning an undercurrent of panic in his normally-imperturbable major domo's voice, Perry spun on his heel.

"What is it, Jeeves?"

"I know you are not receiving, but a most insistent young lady refuses to leave the premises until she speaks to you. I might add the hatchet-faced servant accompanying her is equally obstinate."

Intrigued, the duke's heartbeat began to quicken. "Perchance is my caller Miss Hester Astell?"

"Exactly so, your grace. Will you see her?"

A slow grin chased away all trace of gloom from features that in repose often seemed a tad too dour. "I wouldn't miss this interview for anything. Show her into the drawing room and shuttle the maid off to the housekeeper's sitting room."

Shortly thereafter, Jeeves ushered Miss Astell into a rectangular room whose walls were hung with light blue silk and whose chairs and sofa were covered in velvet of the same hue.

Hester was endeavoring to calm her jumpy nerves by inspecting a Derbyshire Bluejohn candelabra on display between two tall windows when the Duke of Alden sauntered into the room.

"Foolish chit! Don't you have more sense than to call at a bachelor's residence, especially without a proper chaperone?"

Hester whirled round to glare at him. He was no kin of hers. So what right had he to scold her? None, as far as she could see.

My, but he was a handsome man, though. When she'd woke that morning, she'd tried to persuade herself otherwise. She'd rationalized that candlelight had flattered his craggy features. That two goblets of champagne had clouded her judgment. That she'd always been plagued with an overactive imagination and that he could not possibly be as virile a specimen of manhood as he'd appeared to be at first sight.

Yet here he stood in broad daylight looking every bit as captivating as she remembered. And every bit as brawny. Plague take him!

But surely a more careful inspection would reveal feet of clay, she reasoned. Her eyes embarked on a bold journey that started at his crown of reddish-brown curls and ended at feet shod in soft leather slip-ons. Her gaze perused wide shoulders and a broad chest that she just knew would be pure heaven to nestle against—especially with his muscular arms wrapped around her.

Her blue eyes skimmed powerful thighs encased in tight breeches that left little to the imagination. Her embarrassed gaze shifted to comely calves clad in silk hosiery that displayed the lower portion of his legs to advantage. All in all, there was no denying his grace had a muscular build comparable to that of a god sculpted by a gifted renaissance master.

"Has my reprimand rendered you mute?"

"Only temporarily," she assured him dryly. "You, sir, deserve a scold for jumping to conclusions."

"I fear you've lost me. What the deuce are you driving at?"

"Your assumption that I've lost sight of the proprieties is

totally unfounded. I brought along the most senior maid on my stepfather's staff to lend me countenance."

"A mere sop to convention!" he scoffed. "Even if you'd brought your mama with you, the high sticklers would still regard your unconventional conduct as grist for the gossip mill. Clearly, if you continue upon your present path, your reputation will soon be beyond redemption."

Hester gamely swallowed the lump lodged in her throat and thrust her haughty up-tilted nose in the air.

"Hang the proprieties! I'm here on a quest!"

Highly amused, he regarded her thoughtfully. "Like the knights of yore?"

"Exactly so! Your grace, my purpose in calling is of a delicate nature. So delicate you must solemnly swear nothing I say will go beyond these four walls."

Perry knew he ought not to encourage the outrageous baggage, but couldn't help grinning. "You have my word it will not. Why don't you draw up a chair and get comfortable whilst I ring for tea."

Tea definitely sounded like a good idea. Certainly her empty stomach thought so, judging by the way it rumbled in anticipation as she seated herself. Which was perfectly understandable, given that she'd skipped breakfast and that all she'd had to eat today was the cup of coffee and buttered roll Iris had brought up from the kitchen.

Glancing up at the duke, she said, "Won't you be seated? No offense intended, but 'tis hard to compose one's thoughts with someone towering over you."

"None taken," he assured her, sinking into a sturdy armchair covered with plush velvet. "I think it best to defer further discussion until we've drunk our tea. Agreed?"

"Of course. 'Tis a capital suggestion!"

Hester felt as if she'd been granted a temporary reprieve. She even dared hope a bracing cup of tea would bolster her flagging courage. Courage, which seemed in danger of melting away just when it was most needed.

Finally, however, the teapot stood empty and all that remained of the plate of macaroons were a few crumbs. Never mind that the cowardly part of her nature wished that she'd never darkened the Duke of Alden's doorstep. The time had come for her to lay her cards on the table.

"Your grace, it is said that you are in the market for a wife. True or false?"

"True," he admitted wondering what this adorable miss was up to.

She lowered her gaze, causing thick dark blonde lashes to fan across her rosy cheeks. "Please don't think me puffed up with conceit, but I fancy I'm one of the candidates."

Her candor enraged him. Miss Astell had gone beyond the line of what was pleasing and deserved more than a mild setdown. He could only wonder at what sort of lax upbringing she'd had that made her assume she might say or do anything she pleased with impunity.

"You topped the list," he confessed coldly. "But thanks to your brazen conduct, you've plummeted to last place."

"Last place? Your grace, you must not let temporary infatuation cloud your judgment. You must face the truth without flinching. The truth is, I don't belong on your list at all."

The duke stared at her. A minute ago he'd been ready to write her off. Now he wasn't so sure.

"Allow me to be the judge of that, if you please."

"How can I, in good conscience? I'm far too willful to make any man a compliant wife, much less a duke."

"Certainly your more impulsive starts must be curbed, but I feel confident I'm equal to the task."

Annoyed by his autocratic posturing, she snapped, "Such arrogance ill becomes you."

"Most women would jump at the chance to become my duchess," he complained peevishly.

"Fortunately for you, I am not one of them. I'd make a terrible duchess."

"I cannot allow you to run yourself down like this. I'm by

no means without flaws myself. I'd no business pressing you
to grant me a third dance. But for your sister's intervention,
your reputation would now be under a cloud."

"Indeed, it was kind of Hannah to switch fans, was it not?"

"I hope you thanked her. I mean to make a point of it the
next time our paths cross."

Hester's blue eyes sparkled. "I plan to do more than thank
her. I plan to do her an enormous favor."

The duke was bombarded by a wealth of misgiving. "See
here, minx, what crack-brained scheme are you about to launch
on us unsuspecting mortals?"

"How astute of you to guess I've something up my sleeve!"

"Never mind trying to butter me up. What are you plot-
ting?"

Exasperated, Hester observed crossly, "Further evidence we
won't suit. I long to savor the moment, whereas you grow testy
if kept waiting a nonce."

Perry pressed his lips into a grim line. "A word to the wise.
Cease baiting me and answer my question."

"My lord, I would remind you that marriage is a lifetime
commitment. You should take great care in choosing your
duchess. After all she will be the mother of your children. I
am a totally unsuitable choice."

The duke sighed. "Very well, Miss Astell, you win. Consider your name scratched off my list of eligible candidates."

"Splendid! Allow me to congratulate you on your good
sense."

"You flatter me, Miss Astell. However, since you've raised
the issue of good sense and since you've an aversion to marrying me, at the risk of seeming uncordial, I feel I should
point out each additional moment you spend under my roof
increases your chances of being discovered in a compromising
situation. One, I might add, which may force us to marry regardless of our inclinations."

"I'm aware of the risk, but cannot leave yet. I need to tell
you about Hannah first."

Perry decided he really didn't understand women. Before Miss Hester Astell crossed his path, he'd assumed he understood them thoroughly—the basis of his arrogant presumption being fifteen-odd years of rakish conduct whilst eluding the parson's mousetrap. But now this nineteen-year-old innocent had forced him to reexamine that conviction. The truth was, he didn't understand a damned thing about the fair sex. And that was doubly true in Hester's case.

"Very well, Miss Astell, I'll bite. What do you wish to say about Hannah?"

"First off, I feel obliged to point out we are identical twins."

"I had noticed."

She'd wounded his pride by pointing out the obvious. Hester was sorry for it, but felt it would be a mistake to gloss over key facts.

"My sister, Hannah, whom I would remind you looks exactly like me, is an infinitely more suitable choice."

"Miss Astell, this is outside of enough! I am perfectly capable of choosing my own bride without benefit of your advice."

"Now, now, your grace, no need to poker up," Hester cajoled. "Of course a man of your vast experience doesn't need a silly chit in her first season presuming to advise him."

"I should hope not!" responded the partially mollified nobleman. "But dusk is upon us. Allow me to see you to your carriage where your maid awaits you."

Hester felt terrible. She'd had a golden opportunity to plead Hannah's case and had somehow botched it. Deeply disappointed in herself, she allowed the duke to escort her to the front curb.

Pausing beside the earl's carriage, he advised, "Don't look so glum, my dear. Failing to convince me to switch my affections to your sister is not the end of the world."

"Perhaps not," she acknowledged with a ghost of a smile. "Still, I cannot help feeling low. You see, Hannah is too shy to put herself forward but she'd make a grand duchess. She's quiet, unassuming and biddable. In short, she's perfect."

"This topic begins to bore me. I suggest you drop it."

"Oh, but your grace . . ."

"Not another word! Do you understand?" he thundered.

Noting that he looked ready to throttle her, Hester took a backward step. "Forgive me for badgering you. It was never my intention to anger you. I was merely trying to be helpful."

The duke gave a roar of laughter. "You, miss, have more brass than wit!"

"All the more reason you should be happy to set your sights elsewhere."

"Yes. Doubtless you'd make my life a living hell."

"I daresay I would. Despite my failure to convince you that you and Hannah are ideally suited, allow me to thank you for granting me a fair hearing."

"Still harping on that string, are you?"

"What string is that, my lord?" she asked with feigned innocence.

"Don't play games, Hester. It doesn't become you. As to your championing of your sister's cause, if will make you feel any better, I promise to give your suggestion serious thought."

Hester instantly perked up. "All I ask if that you judge her on her own merits. If you do, I truly think you'll soon agree Hannah will make you a splendid duchess."

His eyes taunted and teased. "Just to be sure we understand each other, are you absolutely certain you don't wish to fill the position yourself?"

"Absolutely!" Hester averred.

Perry raised an eyebrow. "Shall we put it to the test?"

Suddenly wary, Hester nervously licked her dry lips. "Test, your grace? Whatever do you mean?"

"Allow me to demonstrate," he said gruffly.

As if she weighed no more than a feather, he lifted her several inches off the sidewalk and planted a kiss on her slightly parted lips. Hester was too startled to put up more than a token struggle. The seemingly endless kiss aroused a myriad of erotic sensations that took her quite by storm. Hester was no longer capable of a coherent thought. She could only feel. She returned his kiss.

Encouraged by her passionate response, he longed to take his exploration a step further, but was afraid if he did, he'd be tempted to continue to take more and more liberties until finally he wouldn't be able to call a halt. And while undeniably a rakeshell, he drew the line at ravishing virgins.

With a frustrated groan, Perry ended the kiss. Eyes still closed, Hester protested with a tiny moan.

Her protest triggered a rueful smile. "Enjoyed that, did you? So did I. Indeed, you are a delectable morsel. But to continue kissing, especially in public view, is sure to curry censure. So open your eyes, my dear."

Her eyelids rose to reveal a bewildered young innocent whose confusion almost unmanned Perry.

"Are you absolutely certain you don't wish to become my bride?" he crooned. "Given your ardent nature, I really think we'd suit."

Hester wanted to deny her passionate response, but how could she with the harsh truth staring her in the face? Her blue eyes regarded him suspiciously. "Is that why you kissed me? To change my mind?"

"Did I succeed?" he asked silkily.

"No, you did not! Your grace, you are a—a—"

"Rakeshell? Yes, I know. And yet you had the brass to show up on my doorstep. This time I contented myself with a stolen kiss, but I give you fair warning. So help me, if you ever show up here again, I swear I'll steal more than a kiss."

Furious with herself for venturing into his den in the first place, furious with him for daring to point out her poor judgment, Hester struggled to break free of him, but his hands at her waist maintained their vise-like grip. And making her position even more untenable, her feet still dangled several inches above the sidewalk. Feeling vulnerable and defenseless, she glared at him.

"Set me down, you blackguard," she demanded.

"Gladly."

Tightening his hold on her waist, Perry swung her up into the carriage and deposited her on the seat. Then, with palpable reluctance, he let go of her. He paid no attention to the cowering maid she'd brought along for the sake of propriety. His gray eyes gave no quarter as they stared into Hester's.

"Now then, Miss Astell, do we understand each other?"

"Absolutely!"

"So be it!" Perry signaled the earl's coachman to drive on.

MASQUERADE . . .

Perry cried out, desperate to escape the tantalizing memory that had haunted his dreams for the past two months. But passion's tentacles proved too tenacious. And no matter how hard he struggled to prevent a recurrence, once again his senses were flooded with an incredible tenderness. The same tenderness he'd felt when he'd kissed Hester Astell and she'd melted in his arms.

He smiled in his sleep. God, but she'd tasted sweet. He reached for her. He woke hugging his pillow.

Disgruntled, he tossed it aside and rang for coffee. When it came, he'd sent it straight back to the kitchen, claiming it was tepid. A blatant lie, yet playing the tyrant took the edge off his temper.

He was still a trifle out of sorts when a fresh pot materialized, but fortunately for his harried servant, he was too desperate for the bracing brew to reject it. Sipping the hot liquid Perry concluded he could no longer function on a few hours rest, which meant he could no longer afford to procrastinate. For surely his constant vacillation between the Astell twins—despite the fact that he was ostensibly courting only Hannah—

was what robbed him of sleep. That and the kiss he'd stolen from Hester, supposedly to teach her a lesson in proper deportment. Perry grimaced. He was no longer sure who had been taught the lesson, but suspected it could well be himself. For certain, he was the one who kept waking up in a cold sweat. Far more telling, he was the one who couldn't seem to forget the kiss they'd exchanged.

There was no denying the pressure was on for the season was winding down. And at five and thirty, he needed to marry and set up his nursery. High time he quit vacillating and chose once and for all which twin he intended to wed.

He drank in the coffee's potent aroma as he poured himself a second cup. Each twin had her virtues; each had her flaws. Take Hannah, for instance. Shy and retiring, but nonetheless quite intelligent—although she was too much of a lady to flaunt it. Living with her would be restful, though perhaps a bit dull. Hester was her exact opposite. More flamboyant, more vivacious, more sensual and most definitely more trouble. But never, never dull, he admitted with a fleeting grin. Also she had a wonderful sense of humor, a virtue her sister unfortunately lacked.

Of course, if he chose her in the end, he'd have a devil of a time explaining to the earl why he'd requested permission to court Hannah if it was Hester who'd taken his fancy. But he'd cross that bridge when he came to it.

Hell and thunder! He was tempted to flip a coin because he couldn't seem to decide which twin would best suit his needs. Yet it was important to make the right decision, because once made, he'd have to stick by it. An hour later, impeccably turned out by his valet, he set off for the Pardo residence in St. James's Square, determined to seal his fate once and for all.

Iris stepped back to admire her handiwork. "You look as fresh as a rosebud in your sprigged muslin, if I say so myself."

Her mind on weightier matters, Hannah awarded the abigail a vague smile. Iris picked up the breakfast tray and headed toward the hall door. She'd almost reached her destination before it occurred to Hannah to ask, "Iris, is my sister up yet?"

"Last time I peeked her morning chocolate was untouched. I must say 'tis most unlike her to sleep half the morning away. Miss Hester is usually up with the chickens."

"I daresay so many late nights have finally taken their toll. And Mama. Is she still abed?"

"Yes. His lordship is up, though. Ate a hearty breakfast off a tray in the library. That he did."

"I see. I'll ring if I need you, Iris."

"Very good, miss."

Hannah waited until the door had closed before she crossed to the lady's writing table she used to answer letters or write in her journal. Today her purpose in approaching the rosewood desk was infinitely more romantic.

She cast a furtive glance about the room. Satisfied she was completely alone, she triggered a hidden catch that allowed a concealed drawer to slide open. Extracting a folded sheet of vellum, she clutched it to her bosom and moved to the tall window where the light was better.

The missive was from Charles, and although she knew its contents by heart, it comforted her to re-read it whenever her spirits were low. But before she got a chance to skim it, approaching footfalls made her scurry back to the writing table. Cheeks flushed, Hannah dropped the much-creased sheet into the secret drawer and pushed it shut.

Rattled, she barely had time to snatch up a pamphlet resting on the desk's surface before the door between her bedchamber and the small sitting room shared with her twin opened with a sudden whoosh. As she spun round to face her sister, the pamphlet slipped from her nerveless fingers.

"Gracious me! Must you always appear like a bolt from the blue? Don't you ever knock?"

"Oh, don't be such a stick in the mud." Hester's blue eyes brimmed with excitement. "I've news that won't keep."

Hannah heaved a long suffering sigh. Would she never learn? Taming a hurricane would be child's play compared to curbing her sister's exuberance. Reaching down, she scooped up the pamphlet she'd dropped.

"What's that in your hand?" asked Hester.

"A broadsheet concerning the evils of slavery."

Hester regarded her sister with consternation. Hannah was something of a bluestocking. A fact Mama was at pains to conceal in the belief it would discourage eligible suitors.

"Really? Wherever did you run across it?"

"Charles lent it to me."

Charles again? Thank goodness he'd just been awarded a fellowship at Oxford and was no longer constantly underfoot, because Hannah seemed to dote on his every word. Though what she saw in such a dull dog mystified Hester, who'd liked him better when he'd been a light-hearted scamp always game for a lark. But that carefree youth had been replaced by sermonizing sobersides with whom Hester had absolutely no rapport. It saddened her, since she'd once been quite fond of him.

"Charles has an avid interest in moral issues," Hannah volunteered.

"Well, good for him!" Hester tried not to sound sarcastic but wasn't sure she succeeded. Adopting a milder tone, she observed, "Doubtless, taking a stand on such issues will help him garner votes when he stands for Parliament."

"Parliament? I don't think so. He speaks of obtaining a Bachelor of Divinity Degree."

"Gammon! Charles is too peace-loving to defy his brother. Miles is grooming him for a career in politics."

Hannah ˙sighed. "You may well be right, but you've kept me on tenterhooks long enough. Tell me the news you claim can't wait."

"Very well. Guess who's closeted with Papa in the library?"

"Really, Hester, you try my patience! One of his whig cronies, I make no doubt."

"Wrong! He closeted with Alden, who's come to make you an offer."

Hannah visibly paled. "How can you possibly know that?"

"I have my ways," Hester averred airily.

"Listening at keyholes, were you? Shame on you!"

"Spare me the lecture. You are on the brink of becoming a duchess. Why aren't you more excited?"

"Excited? I'm dumbfounded. We scarcely know each other."

Hester glared at her twin, exasperated. "Must you ever behave like a wet goose? You've had two whole months to get acquainted. During which time, he's wooed you with flowers and showered you with gifts. What more do you expect?"

Hannah resisted an urge to wring her hands. "How I wish I could turn back the clock. How I wish I'd put my foot down when he asked Papa's permission to pay his addresses. Oh, Hester, I envy your strength of character."

The passion in her twin's voice shook Hester to the roots of her soul. She'd grown so used to her sister's placid acceptance of whatever chanced to befall her, it had never once crossed her mind that Hannah might balk.

"Hannah, you cannot possibly reject him. The season ends in a month. Mama and Papa will be beside themselves."

"Yes, I know they think it a splendid match. But Hester, I truly don't wish to be a duchess. I don't like the limelight. What I crave is solitude."

"But, dearest, a duchess does just as she pleases. If you want solitude, I'm sure Alden will respect your wishes."

Hannah responded with a scornful laugh. "Pray do not insult my intelligence. Alden expects a paragon. And I tell you I don't think my shoulders are broad enough. But that's not the worst of it. 'Tis conjugal intimacy I dread most."

Hester dare not crack a smile. Conjugal intimacy indeed! Only a quaint bluestocking such as Hannah would come up with such an outlandish phrase.

She sobered. While Hannah's phraseology might be odd, the point she raised was valid and deserved a carefully reasoned response. Only Mama should be doing the talking—not Hester, who knew next to nothing in regard to the subject. Unfortunately their mother wasn't present so it fell to Hester to try and assuage her sister's qualms.

"But, dearest, unless one chooses spinsterhood, such intimacy is unavoidable, since all men desire an heir."

"That may well be. But it is Alden whose offer I must consider. What he desires is a marriage of convenience. Which I am not at all sure I wish to settle for." A note of despair crept into Hannah's voice. Besides, he is so . . . so very large, it quite puts me in a quake to contemplate my wifely duties."

Hester felt a wrenching sense of guilt. Was there no end to her self deception? Although strongly attracted to the duke herself, his overwhelming masculinity had unnerved her. And if she, who was usually so fearless, had been too scared to contemplate co-habituating with such a great bear of a man, her overly-timid sister must be terrified.

Had she mustered the courage to honestly face up to her fears, she might still be able to hold up her head. Instead, coward that she was, she'd urged Alden to court her twin. Far worse, she'd somehow managed to convince herself she was doing her shy, retiring sister a favor.

She rolled her eyes. Some favor. Thanks to her meddling, Hannah was headed straight for disaster, and it was all her fault.

The light tapping on the bedchamber door provided a welcome diversion. Hester called permission to enter.

Iris walked in. "Miss Hannah, the earl wishes you to join him in the library."

Despite being pre-warned, the summons drained every remaining drop of color from Hannah's already pale face.

"You're white as a sheet. Shall I go in your stead?"

"Would you really do that for me? If Papa finds out he'll be livid."

Stomach churning, Hester squared her shoulders. "I'm willing to chance it."

"I can't face the duke. Nor Papa either. What I wouldn't give for a smidgen of your pluck."

"What do you want me to tell Alden?"

Hannah emitted a deep sigh. Charles would be so very disappointed in her when he learned of her defection. But if he truly loved her, he'd eventually realize she simply didn't have the intestinal fortitude to go against her parents' wishes.

" 'Tis too late to cry off. Tell his grace I accept his flattering offer."

Minutes later, gliding down the curved staircase, Hester espied her five-year-old stepbrother with his eye smack against the keyhole of the library door. Her lips curved into an amused smile. The scamp had once again escaped from his nanny.

Before Hester got a chance to take him in hand, her brother, Toby, home from Harrow until the Michaelmas term commenced, stole up behind Marcus and scooped him up into his arms.

"Slipped your leash again, have you, Mark?"

"Curse you, Toby. Turn me loose."

"You know I cannot. Tell you what, though. If you go back to the nursery without a fuss, this afternoon I'll take you for a turn in your pony cart. How does that sound?"

"Will you carry me there on your shoulders?" Marcus wheedled.

Toby almost choked on his own laughter. "Very well, you imp. It's a bargain."

Hester watched Toby, a tall and gangly youth, swing his brother high in the air and settle him on one shoulder.

"Hang on, sport."

Whirling about, Toby almost collided with Hester, blocking the curved staircase.

"You startled me. Almost dropped Marcus on his noggin. If I had, there'd be the deuce of an ugly scene."

"Gammon! Your hold on the squirmy tadpole is too deft."

Marcus beamed Hester a smile from his high perch. "Toby's giving me a ride back to the nursery."

"How about that?"

"Where are you bound, sis?" Toby queried.

"I've been summoned to the library by Papa."

"Really? I could've sworn it was Hannah he sent for."

Chuckling at her chagrin in being caught telling a fib, Toby raced up the stairs, careful to keep a firm hold on his little brother. Marcus's squeals of delight trickled down to Hester who gazed up at the carefree scene.

Toby peered at her from the upper landing. "It's not too late to change your mind."

"I know, but I gave my word."

"Well, it's your neck. But I shouldn't like to be in your shoes when Papa realizes you've hoaxed him."

Hester waited until Toby and Marcus passed from sight before she rapped on the library door, then entered before being granted permission. Her forward momentum took her several steps forward before she paused at the room's center to assess her reception.

Her worry that her stepfather would take offense at her small indiscretion faded when both noblemen jumped to their feet, their faces wreathed in warm smiles. Hester smiled back but feared the result more closely resembled a grimace.

"You sent for me, Papa?"

"Yes. Move closer, Hannah."

Heart in her mouth, Hester advanced on leaden feet. With each step she took, she wished she'd never offered to switch places with her twin. Toby was right. Papa was sure to see right through her subterfuge, and when he did she'd be lucky if he didn't beat her. Not that he'd ever raised a hand to her before, but still . . . The pulse at the base of her throat pounded as she halted before him.

Expression jubilant, the earl placed a hand on each shoulder and gazed down at her kindly.

"I've given his grace permission to speak to you in private whilst I fetch your mama."

Hester experienced a rush of panic at the realization that her stepfather was about to leave her alone with Alden. Anyway, once Papa left, the duke would be sure to make her an offer—or rather make Hannah an offer, since that is whom he assumed she was. She winced at the sharp, searing pain that coursed through her at the thought of having to listen to the duke earnestly pouring out his heart to her in the mistaken belief that she were Hannah.

Lord save her! Whatever had possessed her to offer to masquerade as her sister? How she wished she wasn't so impetuous. That just once she'd taken time to look before she leaped.

Papa, of course, would be furious if he ever discovered the switch, but the duke was an unknown quantity. Should he ever get wind of the ruse, she had no idea if he'd react violently or not. For certain, he'd never forgive her, or Hannah either.

When her stepfather planted a kiss on her left cheek, Hester almost had heart failure.

"Sly puss. Your mama will be in the alts."

The earl buzzed his stepdaughter's other cheek, then released her shoulders and turned to shake the duke's hand.

Watching them pumping each other's hands, Hester tried to calm herself. As their hands broke apart, she stared at the duke.

"I'll return in a bit with Lady Pardo and a bottle of vintage champagne. Meantime, carry on."

Chuckling with glee, he began to stride toward the door. Only then did Hester dare let out the breath she'd been holding. She could scarcely believe her luck and was tempted to pinch herself. For once, Papa's eyes weren't as sharp as they usually were. Wonder of wonders, she'd actually managed to pull it off.

She hazarded a discreet peek at the Duke of Alden. He was eyeing her as if puzzled. Her heart plummeted to her toes. With the benefit of hindsight, she now wished Papa had caught on to her game. Because something told her if his grace ever discovered he'd been duped, he was the type to hold a grudge.

His grace cast Hester a friendly smile intended to assuage her misgivings. "Calm down, m'dear. Rest assured I hold you in the highest esteem and will do nothing to frighten you."

Hester stared at him incredulously. Of course, he assumed he was speaking to Hannah. Nevertheless, she couldn't go through with this masquerade. Not because she'd lost her nerve, either. But because she'd suddenly realized she'd fallen in love with Alden. How, when or where it had happened she couldn't say. All she knew was that she couldn't bear to hear him propose to her sister.

Her eyes widened at the magnitude of her self deception. In comparison to her timid sister, she'd come to regard herself as fearless. Yet she'd been frightened of the duke's magnetism, fearing that if she surrendered to it she would lose her identity. And now he was about to offer for Hannah. And thanks to her unwillingness to face up to her fears early on, she was about to receive her just deserts.

"Devil a bit!"

Papa's oath sent Hester's anxious glance winging toward the library door. The earl's hand had already begun to turn the knob when it fell away.

"Damnation! Hester Elizabeth Astell! Have you no sense of decorum?" Breathing fire, the earl covered the distance between himself and the now-quaking Hester in a trice. "What have you to say for yourself?"

"Papa, I—I . . ."

"Speechless for once, are you?" He seized her shoulders. "God, I ought to shake you 'til your teeth rattle."

Hester could not remember her stepfather ever being so furious. Even the time that Toby had tossed a frog down his back, causing him to hop about like a demented moonling, palled in comparison. On that occasion, he'd quickly recovered from his temporary loss of dignity, and after meting out suitable punish, had been eager to forgive and forget. But this time was different. This time his eyes contained spitting embers. Hester was scared witless.

"You are too old to shake and too old to spank. Go," the earl snarled.

Tears coursed down Hester's cheeks. "Papa, I am so very sorry. Do forgive me."

"Go, you incorrigible baggage. Tell Hannah to come at once, then stay in your room until further notice. Is that clear?"

"Yes, Papa, I'm g-going."

Gulping back tears, Hester fled.

As she stumbled blindly up the stairs, the floodgates opened and she could scarcely see where she was going. That the duke had witnessed her sorry performance was the last straw. Why oh why, Hester lamented, hadn't she realized his opinion meant the world to her before it was too late? Never would she forget the shock she'd seen in his grace's eyes. Never ever had she been so miserable. Oh, why had fate been so cruel?

With Hester's departure, a heavy silence fell upon the room's occupants. Perry tried to think of something diplomatic to say, but his mind was a blank.

The frozen tableau ended when the Earl of Pardo strode purposely over to the decanter of brandy and poured an inch of amber liquid into two goblets. Handing one to Perry—who by now was willing to swallow hemlock if only to relieve the unbearable tension—the earl tossed the contents of the other down his own throat.

"Ah, that hit the mark!" he exclaimed.

"I daresay there's nothing like a spot of brandy to calm one down," Perry agreed.

"I seldom lose complete control of my temper. Not that I expect you to take that statement on faith," the earl said ruefully. "But that intrepid little hoyden's antics are enough to topple a saint."

"I quite agree she's incorrigible. Which is why I decided to settle for Hannah. But personalities aside, I trust you will satisfy my curiosity on one point."

"Certainly, if I can. But before I do, my apologies for the scene you just witnessed. Hester does not usually try my patience quite so far, but that is neither here nor there. What is it you wish to know?"

"Well I don't wish to pry, but feel I must ask you something in the interest of self survival."

"How may I help?"

"By revealing how you can tell one twin from the other."

The earl smiled faintly. "Nothing could be simpler. Hester has a tiny beauty mark on her right earlobe. I don't mind admitting before I learned of it those naughty minxes lead me a merry dance. But they haven't been able to hoax me for years—at least not until today. And Hester did not succeed, did she?"

"No she didn't. I confess I don't envy you the responsibilities you assumed as a stepfather."

"Ah well, in all fairness, Hester has many endearing qualities. Truly, most of the time I enjoy playing father to the offspring I inherited along with my dearest wife, whom I love madly. Still, I shudder to think what I'd have done if Miles hadn't married Margaret's eldest daughter, Henrietta. Now there was a brazen wench who wanted taming, if ever there was one. Even so I must admit Miles seems to manage her with admirable grace and be quite happy in the bargain."

A timid tapping on the library door interrupted the earl's monologue. "Ah," he said, equanimity restored, "that will no doubt be Hannah."

FUGUE . . .

A soft persistent patter woke Hester. Rubbing sleep from her eyes, she probed the inky darkness, bent on pinpointing its origin. A stiff breeze wafted into the room from the tall casement window she'd flung open before she'd retired with a blinding headache.

Her ruffled brow cleared. Her sleep had done her the world of good, and the dreadful headache that had plagued her earlier was gone. But while the patter of rain was music to her ears, a blast of chill air made her shiver.

Hester pulled her covers up to her chin. She had no desire to leave her warm bed. Yet, unless she roused herself, the slanting rain would soak through the Axminister carpet and cause it to mildew. Wrinkling her nose in distaste, she threw off her covers and padded barefoot over to the hinged window. She managed to tug it shut on the second try.

Mission accomplished, she huddled again beneath her covers, listening to the rain in the hope it would lull her back to sleep. But no such luck. She was wide awake. With a sigh, she rose and lit a candle.

Two flights below, the long case clock chimed eleven times. Wednesday, all those with vouchers flocked to Almack's. Just about now, the patronesses would bar the doors to any stragglers. Of course, Hester acknowledged, Mama and Hannah were already inside. She'd be there with them, but for a headache that had forced her to dose herself with laudanum and take to her bed.

Not that she'd wished to go. Orgeat punch and stale biscuits held no appeal. Besides, Alden would be there, ostensibly to dance attendance on his betrothed, which he had every right to do. What Hester took exception to were the sultry glances he threw her when he thought nobody else was looking. Conduct which only served to confirm the low esteem in which he'd held her ever since Papa had unmasked her in his presence a fortnight ago. Hester shivered. The duke put her in mind of the big bad wolf on the brink of gobbling up little red riding hood.

Still, she hesitated to make a fuss. After all, it would be his word against hers, and at the moment she feared her credibility was at an all-time low. But regardless of whether or not he had seduction in mind, what really cut up her peace was not his conduct, but rather her own.

It vexed her that she could sense his virile presence before she actually saw him. It vexed her that she couldn't seem to control her own actions. That no matter how hard she tried to curb them, her traitorous eyes kept straying to him. She knew she was just asking for trouble.

Far safer to stay home with a good book, thought Hester. That way she'd be sure to stay out of harm's way. Something she was trying very hard to do, since she was anxious to get back in Papa's good graces.

Her mind was a churning caldron. Perhaps a glass of warm milk would relax her. By now the servants would be in bed, allowing her free access to the kitchen. Hester donned a light wrapper over her nightrail and tied it securely at her slender waist.

While Hester scalded a saucepan of milk on the kitchen range, Ned Astell entered the town house with Charles Stuart. Both youths were three-parts disguised, due to imbibing blue ruin whilst touring the gin shops.

His slight figure swaying unsteadily in the dimly lit anteroom, Charles knocked over the suit of mail, passed down to successive generations since medieval times. The din created took the form of discordant clatter that could be heard as far away as the kitchen. Showing no mercy, it continued to echo in the hollow chamber.

Ned, who'd grown increasingly testy as the evening advanced, snarled, "For lord's sake, Charles, mind your step. That's a family heirloom you bumped into."

"Well of all stupId places to park it—smack in the middle of a chap's path takes the palm!"

"Shush! You'll wake the entire household!"

Charles snorted. "Don't be ri-ridiculous. If the crash didn't rouse them, raised voices sure as hell won't."

Grouchier than ever, Ned grumbled, "Talking me into smuggling you in here is outside of enough! Especially jug-bitten. The earl'll pin my ears back if he gets wind of this. Besides, Hannah won't get in 'til the wee hours."

"Good. Should be cold sober by then."

"I trust so. But why call on her at such an ungodly hour?"

"Hen-hearted chit's been avoiding me ever since her betrothal to the debonair duke. Her shabby treatment is driving me to drink. Refuse to be put off any longer."

"But, Charles, Mama is chaperoning. Mark my words, she'll send you packing."

"Humbug! Can't give me my walking papers if she ain't aware I'm here. Don't intend to rat on me, do you?"

"No, but you're pressing your luck."

"A gamble I'm willing to take. Hannah and I must talk. Can I rely on you to bring her to me?"

"Oh, very well. I'll do my possible. Now then, let's adjourn to the library."

However, no sooner had they settled in commodious chairs in the bookroom than Ned recalled the fallen armor.

Rising, he said, "Papa may decide to cut his evening short. I must aright Sir Galahad before he comes home. Otherwise, he's sure to fly into a pet."

The instant the door closed behind Ned, Charles ambled over to the sideboard when he lifted the brandy decanter and poured an inch of the amber concoction into a snifter. Warming it with both hands, he wandered disconsolately back to the chair he'd just vacated and plunked himself down.

Dash it all! He'd had his entire future all planned. Despite Miles's urging, politics were not to his taste. What he desired was a career in the Church, first as a country parson with Hannah as his wife and helpmate. Later on, in a higher position that freed him to follow his scholarly pursuits.

Charles sighed. Now that Hannah had thrown a spanner into the works he didn't much care what he did. His sole glimmer of hope lay in persuading her to break her engagement and marry him instead. His only chance was to speak to her in person. Once he passed that hurdle, he was reasonably confident he could convince her to change her mind.

Still, a tiny doubt persisted, which explained why he needed a brandy to buck up his spirits.

Ned proceeded without incident back to the site of the earlier debacle. Crouching, he lifted the armor off the marble floor and propped it upright.

"Looks a bit lopsided, Ned."

Startled to hear a feminine voice, his hand bumped against the helmet causing the armor to topple over a second time. "Devil take you, Hester. Look what you made me do?"

"What a silly goose I am, to be sure! Let me help you reassemble him."

Working together, the siblings soon had the suit of armour standing upright.

"Looks almost as good as it did before it keeled over the first time," Ned observed.

"So it does. Am I forgiven?"

"Of course. But I thought you had a headache."

"I did, but my nap cured it. The rain woke me and I couldn't get back to sleep, so I came down to warm some milk."

"Well, I advise you to scurry back to your bedchamber. Because if Papa catches you roaming the halls in your delightfully dishabille state, I guarantee your stay in the room will be extended."

"How kind of you to take an interest in my welfare, brother mine," Hester responded, tongue-in-cheek. "Allow me to return the favor. Have a care what you're about, else you're sure to find yourself in his black books."

Ned's gaze grew pensive. Obviously, she'd heard the earlier crash. But given the distance from the kitchen, it was doubtful she'd heard Charles's outraged bellow.

"Are you foxed?"

"Just a trifle bosky is all."

"Whatever. You'd best retire before Papa gets a whiff of your breath."

Ned hesitated. If he revealed Charles's presence, Hester would insist on joining them in the library. She was already in dutch with their stepfather. He didn't want to get her in any deeper. No, he decided. Far better to keep mum.

"Quite right. Come," he said, cupping her elbow. "We'll mount the stairs together."

While not precisely besotted, there was no denying Ned's wits were not as sharp as they would've been if he hadn't been drinking blue ruin all evening. Which explained how he came to be caught flat-footed in front of his bedchamber.

Ned willed Hester to walk on. Instead, she dug in her heels and refused to budge. Quelling a sigh, he decided a strategic retreat was called for.

Inside his bedchamber, he marched over to his bed and threw himself down. Lying supine, he cradled the back of his head with his hands and gazed up at the ceiling. Patience was not his forte. But even in his befuddled state, he knew better than to pop out of his room and rush back to Charles in the library. To be sure, Hester was clever. Just the same, all he need do was outwait her.

After her brother slammed the door in her face, Hester continued on to her room. However, she had no intention of going to bed. Ned's behavior had roused her suspicions. She couldn't begin to guess why he hadn't told her at once that he had every intention of rejoining Charles in the library.

By the time the clock chimed twelve thirty, Hester's vision had long since adjusted to the murkiness. She tiptoed down the hall to her brother's room and cautiously turned the knob. Entering, she stole over to the bed. Fully clothed, Ned had fallen to sleep. She covered him and carried a spare quilt to the library, where she found candles sputtering in their sockets whilst Charles emitted stentorian snores.

Hester considered it a blessing that he was fast asleep. Even so, her reputation would be ruined if caught alone—especially dressed as she was—with a gentleman only vaguely related by family ties. She'd best cover him and leave.

But first things first. She'd removed the brandy snifter dangling from his hand and was all set to spread the quilt over him when Charles opened his eyes.

"Where's Ned?"

Hester cast him a friendly smile as he swung his feet off the sofa and sat up.

"Gone to bed. Go back to sleep."

"Sleep be damned? We need to talk," Charles bellowed.

Hester shook her head. "You reek of strong spirits. Sleep it off. Whatever you have to say will keep until morning."

She'd already begun to turn away when Charles grabbed hold of her sleeve and gave it a good tug. Yanked off balance, she wound up in his lap, the breath knocked out of her.

Unable to speak, she observed the expression in his eyes soften. "We'll talk now, Hannah," he said gently. "Not later."

"Nodcock! Hannah's still at Almack's. Release me."

The lover-like gleam in Charles's vivid blue eyes gave way to dismay. "Hester?"

She nodded curtly.

Charles heaved himself off the sofa and stood her on her feet. "Sorry, m' dear. I was waiting to speak to Hannah, so naturally I thought . . ."

Hester marveled at her own obtuseness. Obviously, Charles was head over heels in love and taking Hannah's betrothal hard.

"Say no more. 'Twas an understandable mistake."

She wondered if Hannah knew how he felt, then realized she probably did. Why else would she look so sad whenever the debonair duke set out to charm her? Why else would she have grown so melancholy ever since the announcement was printed in the Gazette?

"But why insist on thrashing out your differences at such an ungodly hour?"

"Because Hannah's been dodging me ever since she caved in to her parents' wishes and agreed to this insane betrothal."

"Insane? That's coming at it too strong, Charles. I would remind you, Alden's a duke."

"Don't care if he's a royal prince. He's not the right man for Hannah. I am. And so I shall tell her, first chance I get!"

A commotion in the hall arrested both occupant's attention. A look of horror flitted across Hester's face as she recognized the firm footfalls.

"Papa," she said in an anguished whisper.

She sprinted toward the door, only to be tackled by Charles. They'd landed on the thick red carpet, his unwelcome embrace pinning her arms to her sides. Hester squirmed in a vain effort to break free.

"Let me go at once! I can explain to Papa. He'll listen to me."

"In a pig's eye," Charles scoffed. "You cannot be seen in here with me. Not dressed in your nightclothes. Your father will hit the ceiling."

Hester glared at Charles. She feared he was right, but knowing in her heart she was innocent, she fought to dispel the traitorous thought. *Papa would believe her. Of course he would!*

"Stop struggling, you little wildcat. We've got to think of a safe place to stash you, else the jig is up!"

Hester decided to try a maneuver she'd once seen employed by a street urchin. She kneed Charles in the groin and when he doubled over, rolled free and scrambled to her feet.

Worked like a charm! Triumphant, she dusted off her palms.

But victory turned to defeat as Charles, struggling to rise, lost his balance and, desperate to regain it, grabbed hold of her. In the ensuing tussle, Charles's spectacles went flying and Hester landed on her back. Which wouldn't have been so bad—since the thick Turkish carpet cushioned her fall—but for the fact that Charles ended up on top of her.

Total disaster struck when the door opened and the Earl of

Pardo stepped inside. An incredulous look dominated his strong features as his dark eyes slowly took in the tangled bodies sprawled on the plush red carpet.

Lucian gave a roar of outrage. Then he groaned, in obvious anguish. "Devil a bit! This time you've gone too far! Have you no shame?"

Blinking like a disorientated owl, Charles groped the immediate area until he found his spectacles that had landed without mishap. Donning them, he climbed wearily to his feet.

"It's not what you think, sir. I can explain."

"Explain, cousin," said the earl in a terrible voice. "What's to explain? You've compromised my daughter. By god, if you weren't kin, I'd horsewhip you."

"Ain't a rakeshell, sir. Not in the habit of compromising young ladies—much less Hester."

"Silence!" ordered the irate earl. "As for you, miss, how could you be so devious as to fake a headache in order to tryst with your lover? Are you trying to break your mother's heart?"

"Oh, Papa, I know it looks bad, but I really did have a migraine. When I woke it was gone. Then Ned created a ruckus while I was getting a glass of milk. He wandered off to bed leaving Charles without a blanket. When I tried to cover him, he woke and, in trying to stand, lost his balance. He pulled me down with him. Which is why we ended up in such a hopeless tangle. But it was all very innocent, Papa, I swear it. Oh, do say you believe me. I cannot bear to have you think me a fallen woman."

The earl's bitter chuckle didn't hurt as much as it would have if Hester hadn't been gazing into his eyes so intently. Because as she watched, initial disgust was replaced by regret coupled with a bleak sadness that left her more shaken than calculated derision could ever accomplish.

"It may well be you are telling the truth, child," he said gently. "However, it matters naught whether you are or not. Regardless of the truth, you are compromised. Furthermore, I expect Charles, who had no business falling asleep on the library couch in the first place, to make you an offer."

Hester stiffened. "He may offer until blue in the face. I won't marry him."

The earl's expression hardened. "Yes you will, daughter. Yes you will."

CRESCENDO . . .

Seated on a cushioned window seat, Hester peered out the attic's dormer window. Beyond the row of elegant town houses aligning the south end of St. James's Square, she caught occasional glimpses of Carlton House gardens. Usually, the profusion of flower beds lightened her mood, but not today. Today she had a fit of the dismals she couldn't seem to shake.

And no wonder. Not only was she betrothed to Charles Stuart against her will, she was about to be dragged off to Aldenwood to spend the weekend. The fact that Alden would be there, too, added to her gloom.

Since Hannah was slated to marry the duke, it made sense for her to go there with Mama to look things over. But Hester didn't see why Papa insisted that she accompany them. Nor did she wish to go where she'd be constantly exposed to the torment of watching the man she adored court her beloved sister.

Several flights below, a door slammed and she heard her name being called. She gave a tiny squeal of alarm, then clamped her hand over her mouth. A cacophony of footfalls, ranging from feather light to lead-footed, caused her eyes to widen. Obviously, the family was seeking her high and low.

Her blue eyes flashed with defiance. Let them look. She was too clever for them. They'd never think to search the attic.

"Ah, there you are, sister! I had a hunch I might find you up here."

Hester clutched her right breast. Beneath her fingertips, her heart palpitated wildly. "Hannah! You gave me quite a fright."

"Sorry. I—I thought you might need a shoulder to cry on."

"Don't tempt me," she shot back, her tone bitter.

"Would you like me to go?"

"Yes, go. And good riddance!"

Hannah's muffled sob tore into Hester's conscience.

"My wicked tongue! I'm so incensed with Papa for resorting to coercion I can hardly see straight. Not that it excuses my behavior. It doesn't. And I'm truly sorry I hurt your feelings."

Hannah's face lost its hangdog look. "Consider yourself forgiven. Now then, may I stay?"

"I fear I'm not very good company at the moment."

"I'm not in exactly in the sunniest of moods myself. Well?"

Hester shrugged. "Suit yourself."

"Move over."

They sat shoulder to shoulder for a good five minutes before Hannah said, "Remember how we used to sneak up here and gaze down at fashionable fribbles on the strut?"

She did remember. The old adage, "misery loves company" was certainly true, she mused, as an incident long buried unfolded in mind's eye.

Wed to Miles, Henrietta had already set up housekeeping elsewhere when dearest Mama married the earl. Immediately after the ceremony, Ned had returned to Harrow and Papa had whisked his bride off to Italy for an extended honeymoon. Toby had gone with them because the earl's Aunt Min simply couldn't cope with a lively six-year-old.

Left behind with their elderly chaperone were the fourteen-year-old twins, who'd found themselves, for the first time in their young lives, cut off from both their other siblings and their beloved mother. Cast adrift, they'd rattled around the earl's enormous mansion for ages before chancing upon their attic aerie, where they'd spent the bulk of their time daydreaming.

"Of course I remember. How could I ever forget?" Hester averred.

"We were very unhappy."

"Very," Hester agreed.

"But we are even unhappier now, wouldn't you say?"

Her sister's genuine concern smashed through barriers erected to protect herself from further pain.

"Oh, Hannah," she wailed, "What on earth am I going to do? Charles and I are no longer on speaking terms. Yet, Papa sent an announcement of our betrothal to both the Gazette and the Post."

"I agree it is very highhanded of Papa, but he truly believes he's acting in your best interests."

"Why oh why do those we love always think they know what's best for someone else?"

"I know exactly how you feel."

"Do you?" Hester asked dubiously.

"Oh yes. You feel harried and rushed. As if you weren't given sufficient time to weigh a momentous decision."

"However did you guess? Or did you read my mind?"

"I'm no mindreader, but I do think being twins predisposes us to being closer than mere siblings. I had the same sick feeling in the pit of my stomach when Alden proposed. Duke or no, I didn't want to marry him. In fact, I had other plans. Yet I couldn't bear to disappoint Mama and Papa, who were so ecstatic."

"Well, of course it would have been better to tell them straight-away. However, it's not too late to bare your soul. Perhaps if you do, they'll relent."

"I tried to tell Mama. She says I've wedding jitters." Hannah's chin wobbled. "I know I should make more of a push to make her really listen. Sometimes, I suspect I was born without a backbone."

The anguish in her sister's voice brought tears to Hester's eyes.

"With each passing day," Hannah continued sadly, "it becomes more apparent that the duke and I are as unsuited as you and Charles are. And speaking of Charles, he won't talk to me either. He's mad as hops at both of us."

"Oh? I can well understand why he's annoyed with me. He thinks I tried to trap him. Bad enough to be faced with a marriage of convenience. Can you imagine how miserable I'll be married to a man who doesn't trust me?"

"I don't understand why Charles is so vindictive. He's equally to blame. He had no business being in the library at that time of night. Especially not foxed."

"Very true!" Hester regarded her sister thoughtfully. "Charles mistook me for you, Hannah. Claimed he needed to talk to you. Any idea what he felt was so urgent he couldn't wait 'til morning?"

Hannah blushed. "I . . . that is, Charles and I had an informal understanding."

"You were engaged to him? Without seeking Papa's permission first?"

"Subject to his consent, of course," Hannah amended hastily.

Her initial shock fading, a knowing smile lit Hester's comely features. "It seems I'm not the only twin who practices deception when it suits her purpose. But why keep Papa in the dark?"

Hannah gave a great sigh. "How could I tell him in the presence of the duke?"

"It would have been awkward," Hester conceded.

"Besides, Papa would be sure to think I'd taken leave of my senses. As a second son, Charles inherits only a modest annuity. We'd planned to confess our mutual regard at the end of the season when we thought Charles's suit would stand the best chance, especially if I received no other offers. Alden's proposal knocked the wind out of my sails. I know I should have refused him, and that I should have told Papa that I care nothing for money or titles. That all I want is to be my true love's helpmate. But I—I just couldn't work up the nerve."

In view of Hannah's distress, Hester did her best to conceal her exasperation. "I daresay Charles felt betrayed when he learned you were betrothed to the duke."

"He did! He blew his top! Which isn't all like him. Normally, Charles is quite even-tempered. I fear he may never forgive me for not speaking up."

"Can you blame him?"

"I suppose not. I've made such a botch of things, I'm not even sure I'll ever forgive myself!"

"Nonsense! There's plenty of blame to go around. And Charles has certainly earned his share. Take heart, Hannah. There has to be a way out of this tangle."

Her twin managed a weak smile. "If there is, I expect you'll find it."

Despite Hester's determination to find a solution satisfactory to both couples, nothing had changed as the Astell twins, accompanied by Margaret, approached the Duke of Alden's country estate for a weekend visit.

To Hester's surprise, Hannah's indifference and Margaret's vexation, the Duke of Alden was not on hand to greet them. That honor fell to Jeeves, the duke's dignified major domo, imported from London for the occasion.

"My lady, his grace asked me to convey his regrets. He'd intended to greet you personally, but a pressing estate matter detained him. However, he plans to join you at the tea table in two hours."

"Quite," said Margaret, still in a huff at what she considered to be an unpardonable slight.

A hour later, having unpacked with Iris's help, Hester knocked on the door of Hannah's bedchamber.

Opening it, her sister bade her enter, and once she had, asked, "How's Mama?"

"Resting."

"Good. She looked burnt to the socket when we got here."

"I agree. I daresay a nap will revive her."

"In time for tea?"

"I doubt it. In any case, she begs to be excused until the dinner bell rings."

Hannah scooped up an armful of books off the bed and crossed to an empty shelf situated between a pair of casement windows. Wide-eyed, Hester watched her arrange them, then chuckled.

"Trust you to bring along your own reading material."

"Exactly so. The footman who carried up my trunk grumbled it weighed a ton."

"He's lucky he didn't end up with a broken back. For once I agree with Mama. You read too much, Hannah. You should have a care for your eyesight."

"Reading is one of the few pleasures I refuse to give up."

"Nobody is asking you to. Just to practice a little restraint. You've always got your nose buried in a book. I doubt Alden will approve."

"Much you know about it," Hannah scoffed. "He doesn't care what I read. I quizzed him on that very point before I accepted his offer."

"Did you now?"

Had Alden really given her sister *carte blanche* to read whatever she pleased? Mischief glittered in Hester's eyes. Perhaps she'd give Hannah a copy of Wollstonecraft's *A Vindication of the Rights of Women* as a wedding gift, then sit back and watch the fireworks.

Her thoughts sailed off in another direction. Hannah's tearful confession of her lack of courage to stand up for herself had wrung Hester's heartstrings. But was that really so? When it came to choosing reading material, she seemed to have no problem asserting herself.

* * *

At tea time, Perry was not altogether sorry that his future mother-in-law had begged off. He cast his betrothed a bright smile. "Care for a cream bun, my dear?"

Always the lady, Hannah shook her head demurely. However, when he offered the tray of sweets to Hester, she amused him no end by eying the bun greedily—even though she hadn't quite finished the tart she'd chosen.

Still, he had no business letting his eyes stray. Hannah was the twin he should be showering with attention. He cast her a warm smile as he dunked a corner of his handkerchief in his water glass. Granted although Hester was the livelier twin, Hannah's disposition was sweeter. Obviously he'd made the right choice. Not for him a saucy baggage who challenged his authority at every turn. No question the more biddable twin was the more suitable bride. To be sure, Hannah was shy and retiring—band face it—just the tiniest bit dull. But at least she wasn't likely to run him ragged trying to keep one jump ahead of her.

Smiling at her benignly, he said, "Hold still. You've a smidge of raspberry syrup on your cheek."

When he thrust the dampened handkerchief forward, Hannah took a deep breath as if steeling herself to tolerate his small, albeit well meaning, intrusion. But despite the care he took not to startle her, the instant the damp cloth he held touched her cheek, she flinched.

Perry's hand stilled. "Did I hurt you?"

Hannah's blush deepened to scarlet. She shook her head vigorously. "I can't think why I am so gauche. Pray don't regard it."

He frowned. His intention had been to render a small courtesy calculated to make her less skittish the next time he touched her. Instead, you'd think he'd tried to ravish her.

Dash it all! He could scarcely be expected to tolerate a wife who almost jumped out of her skin whenever he touched her.

Patience, he counseled himself. With patience, she'd soon settle down. He mustn't be discouraged by this small setback.

Forcing a smile, he said, "My dear, I'm pleased your mama agreed to bring you to Aldenwood for a visit. I look forward to showing you around. The grounds were designed by Capability Brown. There's a lake and a summerhouse. I assume you ride. We can tour the estate on horseback if you like."

Hannah blanched. Now what was bothering her, he wondered. Her temperament was that of a high-strung filly. Too sensitive by half! God grant him patience!

"What's overset you?" he asked quietly.

"My lord, I don't care to ride."

"What, never?" he teased. "Not even if I arrange for a gentle mount?"

Hannah's eyes glistened with unshed tears. " 'Tis no teasing matter. Horses are unpredictable creatures. I'd sooner slit my throat than climb up on one's back."

Up to now, Hester had elected to bite her tongue but once she glimpsed pain in her twin's eyes, her priorities shifted.

"My lord, give over. Hannah said she does not care to ride. That should end the matter."

Perry glowered at the audacious minx. "Stay out of this."

"What? Let you bully my sister with impunity? Never!"

"By Jupiter, I'll teach you to meddle!" Rising, he loomed over Hester like an irate demon. "I suggest you finish your tea before it grows tepid." Then, gentling his voice, he said, "Come, Hannah, I'll see you to the foot of the stairs. Doubtless, you wish to rest before dinner." Glancing back at Hester, his jaw set in a rigid line. "Stay put. I'll return in a nonce."

Perry whisked his cowering fiancée out of the drawing room and left her in the capable hands of his housekeeper before he returned to confront Hester.

Still seething, he stared in awe at the full cup of tea she'd shoved aside. All his bluster had failed to intimidate her. How could one sister be so timid and the other so intrepid?

"You didn't drink your tea," he observed with deceptive softness. "To spite me, no doubt."

"Don't flatter yourself. Bullies tend to sour my appetite."

Thank goodness Hannah was his chosen bride, thought
Hester. Had it been the other way round, by now he'd probably
have strangled her.

" 'Tis useless to try and intimidate me. Unlike my sister,
I'm made of stern stuff."

"Damnation! I am not a bully. That sister of yours is afraid
of her own shadow. I was merely trying to coax her out of
her unreasonable fear of horseflesh."

"Good luck to you. Her fear is deep rooted."

"Your faith in my persuasive powers overwhelms me."

"Your grace, there is no need for sarcasm. Hannah took a
bad fall when she was fifteen. Her mount had to be destroyed.
From that day to this, she refuses to ride."

That evening, long after Lady Pardo and her daughters retired, found Perry seated at his fireside getting steadily drunk.
Hell and thunder! He now understood the reason behind Hannah's aversion to horses. Still, it saddened him that his chosen
bride was so henhearted. Had it been Hester who'd taken a
tumble, he'd bet his last groat she'd have long since conquered
her fear. Game as a pebble, had she consented to be his duchess, he'd be willing to wager she'd have relished their morning
gallops. With a bittersweet smile, he forced himself back to
earth. Hester had discouraged him from courting her, whereas
Hannah had agreed to wed him. And to complicate matters
even further, Hester was now engaged to Charles Stuart. So
he'd best stop mooning over what might have been and concentrate on his intended. Actually, the fact that Hannah took
no pleasure in a brisk gallop could be glossed over. What could
not be overlooked was the fact that she shrank from his touch.
Indeed, the very idea of making love to a frigid bride turned
his stomach.

A wistful smile chased a scowl from his rugged features as
he recalled the way Hester had melted like warm butter when

he'd kissed her. Now there was a filly with a passionate core just waiting for the right man to bring it to fruition.

The scowl returned with a vengeance. Fool that he was, he'd let such a rare treasure slip through his fingers. When he'd decided to marry it had been with extreme reluctance. What he'd envisioned was a marriage of convenience. Curse him for being a blind fool! Never in his wildest dreams had he envisioned a love match. Nevertheless, he'd fallen in love with Hester.

For all the good it did him, he loved her very much. But his hands were tied because it would hardly be honorable to call off his wedding to Hester's sister. While Hannah could cry off without incurring the censure of the *ton,* a true gentleman did not treat a gently bred young woman so shabbily. Besides, his own sense of honor wouldn't permit it.

The realization that he loved Hester but could never claim her almost unmanned him. Rising, he tossed off the rest of the brandy and smashed the empty glass against the brick fireplace.

Perry's temper tantrum was cut short by Jeeves, who informed him a Mr. Charles Stuart had arrived on the premises an hour past and desired a word with him before retiring.

Curiosity piqued, he said, "Show him in, Jeeves."

Minutes later, Charles stormed into the duke's private sitting room like an ardent crusader determined to give no quarter.

"I can't get a word of sense out of Hannah. Whatever did you say to her to overset her?"

Amazed at Stuart's gall, Perry said icily, "How dare you presume to question me? Whatever I said to Hannah is none of your business."

"Well, I choose to make it my business as of now. I can't have my dearest love crying all over my new waistcoat. This farce has gone on long enough."

Perry rolled his eyes. He could make neither head nor tail out of his irascible guest's ramblings. Yet his interest was caught.

"Farce, sir? Are you implying my engagement is a farce?"

"I ain't implying," Charles fumed. "I'm telling you to your

face Hannah loves me—not you. And if you hadn't turned her mama's head by making her an offer, she and I would now be betrothed."

Perry's eyebrows raised so high they almost met with his hairline. "Would you now? That would certainly be a cozy arrangement, being as you are already engaged to Hester?"

"Hester?" Charles stared at him blankly.

"Purely as a matter of idle curiosity, what did you plan to do about your present fiancée? Drown her, mayhap? Or does your taste run to being engaged to both twins at once?"

His grace's sarcasm passed right over the head of the pre-occupied scholar.

"Mind you, I'm fond of Hester. But I love Hannah. Besides, she'll make an ideal parson's wife, whereas Hester would be an abysmal failure."

Perry experienced a poignant rush of tenderness for Hester. How mortified she'd be if Stuart cast her aside in favor of her sister. Stuart's indifference to the one woman on earth he'd give his eye teeth to be in a position to cherish infuriated him. Indeed, the duke was so incensed he was forced to clench the arms of his wing chair with both hands to keep himself from drawing the insensitive clod's cork.

"See here, Stuart, you can't mean to reject Hester and take up with her sister. It simply isn't done."

"Gammon! Hester would cry off in a minute if the earl would permit it. With my blessings, I might add. But never mind about her. We need to discuss how best to convince Hannah to end your farcical engagement."

Perry's head reeled. His sitting room had suddenly turned into bedlam. Still, he desperately wanted to believe Hester's betrothal to Stuart was every bit as farcical as his own. And that Hester regretted agreeing to it as much as he regretted making Hannah an offer.

Indeed, while perfectly charming, Hannah was entirely too meek for his taste. Far better the challenge of a saucy wench, who had the bottom to stand up to him whenever he became overbearing. And far, far better a wife with a bit of fire in her blood.

"Quite right. I suggest we put our heads together and see if we can find a way out of this muddle."

"By George, that's a capital notion! When do we start?"

"Immediately, my dear chap, immediately. Time is of the essence."

Charles favored him with a boyish grin. "Just so, your grace, just so."

FINALE. . . .

On the last day of June, the sun shone brightly and the sky was cloudless. Would that the minds of the four participants scheduled to be united in holy matrimony that morning were equally as bright and free of storm clouds. But such was not the case.

Hannah and Hester slumbered on, oblivious to the fact that their wedding day had dawned. True, it was barely eight o'clock. But brides need plenty of time to ready themselves for such an important turning point in their lives.

Hester, being the early riser of the two, was predisposed to wake first.

She emerged from her dreamlike state with a wistful smile on her face. At Aldenwood, the cunning rogue had used blackmail to soften her up. Last night, she'd fallen asleep recounting every facet of his campaign in delicious detail. The clever way he'd crept past her defenses to steal a half dozen kisses. And the way his slightest touch made her feel all tingly inside. This morning, she'd woke with the endearments he'd whispered into her ear at Aldenwood replaying in her subconscious.

Drat the man! Bad enough that he haunted her waking hours. Did he have to rob her of sleep as well? Silly question. He'd keep pouring on the pressure until he got his way.

The sense that the walls of her bedchamber were closing in

on her sent Hester rushing over to the open casement window. Peering out, she noted a soft rain had fallen during the night. She drew a deep breath. The air smelt sweet. That the sun shone was considered a good omen on one's wedding day. A glimmer of hope flickered.

Turning with resolution from the view, Hester rang for her morning chocolate.

By eleven o'clock St. Margaret's Westminster was packed to the gills with the cream of society come to witness the nuptials of the Astell twins. Many families had postponed their departure to the country, for although rather late in the season, the earl was held in high esteem and no one wished to offend him.

Both prospective bridegrooms stood at the chancel rail, their expressions strained and anxious. By rights, Ned Astell, who was Charles's best man, should be standing beside him. But the Astell twins hadn't arrived yet. Nor had the rest of his family. So he'd gone outside to wait for them.

Standing shoulder to shoulder with the debonair duke was Lord Buxton, a longtime friend who'd agreed to be his best man, even though it entailed making a special trip up to London from his Devon estate. It meant a great deal to Perry that Andrew and Jenny had agreed to come because, despite a rocky start, they were happily married and his grace considered their attendance a good omen.

The church's east wall boasted a beautiful stained glass window dating from medieval times. However, there was only so long those gathered could stare at a window depicting the crucifixion without becoming cross-eyed. Thus, the increasing restlessness of their captive audience came as no great surprise to Perry.

Hester frowned. She disliked riding backward because she like to see where was she was going. But to sit beside Hannah was impossible. Dressed in their finery, it would be too much of a squeeze. Nor did she dare switch places. Her sister was prone to motion sickness and, if coaxed to ride backwards, would in all likelihood cast up her accounts, which would certainly put a damper on what was purported to be the most important day in a young woman's life.

Besides, she had more important concerns. It was her job to see to it that Hannah did not lose her resolve. So far she'd managed to distract her, but they had a ways to go yet before they arrived at St. Margaret's.

Normally, Hester mused, their parents would have ridden in the same carriage. But having spent a small fortune on their satin cream wedding dresses, neither had wanted to take a chance that their daughters' gowns would be crushed en route. They, along with Toby and Marcus, had gone on ahead in the family travel coach.

Thus, she and Hannah had the smart town carriage all to themselves, which was just as well. To be honest, Hester's normally cast-iron stomach was experiencing a few flutters, chiefly because they were running almost three quarters of an hour behind schedule due to an overturned hay wagon that had blocked the intersection at Charing Cross.

"H-hester, are you sure we should go ahead with this?"

She lifted an eyebrow. "Cold feet, sister?"

Hannah nodded. "Charles will never forgive me if I let him down a second time. So if I balk, promise to give me a sharp nudge."

"Of course I will. Try not to worry, dearest. Either it works like a charm or it doesn't."

Hell and thunder! Perry muttered. This waiting was a torment akin to purgatory. Perspiration trickled down his spine and his neckcloth was choking off his windpipe. He'd assumed that he and Hester were now of the same mind, just as Charles and Hannah were natural soul mates, but as the moments snailed past his confidence had steadily eroded. For something had clearly gone awry, because their brides were almost an hour late.

Nor was the duke the only person inside the church who was ill at ease. Beside him, Charles shifted his weight from one foot to the other, and the rector scowled at Perry as if he held him directly responsible for his bride's tardiness. He could only suppose Hester was having trouble shoring up her more timid twin's nerve. If that was the hitch, he had faith in her powers of persuasion.

His thoughts darkened as he faced his worst nightmare. What if Hannah wasn't the problem? What if Hester herself had changed her mind? What if in the end, she wouldn't have him? Life without his delightful deceiver would be bleak indeed.

Adding to his sense of doom were the wedding guests, who had progressed from bored to resentful. Hell and thunder! Some squirmed in their seats, some coughed. A more mean-spirited segment explored possible ramifications of the Astell twins' tardiness in an waspish undertone, thus setting the stage for a cynical wag to remark in a voice loud enough to carry to the prospective bridegroom, "poor sods looked as if they're facing the guillotine instead of the altar."

His compatriot gave a rude guffaw, which echoed throughout the acoustically enhanced structure. "Their fate is far worse. They're about to be leg shackled."

Someone else chuckled, but Perry had had quite enough. He gazed at the original wiseacre, the light of battle in his steely gray eyes.

The offender fell silent. The audience quickly followed suit. God knows no one wanted to get on the wrong side of the powerful Duke of Alden who, while not precisely a grudge-older, was said to have a long memory.

But while he'd managed to curb the tongues of the mean-spirited elements, the mood of the congregation had turned ugly. And there wasn't a damn thing Perry could do to turn

them up sweet. Only the arrival of the Astell twins could do
that. And if they didn't show up soon, even they were liable
to be caught up in the backlash.

Once the liveried footman helped her alight, Hester found
herself surrounded by the rest of her family, who'd gathered
in the churchyard.

"Such a backlog on the road," Margaret complained. "I
thought we'd never arrive."

"Don't fret, dearest," said the earl. "We're all here now,
which is what matters." He turned to his oldest stepson. "Ned,
you may escort your mama to the front pew. Toby and Marcus
shall follow in your wake. Then after a decent interval, I'll
make my grand entrance."

Hester had to smile. To be sure, St. Margaret's was a gem
of a church nestled within the shadow of the famed Westminster Abbey. But that was not the reason it had been chosen for
the twins' wedding. Papa fancied himself striding down the
aisle with a twin on each arm, and St. Margaret's aisle was
wide enough to accommodate three abreast without crushing
either bride's gown.

His grace's craggy countenance resembled that of a disgruntled bear with a sharp thorn in its paw. He's been standing at
the altar for well over an hour in full view of a church packed
with wedding guests. Never had he been more mortified.

Face it, you lovesick nodcock! Hester isn't coming.

Perry felt as if the ground had suddenly crumbled beneath
him. Hester meant the world to him. Had he really lost her?
And if so, how could he go on without her?

Suddenly one of the church's huge doors widened enough
to allow a shaft of sunlight to cut a broad swath across the
narthex and Ned appeared in the nave with Lady Pardo on his

arm. As they glided down the aisle, Perry felt as if a great weight pressing against his chest had been lifted.

Ned settled his mother in the front pew, and after acknowledging Miles and Henrietta—who was making her first appearance in public since the birth of her third daughter—continued on to the chancel rail where he took his rightful place beside Charles Stuart.

Next to appear at the nave were the Earl of Pardo and the Astell twins. Proud as a peacock, he proceeded to strut down the aisle with a radiant daughter on each arm.

Once the threesome reached the chancel rail, the earl gently disengaged himself and retired to his seat next to his wife. The sudden withdrawal of his support seemed to momentarily astound both twins, who now seemed hesitant to take the final step.

Perry sucked in a breath. Great God almighty! How would either he or Charles cope if they wound up with the wrong bride?

It wasn't to be thought of. Yet if either twin lost her nerve at the last minute, that's exactly what would occur. And should that actually happen, there'd be hell to pay with the rector. Because he and Charles had called on him earlier and fed him the tarradiddle that the twin's names had been accidentally switched and that they'd come to set the record straight.

On the other hand, his grace reflected, if his dearest madcap could just muster the courage to execute one more deception the records of both marriages would be entirely correct, and Perry need not contemplate a painful interview in which he tried to calm an irate rector.

Perry stared at Hester as if willing her to take the final irrevocable step. Starved for air, his lungs ached, but he dare not break his concentration. The moment that tested a man's soul was upon him! Never in his life had he felt so helpless!

The twins exchanged a meaningful glance, then Hester nudged her sister and, quicker than the blink of an eye, they switched places. In the front pew, the earl's eyes glazed over.

Tensing, he started to arise, but Margaret tugged on his sleeve and smiled at him so serenely, Lucian decided his eyes must have been playing tricks on him and slowly relaxed tense muscles.

Once Perry sensed Hester's presence beside him he let out the breath he'd been holding in a long sigh. Finally all was in train. Gazing down at his beautiful bride, he discovered she was trembling like a leaf. Taking her hand in his, he gave it a gentle squeeze as if to say: "Never fear. I'm here beside you. Nothing can harm you."

Hester cast her husband-to-be a tremulous smile. She couldn't be happier. In a few minutes they'd be wed, as would Hannah and Charles.

Both couples were poised to live happily ever after, Perry reflected. Or were they? He was seized by a terrible premonition. What if the twins had gotten mixed up, and even though they'd switched with each other, he was about to marry the wrong bride? Hell and thunder! Where had such a nightmarish thought risen from?

Well never mind. There was a surefire way to reassure himself. Yet he was afraid to take action.

Finally, however, Perry simply could not bear the suspense any longer. So putting his entire future happiness on the line, he cast a sharp look at the beautiful young woman whose hand rested so trustingly in his.

In that instant, all his misgivings magically vanished. He knew he was marrying the right twin, and that standing beside him, looking surprisingly demure, was Hester Elizabeth Astell. And the reason he could be absolutely certain was because of the tiny beauty mark he'd spotted on her right ear lobe.

"Dearly beloved. We are gathered here . . ."

Perry smiled. All was right with the world. He was about to marry Hester. And by God, if he had anything to say about it, they'd live happily ever after.

The Vicarious Bride

by
Winifred Witton

Moonlight glimmered fitfully over the grounds of the Misses Grimbeys' Select Academy for Young Ladies of Bath. Breaking through scattered clouds, it picked out a pale figure flitting across the back lawn. Moments later, branches bent and leaves rustled as the runaway climbed the elm tree that leaned against the wall. In another moment the wall was scaled and a flurry of muslin skirts vanished over the side.

Miss Abigail Fordham, the literature mistress, stood on the lawn, uncertain. She was fond of the rebellious Kitty Wellfleet and was tempted to let her go, for she quite understood the girl's longing to break out and be free of the strict confines of the school. Besides, she anticipated a comfortable coze with Kitty, learning all the titillating details of this latest escapade, for without a romantic life of her own, Abby lived vicariously in Kitty's adventures. Being the offspring of a devout vicar who named his daughter Abigail—a term for a lady's maid—to remind her that all humans live in servitude to a Higher Being, she sympathized with the wayward Kitty.

For the past year, since obtaining her position at the Misses Grimbeys' establishment, Abby had covered for Kitty as best she could while that damsel slipped out to visit the famous Pump Room, shop in Milsom Street, and even, she suspected, to meet with officers from the regiment currently quartered far too close by. She imagined a braver version of herself taking Kitty's place, flouting authority with zest.

But that was not for a penniless school mistress with her way to make in an uncaring world. And if Miss Wellfleet was caught one more time, she would be expelled for certain and

Abby would lose the volatile girl who had become her one alleviation in the dreary cloistered halls of the Select Academy for Young Ladies. She'd best go after her and sneak her back inside.

She dared not take the time to run around to the gate at the front. She eyed the elm tree, undaunted. It had been fifteen years since an eleven-year-old Abby had last climbed a tree, but the old skill must remain. Hitching up her narrow skirt and petticoat, she rolled them up and tucked the hems in front, under the bodice of her simple gray gown. Her lower portion, should anyone see, was covered almost to her ankles by her cotton pantalettes. She attacked the tree confidently.

She soon discovered house slippers were not designed for scrambling up limbs and she had reckoned without her grown-up skirts. They showed a regrettable tendency to slip loose from under her bodice and unroll. Attempting to secure them before she was tripped up, she missed her footing and tore a rent in her second-best stockings. Then one of the tapes that tied her two-part pantalettes at her waist came undone and she lost the legging in a tight tree crotch.

It might be the dark of night and no one to see, but she hastily let down her skirts, blushing furiously. Try as she would, she could not pull the pantalette free. The crocheted edging she had worked at the hem, not being able to afford real lace, had snagged on an unusually twiggy branch and her pulling succeeded only in wedging the recalcitrant garment more solidly into the crotch of the tree limb. She had no time to waste struggling with it if she was to find Kitty before the confounded chit was out of sight. Fortunately, the top of the wall was now within easy reach. With only one leg properly covered, she crawled along a sturdy branch that might have grown there for the purpose, gaining that next step.

Only to face a new dilemma: the wall was high. How would she get down on the other side? The moon broke through again and she saw someone had placed a wooden crate on the ground below, in a strategic spot to act as a stair. Ah, she had stumbled on a frequently used escape route.

Ahead was not a lane leading to the town road, but rather an orchard—and the moonlight, now bright and clear, revealed the white of a gown and the red of an officer's coat among the trees. Just as she feared, Kitty was having a rendezvous with a man.

This would never do and Abby knew her duty. Pulling down her rumpled skirts to hide her missing pantalette, she hurried up to the couple. The young man pushed Kitty behind him and faced her bravely, but Kitty had seen who had caught them.

"It is all right, Harry," she exclaimed. "It is only my dear Miss Abby. She is a Trojan and will not carry tales on me."

"Kitty, you will be expelled!" Abby shook her head in despair. "And I will be dismissed as well if we are found outside."

The young man assumed a belligerent pose, his arm protectively about the girl. "Madam," he declared stoutly, "we love each other."

"Yes, yes, of course you do," said Abby, "but not now and here. Kitty, come with me immediately. You know you must never sneak out to meet a man or do anything like it again."

"Oh, but I must."

"No, my love." Her Harry released her and stepped away. "Go quickly. I'll not have you in trouble because of me." He saluted Abby as though she were an officer, turned sharply on his heel, and marched off.

Kitty sighed dramatically. "Is he not noble?" She clasped her hands to her heart like the heroine in a melodrama she imagined herself to be. "He is so romantic."

"That is neither here nor there, young lady," Abby told her, trying her level best to sound stern—but would it not be heavenly, she thought, to be so young and in your first love . . .

Kitty hung back as Abby tried to steer her around toward the front gate. "It's quicker over the wall," she pointed out.

"I don't care. I am not clambering about in that tree again."

She took Kitty's hand and pulled her along. "If we hurry we may still slip in through the front gate."

"It is easier climbing down," Kitty told her, but she trotted meekly by Abby's side. "I expect you are wondering who that was," she said.

"Not at all. I only wonder at your daring to meet him. Kitty, such clandestine affairs are not at all the thing for a respectable young lady of quality."

"He is Lieutenant Harry Boardman," Kitty went on happily, ignoring the reproof. "Do you not think him handsome?"

"I only think we'd best be quick."

They were not quick enough. When they reached the gate, the school porter had already locked it for the night, leaving them no alternative but going back to scale the wall and coping with the tree.

A cool breeze blew up the back of Abby's skirt and she stiffened suddenly. It was a very good thing that they had to go back! Her lost pantalette would be waving in that breeze, a betraying white flag among the branches.

Kitty had gone up first and she stopped short on top of the wall, pointing a shaking hand. "Abby—Oh, Abby, what is that?"

Abby joined her. Just as she feared, the pantalette flapped below the leaves. "I'm afraid it's mine," she explained, lifting her skirt so Kitty could see her one bare leg. "The tapes came untied, and—"

The rest of her sentence was lost on Kitty, who nearly toppled from the wall, giggling. "Oh, I thought one of the Miss Grimbeys had seen me climb the tree and left a marker to catch me coming back. I nearly died of fright!"

"They may catch us yet," Abby admonished. "Do hurry down and help me get it loose."

They negotiated the tree without further calamity and nimble-fingered Kitty, sitting astride the limb, managed to separate the lost pantalette from the twigs and the rough bark of the crotch.

"The trim is quite ruined," Abby mourned. "I must crochet a whole new border, all because of you, you hurly-burly young baggage."

Still overcome by unrepentant giggles, Kitty helped her put it on and retie the tapes about her waist. They were both in disarray, their garments grimy and snagged by twigs.

"Let us hope," said Abby, "that we may get in unseen."

"Should I pray?" asked the incorrigible Kitty with yet another giggle.

"I fear we are undeserving of grace. Do be quiet, we must pass the Miss Grimbeys' quarters."

Their luck, if one could call it that, had run out. Kitty caught Abby's arm. "The parlor casement," she hissed in her ear. "It's open, and is that not a light?"

It was. A wavering candle sent a faint glow out onto the lawn they were about to cross. They ducked behind the row of flowering shrubs.

"Oh, Abby," Kitty whispered. "It is Miss Matilda and she is waiting for us. I was about to leave here in a few months anyway but, Abby, I am so sorry to have involved you. You may lose your position—but, really, you should not have followed me."

Before Abby could think of a suitably crushing reply, the eldest Miss Grimbey leaned from the window, playing the weak beam of her candle on the shrubs.

"I see you, Miss Wellfleet," she said. "You may as well come out. And is that you, Miss Fordham?" She smacked her thin lips in satisfaction. "I thought as much."

Fairly caught, the two miscreants rose from behind the bushes and stood on the lawn. Miss Matilda eyed them with grim pleasure.

"I did not approve of my sister appointing you Mistress of Literature, Miss Fordham. Encouraging impressionable young females to read novels and absorb romantic notions! I told her no good would come of it, and I was right."

She looked the silent figures on the lawn up and down,

taking in Abby's torn stocking hanging about her ankle and the dangling ends of her crocheted pantalette trim on the other leg. Both their gowns were filthy and stuck with leaves and twigs.

"It is late," said Miss Grimbey. "I will deal with you in the morning. Meanwhile, may I suggest you both pack your trunks."

"Both?" cried Kitty. "But Miss Fordham was only bringing me back!"

Too late. The casement slammed shut.

Miss Abigail Fordham perched on the edge of a hard-backed chair in the best front parlor of the Misses Grimbeys' Select Academy for Young Ladies of Bath. Her fingers twined and untwined in the lap of her dove gray gown, and a cap—so suitable for her lowly situation—covered the soft brown hair pulled tightly back into two neat buns. She looked questioningly at the two elderly school mistresses, waiting for the axe to fall. Where was she to go? What was she to do? And who was this man?

The impeccable Corinthian who stood before her raised his quizzing glass and inspected her critically. Suddenly he addressed a remark to the air above her head.

"She appears far too young."

This ruffled Miss Fordham's feathers. He was not so very old himself! She judged him to be near her own age of twenty-six, though possibly some years her senior. And quite the most romantic hero-image she had yet encountered! She studied him carefully, memorizing his features and gestures to add a new character to her meager collection of daydreams.

His tall figure seemed to fill the dainty parlor, his breadth increased by the caped driving coat he still wore. He had removed his curly-brimmed beaver, dropping it casually on a gimcrack-filled table to the obvious horror of Miss Jane Grimbey, who had rushed to the rescue of her precious ornaments.

The only damage had been to his dark hair, now rumpled and creased at the back where his hat had rested. Abby wondered if he knew the way it lay in damp ringlets on the nape of his neck. Probably not, his aspect being so forbidding and dignified. His brows frowned over piercing blue eyes, his wide mouth was set in a grim line, and his nose and jaw appeared chiseled rather than smoothly carved. Truly, he was worth taking part in her dreams—but what had he to do with her losing her position?

He repeated his flat comment. "Far too young."

Miss Jane Grimbey twittered and fluttered, shaking her head at him. "Indeed, she is not too young!" she exclaimed anxiously. "Miss Abigail Fordham has been one of our best teachers."

Abby blinked, surprised. But she was being sent off! Why did Miss Grimbey sing her praises to this man?

Miss Jane had the temerity to add a rider. "Yes, and the only one to whom *that girl* will pay the least heed!"

Miss Matilda frowned at her sister. "You must understand, my lord, we demand strict adherence to our rules. Unfortunately, your ward's conduct does not match her pretty face."

His ward! Abby eyed the man with renewed interest. So this was Lord Ashley, Miss Kitty Wellfleet's guardian. She would have thought him to be a much older man, for Kitty, though generally a care-for-nothing damsel, seemed to hold him in some awe. Part of the mystery clarified, she now knew who he was, but had she been called in to take the blame for Kitty's wayward behavior?

The Corinthian raised haughty eyebrows. "Am I to gather Kitty is being—er—sent down?"

This direct approach flustered Miss Jane. "Oh, no—well— but you see . . ."

"Indeed, I do see. In that case, I have no choice but to remove her from your care. However, as I have informed you, there is currently no resident female in my establishment and the chit must have a chaperon." He returned to Abby and the quizzing glass came into play once more. She began to feel like an ant on a cheese board.

He dropped the glass, letting it dangle on the end of its black grosgrain riband. "I would prefer an older woman who would keep a strict attendance on her."

"Then the girl will run away," muttered Miss Jane.

Miss Matilda primmed her thin mouth. "I am afraid she always does so when she is bored, my Lord Ashley."

"She does, does she?" His deceptively quiet tone boded ill for the unfortunate young lady under discussion.

If the Misses Grimbey expected her to give a report on the escapades of Miss Kitty, Abby knew not what she would say to the shatteringly dignified peer who had raised his quizzing glass at her. That Kitty was so fond of currant cakes she slipped down at night to raid the kitchen and that she played truant on every possible occasion? That she refused to learn her French verbs and had absolutely no aptitude for either pianoforte or harp?

Abby was no tattle-tale, one reason why her students held her in such high regard. As Kitty's instructor she might have despaired, but she had formed a deep affection for the restless child. Child! Miss Kitty Wellfleet had just passed her seventeenth birthday, far beyond the age when she should have left the Misses Grimbeys' Academy. One could hardly blame her for becoming bored with schoolroom occupations and escaping whenever she could.

Miss Matilda still held forth. "We can only hope that her want of conduct may not put her beyond the pale. You must see, my lord, that we can no longer keep her here."

"We cannot be responsible for the actions of such a sad romp," added Miss Jane, with an air of washing her hands of the whole affair.

The frown that creased Lord Ashley's brow became a veritable thunder cloud. "I collect she is hot-at-hand, but not yet ready to tie her garter in public."

Miss Matilda's mouth set in a thin line. "Well, as to that,

you must know a regiment of His Majesty's Finest is now stationed quite near Bath. I am afraid the scarlet coats have caused a number of heart-stirrings among the older girls and we have discovered that your ward has been slipping out at night. We cannot feel she is a good influence on the younger girls."

Lord Ashley took a rapid turn about the room and from the expression on his face, Abby suspected him of cursing silently. "What the devil I'm to do with her, I don't know. I shall have to take her to Ashland Court and hope that the prospect of five miles on foot will keep her from the attractions of Bath, for she will be forbidden the use of horse or carriage. You may be sure that once she is under my control, she will be more circumspect in her behavior."

"She'll be gone in a week," Miss Jane muttered to herself, and his lordship turned his frowning eyes on her.

"She likes Miss Fordham," Miss Matilda offered. "Kitty may never run away if she is in Miss Fordham's charge."

He stopped in front of Abby, who still felt confused. "In that case, Miss Fordham, it must be you. I am told your trunk is packed. I'll have it strapped to my traveling coach at once along with Kitty's. We shall leave within the hour for I do not care to put up here for the night."

Abby gasped. "Leave? With you?"

He slapped his thigh impatiently with his driving gloves. "Yes. Have you not been informed? You are to enter my employ at once as a companion to my ward. I could wish you were an older female. It will be impossible for me to remain at Ashland while young unmarried ladies are in residence, so I will have to remove to the York. Meanwhile, Miss Wellfleet must have a chaperon. I had hoped to keep her here until the wedding."

Wedding? The rest of his speech was lost on Abby. Was Kitty then to be married? Or was he? And waiting to remove his ward from the school until he had a wife and a proper home for the girl? For some reason the thought of this romantic-

looking man being betrothed caused her to feel a genuine pang
of regret. As if it should make the least difference to her! Nor,
she added to herself, would it interfere with his becoming part
of an impossible fantasy in her daydreams. Still . . .

Perhaps not precisely within the hour, but in a surprisingly
short time Abby found herself seated in Lord Ashley's comfortable traveling coach, with a hot brick for her feet and a
fur-lined carriage rug over her knees. Ashley himself remained
at the York, awaiting the arrival of his valet and curricle.

Miss Kitty Wellfleet sat beside her in a quiver of excitement
and delight. Abby wondered who was better pleased at their
departure, Kitty or the Misses Grimbey. She felt a small thrill
of pride in her pupil. The girl presented a delectable picture
in a sky blue pelisse covering a dainty sprig muslin gown with
a high waist and tiny puff sleeves. Her dusky curls peeped
from beneath a modish bonnet that must have cost all of fifty
guineas. More than Abby's entire outfit, she was sure.

Kitty turned to her impulsively and gave her a hug. "Oh,
Abby, my darling Abby, I can't believe I'm free! And I'm so
happy to have you all to myself!"

Abby disentangled herself from the arms that threatened to
knock askew her one decent hat.

"You may not have me long if you do not mend your hoydenish ways. My Lord Ashley will expect you to behave like
a lady or I shall be laid off once more. He seems very stern.
Tell me, Kitty, how came you to have such a young man for
a guardian?"

"Why, he is not young! Nearly an old fogey. He must be
fully as old as you."

Abby choked. Old, indeed!

"He inherited me," Kitty explained, as if that made all clear.

"He what?"

Kitty rattled on, a regular little bagpipe once started. "Yes,
he is the son of my first guardian who was my father's dearest

friend. When he died last year, there was no one but Ashley to take over. But that is not the worst! You see, I must marry Ashley or be a penniless orphan, thrown out into the street."

Kitty was to marry Lord Ashley or be disowned? Abby stared at her, startled. "Good God, it cannot be as bad as all that!"

"Oh, but it is! It is the most monstrous thing. You see, my father and his father betrothed us to each other when we were children and to insure that nothing went wrong, my father left my estates and my entire fortune, free and clear, to Ashley. To get them back, I must marry him."

"But—but do you wish to?" Oh, dear, Abby thought, Kitty could never survive without the luxury she was accustomed to! She *must* marry the man!

Kitty seemed sublimely unconcerned. "Well, Ashley will insist on it. It is just the sort of nonsensical notion he'd cling to. However, he won't wish to be leg-shackled for years and something is bound to come up before then."

Abby corrected her almost mechanically. "Kitty, you must not talk cant."

The girl smiled happily. "I can if I wish now. It doesn't matter any more. Oh, Abby, you will love Ashland. It is the most beautiful place, and is it not lovely that it lies so close to Bath now that the regiment is quartered there—for escorts, I mean, to the concerts and assemblies."

As Abby heard those fell words, she had a presentiment of disaster. In a tone of deep foreboding, she came directly to the point. "Do pray tell me, Kitty, at once! Is there one particular scarlet coat?"

The rosy blush that mantled the girl's cheeks belied her next words. She spoke carelessly. "Oh, not seriously. Though I do know one quite delightful officer. You met him last night."

"However did you manage to scrape an acquaintance with one of the soldiers?" And, Abby added silently, however shall I put a stop to it? The girl was in the throes of first love.

Kitty caught her hand in a rush of confidence. "Oh, Abby,

darling, it was so romantic! We met in the bookstore where I went with Melissa. He was on the other side of the table and when we looked up, our eyes met over duplicate copies of *Marmion*. Abby, he is just like Lochinvar. 'So faithful in love, so dauntless in war . . .' Abby, it was love at first sight!"

Oh, dear God, thought poor Abby. I should have known when I caught her slipping out at night. "But, Kitty, what about Lord Ashley?"

Kitty smiled sunnily. "Oh, I shall not tell him and I know you will not give me away."

Although greatly disturbed, Abby kept her tone casual and practical. "No, of course not. I am no addle-plot. But you must not see that officer again! I can only hope you may not have sunk yourself beyond reproach."

Kitty hugged her again. "Do not put yourself in a stew, darling Abby. No one has ever seen us together."

Abby pressed her hands tightly. "No, Kitty. You must promise me to end this affair at once. I cannot set the least store by your acting with any discretion."

Kitty merely laughed, and their arrival at Ashland prevented Abby from saying more.

Ashland Court was everything and more than Abby had dreamed. They drove for a mile or so along extensive grounds enclosed by a high stone wall topped with urns and curlicues of black wrought iron. When they drew up before a pair of towering gates, Abby let down the glass on her side of the coach and peered ahead through the decorative iron work while they waited for a porter to throw them wide.

She saw a long drive, edged with rhododendrons and paved with freshly raked gravel. The manor house itself was still invisible as they entered, hidden by a stand of elms that bordered a lake as blue as the sky. Three white swans and a black one floated amid pink and yellow water lilies and swaying reeds, disrupting the reflection of a single fluffy cloud. On the far bank was a gazebo, constructed of green and white marble in the style of a Greek temple, and behind it, another grove of trees with a flower bed blazing with color at its base. Abby let out a sigh of sheer pleasure. It lacked only a strutting peacock or two, but then even that was granted her a few minutes later when the drive curved around the elms and the manor itself came into view. Not one but four of the magnificent birds scattered before the carriage, squawking.

The manor was not over large. It must be one of his lordship's minor establishments, she decided. An elegant rectangle of native stone, ivy covered, with three rows of mullioned windows and topped with a crenelated roof decorated with hideous gargoyles, it fulfilled her every expectation. A broad, stair-stepped, semi-circular terrace paved with red brick led down to the drive from the entrance.

As the carriage drew to a halt, the great double oaken doors were thrown wide, revealing a liveried butler and a black-clad housekeeper waiting to welcome them. To Abby's intense delight, two footmen in knee breeches, white wigs, and gold-laced coats ran to open the carriage door. Kitty, who had taken advantage of the long trip to catch up on the sleep she'd lost the night before, tumbled out almost before the steps were let down, to be greeted with open arms by the housekeeper.

Abby followed her across the terrace, hesitant, unsure of her position in this elegant household. Kitty at once made it clear.

"Fenny, this is my beloved Abby—Miss Fordham—who has come to keep me company while Ashley stays at the York in Bath. Mrs. Fenton, Abby. She'll see that you are always comfortable. And here," Kitty turned to the butler, catching his hand and pulling him forward. "This is Fenton, who saw to it that I never wanted for sweetmeats. He's a darling."

The butler, flushing with pleasure, bowed formally from the waist, just in time for Abby to stay the hand she'd been about to offer him.

She and Kitty were bundled inside by Mrs. Fenton while

the butler remained to oversee the footmen struggling with their trunks. Abby had no time to admire the tapestries, paintings and suits of armor in the sumptuous hall before she was escorted up a broad flight of carpeted stairs with carved balusters. On the first floor, she was shown to a bedchamber next door to Kitty's and left to freshen up and change her gown as dinner was ready to be served, Ashland Court being on country time.

After her bare cell at the Misses Grimbeys' academy, Abby found her room luxurious beyond her imaginings. She sank down on a feather bed and ran her hands over the blue and gold cover that matched the hangings from the tester above her head and the draperies at the window overlooking a rose garden. The setting sun glowed on walls papered with a pattern of vines and leaves against a blue dotted background. It glinted off the gilt frames of several delicate flower paintings and the shining brass of a pair of candlesticks flanked with porcelain figurines on the mantel. A mantel—and a hearth with a real fire, just for her!

A tap on the door preceded the footmen, who carried in her shabby trunk. They were followed by a maid who curtsied to her as though she were an honored guest.

"My name is Betsy," the girl said. "Would you like me to unpack for you?"

And see her home-made undergarments? Abby shook her head, too dazed to speak. The maid curtsied again and left with the footmen.

At dinner, she and Kitty sat in solitary splendor at one end of a vast mahogany table meant to seat thirty or more.

"When only Ashley is here, we usually have all our meals in the morning room," Kitty explained with an impish grin. I ordered dinner in here just to impress you."

Abby had been staring, awestruck, at the paneled wainscoting and deep red silk covering the walls up to the ceiling. Dark paintings in ornate frames stared back at her. She wrenched her eyes from a repellent depiction of dead pheasants and rabbits that hung directly before her.

"You have succeeded," she admitted with a reluctant smile. "But if I am to enjoy my meals, please let us use that morning room where I won't be faced by defunct fauna!"

Kitty giggled, inordinately pleased. "I knew you'd be overwhelmed. Isn't Ashland Court a lovely place? It is my favorite, and Ashley is rarely here, preferring London, so we shall have it mostly to ourselves."

This did not seem as delightful a prospect to Abby as it did to Kitty. She realized with a touch of surprise how much she looked forward to seeing a great deal more of her dashing Corinthian. Yes, *her* Corinthian, in that she had already cast him in a prominent role as the hero figure in her vicarious dream life. The man was worthy of a great deal more study.

As a matter of fact, she met him again the very next day, when he arrived just as the ladies were about to go in to luncheon. Kitty had already entered the morning room, but Abby was still in the hall when he came in. He walked directly up to her, put a finger under her chin and inspected her features with a slight frown. In spite of herself, she felt her cheeks flush.

He shook his head. "Definitely too young. And too serious to be a companion for a child like Kitty. Let me see you smile."

There he went, harping once more on her lack of years. Abby was proud of her competence as a teacher and her temper got the better of her. "Are you under the impression, my lord, that you have purchased a horse whose teeth you wish examine? I assure you, I am of age."

He stepped back and his eyes traveled over her defiant figure. "Good. You have spirit. You'll need it to control my wayward ward." Then he grinned, and his entire face was transformed.

Abby stifled a gasp. Never had she encountered such an attractive male. Gone was all trace of the austere gentleman of the Misses Grimbeys' parlor. Instead, she faced the embodiment of all those daydreams with which she had endured her dreary days at the academy.

"You're a pretty little thing," he remarked, "but must you go about in mourning? Surely you possess more suitable raiment for dining."

"I am wearing a *most* suitable gown, my lord," she exclaimed, somewhat taken aback. "I am a companion, not a guest in your home."

"Yes, that is what I came to see you about. I wish you to accompany Kitty at all times, and I fancy that requires a new wardrobe. You will take the troublesome chit to Bath on the morrow. I'll order the carriage for you. Select whatever you need to appear well-dressed before any of my friends who may call. Have the bills sent to me."

Abby was shocked into remonstrating. "My lord, I could not!"

"You can and will. I'll not have Kitty embarrassed by your appearance. Now, come off the boil, young lady, and remember you are my employee and must follow my orders."

Once more, he tipped up her chin with a finger, nodded approval, and left as quickly as he came. Abby had to wait several minutes to regain her composure before going to report this singular conversation to her young charge.

Kitty greeted the news with squeals of pleasure and the upshot of the matter was a thoroughly satisfying trip to Milsom Street for an orgy of shopping. When the amount of the expenditures began to worry Abby, they made another journey, this time to Stall Street, where bargains abounded. Here, from a ready-made modiste in one of the less expensive shops, they acquired several new gowns for Abby, including one she felt unnecessary, a lovely evening gown to wear when Lord Ashley dined with them. Abby felt it far too expensive, but Kitty reminded her Ashley said she was not to be ashamed of her companion.

"As if I ever could be! And as for expense, my darling Abby, the entire cost of the garments we have ordered here for you would not equal the sum Ashley paid for one of my party dresses last year when I spent the holidays with his sister."

The gown was so lovely, and so becoming, that Abby had not the strength or will to refuse it. It was constructed of the new machine-made Urling's net, worn over a slip of rose satin, and trimmed at the hem with a deep, full flounce of blond, a lace made of fine mesh with a pattern of flowers worked in shiny silk thread. Above the flounce, a row of satin roses in the deep pink of the slip was joined all around the skirt with a rouleau of the rose satin, twined with a rope of *faux* pearls.

The corsage was cut very low, and so short that vicarage-bred Abby flushed when she looked into the glass, but she could not resist its beauty. Made of the rose satin, it was edged with a ruffle of blond and a ring of matching roses that continued across the tops of the sleeves and on around, creating a garland of blooms to frame her neck and bare shoulders. The tiny puffed sleeves of Urling's net were finished at the bottom with more pink satin roses. A headdress came with it, a Kent toque of pink Parisian gauze topped with three satin roses. It flattered her soft brown hair and brought out the color in her complexion, making Kitty clap her hands in delight.

"Oh, Abby," she exclaimed. "It was designed for you. You are positively lovely!"

Abby, staring at the fairy tale image that gazed back at her from the mirror, could not deny that she might be right. Fine feathers, her stern father's words echoed in her mind. Fine feathers make fine birds.

And why not, his rebellious daughter thought back at him. *Just for once, let me shine.* She firmly stifled the realization that it was Lord Ashley for whom she wished to shine. Just for this once, she repeated to herself. This fabulous period in her life would be finished when Kitty married him and no longer needed a chaperon, but the dreams of this incredible present, lived over and over, would last her a lifetime.

"You shall have my last year's long gloves," Kitty babbled on, walking around her. "I shall buy a new pair, this time of

Limeric leather, which I wanted in the first place. And you may wear my white grosgrain slippers, for they became only a bit scuffed and I am sure Ashley will allow me to purchase the satin ones we saw with the rhinestone buckles. We must go back to Milsom Street at once."

The needed alterations on Abby's new ensembles were minimal and the modiste, obviously flattered to obtain Lord Ashley's custom, promised the gowns in two days' time.

Kitty herself made only one purchase, a delectable travel gown with matching pelisse and bonnet. When Abby questioned this purchase, Kitty explained it was for her future trousseau for she was certain she would be taken to Paris or Vienna or even Italy.

Back they went to Milsom Street where Kitty soon found her new gloves and possessed herself of the buckled slippers.

Abby, who had caught glimpses of a scarlet coat among the crowds that thronged the popular street, was relieved when Kitty suddenly suggested entering a book store. She was not relieved for long. To her dismay, the gentleman in the red coat was inside. She recognized Lieutenant Harry Boardman at once. How could she fail to know him again?

Tall, blond, handsome, set off by his scarlet uniform, Lt. Boardman was a young girl's dream. He had an air of quality about him, no doubt someone's impecunious younger son. She could see his attraction for Kitty. In Kitty's place, she thought guiltily, she'd be quite taken with him, too. She stiffened suddenly, seeing him in the act of placing a folded scrap of paper inside a book of love sonnets bound in lavender leather. When he saw Abby and Kitty enter, he ostentatiously laid the volume on top of the pile, removed his hat, bowed politely, and left. Kitty promptly ran forward and picked up the book.

"Kitty!" Abby exclaimed. "That man left a note for you."

"Yes," said Kitty with a sentimental sigh. She clutched the lavender love sonnets to her bosom. "Is it not romantic? You must know, we met in this very store and he has not forgotten."

What could Abby say or do? It *was* romantic. The lieutenant was so very handsome, and she had intercepted a glance that might as well have been a kiss passing between them when he set the book on the table for Kitty to find. Abby sighed, her eyes on the book, now held close in Kitty's arms. She could almost feel the love words on that folded paper burning through the lavender leather cover. Her heart went out to the love-lorn lieutenant and for a few minutes, she allowed herself to bask in the reflected glow. But in her role as chaperon, she could not let this pass. Storing the sensations in her memory to live over later, she spoke firmly to Kitty.

"Young lady, I forbid you to answer that missive. It is not at all the thing to correspond in any way with gentlemen who are not of your immediate family. Especially," she added, a bit regretfully, "gentlemen in His Majesty's service."

"I know." Kitty dimpled cheerfully. "Do not distress yourself, Abby. I have no intention of writing a reply."

With that, the chaperon in Abby had to be satisfied, but she could not dismiss a niggling foreboding.

Kitty seemed to be accepting the quiet of the country estate with a good grace, and Abby began to relax. Several days went by before they saw Lord Ashley again. She and Kitty were sitting on the side of Ashley Court where the terrace curved round. Steps led down to a rose garden and ornamental reflecting pool. Carved stone benches were placed at strategic spots for meditating on the peaceful beauty of the scene, and several life-sized statues of mythological beings in an embarrassing state of undress posed here and there.

Abby was occupied with replacing the tattered crochet edging on her pantalettes with new lace acquired on their trip to Stall Street—really, such a bargain!—and Kitty had abandoned her book of sonnets in her lap temporarily, to stare dreamily into the water. Suddenly, his lordship appeared on the terrace.

For a moment, all was chaos. Kitty sat on her lavender-bound book, sadly mashing two of the pages, and Abby, mortified, bundled up her unfinished undergarments and stuffed them into her mending basket.

"Am I interrupting something?" he asked, raising his eyebrows as he strolled leisurely down to join them.

"No, no. Of course not," they both assured him, speaking at once.

Kitty quickly regained her composure. "It is only that you startled us. We did not hear you drive up."

He seated himself on a bench near them. "Possibly," he said, "because I rode over."

Abby belatedly noticed that indeed he was dressed for riding, in buckskin breeches, white-topped boots, and a bottle green coat with a slit tail. It fitted so perfectly over his broad shoulders that Abby wondered if she was viewing an example from the legendary hands of Mr. Weston of London. She herself was wearing one of her new gowns, a most becoming rose-embroidered muslin that emphasized the fresh bloom on her cheeks, and he sent an appreciative glance toward her.

He had hardly settled down when Fenton trod from the house at his most butlerian. He was closely followed by a rotund gentleman in somber garments who missed the top step of the terrace and only saved himself from pitching into the shrubbery by grabbing at a pot full of geraniums standing on the low wall. It came away in his hands and he juggled it while performing a sort of jig until he regained his footing. Fenton, unperturbed, relieved him of the pot and carefully replaced it on the wall.

"Oh, the devil," Ashley remarked in a low voice. "Or no, I should have said the opposite, since it is old Elmgrove the vicar, and I suppose we cannot escape."

Mr. Elmgrove, when he arrived, flush-faced, at their sides, proved to be not so very old, no doubt in his late thirties. His hair, barely touched with silver at the temples, was thinning, and his round cheeks were rosy with health. He bounded forward, beaming, to offer his hand to Ashley, only to discover it covered with dirt from the geranium pot. Scrubbing his fist on his immaculate breeches, he bowed instead.

"My lord," he began with yet another bow. "I have ventured to call and pay my respects, having heard the master of Ashland Court is in residence." He bowed again.

"I'm not in residence," said Ashley. "I'm staying at the York in Bath while my ward is living here."

"Ah, yes, the little Miss Wellfleet." Mr. Elmgrove bowed at the waist toward Kitty, as deeply as his *embonpoint* would allow, but his eyes had drifted at once to Abby. "Never," he intoned, "has it been my pleasure to discover a lovelier pair of roses in this earthly garden we must inhabit, forbidden as we are the glory of Eden."

Ashley introduced Abby, straight faced, and the vicar bowed once more, so deferentially as to almost lose his balance. "Charming," he said, and the warm admiration in his eyes put her to the blush. "Truly," he continued, "an angel has descended from heaven to light our lives."

He held out his hand. Abby, uncertain what to do, offered him her own, only to have him bow over it and place a lingering kiss on her fingertips. "In another age," he informed her, "I would touch the hem of your gown to my lips and go in search of a dragon."

Really, the man was preposterous! Embarrassed, and fighting an urge to giggle—as Kitty was doing behind a fold of her own unkissed skirts—Abby glanced toward Lord Ashley. A most sacrilegious amusement glinted in his eyes and met the laughter she struggled to keep hidden in her own. For a giddy moment the two of them were joined in a warm flush of kinship. Startled, Abby dropped her gaze, suddenly sober. To her annoyance, his lordship made no attempt to disguise his obvious amusement at her discomposure.

Fortunately, Mr. Elmgrove was too full of his own romantic rhetoric to notice anyone else. By the end of the prescribed half-hour of his visit, and a dozen bows later, it was apparent that the reverend gentleman was quite bowled over by Miss

Kitty's companion. He begged permission to call upon the ladies soon again.

"Certainly," his lordship agreed, with a grandly welcoming gesture. "Come when you will. I am sure the ladies, living here solitary as they are, will be grateful for your attentions."

Quite overcome by such condescension, Mr. Elmgrove bowed three times more and fell over a bench as he backed from their presence.

"Oh, Ashley," Kitty complained when he was out of sight. "How could you? He will be popping in forever!"

His lordship raised astonished eyebrows. "Why, I thought you'd be pleased for Miss Fordham." His laughing eyes quizzed Abby. "I do believe she has made a conquest of our good vicar. I'll lay a monkey he means to fix his interest. I hear he is hanging out for a wife."

She knew he merely teased her, but as a vicar's daughter, Abby also knew very well what the life of a clergyman's wife would be. One she was well fitted for—but what a come-down it would be after the glories of Ashland Court! For that she chided herself. It was not as if she couldn't live over the luxury of Ashland forever in her daydreams. This was but a short, magnificent interlude in her life and she should be prepared to face whatever came next with fortitude and a grateful heart as her father had taught her. But, oh, would it not be heaven to also know love! Mr. Elmgrove, she was sure, merely felt the need of a female helpmate in his parish. Abby was not ready to settle for so humdrum an existence, nor could she feel comfortable with the thought of the bumbling reverend gentleman as a suitor.

Days at Ashland Court settled into routine, enlivened only by the occasional visits of Lord Ashley and almost daily calls by Mr. Elmgrove. The sameness began to make Abby nervous, for there was little to entertain the intrepid Kitty.

Then one moonless night, Abby was awakened by a noise. It came again, the loud hoot of an owl, obviously from the throat of a human not bred in the country. It was followed by the sound of the door to the next room—Kitty's bedchamber—opening and closing. That note in the book of poetry . . . the confounded girl must have answered it and told her soldier where she had gone!

By the time Abby had donned her dressing gown and slippers, Kitty had let herself out by the front door, leaving it ajar. Abby hurried out into the dark in pursuit.

She paused on the bottom step. How different everything looked at night, especially with no moon to see by. How ever was she to find her errant charge? The rose garden seemed the most obvious choice, and she ran around the manor and across the side terrace. The bricks were damp and slippery. Like Mr. Elmgrove, she missed the top step. Instead of catching at the potted geranium on the wall, she sat down hard.

This was being idiotic. She remained sitting on the cold stone and waited for her eyes to adjust to the darkness, which she should have done in the first place.

Peering ahead into the rose garden, she made out two pale figures by the ornamental pool and jumped up. She started forward in a hurry, luckily banging her knee on one of the stone benches before she walked straight into the water. Really, she thought, exasperated, she was proving herself a fit mate for the blundering vicar. And now that she was closer, the vague shapes before her became not living people but a pair of the life-sized Grecian statues, standing ghost-like in the night.

Listening quietly, she could sense no life around her, only a stillness that was almost audible. There was no sign here of a red coat or pale gown. Had Kitty and her paramour heard her and run away? No wonder if they had. She'd certainly made an entrance, falling on the steps and bumping into the bench. She made her way cautiously around the reflecting pool, superstitiously avoiding the statues that loomed twice as large in the dark. They had never seemed alive before, at least not in the bright daylight, but now in the eeriness of night she didn't want to touch them—or let them touch her. Their hands could not move, she told herself, they only appeared to be reaching for her. She knew she was acting like a silly child, but she ran past the pool and the menacing figures on flying feet.

Where could Kitty be?' And how *could* the girl break her promise? She had been so sure she could trust Kitty's word—they had become friends! Kitty knew what would happen, and not just to herself. Lord Ashley would cast them both out if she were caught. Abby had to find her.

The yew alley on the other side of the rose garden beckoned, but somehow she felt she'd rather not go into that black tunnel. Then where? It was some time before she remembered seeing a gazebo by the lake. She set off at a trot, skirting the menacing shadows of the bordering trees. It seemed a very long way, much farther than in the daylight. Looking over her shoulder, she stumbled and lost a slipper. It evaded her groping hands for a nerve-wracking minute, then when she jammed her foot back in she didn't take time to brush away the accompanying twigs and gravel, for she saw the gazebo ahead. There, as she suspected, she discovered Miss Kitty Wellfleet in the arms of her scarlet-coated officer.

At that odious sight, she lost more than a shoe. Her temper, fueled by raw nerves, erupted.

"Kitty!" She exploded, hopping on one foot as she dragged off her uncomfortable slipper. She waved it at the offending couple. "Have you parted company with your mind?"

The aggravating chit untangled herself from the gentleman in the red coat. "Abby!" she exclaimed. "However did you know?"

Abby had by now emptied her slipper and replaced it. "Never mind that. You," she addressed the young man. "Go. Now."

As before, Lt. Harry Boardman put his arm about Kitty's waist and tried to shove her behind him. She was not to be shoved. She put a hand firmly over his mouth.

"Do not blame Harry," she pleaded. "It is not his fault. You said I could not warn him not to come."

The lieutenant pulled her hand away and faced Abby bravely. "Nothing could keep me from her side. Nothing!"

Kitty had been assessing Abby's mood and eyed her warily. "This is not the time, Harry. You'd best leave." She pushed him out the other side of the gazebo, ordering him fiercely to go when he resisted. Reluctantly, the red coat vanished into the night.

Abby's anger had by now subsided, leaving only her disappointment at Kitty's betrayal.

"You promised me you would not reply to that message," she mourned. "You promised!"

"I did not answer it," Kitty told her, all innocence. "You told me not to, and that is why Harry came. Besides, there was no need. His note merely confirmed the night he would next be free to come to me. And now you have frightened him away before we made another plan! He may not come again!"

"I should hope not!" said Abby, stung. "Only think of the disgust of you Lord Ashley will feel if you are caught. You will be cast off!"

Kitty only shrugged. "Oh, he will never let me go. He has sworn to our fathers he will take care of me—and my fortune."

"How can you speak of him so?" Abby was scandalized. "I am sure he has no such mercenary motive. He means only to protect you."

Kitty shrugged again and turned a petulant shoulder. "Oh, I know that. It is only that I am bored. I met Harry just for a lark. I cannot stand being shut away here from all the pleasures I knew in Bath."

Abby could only sympathize with her for rebelling against the restraints set by her guardian. "But Kitty," she pointed out, "do remember that while he cannot fire his ward, he can—and will—send me packing, and bring in a veritable gorgon to keep watch over you, probably under lock and key."

Kitty threw her arms about Abby, completely disarming her.

"My darling Abby," she vowed. "I do not wish to lose you! I swear I will behave from now on!"

Abby begged her to do so, for she could not go back to her position as mistress at the Misses Grimbeys' Select Academy after being sent off in disgrace. Oh, why must her very livelihood depend on the actions of this wayward miss? First the debacle at Grimbeys', and now when she will need a letter of recommendation from Lord Ashley, that bored damsel was certain to plunge them both into another catastrophe. To add to her discomfort, rain began to fall, drenching them as they ran for the house. Kitty's only worry was for the soaking of poor Harry's uniform.

When next Lord Ashley came to visit, Abby sought an audience with him alone and told him she felt Kitty stood in need of more entertainment. "A girl of her lively disposition becomes easily bored and is bound to attempt to break out, if only to cut a lark to break the monotony."

"Think you so?" The quizzing glass came in to play, the eye behind it suspicious.

Abby's heart fluttered. Could he know about Kitty's lieutenant? She stood firm. "Indeed I do. Hers, I am afraid, is a naturally rebellious nature. She will not suffer long to be so 'cabin'd, cribb'd, confined,' my lord."

He looked at her with sudden interest. "I never thought to meet a pretty woman who could casually quote Macbeth."

Abby's color rose. "I am a school mistress, my lord, and for that very reason I have some knowledge of young ladies Miss Kitty's age. If she has no amusements, she will create her own."

His brow gathered in a frown. "I see. I daresay you speak from recent experience." He tapped his ornate glass against one palm. Abby quailed at his shrewd glance, but he continued in a mild tone. "Then we must find the means to distract her.

I see no harm in her attending the concerts in Bath, or visiting the Pump Room as long as she is in your company."

"Oh, thank you, Ashley," Kitty cried when she heard the news. "You cannot imagine how dire it is here with only a visit from Mr. Elmgrove to look forward to."

"Ah, the good vicar." His lordship's eyes met Abby's with that glint of unholy amusement she had seen before. "We must not forget Miss Abby's conquest. What say you both to inviting him to be one of our party at the next concert?"

Abby felt herself blush, but Kitty pounded him on the arm. "You are quizzing us, you must be!"

He fended her off, grinning at Abby. "What, do you not wish me to encourage him?"

"That we do not," said Kitty. "He needs no encouragement and he is very hard on our flowers. Only yesterday he fell over another rose bush and quite crushed it."

Ashley frowned. "He was here again? He made his duty visit only a few days ago." He transferred the frown to Abby, then suddenly dropped the subject. "Well, Kitty, how would you like to attend a play tomorrow evening? I understand there is to be a performance here in Bath. We could visit the Pump Room in the morning and then go to Sydney Gardens before dinner—" The rest of his words were lost to Abby under Kitty's gleeful shouts.

Having driven to Bath from Ashland Court in the early morning, they entered the famous Pump Room as the long case clock, made by Tompion especially for the Room, struck noon. Ashley led them rapidly past the counter where the ghastly waters were served up by the glass to portly gentlemen with the gout and hypochondriac ladies who came for the gossip.

He found Abby a table where she could sit beneath the daunting eye of the statue of Beau Nash and admire the passing parade while he procured for her a cup of tea. As she sipped it, an orchestra in the musicians' gallery played tunes that could almost be heard over the general hub-bub.

Abby was very conscious of wearing one of the prettiest of the walking gowns Kitty had insisted on choosing for her. Looking around at the promenading crowd, she was aware of an unaccustomed thrill, the knowledge that she—Abigail Fordham, vicar's daughter—was as well dressed as any in the room.

Lord Ashley and Kitty had joined the strollers and Abby saw that his lordship made a point of making his ward known to several opulent matrons accompanied by young ladies her age. Nobly doing his duty, she surmised, by the stiffness of his back and his bored expression. He soon left Kitty in the charge of a lady who had two daughters with whom Kitty seemed to have struck up an immediate friendship.

Seeing Kitty properly occupied, Abby let her eyes wander about the famous meeting place and suddenly noticed the number of scarlet coats mingling with the crowd. Did none of them have duties to keep them at their posts? Was Lieutenant Harry Boardman among them? Would she recognize him again? To her eyes, dazzled by the red of so many uniforms, the men looked much alike.

"Searching for a friend?"

Abby looked up, startled, to find Lord Ashley standing beside her. "No, oh no. It is only—only that there are so many people."

He offered her his arm. "Would you care to walk about?"

And perhaps walk right into Lieutenant Boardman? What should she do if she did? Cut him cold, and pretend not to know him? Suppose he bowed to her, how would she explain it to Kitty's guardian? As she sat dithering, they were interrupted.

Kitty came dancing up, bringing the other girls. "Ashley," she cried, raising her voice above the babble. "Did you not say we might visit Sydney Gardens?"

He nodded his acquiescence and the trio squealed with delight. It proved they, too, were bound for the same treat. They left the Pump Room in a party, and soon were admiring the waterfalls and grottoes, and laughing like children as they lost themselves in the labyrinth. Abby forgot Lieutenant Boardman, enjoying one of the happiest days she had known.

The next week passed like one of Abby's daydreams, as she lived the life of a lady of quality at Kitty's side. Lord Ashley graciously took them to the play and later to a concert to hear the great Catalani sing at a special performance. While Kitty happily joined her new friends in the Pump Room, he devoted himself to conversing with Abby in a most flattering manner, and complimented her, saying that seldom had he discovered such a well-informed mind in a female.

She, however, was in a constant flutter of nerves, for wherever she looked, scarlet coats abounded. If Lieutenant Harry Boardman was among them, he managed to keep least in sight, and Kitty pretended a disarming indifference. Too disarming, for one who knew her as Abby did. Had it been a mistake to suggest to Lord Ashley that Kitty be given more freedom? Abby began to fear it was, and redoubled her efforts to guard the girl. Kitty, meanwhile, smiled sweetly and remained on her best behavior, displaying such grown-up dignity and pleasing manners that Lord Ashley was completely hoodwinked. He came to a decision.

"I had not realized she is no longer a hoydenish schoolgirl," he said to Abby, one morning at the Pump Room. "She has not yet come-out. I see that must be arranged at once. My sister, Lady Agatha Penrose, will know what to do and there is an excellent ballroom here at Ashland Court. We will pick a date in the near future and see that the proper invitations go out immediately."

Kitty was thrown into transports of rapture and Abby, though she remained quietly in the background, was no less excited. A ball. Never had she been to a ball, much less a come-out, and surely, she would be allowed to watch the proceedings from a front row seat on the musicians' gallery where she could pretend it was all for her.

"I shall need a new gown." Kitty clapped her hands and skipped about Abby. "A very special gown and you shall wear your rosebud evening dress which you haven't had a chance to don as yet. Oh, Abby, I cannot wait! We must make plans at once."

Abby felt a moment of terror. She knew nothing of planning balls, but Lord Ashley put her at ease.

"No, you don't," he declared. "Agatha will manage all and love doing it. Come to think of it, I'd better send for her at once and give warning. I believe scheduling these affairs takes time."

A letter was dispatched immediately by messenger and the answer came the following evening in the form of a carriage bearing the Penrose crest. Kitty, on hearing coach wheels crunch on the gravel drive, ran to the front entrance and Abby, wondering that Lord Ashley would come so late, came on her heels. She stopped at the door when she realized her mistake.

Both footmen, summoned by Fenton, came on the run. The moment the carriage steps were let down, a petite lady descended in a flurry of velvet pelisse, ruffled skirts and ostrich-plumed bonnet. She tripped up the steps, followed by her lady's maid, and enveloped Kitty in a scented embrace.

"I have been waiting *ages* for Ashley to call on me!" she cried. "What a young *lady* you have become in this past year—and are you not *lovely!*"

Kitty, tickled by fur and feathers, sneezed, while Abby stared, wide-eyed. All fluffy blond curls, sparkling blue eyes and a constantly bubbling well of laughter, Lady Agatha was nothing like her brother.

She turned to Abby and caught both her hands. "And you must be Miss Fordham. Dear Ashley has told me *all* about you. He relies on you for *everything*—but *not* this ball." She shook the hands she held, playfully. "It is to be all *my* doing, and I cannot *tell* you how I have been looking forward to this event. Such excellent *practice,* for you must know I have *three* daughters of my own, though it will be years before my oldest will be out of the schoolroom." Turning back to Kitty, she demanded, "But where is Ashley? Why is he not here to greet me?"

"He is staying at the York." Kitty managed to find a break in the flow of words. "He will come immediately now that you are here."

"No matter. He is only a man and not *needed* in the plans we must make." Lady Agatha saw Fenton and Mrs. Fenton hovering in the hall behind them and bustled inside. "My *usual* room, Fenny, and have the men carry up my trunks *quickly.*" She made a rueful moue at Fenton. "As *always,* I have brought *entirely* too many trunks." She waved her abigail forward. "Mrs. Fenton will show you where, Marsden." Taking a box from the maid, she hurried ahead. "Oh, Kitty, only *wait* until you see my new gowns! From *Paris,* for the Season. I have brought them *all* for you to admire. And you, too, Miss Fordham."

A miniature whirlwind, she swept Abby and Kitty before her into the hall, stripping off her bonnet and pelisse as she went. "Tea, Fenny, and perhaps a *very* small sherry. It has been a *tiresome* trip. I was *so* anxious to arrive. Is it not *fortunate,* I happened to be near in Pen Hall and not in London?"

She carried the box into the library and emptied it out onto a table. Kitty squealed with ecstasy for it contained fashion plates curried from *La Belle Assemblée, The Lady's Magazine, Le Beau Monde,* and *La Miroir de la Mode.* It was late before the three ladies retired.

Abby mounted the stairs after them, floating in a blissful cloud. The ball had become a reality, and she would be a part of it. Her head was filled with dreams of the marvelous gowns they had studied. Kitty, of course, would be in white muslin, but in a wondrous design; Lady Agatha was no less excited in planning her own ensemble because, naturally, none of her London gowns would do—and Abby herself had the rose satin and lace Kitty had insisted she buy. And she need not do a thing toward managing the ball. A heavenly vista lay open before her.

Lady Agatha proved to be far from the feather-head she appeared. Once Ashley managed to talk his sister out of holding the affair in London, the plans for Kitty's ball went forward at miraculous speed. Ashland Court bloomed under her direction. Modistes, caterers, decorators, and musicians were handled with an incredible efficiency and she managed, all smiles and gracious thanks, to keep them from each other's throats.

Abby walked about in a daze of wonder and delight, imagining it was she and not Kitty for whom the plans were being made. It was everything she had ever dreamed, and she busily stored the memories in her heart to live over for years to come.

Mr. Elmgrove continued his almost daily visits and, everyone else being too busy, it fell to Abby's lot to entertain him in the haven of the garden, away from the chaos in the house. As he stayed only the correct thirty minutes allowed for a morning call, this was not too harrowing, and she even began to enjoy the peace of their quiet talks, despite his flowery phrases.

Though it was short notice, quite a respectable number of guests responded to their invitations. Far more, actually, than the ballroom at Ashland could comfortably hold. Lady Agatha was in ault for it was certain to be a sad crush and an overwhelming success. Every domestic was involved in the cleaning and refurbishing of the entire Court and the polishing of the lusters of the three great chandeliers that had been lowered to the floor of the ballroom. Abby's days were soon filled with conferences with the modiste's seamstresses working on Kitty's gown, and overseeing the tedious fittings.

Though of white muslin, it made Abby's satin and roses seem quite simple. The fad of the season was for cockle-shell decoration, rather than flowers. Kitty's skirt was trimmed with rows of the shells worked in gold thread, a band of them above each of the three deep flounces at the hem, interspersed with a pretty play of frolicking fish in silver. All were joined together by a twisted rope of *faux* pearls, a concept they thought most daring and different. More golden shells edged the minuscule corsage and tiny puffs of stiffened muslin that formed the pretense of sleeves. The new white Limeric gloves reached past her elbows and were stitched with a cascade of the silver fish, and golden sea shells were clipped to her *Gros de Naples* slippers.

It was with difficulty that she was persuaded not to wear a diamond choker left her by her mother, which would not be at all the thing for so young a maiden making her first appearance in society. Abby finally turned the trick at the last hour by saying it was a shame Kitty had no pearls, for they were the true gems of the sea and the only jewels to go with the cockle-shells and fish.

"But I do have pearls!" Kitty exclaimed. "Only a necklet, but they are very beautiful. Ashley gave them to me for my sixteenth birthday last year. You must remember, Agatha, for you said how lovely they were when I wore them while I visited you at Christmas."

"Why so I did! I had *quite* forgotten. But how fortunate! They will be *ideal.*"

As well as, Abby thought with relief, being the only proper adornment for the occasion.

The final touch was added, a headdress of foaming white gauze, garlanded with more of the *faux* pearls and studded at her forehead with a buckle in the shape of a gold shell. Kitty looked a dainty fairy princess, all in white with silver and gold sparkles catching the light when she twirled for their approval.

Both Kitty and Lord Ashley insisted on Abby's attending the ball as one of the guests, surpassing her wildest imaginings. She wore the evening gown Kitty chose for her on that memorable shopping trip in Bath, complete with Kitty's donations of gloves and slippers, and prepared to treasure every moment as she watched from behind a potted palm. The hundreds of candles in the chandeliers glittered on the satin and jewels of the dancers and the orchestra played in the gallery above without her company. Kitty, surrounded by young gentlemen—none of whom wore a red coat—was quite the acknowledged belle of her ball.

Oblivious to all but the entrancing scene, Abby was startled when Lord Ashley spoke suddenly behind her.

"So here you are," he said. He took her hand and led her onto the floor—and into paradise—when he stood up with her. The set for a promenade waltz was just forming.

In one movement of the dance, the gentlemen actually put their hands on the ladies' waists and drew them close while whirling them around several times. Abby knew the steps, for one of her duties at the Misses Grimbeys' Academy had been to fill in for the dancing master who had eloped with one of the students the year before. This, however, was nothing like those lessons.

Abby had never been in a man's arms before and she felt dizzy from more than the dancing. She glanced up at Lord Ashley's face, so shatteringly close above her. He was looking down with an odd glow in his eyes that sent her pulse racing.

"I do not wish to infringe upon the role played by our good vicar, my dear Miss Fordham," he murmured in her ear, "but I must tell you, you are a most lovely rose yourself in that delectable gown."

There was a warmth in his smile that brought a blush to her cheeks. For a mad moment, she imagined he might kiss her—but they were in a ballroom, surrounded by over a hundred people. Abby wouldn't have cared what they thought if he kissed her, but that had to be saved for a dream.

He removed his hand from her waist as the music ended and steered her to the rout chairs along the wall where the matrons were seated. He left her, bowing a smiling thanks. Shaken and flushed, Abby averted her betraying face from the row of ladies and took shelter once more behind the potted palm. The heat of his hand on her waist stayed with her, sending shivers up her spine. Never would she forget this evening; it would live in her daydreams forever.

It was but the machination of perverse fate, lulling a victim before it intervened. That night, Abby was so full of the ball that she could not waste precious hours in slovenly sleep that were better spent in going over every aspect of the evening. Thus she was awake, and heard the rattle of pebbles against the window of the room next door. She flew to her own window and saw, by the moonlight, a scarlet-coated military figure standing on the lawn below.

Once more, she heard Kitty's door open and close quietly.

Abby went back to her bed and sat on the edge. The girl was incorrigible! What was the use in trying to save so wanton a miss? Kitty did not *care* if she were caught. But while Kitty had no fear of losing her home and fortune, Lord Ashley would dismiss her companion on the spot—and then what would Abby do? Positions were not easy to find for impecunious vicar's daughters with no recommendation from their two previous employers! She was almost ready to give up, but too much was at stake. Instead of chasing about outdoors in the night, she went into Kitty's room and sat down to wait. It could not be long, for dawn was breaking and the servants would soon be about.

Indeed, Kitty was back very soon, her face flushed and her eyes sparkling. She stopped inside the door when she saw Abby by the window, and broke into tumbled speech.

"I know you do not approve, Abby, but I had to meet him this one last time. His regiment has been ordered to the Continent to keep the peace and he is leaving! You would not want me to be so remiss as not to bid farewell to one who has been a friend."

Only a friend? But Abby could detect no despondence at the parting in Kitty's manner. The aggravating girl seemed actually cheerful. Apparently her heart had not been touched by

what had been only a schoolgirl lark, and Lieutenant Board-
man would be passing out of the girl's life without regrets.
Abby took in a deep breath and let it out in a sigh of relief.
She, too, would bid farewell to the handsome officer, and with
pleasure. Kitty's marriage to Lord Ashley was not in danger.
At least, not this time . . .

Kitty's come-out ball had been the loveliest time Abby had
ever known; why did she become stupidly blue-deviled and mum-
pish afterwards? She blamed her depression of spirits on the fa-
tigue from all the excitement and her sleepless night. It could be
nothing else. It was only that Ashland Court had become oppres-
sively quiet after the departure of the ebullient Lady Agatha.

As she and Kitty took refuge in the rose garden, she saw Lord
Ashley's tall, well-knit frame coming toward them. He took
Kitty's hand and playfully kissed her fingers as if she were a
grande dame before greeting Abby with a slight bow and a warm
smile. He turned back to Kitty at once, with a teasing remark
about the uneven daisy chain she was attempting to make.

Abby had been concerned that Kitty would not accept her
betrothal to Lord Ashley, but the two of them seemed to be on
excellent terms. This pleased Abby; she told herself that it did,
for their marriage must eventually take place. Lord Ashley was
in every way exactly what one would desire in a husband—for
a damsel of whom you were fond, that is. Abby's spirits, which
had taken an upward bound at his arrival, sank unaccountably.

On his lordship's heels, came Fenton with a dire announcement. "The Reverend Mr. Elmgrove," he intoned, a sympathetic note in his voice.

Kitty giggled. "Oh, dear, here comes Abby's worthy suitor."

Ashley frowned. "The man is making a nuisance of himself.
Has he taken to infesting our rose garden?"

Abby felt herself flush and realized he was looking directly
at her. He transferred his glare to the vicar just as the man
started down the steps.

Seeing his lordship glowering at him, Mr. Elmgrove broke his confident stride and barely avoided stumbling. He came forward bravely, however, and bowed to Lord Ashley with undue reverence before turning to the ladies. He bowed twice more, kissing their hands.

"I see this beautiful garden enriched," he proclaimed. "Here are two roses lovelier than all the rest."

"Indeed," said Ashley. "That is now my line."

Abby hastened into speech, seeing the vicar nonplussed. "Will you not join us, my dear sir? It is most pleasant, sitting here."

Ashley, who had seated himself by Kitty, came to his feet.

Mr. Elmgrove backed a step. "No, no, but my deepest gratitude for your graciousness, Miss Fordham. I—ah—cannot stay. I came only to tell you I could not be with you today. Tomorrow, perhaps." He bowed again, and getting no response from his lordship, bowed once more.

Abby grew thoroughly embarrassed, for the vicar was becoming most particular in his attentions. He had not acted such a buffoon in her company. The awkward change in his manner was no doubt brought on by the cold comportment of Lord Ashley and she resented it on the part of the reverend gentleman. There could be no need for Ashley to be so snobbish. Mr. Elmgrove was a respectable man of the cloth. It seemed almost as though his lordship disliked the poor man for some reason other than mere boredom in his presence.

He continued to glower and Mr. Elmgrove hastily took his leave, bowing to each of them and giving Abby a most speaking glance. He retreated, colliding with one of the statues and apologizing to it. At the sight of its unclothed condition, he turned scarlet and fairly fled, while Kitty smothered her giggles.

At the ignominious departure of the vicar, Ashley's good humor returned. He seated himself once more beside Kitty.

"You were quite the belle of your ball, my girl," he said, gently teasing.

Abby watched them. He sat so close to the girl that his

shoulder brushed hers and Abby, to clear the unfortunate vicar from her mind, slipped into one of her vicarious dreams, experiencing what she knew Kitty must be feeling.

So close—their shoulders touched, and their fingers met as he retrieved her daisy chain and handed it to her. Abby felt the tingle that would run up Kitty's arm—now, Kitty, she thought, look up at him slowly, flutter your lashes, he's going to kiss you—close your eyes, part your lips . . .

Kitty did. She parted her lips and spoke.

"You have a caterpillar in your hair, Ashley," she remarked. "Here, let me take it off."

He drew away. "You'd better not be planning to drop it down my back." He fended off her reaching hand. "I'll cope with it myself." Bending over, he ruffled his hair, dislodging something small and green that landed on the path.

"Ooh, don't tread on it!" Kitty cried.

"Of course I'm not going to squash it." He crouched beside the wriggling object. "Get me a leaf, girl, so I can move it over to the bushes."

At first disappointed by the sudden divergence from her scenario, Abby realized that all was as it should be. They were friends, which augured well for their marriage. Love would come later, when Kitty was more mature and handsome redcoats a thing of her past. Somehow the thought of that faraway day brought her no pleasure. A queer little pang shot through her as she saw how comfortable they were together. Almost as if she were jealous!

It was at that moment she realized, with a heart-piercing despair, she had fallen in love with the man Kitty Wellfleet must marry.

It was much harder after that devastating discovery to take part in their expeditions to Bath with any semblance of pleasure. She forcibly blanked from her mind the thought that only too soon she'd never have cause to see Lord Ashley again, but the thought wouldn't stay blanked. Gradually her love assumed the proportions of a major tragedy, an oppression that threatened to overwhelm her.

She accepted the fact that she loved him. Her love was hopeless, but at least, for now, she had his friendship. She sat with him at the Pump Room next day, and talked with him for an hour, knowing she headed for heartbreak but willing to pay the price for the sheer joy of having him sit by her side companionably, and look at her with that warm, friendly light in his smiling eyes. For now. Empty years stretched before her, filled with empty dreams. At the thought, her heavy heart felt as though it would roll over in her breast and turn up its toes. Her life would be finished—unless she was offered for by the pudgy Reverend Elmgrove, who was showing alarming signs of coming up to scratch.

Depression settled on her like the onset of a bad cold in the head.

Kitty was in her bedchamber having a gown fitted, and Abby wandered alone in the rose garden when the Reverend Mr. Elmgrove made one of his frequent morning calls. He came, bowing his way between the flower beds, pausing only twice to unhitch his garments from the grappling thorns. She saw no escape and returned his greeting a trifle nervously, for his usually rosy face was pale with determination.

"How—how nice to see you, Mr. Elmgrove," she faltered.

He shook his head at her, with another bow. "Ah, be not so distant, my dear Miss Fordham. It is my fondest desire that you will one day address me as Arbuthnot."

"Good gracious," said Abby, before she thought. "Whatever for?"

He seemed a bit startled. "Why, it is my name!" Brushing aside this slight setback, he returned to his formal manner. "Miss Fordham, my dearest Miss Fordham, it cannot have escaped your notice that I have become most particular in my attentions." He caught both her hands. "You have led me to believe my suit would not be displeasing to you."

"Oh, dear!" said Abby. "I had no intention of leading you on."

"No, no," he exclaimed. "I did not mean to insinuate—that is, in your maidenly innocence—ah, I fear the violence of my sentiments has caused me to be premature."

Abby could imagine nothing less violent than Arbuthnot Elmgrove. "Oh, please—" She tried to pull her hands away. "Of course you are not—" She realized too late she'd said the wrong thing.

He apparently decided to put his fate to the test, for without further ado, he spread his handkerchief on the ground at her feet. Before she could stop him, he dropped on one knee, unfortunately missing the handkerchief and coming down on a particularly soggy patch of moss. He rose above this paltry annoyance, pressing her reluctant fingers to his lips.

"Miss Fordham, I am not an articulate man where my innermost longings are concerned, but you must know I harbor in my bosom feelings for you far warmer than mere friendship. Miss Fordham, I pray you, I beg you, to grant me the honor, the inestimable joy, of becoming my wife."

For a wild moment, she seriously considered marrying the vicar. He was a good man, kindly, and well-meaning. She understood what would be expected of her; she could live with him—or could she? Even more to the point, she realized how unfair it would be to accept one man when her heart belonged irrevocably to another, as unfair to herself as to Arbuthnot.

She looked down at his eager face and a wave of revulsion washed through her. No. She could not bear to lie in his arms while dreaming of Lord Ashley. Nor could she hurt this gentle man. What should she say? Inspiration was granted her. She turned away, her hand at her heart. "Mr.—that is, Arbuthnot—this—this is so sudden."

He would not take no for an answer. "It is only that I am too importunate," he told her, undiscouraged. "Now that you are aware of my intentions, I have but to await a more favorable answer."

They were interrupted, greatly to Abby's thankfulness, by the appearance on the nearby terrace of Lord Ashley, who had also come to call. Conscious of being caught in an embarrassing situation, Arbuthnot Elmgrove rose hastily to his feet, scooping up his handkerchief, and backed into a rosebush.

"I must leave you now," he told Abby, prying his coattails loose from the thorns. "Believe that hope fills my heart. Think on me with kindness, my dear Miss Fordham. I live only for your decision."

Bowing three times, he departed the rose garden by way of the yew alley, in somewhat of a hurry, for Lord Ashley was bearing down on them, his face grim.

"What is that smarmy palaverer up to?" he demanded. "Don't think I have not seen that confounded bobbing-block making you the object of his misguided gallantries. I sincerely trust we are not to see you wedded so far beneath you—throwing yourself away!"

This Abby could not let pass. She might not wish to marry Mr. Elmgrove, but the vicar was a perfect gentleman and it would be a highly respectable match. "Lord Ashley, I must remind you, a schoolmistress can look no higher—"

She stopped, frightened by the way Ashley was glaring at her. His mouth worked, but no words came out. In a fury, he strode away, leaving her in a turmoil of confusion.

When next Lord Ashley came to the Court, he handed Abby a small box. "Brought you something," he said brusquely.

She opened it and gasped. On a bed of cotton, lay a brooch, a single rose wrought in gold filigree and set with a faceted pink stone. She touched it with a tentative finger. "But—but it is beautiful! How can I ever thank you? It is too much."

He shrugged. "A bit of trumpery. I happened to see it and was reminded of the roses on your ball gown."

Happened to see it? How? Not unless he frequented a jeweler's establishment. Abby's heart fluttered.

"Oh, Ashley!" cried Kitty, looking over her shoulder. "It is lovely, so dainty. Will you not give me one like it for my birthday?

"No," he said shortly. "There is not another such in the world." For a fleeting moment, his eyes met Abby's with an expression that sent a wild hope surging through her.

He looked away quickly. "Thought you might like it," he said, his tone casual, as though dismissing the wondrous gift as merely a friendly gesture.

Her wild hope crashed. Really, Abigail Fordham, she scolded herself. What did you expect? You had best stick to vicarious living, where all can be made to turn out as it should!

Kitty prepared to pout, but she had something of far greater importance to put forth.

"Now that I am officially out," she announced, "I wish to be taken to the next assembly in Bath."

She was once more doomed to disappointment.

"Not this week, Kitten," he said. "I mean to stay in London for a while. I'll take you when I come back."

She was dismayed. "But I want to go to *this* one! I—I have promised someone I'd be there."

Abby looked up sharply. Her lieutenant? He was leaving. No doubt she wanted to go to the assembly to dance with him, and probably stand up more than twice and set all the Bath quizzes gabbling.

Ashley was frowning at Kitty. "Who?" he demanded. "Who were you planning to meet?"

"Why, the Riddleby girls," she replied brightly, and too quickly. "You remember them, Ashley. We met at the Pump Room and went to Sydney Gardens together. They say the assemblies are the greatest fun."

Yes, thought Abby, clutching her brooch. Dancing with the military. Not if she could stop it. To her relief, Lord Ashley shook his head.

"It will not hurt you to stay home this once. I'd rather you didn't go until I can take you and Abby myself."

"Abby!" Kitty exclaimed, a desperate note in her voice. "Abby is my companion, she can chaperon me."

"What?" exclaimed Ashley. "Two young unmarried ladies attending a public dance alone? Your reputations would be dished up as scandalbroth for every gossip monger in Bath! You will neither of you stir a step from the Court until I return."

Kitty, white-faced, trembled with anger. "Is this how it will be when we are wed? Your pleasures to take precedence over *my* entertainment?"

His eyebrows rose. "Certainly. As my wife, you will naturally be expected to take second place to my activities."

She stared at him, too furious to speak, and stormed off to her room, her lips compressed in a mutinous line.

His lordship turned to Abby who had shrunk back, hugging her rose in its box. "I trust you will keep an eye on her," he said, and took his leave.

Abby took out the brooch and pinned it to her light gown, over her heart, where she could feel its warm weight. It was the most beautiful jewel she had ever owned, and thrice beautiful because of the giver. She would earn the right to wear it, she vowed. She would see to it that Kitty did not stray.

After he was gone, Kitty seemed to regret her behavior and regained her cheerful spirits. May had turned to the first lovely days of June, and that afternoon she seemed quite content to walk in the garden, poke innocent fun at Mr. Arbuthnot Elmgrove, and play at battledore and shuttlecock on the lawn with Abby before supper. In the evening, they read by the fire and retired early. No pebbles rattled on the windows in the night; Abby heard no stealthy opening or closing of doors. All was too peaceful, and remained so for the following day.

Abby found she should have been suspicious when on the third day, Lord Ashley returned suddenly from London. He strode into the parlor where she sat alone, his face dark with anger. His voice, when he spoke, was tight with his effort at control.

"I assumed, Miss Fordham, that you were to be trusted. Instead I find you aiding and abetting that troublesome wench to make a byword of herself."

Abby rose, trembling with apprehension. "I don't understand, my lord. What has she done?"

His eyebrows clamped down in a ferocious frown. "Do you tell me you do not know? Well, let me inform you, ma'am, that your betrayal of your duty has caught up with you. I have only just been asked by an infernal busy-body why I permitted my ward to attend the assembly last evening—unchaperoned, and in the company of a military gentleman!"

Abby sank into her chair, feeling the blood drain from her cheeks. "Kitty? But she was here last night. She—she retired early . . ." Her voice trailed off.

"And you did not feel encumbered to check on her?"

"No—she has been so good the last two days—oh, dear God, I should have suspected something. She has been *too* docile!"

His mouth was set in a grim line. "She'll be good from now on. She'll have me to deal with. I'm afraid there's nothing to be done but for me to marry the girl before she ruins herself. I'll make the arrangements at once. I'm leaving it to you, Miss Fordham, to inform her of this—and why!" He turned on his heel and she was alone again.

When Abby taxed Kitty with her indiscretion, the girl seemed strangely unperturbed. "Can you not see what you have done?" Abby cried. "Nothing is more fatal to a girl than to have earned the reputation of being fast."

"Yes, dearest Abby, I know."

Abby felt helpless. Kitty didn't care! "You must know my Lord Ashley means to marry you immediately, before your reputation lies in shreds."

Amazingly, Kitty merely smiled. "That is the only solution, of course. I believe I shall be quite happy as a married lady."

She left the room, walking as though in a dream and Abby threw up her hands.

Lord Ashley returned in the morning. "I have sent for Agatha," he told Abby, his tone cold. "And I have scheduled the ceremony for the twenty-fifth of June."

Only two weeks away. Abby's heart began to pound. Then it was true. He meant to marry Kitty immediately!

"Close your mouth," he ordered. "Why are you so surprised?"

Abby collected herself in a hurry. "It is hard to believe—happening so suddenly."

"You may believe it. I am at my last hopes. I know of nothing else to do." He ran a hand through his hair, sadly disordering it. Abby longed to tuck back the lock that fell over his brow. Anything, any excuse, to touch him.

"Agatha should be here tomorrow," he went on. "She will put all in track." He squared his shoulders. "This has to work."

Abby licked her lips. "It—it will," she assured him. "Kitty likes you very well." But she doesn't love you like I do, she wept silently. She longed to sob aloud. The wedding would go ahead, she would leave Ashland Court—and Ashley. She squared her shoulders as he had done and held up her head, but her heart had sunk into some cold, dark well. No matter. She would survive, and she'd best give a thought as to how. "My lord, I have a favor to ask."

"Well?"

She hesitated. "After all this—after what I have allowed to happen—could you still see your way to giving me a letter of recommendation?"

She half expected him to laugh, bitterly perhaps, but instead he frowned as though puzzled. "What?"

"I shall need to seek a new position after Kitty is married. I'll no longer be needed here, and I'll honestly try to do better next time."

"Don't be a fool. You'll remain here. How could I—we—go on without you?"

"Quite well, I assume. I do nothing but keep Kitty company, and not very well at that. And once she is wed, she'll have no need of a chaperon. I thought perhaps, if you'd be so kind, you might speak to Lady Agatha. She has three girls and I was once a schoolmistress. I could be a governess."

He hesitated. Did he fear to inflict so flighty a female on his nieces?

"We'll see about that," he said. His jaw tightened as though he clenched his teeth and he looked at her oddly, with eyes haunted by a dreadful anxiety. What ailed the man? "We'll see," he repeated. "In two weeks."

Two weeks until the culmination of all her vicarious dreams. The wedding of the man she loved to another woman would be a fitting end. Abby turned away, blinded by tears. Kitty would have the wondrous wedding she herself would never have. It would be agony, but she vowed to live every moment of it through Kitty.

Lady Agatha arrived, rather subdued, with lines of worry creasing her ivory forehead. "Ashley," she kept asking, over and over, "are you *sure?*" His sister was not happy but she saw to it the plans for a sumptuous wedding breakfast proceeded with a vengeance. Ashland Court was cast into chaos once more as the domestics scurried about preparing for the grand reception. Lady Agatha fluttered here and there, ordering all, interviewing caterers and decorators. Abby she set to work listing the guests who sent acceptance cards. Through all of this, Kitty remained too complaisant, but Abby, taken up with her misery, was only relieved not to have to cope with tantrums or hysterics.

The fatal day drew near. All too soon Kitty would have no more need for a companion, and Abby determined to make the most of the time she had left at Ashland since these few hours would be all she had with which to rekindle her dreams and memories.

Memories—already they were only memories. She scarcely saw Lord Ashley. She stored away the precious moments she'd known—his tall, broad shouldered figure coming toward her, dancing with her at Kitty's ball, sitting beside her at the Pump Room, his warmth, his sudden laughter when she made a clever remark in his presence. She engraved in her mind the way his hair curled up at the nape of his neck, the humorous lines about his eyes and mouth, his glowing smile—which she had not seen lately.

She tried to remember when she last heard his laugh. Surely it had been several weeks, and he had not been around much for all that time. No wonder Kitty had broken out while he was in London. Life at Ashland was dull and time dragged interminably when Ashley was not there. And now when he did come, Abby realized he avoided her. He seemed worried, distracted, as though his approaching nuptials were preying on his mind. It was agony to endure his coolness on his infrequent visits—but a worse agony when he failed to come at all.

She found unexpected respite. Couturiers brought samples of fabrics and began the measuring for Kitty's trousseau. The girl soon became bored, standing for hours while seamstresses cut and draped a series of delectable ensembles on her wilting figure.

"You must do this for me, Abby darling, will you not?" Kitty pleaded. "Fortunately, we are much of a size."

Thus this chore gradually descended upon Abby, who reveled in the vicarious pleasure of posing for the fittings of the lovely gowns, modeling them for Lady Agatha, who circled about her, changing a flounce here, discarding a clashing bit of trim there, adjusting the hems and shaking her head over an ill-set sleeve. The wedding gown in particular reawakened all Abby's daydreams, a fabulous concoction in the bride colors of silver, white, and pale celestial blue worked in a marvel of lace and satin. She was soon pretending Kitty's entire wedding would be hers and she lived in the fantasy, imagining herself wearing that heavenly gown and standing beside Ashley before Reverend Elmgrove—which reminded her of the vicar, who presumably awaited her answer.

Mr. Elmgrove had been turned away at the door repeatedly, for Abby had no time for idle chit-chat—or for a nerve-wracking session with a would-be suitor. She had been sending her apologies by way of the butler and hoped the reverend gentleman would not believe she was being coy. That thought returned her to reality. It was unfair to dangle him on a string.

She agreed to meet the poor vicar. They could be alone in the rose garden. Lady Agatha was in the ballroom, berating the decorators who had brought the wrong shade of muslin to drape the arch beneath which the bride and groom would stand to receive their guests. The would-be bride herself had curled up in the conservatory with a marble-backed novel. Abby slipped out the side door.

Arbuthnot Elmgrove awaited her in the garden, standing in front of one of the stone benches that bordered the ornamental water. Dismayed, she saw he was wearing his best waistcoat and carrying a large bunch of daisies.

"My dear Miss Fordham," he exclaimed, bowing over the hand she held out as she walked up to him. "As you may have guessed, I am come for my answer."

Abby steeled herself. It was best she told him at once that she could not marry him, and she had her speech prepared. She launched into it, gently removing the fingers he was kissing one by one.

"My dear Mr. Elmgrove," she began.

He looked up from the last finger. "Arbuthnot."

"Very well, Arbuthnot." She tried again. "I am so sorry, but I have been thinking deeply these last few days—" now there was a falsehood. She had not thought of him at all "—and I have come to a painful decision. I am a teacher, Mr. Elmgrove, and I feel I must devote my life to instructing the children of England that we may have—" she floundered, forgetting the words "—that is, they are the future of our great nation," she finished lamely. "In short, I shall never marry."

Mr. Elmgrove stepped back dramatically, and Abby shrieked as the stone bench caught him behind the knees. He flailed his arms, casting his bouquet of daisies to the winds, and sat down hard on the bench, saving himself from landing on his back in the reflecting pool.

"Dear me," he remarked. "I have quite lost all my flowers."

Abby had hurried to catch his arm. "Are you all right, sir?"

"My dearest Miss Fordham," he said, getting to his feet. "Your tender solicitude does credit to your noble character, as does your selfless decision. Must I then accept this as your final answer?"

"Indeed you must!"

"I see." He was taking it very well, far better than she expected. "Well, then," he said, resigned. "It must be the butcher's daughter. She is not as comely as you, Miss Fordham, but she is an excellent cook." Taking her hand, he kissed her fingertips lightly. "I bid you farewell."

On the point of departure, he turned back for an instant and saw that Abby had begun to pick up the scattered daisies. "You may keep the flowers," he informed her magnanimously, and bowed his way out of her life.

Abby watched him go, shaking her head helplessly. "Well, really!" she exclaimed aloud. She did not know whether to laugh at the absurdity of the whole affair, or cry because she had been as good as jilted. She decided to laugh and went on picking up the daisies.

The Reverend Mr. Elmgrove was soon forgotten for Kitty's trousseau began to arrive, and the gowns had to be admired and tried on by both Kitty and Abby, for Kitty wished to see how they looked from all angles.

While Abby was being divested of a soft blue merino carriage dress by Lady Agatha's abigail, the lady herself spoke casually.

"It is an excessive *shame* that Ashley will *not* live in London. These lovely gowns will be positively *wasted* in this backwater of Bath. You must know, my brother has *always* been a homebody, never caring to grace the *simplest* of balls with his illustrious presence."

"He does not go to balls?" Kitty dropped the *jonquille* yellow lustring she had been holding before her in front of the mirror. "Whatever does he do?"

"He virtually *hibernates* during the Season, my dear. But do not fret, you will become quite *inured* to it in time."

From the incredulous expression on Kitty's face, followed at once by one of determination, Abby surmised that a change would soon be in the air.

"Of course, there *are* the assemblies in Bath." Lady Agatha tried on a plumed bonnet, turning this way and that, admiring her reflection. *"If* you can convince him to attend one." She glanced sidelong at Kitty, whose mien had now become very thoughtful.

The wedding gown arrived, and they crowded about the box, eager to see the result of all their planning. To a chorus of oh's and ah's from Kitty and Abby, Lady Agatha lifted it from the folds of silver paper in which it was wrapped. It was all Abby's dreams come true.

"Kitty must see it on someone else to *properly* appreciate the full effect," Lady Agatha decreed. "Abby, you must once more be our model, for I am far too *plump* to wear it."

She and Kitty sat back and watched while the abigail adjusted the dress on Abby, who felt herself trembling with awe. As she pirouetted slowly before them in the wondrous wedding gown, she was gripped by a hopeless longing, and had to blink rapidly. She smoothed the luxurious satin of the cerulean blue underdress and touched the silver roses that bordered the open white lace robe from corsage to her feet and on around the hem, including the three-foot-long train. If only it were hers . . . if only he . . .

Kitty broke into her thoughts, clapping her hands. "It is perfect, Abby. You look a veritable angel!"

Indeed it was lovely. Just what she herself would have chosen. She looked at Kitty's ecstatic face and the tears she thought she had blinked away filled her eyes. "I—I pray you will be happy."

Kitty seized her in a bear hug, endangering the delicate silver roses. "Darling Abby, you must not worry about me. Only think, I shall now be allowed to wear my diamond choker!"

And that, Abby felt, was her answer.

The fatal day dawned. On the wedding morn, Abby went to Kitty's bedroom to awaken her—and stopped on the threshold, a chill fear catching at her heart.

The bed had not been slept in, and a note lay pinned on the pillow. No wonder Kitty had accepted all the marriage plans so quietly—she had no intention of going through with the ceremony! With shaking fingers, Abby unfolded the single sheet and spread it flat.

Dearest Abby,

Forgive me, I know you will, for you at least have my happiness at heart. Please tell Ashley I am sorry, but I do not care a snap for my fortune and he is welcome to it. I would rather follow the drum with my true love. By the time you find this, we will be well on our way to London. My darling has a special license and we shall be wed as soon as the registrar's office opens . . .

Abby looked at the clock on the mantel. Good God, it was after eight already—in no way could they be stopped in time! She crumpled the note in her hand, the rest unread, and she ran from the room to dispatch a message to Lord Ashley at the York, begging him to come at once.

Panic overtook her as she imagined what he would say after this. How could she tell him? How could Kitty do such a thing—oversetting all their plans? Why, why, oh, this was the end of everything! There would be no wedding at Ashland Court. She would miss the greatest vicarious thrill of her life, living through Kitty the dream wedding she would never have herself.

And Kitty! How could she survive on a soldier's pay, even that of an officer, accustomed as she was to every luxury? Guiltily, Abby admitted she had carelessly allowed herself to become accustomed to that same luxury, and thereby to be inordinately spoiled for whatever life was to come. Truly, this was the end of comfort for both of them. What was she to do? Lady Agatha would never offer her a position after this debacle, even if Ashley would beg her, which he assuredly would not do now. And worse than being sent off once more in disgrace, she'd never see Ashley again.

After being sunk in melancholy for weeks, this last straw broke her reserves and she collapsed on a sofa, indulging in the hearty bout of weeping she had held back so long. It brought no relief.

Far sooner than she expected, she heard Lord Ashley's quick steps in the hall and he burst into the room.

"Good God, Abby, what has occurred to distress you so?" He dropped on one knee beside her, pulling her hands from her tear-streaked face.

She gave him the crumpled letter. "Oh, my lord, you have every right to blame me. I should have foreseen—but I never dreamed—"

Ashley read the first part silently, and then the last sentence aloud. ". . . And Abby, darling, I wish you happy too, as happy as I am to be."

Abby glanced up, surprised. What could Kitty mean by that? Did she think Abby planned to marry the vicar?

"The little minx!" Ashley exclaimed. "So she knew all along." Sitting back on his heels, he blew out his breath in a great gust of relief. "Thank God! I had begun to think they would *never* carry it off! I've been in the devil of a stew."

Abby stared at him. "You do not mind? But her home—her fortune! She'll never survive as the wife of a penniless soldier!"

He rose to his feet and grinned down at her. "Oh, as to that, if they care for each other enough to give up all for love, then they deserve to have their happiness. I shall deed over the property to them as a marriage gift, and at last I shall be rid of my blasted obligation."

Abby mopped at her cheeks with her damp handkerchief, her mind in turmoil. "But all those lovely gowns—and the wedding—it's all arranged!"

"The gowns fit you, do they not? I doubt she'd want them on the Continent. You may keep them, and I have every intention of going through with my marriage."

Abby's heart contracted. He had another bride in mind. No wonder the necessity of wedding the wayward Kitty had so upset his peace.

She stood, balling the wet handkerchief in one hand and looking away. "I—I wish you happy, my lord," she stammered.

Catching her arm, he turned her to face him. "Oh, no fear. Of more importance, will *you* be?"

"I? Oh, yes. I suppose so." She raised a forlorn face, still not comprehending. "Oh, dear. Perhaps I should have accepted Mr. Elmgrove."

Ashley frowned. "Good lord, what for?" Suddenly he gripped her shoulders, his face paling. "Abby? Abby, you cannot mean you are turning me down? Have I been fooling myself? I thought—I was so sure—oh, damn, I'm making a botch of this, but you see, I've never proposed to a lady before."

Bereft of her scattered wits, Abby let the tear-soaked handkerchief drop from her nerveless fingers, not daring to believe his words. The tumult in her mind became utter confusion. It was inconceivable that she might yet experience—and at first hand!—the wedding she had dreamed of for Kitty . . . Lord Ashley to marry *her!* It *must* be one of her dreams, too incredible to be true. "You—you cannot mean—*me!*"

"My love, can you doubt it?" He captured her fluttering hands and pressed them to his chest.

"Oh, this is insane! Only think what people will say if the bride is changed!"

"Who cares? Let them talk."

Drawing her into his arms, he held her as if he never meant to let her go. Abby's heart pounded until she feared she would faint, but she made one last effort to bring him to his senses. "You should wed a real lady, not your ward's companion . . . oh, what should I do?"

"Why, you should kiss me," he said simply.

So she did. His warm lips met hers and enveloped in his strong arms, Abby abandoned herself to a heaven more wondrous than she ever expected to know. So this is real, she thought, dizzily, this is reality . . . Without a qualm, Miss Abigail Fordham bade farewell forever to vicarious living.

ZEBRA'S REGENCY ROMANCES
DAZZLE AND DELIGHT

A BEGUILING INTRIGUE   (4441, $3.99)
by Olivia Sumner

Pretty as a picture Justine Riggs cared nothing for propriety. She dressed as a boy, sat on her horse like a jockey, and pondered the stars like a scientist. But when she tried to best the handsome Quenton Fletcher, Marquess of Devon, by proving that she was the better equestrian, he would try to prove Justine's antics were pure folly. The game he had in mind was seduction — never imagining that he might lose his heart in the process!

AN INCONVENIENT ENGAGEMENT   (4442, $3.99)
by Joy Reed

Rebecca Wentworth was furious when she saw her betrothed waltzing with another. So she decides to make him jealous by flirting with the handsomest man at the ball, John Collinwood, Earl of Stanford. The "wicked" nobleman knew exactly what the enticing miss was up to — and he was only too happy to play along. But as Rebecca gazed into his magnificent eyes, her errant fiancé was soon utterly forgotten!

SCANDAL'S LADY   (4472, $3.99)
by Mary Kingsley

Cassandra was shocked to learn that the new Earl of Lynton was her childhood friend, Nicholas St. John. After years at sea and mixed feelings Nicholas had come home to take the family title. And although Cassandra knew her place as a governess, she could not help the thrill that went through her each time he was near. Nicholas was pleased to find that his old friend Cassandra was his new next door neighbor, but after being near her, he wondered if mere friendship would be enough . . .

HIS LORDSHIP'S REWARD   (4473, $3.99)
by Carola Dunn

As the daughter of a seasoned soldier, Fanny Ingram was accustomed to the vagaries of military life and cared not a whit about matters of rank and social standing. So she certainly never foresaw her *tendre* for handsome Viscount Roworth of Kent with whom she was forced to share lodgings, while he carried out his clandestine activities on behalf of the British Army. And though good sense told Roworth to keep his distance, he couldn't stop from taking Fanny in his arms for a kiss that made all hearts equal!